# *Killing Daniel*

## SARAH DOBBS

UNTHANK BOOKS

First published in 2012
By Unthank Books
www.unthankbooks.com

Printed and bound in Great Britain by Lightning Source, Milton Keynes

A CIP record for this book is available from the British Library

ISBN 978-0-9564223-8-5

Cover design by Tom Collin

Cover image 'Killing Daniel' © Tom Collin 2012

For my brother

# PART ONE

# 1

This time Fleur imagines it like this.

He bursts out of brown water. Sucks air. The tension in the teenager's face relaxes; oxygen, life, momentary relief. He is *not* going to die, not this second at least. But he's forced under again. A boot - or is it a trainer? - on his chest stakes the teenager underwater. His hands slap against the boot, scrabbling at the leather and the bare leg from above it. Bubbles fizz out the boy's nostrils, jetting upwards, desperate for the surface. Eyes stinging, he sees a smudge of black on a calf hard as limestone. A tattoo.

The boot withdraws. The young man, gasping, arcs out the water.

He shakes his head, signing: *I never touched her. Please, I never touched her.*

He's trying to speak as he signs, no breath. His wrist – so painful – he wants to scream. Fleur struggles to remember the signs he taught her. Something about hurt. No, it was about *not* hurting. Not making pain. Not hurting Fleur?

But he isn't really signing that, is he?

3

The older man at the lip of Mesnes Park pond blinks as the boy drags himself out of the pond. The man's anger is loose electricity; his nostrils flare. His fists are red and white. Water drips from his knuckles. He's waiting.

At seventeen, the teenager is tall but still skinny. His chest heaves, sounding like a kid with whooping cough. The man draws his knee up to his chest, drives his boot down onto the younger man's head. The teenager crumples. The man wedges a boot against the teenager's shoulder, kicks out. He crashes back to the pond, striking the water so hard it's like hitting bricks.

Now, the teenager's eyes are fixed. He doesn't blink. He bobs on the water, cushioned by it. But he can feel himself sinking, sodden clothes dragging him below the surface. Water trickles into his ears. Unable to move, he watches as the man approaches. Panic streaks through his body. His toes tingle. His neck feels odd, like it's not part of him. The water isn't cold anymore.

His eyes are the sort of blue you notice from very far away; blue as the skies you fly kites in. The man wades into the pond. He raises his boot and pins the boy down. The teenager's body folds into a V shape, and disappears.

His lungs are filling with water. He's got to – needs to – has to breathe, but if he does, he'll choke. He holds his breath, mouth buttoned tight, eyes bulging. He wants to thrash and flail, get out, get away. Get home. Why did he take the short cut? Why didn't he just go round? But his body stays still, barring small random spasms that make tiny fan-like ripples in the pond. Water laps against the *Happy Meal* box he's just dropped in surprise.

The pressure on his spinal column is about to reach a maximum. From beneath the water, the teenager sees his murderer, blurry and indistinct. He'll never know who and he'll never know why.

Did he think of Fleur in those final moments? The plans they'd made.

The teenager can't hold back any longer. He breathes in. Snorts water slimy with algae. Pins and needles wave over him.

She remembers something from First Aid at work, or one of those docu-soaps. Within six to eight minutes he would go into cardiac arrest.

This body, this person.

Through the veil of water, his blond hair is the colour of undulating rapeseed. His hair is just a shade lighter than the wings of the moth, or maybe a horsefly that hovers nearby, emitting an audible hum. The teenager's foot jerks, splattering the moth with water. It skips to the right, away from the pond and the clearing.

The boot pinning the body down is withdrawn. If this had been done just a minute earlier, if someone had come, the boy may have risen, spluttered, and restarted. But it wasn't, they didn't, and so it is that a body rises to the top of the small pond, not a person.

His features peek out of the disturbed, murky water: an inch of nose, half an inch of chin, a millimetre of a full, purpling bottom lip. His eyes are open; an unnaturally rich blue. The pupils are fully dilated. She's heard that somewhere. *ER?* Water forms shallow pools in the teenager's eye sockets. A pond skater stands in the pool of the teenager's left eye, its legs like eyelashes, dimpling the water's surface.

The moth – or the horsefly – jerks again, cutting further away from the pond. As it moves, a scribble in the clearing dense with midges, it looks like an aeroplane with engine failure. It could either restart, or spiral suddenly to the ground.

With the boot removed, the leg and the man attached, is also gone. All that remains in the clearing is the teenager in the pond. His arms are drifting forwards, curving towards meeting as if in prayer, nudged along by the internal rhythm of the pond. The muck is settling, the water clearing.

His name was Daniel.

# 2

Fleur walks home after another midnight finish at *McDonalds*, frowning deeply. The other girls had their boyfriends pick them up. Marcus would be too drunk. Her flat shoes clap against her heels as she walks. Trimmed with silver sequins, they're the most extravagant thing about her. She clutches the worn strap of her handbag, spine impeccably straight. The leather has been bleached the colour of sand by the sweat of her palm. The scent of impending rain stings the air. She shivers.

If Fleur carried straight on she would be following the path Daniel took the day he died. Hard to believe it was ten years ago, almost to the day. The day had been spring-bright, edged with that chill of winter. She wishes there'd been something remarkable about it. That she could say, I *knew*. I sensed something. Because if she'd known, she could have stopped it. But that wasn't totally true. There'd been that guy walking after Daniel. The one who looked like her mother's old boyfriend. Had it really been him? She'd looked away, gone back into *McDonalds*. Served fries as Daniel was murdered.

Fleur veers right instead, towards the only scrap of green field this close to the town centre, where the skate-boys gather with spliffs and *White Lightning*. Her back bedroom looks out onto the park. There's a light on, glowing through thin cotton curtains. She reaches the front of the house. Why can't she go any further? She looks up the street, the seemingly unending row of red, *Coronation Street* terraces. All the cars sleek and quiet under a dull-eyed moon.

A crash splinters the night. It's from the house opposite; someone having a domestic. Fleur's stomach lurches. Should she go over? She's about to cross when her hand goes to her own stomach. There's a baby under there, filling out and taking shape. Marcus doesn't even know about it. Yet.

A breeze fingers her hair. The touch is so gentle. She closes her eyes. God. Imagine, being touched so carefully. She craves a delicate touch, an expression of care. Daniel would have been a gentle boyfriend, wouldn't he?

The front door pulls back.

'What the fuck are you doing out here? Want the neighbours to catch you standing around, gawking like some gormless twat. Get in, woman.'

Woman. At nearly thirty, she still felt like a girl. Still wanting someone to come and rescue her, to take her out of this place, let her be the person all the teachers used to hope she could be. She *could* leave Marcus. Pack a bag, go back to her Nan's, tail between her legs. Start university. People do that, don't they?

Anger tightens her skull. She forces a smile. 'It's a nice clear night. I can see the stars. Look.'

'You're bonkers, lass. The only thing I want to look at is my tea on the table.' He jerked a thumb.

Her feet move; her body goes inside. She imagines she leaves part of her out there on the pavement. Another self, escaped. In her mind, she waves at that other half. The other half sighs and waves goodbye. Fleur shakes her head. Marcus was right, she *was* crazy. Stepping around him she catches a whiff of alcohol. Drinking all night, sat on his fattening arse waiting for her to come in and cook.

She fixes something mechanically, puts it on the coffee table. He's watching porn on pay-per-view. Who was going to pay for that?

The cutlery looks doll-sized in his hands.

'Is it okay?' she asks. 'Marcus?'

'Eh? Aye. Salt.' She gets it. His ears look shockingly red as he shakes salt into his food.

She stares at the round, gold stud nestled in the fat of his left earlobe. Could he take it out even if he wanted to, or was it wedged in for all time? Crusting over.

She eats on the couch next to him, careful not to let the cutlery touch her teeth. He hates that sound. She watches a pretty brunette giving a blowjob on all fours in a cellar. There's steam and funky music, bizarre camera shots. Men would never see how sad porn is. Fleur was willing to bet that 'sucking a stranger's dicks for money' was not one of this girl's initial career aspirations. What happens along the way?

Marcus stabs a knife at the television. 'Your arse is better than that.'

Is it wrong to be pleased by this comment? She feels a little sick, but forces down the food and shows Marcus her plate. He nods and she carefully scrapes her food into the bin. She washes and stacks the dishes before heading upstairs. Walking on tiptoes, she makes no sound on the carpets, and takes out the box she keeps under the spare sheets in the bed drawer.

She removes a piece of paper like she's playing KerPlunk, that game where you take out straws, trying not to dislodge the marbles resting on them. The paper is yellowed, thinning a little, but still crisp. The tail looks tattered from afar, but that's just the wing flap. She puts the paper to her nose and inhales. It smells like library books and the lavender fabric-softener she uses. The only presents Marcus ever really got her were a vibrator, and her engagement ring. But Daniel gave her this present years ago. It's just a plane, some piece of paper, but she treasures what she has left of him. She traces her thumb over the wings, still strong. It reminds her of him, of the life she could have had, the choice she might have made. She turns the plane onto its belly, sees the words he wrote: 'So you can fly. Love Daniel.'

Footsteps sound on the stairs, growing louder. They are heavy, as if weighted by the sheer amount of food Marcus has ingested.

Fleur tucks the aeroplane away.

He goes to the loo. She can hear his piss streaming, then dripping jerkily until he stops all together. No flush. She imagines drops of piss congealing on the toilet seat.

Quickly, she pulls out a photograph from the same drawer. Two girls; one English, one Japanese. Their hair is in plaits, knees in the same position, peeking out under school skirts. There is no gap between their bodies. They look entirely different. Chinatsu is delicate, so flawless that she seems like a drawing, whereas Fleur is scrawny and ablaze with freckles. And yet, they look like sisters; the same posture, the same sadness in their eyes. She remembers that day. It was the worst and best of her life.

She slips the photograph back; Marcus is coming. The newspaper clipping is below the photograph. She only sees the edge of it: 'Pond'. But the headline and even the article itself is written into her brain: *Teenage Boy Killed in Mesnes Park Pond*. She pushes the drawer to rest with a tap, smoothes the bed's peacock-blue valance.

Just in time.

Her shoulders hitch sharply when Marcus repositions her ponytail, a thick switch of hair, which has fallen forward over her right shoulder, back down the centre of her spine. She is still as he kisses her ear, controls a shudder as his tongue investigates the small nook, catching the back of her earring. He runs a palm over her stomach, which cinches in. His fingers are icy. He pops the button on her high-waisted jeans and she helps him with the rest, pulling off the jeans and knickers herself, before kneeling back down. Eyes to the right, she waits. As Marcus drags her hips back, she adjusts into a practiced position, both hands on the stubbly blue carpet. Waits. When he enters her, her face looks as though she has just trapped her finger in a door. By the end of it, she's flat on her stomach, chin propping up the rest of her head, the pink skin there becoming red. She has two fingers on the bed drawer, curling the bobbled fabric of the peacock-blue valance into a knot.

*Is there anything, absolutely anything you can remember that might be able to help us, Ms Johnson?*

She remembers the policeman's words. Two coppers had come into the restaurant after Daniel disappeared. She'd told them she thought someone was following him. Her mother's ex-boyfriend.

Red-faced, she'd given up her fiercest secret to strangers, the one knitted into her bones and skin, the one that built her this way. The one about the nights spent in the airing cupboard, the scalding pipe. And she told them, about Derek creaking into her room in the folds of the night. They'd crosschecked with each other, denouncing her information even before she was finished; she was not credible, her story was halting, half-imagined. Emotional. Not important.

*And did you see this . . . Derek's face?*

She'd shaken her head.

Pause.

She'd caught the brown eyes of the female officer, the heavy-lidded 'seen-it-all-look.' She'd felt acutely betrayed. How could a woman ignore this sort of information? The male policeman was attractive, and that had just made it worse. He'd asked whether she had informed the police of this at the time. The question was a wagging finger. The suggestion: It's your fault. You should have spoken up then, so what do you expect? The embarrassment seared her. Before they left, the male officer had given her the perfunctory police line: Well, if you do wish to make a formal statement on the matter. But she'd tuned him out, closing up.

Marcus is twisting her hair now, gearing up, slamming. It will be over soon.

Her mind went back to the police visit. They had left with her secret; it dissolved over them, leaving her bereft. Over the years, she told herself that it probably hadn't been Derek. She'd imagined it; it wasn't important. But what if it had been? What would that mean?

As Marcus is fucking her, Fleur thinks about Chinatsu. What did she look like now? She imagined a poised and elegant woman, an office worker maybe, something powerful. Her features would still be cartoon-like in their absolute clarity. She longs to know her again. Was she married? Was her husband everything Marcus was not, their lives coloured in connection and whispered conversations at night, breath hot on each other's lips? The familiarity of a draped limb, a random kiss. Inhabiting their Sunday mornings in quiet intimacy, one starting the kettle, another brewing green tea? Or were they just the same?

Outside, there's the sound of scraping. A kid peddling a go-kart down the pavement, out of the street, maybe towards the park. Maybe towards the pond where Daniel was drowned.

# 3

Yugi Hamugoshi raises one eyebrow, observing the woman on the narrow bed. Her house is as small as Tokyo flats. It stinks of female things; antiperspirant, talc, flowery soap, laundry – unwashed knickers? There's a blue bear on the worn carpet at the side of the bed. It's supposed to be tucked out of sight. The idea of a whore who sleeps with a teddy bear at night makes him somewhat uncomfortable.

Yugi's eyebrow is black and sparse. From the marks on the woman's skin, Yugi can see all the places he has been. His fingerprints blur the white column of her throat with red. His right hand trembles. He clutches his wrist to still the shakes. It's not nerves. It's adrenalin. Still, he needs a moment. The women here were far less savvy, much more grotesque in a warped sort of way. And yet they were somehow innocent. It was almost crueller.

Naked, Yugi shoulders open the bathroom door. He uses the back of his hand to flip up the tap. He splashes his face with water. The water is foamy and tiny bubbles pop against his cheeks. He checks his watch. It's 2.25pm.

Yugi stares at the watch. The bronze face brandishes the words *Ulysse Nardin* in raised Bodoni font. It has a crocodile-leather strap and deployment clasp, its blue skeleton hands resemble the wings of a butterfly. Yugi blinks, lips tightening. The watch reminds him of the

11

mother he barely knew and the moths he used to suffocate in glass jars after her death.

Yugi pads into the bedroom. The whore is just a body to him; it raises its head. The face is slack and bored, eyelids heavy. She may have started to wonder why he didn't untie her after sex. The thought makes Yugi feel strong. He roots in his suit jacket pocket, the sole item hanging from a rail near the door. Removing his mobile he returns to the bathroom.

The phone clicks, burrs and connects.

'Chinatsu, hello,' he says in Japanese.

There is a small pause.

'Yugi. Something is wrong?'

'No. Nothing.' He nudges the bathroom door to with the side of his knee. 'I was just calling to let you know my plane is on time. I shall be arriving in Tokyo at 7.25pm. All being well.'

'Would you like anything particular for supper?'

'I will eat beforehand.'

'Well, have a safe journey.'

Yugi hangs up first. He re-enters the bedroom and the woman raises her head again. Her hair is wavy and just short of black. The tendons in her neck stand out like a letter H without the middle step. His tie is a black gag between her lips.

*Click.* He opens his briefcase. Ah. There. The whore is twitching now, her nostrils wide. Alarm streaks towards terror. She jerks against her binds. She tries to speak but the gag makes the words mushy. He can't be bothered translating. His cock is hardening. *Click.* He shuts the briefcase.

A stray breeze disturbs the slatted blinds, and a dart of light intrudes into the grey room, pinging off the metal in Yugi's fingers. He looks up at the squirming whore. Brackets of sweat glisten either side of her nostrils, her cheeks flash wet. Her earrings are studs. The jewellery winks at him, the colour of tongues.

He strokes the whore's puffing cheeks. 'There, there, Chinatsu. I'm going to make you feel good.'

The plane lifts with inevitable force. When the g-forces slacken and the plane balances out, Yugi turns to look out of the window-seat. Using one thumb, he circles a pink stud around and around in his palm. He feels extremely close to his wife, yet also increasingly distant.

# 4

Phone in hand, Chinatsu stares at the kitchen sink, her image grossly warped. Beads of water spot the metal. She slots the phone onto its holder next to the bonsai and reels in her breath. The phone beeps, rings again suddenly.

Chinatsu jumps and puts her fingertips to her forehead. She calms herself, rubs the arch of one eyebrow as if to check its precision and straightens her blouse's ruffles. Will this be the Chinese Madam?

She holds the phone with both hands, close to her left ear. 'Yes?'

'You can speak with me?'

'Yes.'

'We must meet for tea to discuss . . . plans.'

'Where?'

She is told the time and place.

'No late,' the caller says, and hangs up.

'Yugi,' Chinatsu says to the sink. In the warped image of her, there is a gash of black where her mouth should be. 'Please, do not be angry with me, but . . . I must tell you something.' The eyes of the image seem darker than her own. Her head snaps up, heart sprinting.

'Mrs Hamugoshi?'

Chinatsu starts, turning at the man's voice. 'Satoshi.'

He bows, looking up at her under a sheaf of dark hair. 'Please excuse

14

me for intruding. I had come to tend the gardens, but found no instructions this week.'

Chinatsu smiles. 'It's not an intrusion, Satoshi. Don't mind the borders today, I am fond of doing those myself. Just cut the grass.'

Of course, the real reason she tends the borders herself is the moonflower, that secret seed she has planted. The moonflower is her money tree. Below the ground Chinatsu plants every spare coin or bill she can conceivably get away with. She tells herself the stash is just in case the plan with Madam Li does not work as she expected and does not deliver the family she so desires. Just in case Yugi gets suspicious and she has to leave swiftly.

Satoshi lingers. Chinatsu raises her eyebrows. Boys in Japan are getting taller these days. Western-tall. His hands are larger than Yugi's, arms thicker from manual work. But he will not stay at this job; she knows that. He is sensitive and clever. The gardening money is to fund his education. He told her once how he loved Japanese poetry and wished to study literature. She sees him in a library working, head bent, hair over his eyes. He will be surrounded by books and admiring glances.

A jolt of pleasure warms her pussy. How would it feel to have his body pressed against hers? Those hands laced into her fingers, hips between her legs? He's wearing mustard-coloured boots and no socks. Maybe it's a very basic response, but the boots are impressively large. They're workman's boots. He can build things. She notices the material bracelet cuffing one ankle. A curious, intriguing mix of masculine and feminine. She realises he's still there, looking politely expectant. 'Yes, Satoshi?'

'I am sorry Mrs Hamugoshi, but the key?'

'Yes of course. Here.' She takes the spare back door key from of one of the kitchen drawers and hands it to him. His nails are a little long. Perhaps he plays an instrument?

'I will only be an hour, Mrs Hamugoshi.'

'There is no rush. I have some business in town. You may leave the key under the mat on the back step.'

He bows again as she leaves. There is a small smile at the corner of his lips; he likes her.

Chinatsu heads to the bathroom with the intention of freshening up, but instead opens the buttons of her blouse, her wedding ring catching the final button. She runs her palm over her stomach which is smooth and firm. She likes the feel of her abdominals beneath. Her fingers disappear underneath the waist of her damson skirt. She circles her clitoris with her index finger; it's already swollen and sensitive. Her touch sends delicious fireworks of pleasure throughout her body. Back to the door, she slides to the cold tiles and lets her legs yawn open. She thinks of Satoshi as her circling gets faster. She applies more pressure. How many girls has he been with? Would he like her body? More mature, womanly? She wants to lick pre-cum off his dick and savour the taste. Wants to look up at him as she sucks the length of him, and see the sheer lust on his face. This thought flicks the switch; her building orgasm spills over.

Her breath is loud in her ears. She gets up and rearranges her knickers, washes the scent of herself from her hands and fixes her face to go out. Stupid. A handsome young man like Satoshi would never think of her in that way.

Jiyugaoka is often referred to as the Japanese Beverley Hills. Chinatsu takes the train from the broad, tree-lined suburban streets of her home into Harajuku Station. Along the way, her head turns at the sign for the Galaxy Language School. She draws a notebook out of an oval purse. Inside, fitted against the spine, is a silver pen. It is as long and slender as her own nails. Uncapping the pen, the metal cool against her skin, she writes her name over and over.

Chinatsu's pen stalls for a moment, as if listening to the train clatter on. A squat man with a downturned mouth drops his mesh bag of oranges. One spills and rests against Chinatsu's heel. She hands it back to him without looking his way. His palms are wispy and dry, no moisture. Remember to get oranges. Don't come home without anything or Yugi will be suspicious.

She goes back to her notebook and draws a picture of an orange. She dots its skin so it seems pockmarked and angles her head. It doesn't seem real. She gives the fruit a shadow, scoring deep into the paper. She would like a shadow too. Was that a crazy thought? Wanting something to connect her to this place, this life?

16

The train stops, doors whooshing. People get off and on. Kogal girls chatter: they're alike in platforms and blonde hair and miniskirts, awash with make-up. They're talking about being offered photographic contracts and paid-for double eyelid operations. To Westernise their Oriental look and smooth out the East. She shakes her head. Is there a country where women aren't paid for looks and sex?

Chinatsu heads for Takeshita-dori, the narrow shopping street opposite Harajuku station. Is she doing the right thing? Perhaps Madam Li's 'plan' is not the answer to her unhappiness.

Despite it being a weekday, Takeshita-dori is seething with shoppers and teenagers made up as *Manga* characters. One girl struts by in platform trainers. She's wearing cat contacts and a pink, baby-doll dress. The red eyeliner she has drawn on makes her black eyes seem to leap out. Her tutu skirt is like an electric shock. The girl's small, quick steps take her over the road towards the shopping street, a wheeled suitcase rumbling over the wide zebra crossing.

But the girl with the tutu skirt is not the figure that attracts attention. Chinatsu is. The girl looks Chinatsu up and down, making a point of looking coolly disinterested before continuing on.

Right before the street's entrance, Chinatsu stops to crumble the notebook paper and drop it into a bin. She walks with the crowd, darting left into one of the restaurants when there's a gap in traffic. The restaurant, tucked between boutiques selling the latest gadgets and outfits, is quiet. It's as if a ceremony is about to begin. The fish tank filter purrs, an irritating soundtrack.

An older woman is already waiting. Her lips are pursed. Her face is broad and she has a rather large nose for a Chinese woman. It's almost Roman.

'Madam Li,' Chinatsu says.

The women exchange pleasantries. They ask about each other's husbands. Tea is brought. Madam Li orders *soba* noodles for Chinatsu and fried fish and tofu *miso* soup for herself. Within moments, the food is placed before them.

'You not drink?' Madam Li was from Shanghai so she spoke, supposedly, very bare Japanese.

'Perhaps I am anxious.'

Madam Li nods. She reaches over the table for Chinatsu's hand. It would look like a gesture of sympathy for a friend. Chinatsu uncurls her right hand and allows the money to be retrieved. The initial wedge of money that Madam Li takes now is more than she ever takes later on. It almost entirely depletes the stash of money she's been saving for years. The woman's magician-eyes are framed by the steam snaking from their tea. Cat-green, they are striking and marred by yellow jelly spots in the whites.

'You no drink you no eat. What you, pregnant?'

'Would I be here?'

Madam Li screws her chin back into her neck. The chair creaks as she sits back, spine straight. 'Well, if you not going eat drink speaking truth, fuck off.'

Chinatsu's eyebrows flick up. She bursts out laughing. Covers her mouth.

Madam Li slaps the table, tea slops onto the cheap paper cloth. 'Ai! Funny? What funny?' But her narrowed eyes soften with amusement.

Chopsticks pause at a man's lips.

Chinatsu glances at him and giggles harder. She wipes the tears from her eyes. 'What happens next?'

'I will for you arrange pictures.' Madam Li leans forward. 'A tip, yes? Choose man who look most like husband. Some people. No think. Stupid.'

Chinatsu blushes. Her body feels clammy.

'You know. If this is just about sex there are other things I can do. We all women. We all have desire. What of it? No shame in this business if it keep marriage. Marriage most important. Yes?'

'No. I – I love Yugi,' Chinatsu whispers. 'I don't want to cheat on him.'

Madam Li snorts. 'Ha. So OK you need to justify. So sad.'

'It's about the child, not the sex. I want us to be a family, to bring warmth and light to my marriage.'

'Having child is not how to do this. But how my problem?' She shrugs, leans back in the chair and scratches at one tooth.

Chinatsu toys with her noodles. She's raising them to her mouth

18

when Madam Li puts her hands on the table, face down. Chinatsu rests her chopsticks. The older woman stares into Chinatsu's eyes, a faint smile on watery lips. This woman, old enough to be Chinatsu's mother, knows her more than Yugi has ever done. Even on their wedding night when she was naked, legs apart, losing her virginity. She can't look into this foreigner's eyes for long. Why? Because Madam Li sees inside her in a way Yugi never will. He does not know the thoughts the Chinese Madam knows, thoughts that take hold of Chinatsu in the nights when Yugi falls asleep without touching her.

It has been ten years since they last had sex.

There have been attempts, yes, but nothing consummated. She has felt his penis hard against her, the tip wet. But each time he tries to enter her, he softens. At these times, she wills it to harden again. She waits, not daring to speak or breathe, until he turns away. She closes her eyes. It is her fault; she is not desirable. If only he would let her touch him, grip his penis and stimulate it back to life. But she knows the very suggestion he required help would horrify him.

Madam Li knows all of this too.

Chinatsu glances down at the soiled cloth, dark with fragrant tea. The Madam's eyes do not leave her.

'So,' she says. 'You are afraid?'

Chinatsu looks up, nods.

'You are not to be.' Madam Li leans close again. 'Listen. Women who come to me think they are being whores, they are being prostitutes. No. If you save marriage, it is honourable thing to do.'

On the train on the way home to Jiyugaoka, Chinatsu takes her notebook out and draws an orange tree. She shades the tree too dark and cannot draw the oranges in right, so they end up looking like big white moons. The tree has branches that droop, hanging down from a centre point that remind her of a long fringe that's parted in the centre. On second glance, she thinks of wings. She smiles; she has drawn her moonflower. Was she really just looking to create a family with Yugi, or had she paid Madam Li to find a man to fulfil less honourable desires? If so, was she now just creating her own nightmare?

As Chinatsu walks through the narrow but smog-free streets of

19

Jiyugaoka, the paper with the orange tree is already torn and in her hand. It has been raining while she was in the restaurant and her heels, damp, make dots on the pavement as she clicks towards home. The rain smells metallic. Throughout the area people are walking their dogs and sipping tea outside cafes, even though the streetlights are on. They eat at French and Italian restaurants, enjoy clotted-cream scones, or sip at the historical teahouse in the grounds of the Kosoan gallery.

Jiyugaoka is the place where East meets West.

Chinatsu posts the screwed-up piece of notepaper into the bin of a sushi restaurant and finally covers the short distance to Yugi's elegant two-story *maison*.

She stops. Oranges. She forgot to buy them. But something else glues Chinatsu to the pavement. The house. There are certain lights the maids leave on when they have tidied themselves away: a sprinkling of lamps and the dimmer in the lounge. The overheads are on.

Yugi is home early

# 5

Daniel had loved Fleur since they were both nine years old. Before the
ear infection his mother, who was in the final stages of nursing his
grandfather, didn't notice until too late. Before he acted up until he got
himself excluded from school, because he was too embarrassed to see
her. Because when he was ten, he thought deafness meant stupid.
Retarded. Disabled.

It wasn't real love then, obviously. He first encountered her in the
playground. She was the new girl, face full of freckles and flaming red
hair. The same shade as the Copper H10 paint he coats his model
aeroplanes with. Nobody understood her name, Fleur, so they had
decided to call her Rosie instead.

'Red rover, red rover, we call Rosie over.'

She was on the opposite team. He saw the determination in her face.
She bared down like a bull and darted forward, trying to burst his team's
defence. She was aiming straight for him. He gripped the other boy's
wrist as hard as he could. The line held; Fleur spilled onto the pavement.
He laughed with them as she righted her skirt. Then he saw the scars on
her legs where her socks had come down. She ran to the toilets.

'Ginger!'

'Fire rocket!'

'Matchstick!'

Daniel detached himself from the group. Mum had had scars like that when she was with dad. Hers were on her arms. She covered them up with make-up stuff but it always came off when she was doing the washing-up. She'd shout at him for noticing and send him off to paint his models.

'We're going to the brook!' someone shouted. 'Baz's blowing straws up frogs. You coming?'

'Got lines to write for Mrs. Hammond.'

Daniel wandered over to the toilets, leaned casually against the wall. When Fleur came out, shaking water off her hands, he straightened up. 'You all right?'

'Yeah. Course.'

'Just asking.'

'Just saying.'

'What you do to get them scars? Impressive.'

She tugged at her socks, dragging them up to her knees. 'Get lost.'

'Only asking.'

'Only saying.'

'You want to go blow straws up frogs? A few of us –'

'That's disgusting.'

'Yeah. I told them that. Said I didn't wanna go.'

'Then why you asking me?'

'Just cos. Did your dad do those scars? My dad gave my mum scars like that.'

She glares at him, shrugs. 'I don't have a dad.'

He picks at the flaking paint on the toilet window ledge. 'Oh. Sorry.'

'Sorry about your mum.'

He shrugs. 'She's happier now. It's just us. You can make dads leave you know, if they make scars.'

'I don't have a dad.'

He rubbed his ear, it felt sticky and annoying today. 'Eh?'

'I don't have a dad.'

'Oh yeah. Sorry. Why'd you move here? You foreign?'

'No. I went to live with my Nan.'

'Why?'

'Get lost.'

'Can't,' he said. 'Live round here. God, I'm starving.'

'You could have some of these jam sandwiches. I suppose. My Nan always makes too much.'

'You've got so many freckles you look like a gypsy.'

She thumps him.

He got called names every day for months for hanging round with a girl. He had to lie and say he was bribing butties off her, and getting snogs in the loo. He started losing words. He made squeaking sounds in class, just to check he could still hear himself. Everyone thought he was playing class clown. But it was like being underwater. He felt off-balance and angry with everyone. Except Fleur. The same day he first saw Fleur's scars, the teacher called his mother and referred him to the doctor.

Another day they were sitting on the steps to the junior playground, eating lemon-curd sandwiches. It was windy. He'd thought that's why his hearing was particularly bad that day. *Cherry Coke* cans and *Space Invaders* packets whirled around, making a racket. Fleur's hair blew in her eyes. Some spaz kicked a football at her. It bounced off her knees. He went to touch her and she elbowed his ribs.

He nipped her arm. She laughed and shouldered him.

'Bully,' he said. 'Telling Miss and you'll get expelled.' But his skin tickled under the clothes from that brief contact. He couldn't explain it, didn't quite know what it was, but when he looked at her legs, the socks having fallen down again, he wanted to punch something. And he also wanted to cry, which he hadn't done since dad was taken away last year. His stomach felt tight and sore.

She carefully pulled up her socks. But he couldn't forget what he'd seen. Her skin was red as if she'd been freshly slapped, and it was bubbly, like it was trying to come away from her body. Some bits were bloody. He thought now they were like burns, not scars. Bits of red had bubbled through her socks.

'You should tell a teacher. Or that *Childline*. It's always on telly.'

'Get lost, will you?'

'Fleur!'

He held her hand and she shook him off, pushing him down so he landed on his arse with a tooth-cracking jolt. Kids were pointing and laughing.

She stuffed the sandwiches into her backpack. He caught her wrist and kissed her cheek. She kneed him in the balls. Crying. What had he done that was bad enough to make her cry? He drew his knees to his chest, crawling in pain.

The next day he tried to rescue a bird that had been mangled by a cat. He fell and blacked out. The hospital called it unconsciousness. It was then they noticed his ear infection and explained why he'd been missing words. That weird underwater feeling. His mother was really upset with herself. Sometimes he was, too, and thought she should go to prison. It was abuse. But then his grandfather died and the smell finally left their apartment, and his mother started cooking again. She made an effort to make nice things. He spent a lot of time in his room, painting aeroplanes, and dreaming that one day he'd be a pilot and get away from this stupid town. Fleur was not talking to him. He could still hear a little, but they'd told him soon he would be severely deaf. Not totally, but still, he would need someone to sit in class with him, and help.

Retard.

He could see it now. All the names. Fleur looking at him, embarrassed. Or worse, pitying.

He asked his mother if he could go to a school where he was the same as everyone else. She said they couldn't afford it, so he rubbed her toothbrush with soap. They still couldn't afford it. He started leaving whoopee cushions on teachers' chairs and fighting. A huddle of kids would surround him – *Fight Fight Fight* – and Fleur would be stood back, away from the crowd, with that quiet new foreign girl. Fleur had that look, like she wanted him to be good again. It inspired him to thump the guy even harder. Soon, Fleur wouldn't even watch him fight. He ripped pictures off the classroom walls, and he wrote 'Mrs Hilton is a prick' on the blackboard. Except he didn't, someone else did, but it was a good opportunity.

He had to travel to his next school, two buses then a cab. He learned a new language with his hands. They called it sign. BSL. It hurt his fingers and looked stupid. There were girls at the new school, but none of them with copper hair and freckles and scars under their socks. They wouldn't share their lunch either.

He saw Fleur around town sometimes, coming out of the baths, or coming out of Stationery Box. She still had her foreign shadow for a while. He tried to talk to her sometimes, but she ignored him. Maybe all she saw was the hearing aid. Maybe she just didn't recognize him anymore.

Lying in bed one night, the smell of model paint and glue making him a little high, Daniel wondered how Fleur got those burns. He fantasised about asking her again, her telling him, and adding that she'd told no one else. That would feel special. They'd grow up and he'd be a pilot and she'd be a businesswoman and she wouldn't have burned legs.

Daniel got out of bed and folded a paper aeroplane. Fleur would probably prefer a flower, but he couldn't do those. So he made sure all the lines were scored and folded perfectly. He tore in precise tail flaps. It would fly. It had been a couple of years since he'd last seen Fleur. The last time he'd noticed her in town, she'd had breasts. Little ones, but a definite bra under her shirt. She would have forgotten him by now. Probably wouldn't even remember his name, but he had to give her this.

The next day, Daniel didn't get the two buses and the cab. He got one bus and went to his old school. He jumped over the fence into the playground and scouted the classrooms until he found Fleur's. The walls were plastered with maps. Fleur had so many freckles she almost looked tanned. But really she was pale as chalk, like those soft bags he bought penny sweets in.

Her face was round; eyes bright and focused on the teacher. She sat very straight. Side on like this, he could see the curve of her eyelashes, barely blinking. So long and thick they looked like feathers.

Next to Fleur was the foreign girl, who was also magnetic. He blinked. And the foreign girl was not there. He moved his head and she was back, skin the colour of the oil in his mother's frying pan. Her eyes seemed to be drawn with a bold hand. They were curious, and seemed to hold some pit of knowledge, coming from a place he didn't understand. Fleur, he understood more. The two girls breathed at the same time.

Perhaps he could just fly it in to her? He crouched, the sole of his plastic shoe crushed a stone. He fished out the aeroplane. Standing, he tapped the window with his scabbed knuckles, and the foreign girl looked right at him. But so did the teacher. Daniel darted out of sight. Crouching below the window, he could just about make out the girl looking for him. She frowned then looked away. He pocketed the aeroplane in his grey trousers and headed off.

He'd give it to her another time.

# 6

Yugi takes the pill and pats his face with water. It runs from the neat planes of his face. He observes Chinatsu's arrival in the bathroom doorway via the mirror. A muscle in his cheek flickers, like a pulse. Did she see him take it? Would she consider him less of a man if she knew what it was for? Or would she appreciate the fact he was trying to redress this issue with their sex life? Liar. Was he really taking those pills for Chinatsu, or to make sure he could keep it up with all the other women?

'You are late home, Chinatsu. Where have you been?'

'I went to buy groceries.'

'What did you buy?'

'The market was closed.'

'On a weekday?'

Chinatsu swallows. He can tell she's lying, but he has things to hide too. He thinks of the most recent prostitute. The imprint of her too-tight knickers on her hips. How he dipped his thumb into her mouth, smearing her lipstick. He'd pressed her shoulders into the mattress, his hand cuffing her neck. Her powder-white skin bursting with colour from the pressure. Her mouth seemed fuller. Had it tingled? Had her vision blurred? He'd bitten her lips, blood releasing from the puncture like a bruised plum. How hard would he have had to bite to make that happen? At this point, the whore couldn't act anymore. Couldn't pretend she desired him. He knew it was only money she lusted for. Were they any different in that respect?

He remembers the tickle of her racing heartbeat under his hands, its urgency. Pleasure warms his groin. He'd let her leave with a few cuts and bruises. Sometimes, Yugi would think about his activities while in bed with Chinatsu. He'd get hard and then she'd turn her innocent eyes on him, so wide and unblinking. And that would be that.

Now, Yugi looks at Chinatsu's long and slender throat. The silver chain she wears constantly, the one he gave her when they were courting. Could he tighten the chain about her neck, see the skin bulge through each metal loop and delicately trace the pattern of red marks it would leave?

His desire goes cold.

Chinatsu is his wife. He cannot think of her this way. He turns to look for her; she is not there.

Yugi dabs his face with a black towel, breathing in the lavender that Chinatsu has scented everything with since his trip to England that March. That trip was the start of his sleeplessness, the reason behind the gap between Yugi and his wife. Whenever he thought back to that trip, images flashed. But stronger were the sensations flushing through his body. The pure, cold sense of power and pleasure.

Yugi heads for his study, wet fingers tapping the lights as he goes. The knotted matting digs into his feet through his slippers. They dim and he disappears into the shadows of the halls. The walls are covered in biscotti paint. Pine-framed pictures are hung at regular intervals. They are all stock photographs, except one. The final picture is a teenaged Chinatsu. She is perched on a swing, head at a birdlike angle. Yugi enters his study and slides the door shut. Chinatsu has watered his fern; the soil smells wet and earthy and glistens like lacquer.

Why does this irritate him?

There is a soft tap at the door.

Yugi looks up from the papers he holds in his neat fingers. His nails are polished moons, no hangnails, no grooves in the shell-coloured keratin. The frosted glass obscures his wife's kneeled shape; it is time for tea.

'Enter.'

The glass slides back as Chinatsu expertly moves the door via the pads of her fingertips. It is an old custom, not even the maids would deliver his tea this way, but Yugi demands it. She understands it is one of her duties.

Kneeling, Chinatsu places the tea tray inside the partition and arranges herself neatly on the other side of the doorway. As she straightens, Yugi imagines the muscles working in her taut white thighs, perhaps a slight click in one knee. She is no longer the teenager he married, yet her movements are fluid, made smooth through practice, like that of a gymnast executing a double salto. She brings the tea tray to his desk.

Her size three feet whisper over the matting in white socks. Such small, perfect feet.

Yugi watches his wife's fingers position his tea. He tries to appear relaxed. Why does she make him so tense? There are spices floating in the clear liquid. The scent of ginger burns his nostrils.

Finished, Chinatsu bows, about to leave.

'Why was the market closed today?'

Eyes downcast, her gaze slides to the right. 'Did I say the market? I meant the herbalist. I thought I was sickening for another head cold. There was a sign on the door. Family emergency, or something.'

Yugi nods.

Chinatsu waits.

Yugi raises his eyebrows.

His wife leaves.

He watches her blurred shape as she walks away. Something has changed. He intends to find out what.

# 7

Chinatsu is tending to the luggage Yugi has left in the hallway when she finds it. The dead end in a pocket, the crackle of paper that shouldn't be in there. She has been folding his clothes into piles, hanging shirts and sorting the remaining garments for the wash. A note – from a woman? Something to justify her meeting with Madam Li, to assuage the guilt of what she is doing? There is that heart-stopping moment, a surety, a cooling feeling of dread deep in her bowels. She had been hungry, and was thinking of slicing up a watermelon, but now has no appetite. She knows that the paper contains something that will unravel her world. Will she have to sew it back together? Does she have the strength to pretend everything is all right?

Her head turns for the bathroom; *clink*. Yugi placing his razor on the glass shelf. Now winding up the tap. Humming? He never hums. The thrill of being caught is half exciting. Her heart pulses in her throat, off-rhythm.

She unfolds the paper, thinking of little white windows opening up.

It's hard to recognise at first, but the paper is a newspaper clipping. The layout is wide and sparse, not Japanese. It's also a printout, not a real copy and the print is too distinct. She almost feels the contents of her head shift as her English dredges up. She looks over the words, her throat and tongue wanting to crease and extend into unfamiliar shapes to pronounce them.

Police have issued a warning to Manchester prostitutes to be extremely vigilant after a prostitute was found dead in her own home.

The naked body of Rachel Roach, 32, was discovered by her mother in the early hours of Sunday morning. Detectives say Ms Roach's throat was cut in what looked to be an almost 'surgical manner' and are looking to question an Asian man in connection with the murder.

Because of her lessons, Chinatsu knows how to enunciate most of the English words, but she does not know what they all mean. She picks out words like wave-crests, sunlight highlighting water: 'Woman', 'murder', 'Manchester', 'Asian'.

There is a picture. The woman's eyes burn out as if she is still alive. Her skin is speckled because of the ink dots, but it is a beautiful face. Sunny. Chinatsu's immediate response is to smile at her: Hello. A cold panic spills through her body. She wets her lips. Murder. *Murder?* Why did Yugi have this article? She scours the paper for dates, clues – anything. She flashes hot, armpits sticky, as if stood over a wok.

*Manchester?* Ten years ago. This was the time Yugi started having trouble sleeping, wasn't it? When she started to dot lavender oil on his pillow, to slip a vial into his luggage when he was travelling abroad. So what did that mean? How did the two connect? Her brain was stubborn, refusing to make the links.

Years before marriage and dinner parties and duty, when she was around eight, her father had been seconded to a small town near the British city of Manchester. She remembers how flat the houses were, all that grey space beneath the grey sky. And that girl with the freckles and the copper hair.

She thinks back. The girl is pale and quiet, her smile tentative, her uncertainty something that Chinatsu just . . . recognised. She had an awareness of her body that no other English girl had. Japanese girls have this awareness from a very early age. They are taught to be poised and discreet and feminine. Both of them stood out in this way, though none

31

of the other children recognised it. Because they were just children. Even now, after all these years, Chinatsu had never had another friend like this English girl. But at that time her family never stayed anywhere for long. This was when her father was still active and working; forging links, building the business that Yugi finally took over. His family had become used to hotel homes and temporary schools. He had lived in offices and meeting rooms, thriving off coded handshakes. Or so she imagined. Chinatsu had felt like an army brat in an American film, always flitting, never connecting. That town was grainy in her memory, just like the picture of the murdered woman in her hands. But the friend she made there is always bright in her mind. Fleur. They had shared a secret, something that had seemed dramatic at the time. Something not to be spoken about, but would bind them together for all time. But what was it? Why couldn't she remember? They'd made a promise to each other, she knew that. They would never marry, but would run away and live in Hawaii and swim with dolphins. They would find each other again, somehow, and be there for the other. The pact seems stupid now and yet she feels acutely guilty. What happened to Fleur?

The bathroom light clicks off, a floorboard giving Yugi's location.

Her chest tightens. She drops the shirt and quickly thrusts the article into the top drawer of the dresser. Yugi might just think the paper has fallen out. Even so, he would definitely search for it. He wouldn't find it below the silk and elastic of the slips in her underwear drawer.

Yugi enters the bedroom smelling of soap. The scent is flowery. His hand brushes her leg when he passes her on his way to the bed. She flinches. Was it an accident, or foreplay? She feels a surge of desire.

The bed is western and made of rosewood. There are grooves in the thick, solid headboard, which give it two distinct sections: here is where you sleep; here is where *you* sleep. A slim silk pillow rests before each section. They are the colour of a wintry *Sukura*, Japanese Cherry. These, the rosewood and the pillows, are the only real colours in the room. The rest is made up of variations of white and grey: polar, arctic, snow, pebble. The opaque rice paper in the *shoji* reminds her of a fogged window; even its frame is chalk-coloured.

Chinatsu wears a silk housecoat. With her back to Yugi, she removes it and hangs it on the *shoji*. Is he watching? Can the sight of her body actually turn him on? Her black hair reaches just below her ears and has been combed into a 20s style. It is curled under; a finger of black drops from the curl, out of place. It tickles the fine, dark hair at the nape of her neck. Chinatsu's top two vertebrae are visible above the square neck of her cotton nightdress. They look like misshapen ice-cubes, melting under the skin.

Chinatsu turns to find Yugi observing her, already in bed, hands folded in his lap over the duvet. She pretends not to notice his gaze, but anticipation swells. She notes the undertone of yellow in Yugi's complexion. She lifts the duvet on her side; it's white like the tip of an owl's wing. She slips inside. Gooseflesh pops on her upper arms.

'You are cold.'

She raises her eyebrows, surprised. Try not to look eager. Sat up, she glances at Yugi over one shoulder, nods. She lies down.

Yugi climbs on top of Chinatsu. His cold toes shock the inside of her ankles. They look at each other. Yugi has red spider veins in his eyes and blunt eyelashes.

She looks at his lips, so tightly pressed. She angles her pelvis to help and can feel him hard against her. His hips fit inside hers, but she knows if he doesn't get inside soon, he will become soft. She wiggles her hips, a millimetre to the left, then the right, trying to find the perfect place. There. She presses his lower back to encourage him. If only she was confident enough to take hold of him. Yugi tries to insert himself. She raises her eyebrows, wincing, as his penis stabs her. Don't make a sound. Yugi's eyes are focused on Chinatsu's collarbone and she watches him, willing him to look up. If only he would look, if he would *see* her. Yugi tries again. She closes her eyes when he enters her, willing herself to relax. She's too tight, not wet. Yugi won't like that.

The blankets lift and fall slightly, like slow breaths, but they do not come away from the sides. How long will he last? Will this be the first time they manage it in years? She feels tense for him, hoping.

Chinatsu raises her left arm and lays it back against the pillow. The palm is up, open. She wants him to lace his fingers into hers. Yugi plants his hand on the right side of her face, trapping a stray hair. She pulls her head to the left to free it, but the strand snaps and the hair coils up into a wire-thin corkscrew.

33

He's going to climax. The thought streaks through her. This should be monumental. It has been so long. But even the excitement of this, something so novel, fades. He ejaculates, just the faintest tension tightening his brow. His seed pulses weakly inside her, a light bulb flickering. She stares curiously at his inexpressive face. Could things be changing? Why did he desire her now? Could she be pregnant, just from that? Pregnant. She does not know how she would feel, after all this ache and longing, should that be true. She blinks, eyes cast away from Yugi's gaze.

Yugi stares at the hair he has trapped, his mouth open, breath hitting her face. It smells like ginseng, dusty and medicinal. Her mother, who was always complaining of impending illnesses, took it habitually. Why is Yugi taking ginseng? There is so much she does not know about her husband. But that article. What could it mean? And what else doesn't she know? There is one obvious reason why Yugi would have an article like that, isn't there?

Yugi arranges himself on his left side and turns off the lamp.

The white room goes charcoal.

He was having an affair. If this was true, surely this is more reason for him not to want her? So why sleep with her now? To dull any suspicion she might have?

In the silence, Chinatsu can hear the faint clatter of a train, a bicycle's bell, and a dog's bark that turns to a lonely howl.

An affair. Why isn't she offended? Perhaps because it gives her a sense of justification, takes away the guilt for seeking out Madam Li. Yugi has desires, and so does she. Excitement builds, static electricity keeping her wide-awake. Any moment now Yugi will ask the question he always asks when they try to have sex. Does it allow him to believe that they have a normal sex life?

Waiting, Chinatsu's thoughts spiral back to England, the girl who explained things with her hands and goldfish expressions when Chinatsu couldn't understand the teacher. They'd giggle together. Chinatsu had spoken the language well, once. But now it was glued down, and would not pop up. She remembered a boy who had pressed his face to the classroom window, so obviously in love with Fleur. And how Fleur had never noticed. How was she? How had she grown up? Had she cut great

34

colourful strokes through life, swathing through university and fulfilling the promise of her quiet fire, with those straight shoulders, a posture Chinatsu's mother would have been proud of? Or had she drowned in normality, bricked down by a man? The idea was almost painful. Chinatsu unfastened an English word, stupidly lost before now: Hello. Another: Goodbye. A sentence bubbled up: How old are you?

'Did you take your pill?' Yugi says.

'How old are you?'

The foreign words are clamouring in the dark. They're like washing suspended on a line between Italian alleyways. The string snaps. The clothes, with their semblance of arms, legs, bodies that aren't there, are poised to fall for a moment, hanging. And then they plummet, clasping nothing to save themselves. The English words were falling through her mind. It suddenly seemed imperative to catch them, and make them real.

There is an attractive growl in Yugi's voice, deepening it. In the dark she can imagine he is someone else, that the growl is lust, and not suspicion. 'Why are you speaking English?'

'There were English tourists on the train today.'

'Why?'

'What?'

'Why would they come here?'

Chinatsu turns to the bedside drawer and pops a tiny cream tablet from its metal row. Introduced just over a decade ago in Japan, the pill was almost frighteningly popular with men. No children. This was why Madam Li's service was becoming increasingly useful. 'I was so excited about you coming home, I must have forgotten to take it.' She slips the tablet between her lips and settles back against the pillow.

Despite the affair, if she is right, and she would be in the minority if it were not the case, Yugi is still her husband. A child will unite them. And if she isn't distracted by her physical desires, she will be able to concentrate on being a good and dutiful wife. Madam Li was right; it is the honourable thing to do.

She whispers the words she says every night. Her ritual, even when Yugi isn't there: 'I love you.'

When she is sure Yugi is asleep, Chinatsu rises and drifts to the kitchen.

Her reflection follows her on white gloss doors, in darkened windows, on every stainless steel and copper appliance and pan in the kitchen. She takes a pad out of the cutlery drawer and a pen from alongside it. The pen is silver, like the one in her purse, and her reflection in it is squashed and elongated down the pen's length. In the centre of the paper she writes one word: 'Amber.' Circles it countless times.

She sets the pad on the counter and the pen back in the drawer. She boils some water, looking at her face looking back at her, flattened and wrapped around the cylinder of the silver kettle. The water boils white against the dark window, coating her blinking reflection.

It looks paler. She imagines the English girl as her reflection, but all grown up. They were, after all, one and the same. Three months. Just three months in England and it left such a significant imprint. Everything in Manchester was familiar, recognisable replicas of her home in Japan, but with enough subtle differences to make the place *foreign*. At first, Chinatsu would hunt out reminders of home. Cheap chopsticks, a *McDonalds*, the iconic yellow and red a relief to see. But only in her friend's face, her smaller nose, the freckles you don't really see on Japanese, her different, milky smell, did Chinatsu feel easy and united. They swapped addresses and wrote once. There were felt-tip hearts on the paper. Who'd written first? Fleur? Or Chinatsu? Who hadn't written back? Was it Chinatsu's fault? Was the bond she'd imagined ever really there? She remembered spotting a tortoiseshell comb gleaming on a market stall. She'd known it should be for Fleur, and was sure she had posted it with such excitement. It was sad. Did she still have Fleur's letter?

Fleur is part of her, she'd always felt it, despite the non-contact. But there is another part of her too. Amber. It's the name she's given to the part of her that has been to ask about English lessons at the Galaxy Language school. The one who reasoned that the meeting with Madam Li would just be a meeting, and that's all. The risk-taker. Evil. The word and the thought are both perverse, yet thrilling. She tingles down *there*, where Yugi has just been. Her thoughts skip to Satoshi: his young body, lean and hard. Would he be eager for her? Something that Yugi has never really been.

How strange to think they had made love tonight. That he was inside her. Now.

The kettle clicks. She straightens and makes green tea, curling her fingers around the china. The burn feels good.

Chinatsu tears out the leaf of paper with Amber's name written on it. She runs her finger over the grooves in the paper where she had pressed hard. With the tip of her tongue, she works the pill out from the inside of her cheek. She tastes the sweetness of its coating and spits it down the sink. It bounces, tinny as it hits the metal. Disappears. She places the paper with the name in the sink and pours water over it, keeping the kettle low so the water isn't loud. Steam rises. Some of the ink is pulled away from the paper, washing away Amber's name. The paper goes see-through, suckers to the steel and separates into wet flakes. She rakes up the sopping paper and slops it into the bin. Looking up, she's about to move back to the counter, ready to slip the pad away under the cutlery basket in the drawer.

Her reflection has doubled.

She puts a hand to her chest.

'Yugi. What are you doing up?'

Via the window, she sees his head tilt in the manner of a headmaster who is quietly amazed his pupil has the gall to answer back.

'You were not in bed when I awoke. Is something wrong, Chinatsu?'

She raises the teacup. 'I woke with a terrible thirst. Would you like some?'

'And that?' He nods towards the sink.

'I was washing a spider away. You know how I hate them.'

He stares at her.

She blinks, waiting.

'Come back to bed.'

Chinatsu glances at the pad still on the countertop.

'It's late, Chinatsu.'

'Yes, Yugi.'

She joins him in the kitchen entryway, and they head back to the bedroom. She doesn't look back.

# 8

Fleur is perched on the back step in the terrace's garden, the first cup of
tea of the day warming her palm. The garden is flagged, but she's filled it
with tubs of pansies. She inhales their scent; they smell of green and life.
She closes eyes and lets the sun warm her eyelids. First signs of
summer. She's gripped by a strong yearning to get out of here. A need
for action. The next time Marcus goes out with his mates, she'll grab her
stuff and get a cab to Nan's. Raise this baby with just women, and
gentleness.

The idea of this sort of life reminds her of Chinatsu, her Japanese
friend, and their promise to each other.

She had talked to Chinatsu in circles, about Derek. There had been
sleet that day she'd told her friend what was happening at home, just
fourteen days before she found her mother hanging in the night. In the
morning, despite how hard she cried, Nan had sent her to school. Fleur
didn't see anything that went on that day but over the years she imagined
what could have happened: there might have been police, people coming
for the body, her *mother*, still and grey and waxen. Everyone upset. As a
child, she'd felt cheated and resentful, torn from her dead mother. In
hindsight, it was probably the right thing to do.

Fleur went back to the earlier memory. She remembers wanting to have someone to tell her story to, of having her chest always full of air ready to speak the secret. Quiet, she'd sat outside with Chinatsu on the playground steps while everyone else was inside on handheld games. Mario, or something. Fleur had really missed Daniel that day. They were such good friends and then he seemed to vanish. No goodbye. In Fleur's mind, he'd gone because he'd tried to kiss her and she wouldn't let him. She wouldn't do what he'd asked. She'd thought he was a friend. Now, if she ever saw him around town she flushed bright red, somehow ashamed and angry. And then Chinatsu had arrived, filling the gap of her loneliness.

The playground was freezing that day and the snow had turned to sleet. They carved out a place to sit on the steps, making a seat of their scarves so their bums wouldn't go numb. Fingers icy, they swapped lunches. Chinatsu loved jam, she wasn't allowed anything sweet. Fleur loved the exotic noodles and boxes and sauces Chinatsu brought. This is *miso* soup, she would say. It tasted of salt and earth. This is wasabi. These are soba noodles, my favourite. The textures and smells were so far away from Manchester. They told her there was a life beyond all this and that one day, she might just be lucky enough to escape.

'My father say we return home to Tokyo soon.'

'You can't.'

Chinatsu looks at Fleur. She pulls a section of her hair, which was loose that day. She plaits it with her own, black and copper.

'There.'

Fleur smiles and runs her thumb over the rope of hair. Chinatsu's hair is silky and is starting to slip already. 'My mum has a new boyfriend,' she says.

'He is nice?'

Fleur looks at her friend. She shakes her head, their hair slips, connected by a small tangle at the very bottom.

'Why?'

'He's still . . . watching me.'

'Still? Watching what? I don't understand.'

'Me.'

39

They look at each other for a long time, for long minutes after the bell rings. They're pulled back by school and the dry radiator-heat of the classroom, of having to get back to reading comprehension and answering questions.

Fleur can hear the buzz in the classroom, chairs clanking. There's a flash, the teacher's swot taking their picture. Something about having a record of Chinatsu's visit. She runs back in.

'One day, we will live in . . . Egypt and take care of each other. It will be sunny each day and no man will say what we cannot do.'

Fleur giggles. Chinatsu's smile makes her eyelashes touch. Fleur stands and Chinatsu follows. They brush themselves off. 'Hawaii. We will live in Hawaii.'

'And how will we live?'

'Off the land. We will have animals and space, and sunshine.'

The next week, Derek did more than just watch. It was early in the morning, just before school. He said he was going to make it so that when she grew up, it wouldn't hurt when she got a real boyfriend. He said he was doing something good and helpful, that she would thank him later on. He said it was OK because he only used his finger.

At school, everyone is getting their swim bags. Fleur's knickers feel wet, but she doesn't know why. She asks to go to the toilet but the teacher says they don't have time. She rides the bus with Chinatsu next to her, quiet. In the changing room she works her clothes off underneath a towel and changes into her costume. She won't look at her body when she dresses.

Queuing on the tiles, Fleur crosses her arms over her body. Her legs feel sticky. People are whispering.

'Fleur's on her period.'

'Ugh. Weirdo.'

'Disgusting.'

Fleur looks down. Her stomach rolls over, she wants to throw up. Her head feels like candyfloss. Blood paints her thighs and knees and calves.

Chinatsu stands behind her. She drapes her with a towel. 'No. Is me. I spill my juice this morning.'

They duck back into the changing rooms and Fleur palms the shower on, letting it drench her. They come back and Chinatsu holds her hand, letting go just before they're in sight. They get into the water via the shallow-end steps, wade up to their necks and clutch the side.

'Tell me,' Chinatsu says.

Fleur cries into the water, shaking her head. She dips down, letting the water rinse her face.

'My father has found me a husband already.'

'Ugh. Will you have to cook all the time?'

'Oh yes.'

'And run his bath.'

'I suppose.'

'And – ' Fleur puts a hand to her mouth, leans over to Chinatsu and whispers.

Chinatsu nods. 'Mother says to think of it as just another duty.'

Fleur squeezes her eyes shut and sticks a finger down her throat.

'Are you ill?'

'Aren't you scared?'

'Of running his baths and feeding him?'

'Of doing . . . *that*.'

Chinatsu shrugs. 'I don't know what that feels like, do I?'

'Oh.' Fleur rests her chin on the ledge. She stares at the water sucking and lapping against the side.

'I might even like that, though mother says I shouldn't. I do know I hate cooking.'

'Yeah.'

Chinatsu bumps Fleur's arm, gently. 'His name is Yugi.'

Fleur sits up. 'What a stupid name.'

'Very stupid.'

'When?'

'When I am sixteen. He wants to meet me when we are home next month.'

'I don't want you to go.'

'I do not want to go.'

'I don't want to go home.'

'I know. Me neither. We should make your mother's boyfriend stop,' Chinatsu says.

41

'How?'

'Get him taken by the police?'

They talk of ways they could make this happen.

'There is also our plan,' Chinatsu says.

'To Hawaii?'

'Anywhere. I will meet you at the bus stop outside school. I have money. Yes?'

They move apart as one of their classmates swims past, then shake their pinkie fingers under the water.

The next day, Fleur is at the bus stop waiting, all her favourite books and six packets of Wagon Wheels stuffed in a carrier bag. She waits until the school bell rings, until even the latest kids have run in. She waits until after Religion has started and then worries she might have missed Chinatsu. Her friend might be sat in class, thinking that Fleur had let her down. She runs, breathless. The classroom door slams open and everybody turns to stare. Chinatsu is not there. She is never there again. In class, Fleur writes Chinatsu a letter. She doesn't ask why she's left, or for an explanation, just talks about life and their promise to find each other and live together one day.

In the middle of the night, Derek asks Fleur to show him what she has learned. He does something to himself as she uses her own finger.

A shout from next door distracts Fleur from her thoughts. She rubs a tear away with one knuckle. The neighbours are arguing about something. She burns with embarrassment. Could people hear her and Marcus arguing too? It got much worse than that, her pleading with him. All the thuds and smashing. Did people sit there wondering what to do?

Fleur puts the mug down; it clinks on the concrete. She massages her wrist. In the main, Marcus was gentle last night, though he'd gripped her wrist a little too tightly. Things could change, couldn't they? If he stopped drinking . . . she shook her head. He'd never stop drinking.

The washing flaps at number 46. A breeze stirs, tickling the leaves on the rhododendrons, ruffling the cuffs of six identical men's shirts. The shirts are bright orange with the words Blacklidge Bros in white font. Blacklidge, the abattoir down the road in the industrial park. She wrinkles her nose and glances up at the sky, tracking the arc of an aeroplane across the blue. It's so far away that it doesn't seem to make a sound, and leaves a foam trail in its wake. She thinks of Daniel again, is thinking of him so much lately. Why? Is it because she's suffocating, and craving escape?

Fleur has just got up from doing the midnight shift. She's had her hair in a long plait. After loosening, it's all wavy, like the way a child draws birds. She squints, flicks off her slippers and wriggles her toes in the warmth of the sun, letting her head fall back so it can wash over her face. She puts a hand to her stomach. She's got someone else to think about now. Nan would help, wouldn't she? She wouldn't be alone. Even if she was, she could do it, be the mother that hers wasn't.

Something jingles, the sound of Santa Claus arriving in a children's movie. She looks to the right. A kitten has just landed on top of the wheelie bin.

She laughs. 'Hello, you.'

The kitten sniffs the bin-lid.

'Here, pss pss. You lost there? How'd you get here?' She reaches out a hand.

The kitten has wide blue eyes and its fur has unusual dots like a mini leopard, a tiny cream mouth. It glances her way, then at the bottom-heavy bee which is investigating the bin. The kitten pats the bee with its white paw and makes a noise like a drill meeting brick. It shoots onto the concrete, hungrily licking the paw.

'Oh-oh.' Fleur approaches the kitten.

The kitten stops licking itself and allows her to pick it up. She brings it to the step and holds it in her lap, tickling its soft ears as it continues licking.

'What's your name then, puss?' She checks its blue collar. 'Bob? Well that doesn't sound right, does it? I'll call you Leo? D'you like that?'

'Oi. How about a bit of consideration? Tryna sleep here.'

Marcus is leaning out of the bathroom, shirtless. She can see the stretch marks on his biceps, remnants of his fledgling rugby career, when he overdid it with the weights.

'Sorry. Although, it *is* eleven o'clock, isn't it puss?'

Marcus' jaw sticks out. 'You fucking what?'

'Nothing.'

'Just keep it down. Yeah?'

43

Fleur rolls her eyes, but smiles at the kitten and takes it into the kitchen. Part of her is pleased at Marcus' behaviour. It's another strike on the leave him/don't leave him tally. He's not the sweet guy she first met, who rescued her from a group of drooling blokes all those years ago. Maybe he never really was?

She runs the tap, takes the smallest Pyrex bowl out of the dish cupboard and fills it with water, shaking in salt.

'Come on. Let's make that paw feel better. Oops. No, come on, it's only water. Won't hurt.' She holds the kitten's paw and dips it into the bowl.

'Fleur? Fleur!'

'What?'

'What you answering like that for?'

She rolls her eyes. 'Sorry. What?'

'Can you come here a minute?'

'Why?'

'Can you not just come up? Fuck's sake. Can't find my rugby shirt.'

Fleur's shoulders sag. She sets the kitten on the floor, flinching as Marcus rolls open drawer after drawer upstairs, only to slam them closed moments later. 'Stay there you. We're not finished with you yet.'

The kitten blinks. As Fleur starts up the staircase, the kitten follows. Pat, pat, pat over the lino.

She collides with Marcus on the landing. His neck is blotchy, as though birthmarks have formed there overnight, or else he's been sucked by leaches.

'Who the fuck is Daniel?'

She freezes, sees the aeroplane in Marcus' grip. She'd preserved it all these years. Looking at it all crumpled in Marcus' thick fingers, something breaks inside her.

'Well? Who is he? You fucking someone else. Eh?'

'Don't be ridiculous.'

'Then what the *fuck* is it doing in our bed?'

She feels so tired. 'It was in the drawer, not the bed.'

'You're hiding things from me. It's not on.'

'It was from a boy I used to know. Years ago.'

'So it means nothing to you, right? He means nothing to you?'

44

She sighs and glances over her shoulder; the kitten is making its way up the staircase. It slips off one step, tries again.

'Well?'

Fleur's mouth is tight.

'Fleur! Tell me he doesn't mean anything.'

'No.'

She can sense his anger building and is tempted to tell him to just chill out, relax, have a beer. But alcohol always has the opposite effect.

'You either tell me now or I knock it out of you.'

She looks at him. In the past, when he's said things like that, her expression has been childlike. She'd been unable to believe what had come out of his mouth. But now her eyelids are heavy, as though unable to keep awake.

'Well that just proves it, doesn't it? Everyone thinks I'm the bastard in this relationship, but you know what? It's you. Lying little whore, just like your ruddy mother.'

She laughs. 'Christ.'

'*What?*'

She frowns. 'Can you just put it back please? You're going to break it.'

Marcus's eyebrows shoot up. He shakes his head, first slowly, then fast. He balls the aeroplane in two hands then tosses it over Fleur's head. 'Go and bloody get it then. If it means so much to you.'

Fleur watches the aeroplane take a nosedive down the staircase. The kitten pauses in its ascent to watch.

'And what the fuck is that?'

'Oh for god's sake Marcus it's just a kitten. What's up with you today?'

'Well what's it fucking doing in here?'

Marcus moves to push past Fleur.

'Leave it alone, Marcus.' She can take whatever he did to her, but the thought of him hurting something else is not OK.

'Why're you being like this?' Marcus grips Fleur's left wrist, the one that's sore from last night. If it had been her right wrist, she might have stayed balanced on the head of the staircase. But it was the left, and Fleur automatically pulls back. Her body opens to the right, shoulder swinging out. Her right heel slips off the stair, her left leg buckles. Now

45

she looks at him, childlike, disbelieving. How could you?

And then she drops, body spiralling down the staircase.

Her body bounces down the stairs, slams into the banisters.

The carpet burns her face.

She doesn't shout for Marcus, or even her mother.

'Nan!'

Her voice breaks with the power of it. She wants to say sorry for all the years of not speaking. For all the pain she'd caused. She wants her child to have a great-grandma. She prays she won't hurt the kitten.

# 9

It was over their lunchtime meetings that Daniel told Fleur about all the times he'd seen her. Especially that time when he was coming out of Riley's Pool Club. It was Saturday night in the town centre. He was sixteen and just starting to reach his full height. His friend Martin had already left, waved goodbye, and signed that he'd call tomorrow. Martin was profoundly deaf, and refused to talk. Most of them at the school were like that, despite encouragement. With them, it was just easier to sign. That upset Daniel's mother. She was worried he would forget. Daniel wanted cochlear implants. She said it was too dangerous. Maybe when he was eighteen he could make the decision himself. Whenever they had this argument, he scowled and slammed his door, knowing she'd be upset. Let her. He would sit down to paint aeroplanes.

It was when he was stepping off the bottom steps that Daniel collided with a group of guys with rugby player frames. One had a gold stud in his left ear, another a gold hoop.

'Watch it, mate,' said the one with the stud.

Daniel clenched his fists. But it wasn't worth starting anything. 'Sorry,' he said.

The group of guys, five in total, laughed and elbowed each other. 'You swallowed your balls, mate?'

'He sounds weird.'

'Ha. Swallowed.'

'Nah, he's retarded. Aren't you mate? It's not their fault though. It's cos his mum fucked her brother. Innit?'

The guy who said this was wearing a neon yellow t-shirt with 'Hero' stamped across it. His hooped earring was fishing-wire thin.

Daniel shook his head and said, enunciating as clearly as possible, 'No, I'm just deaf. What's your excuse?'

The one with the gold stud sneered. 'Easy, Ellison. We're not out to twat about with retards.'

The guys headed towards a club on the corner, a couple of them shouldering into Daniel as they passed. The club used to be a bank, then an Irish bar, now it was a *Reflex* – total 80's cheese. Daniel waited until they were inside, then followed. These past few years he'd shrugged off tons of comments from arseholes like this. He'd had enough. His arms felt hot. He wanted to punch something, or someone.

He dodged the chip cartons clogging the gutters. A taxi made a U-turn down a one-way street. He felt its engine thrumming through his soles. A girl, who couldn't be much older than Daniel, looked up from kissing a bearded man in the doorway of a solicitors. She was wearing fur and platform boots and not much else.

Daniel stopped at the *Reflex*. His shoulder touched the brick of the doorframe, the music vibrated through him. He might be wrong, but it felt like the bass of a Michael Jackson song. He could see Fleur. It had been a while since he'd seen her, and she'd stretched out. Tall, a little too thin. Her shoulders seemed extremely vulnerable. She sat extremely straight, as though attending a job interview. He liked her dress. It was electric blue, stark against the dark copper of her hair. It was tight, and quite high above the knee. She kept tugging it down, arms cuddling her waist. Her breasts were small, but he could see the shape of her nipples through the dress. He liked her hair; she'd curled it properly. It was not just frizzy like it used to be. She sipped from a bottle of blue WKD. She looked young, a girl dressed up in women's clothes with women's make-up. Her face still had a childish roundness to it, despite her slimness. To Daniel, the vulnerability was endearing. But he knew how men's minds worked; she'd just look like an easy target. He had a sudden desire to protect her.

Lately, Daniel had got massively into *Star Trek: The Next Generation*. He had a small moment where he thought it might just be possible to reach out to her in his mind. He concentrated hard. Look at me. *Look at me*. She sipped her drink and glanced over to the dance floor. He cringed. Idiot.

One of the guys Daniel had encountered in the street blocked his view of Fleur. Her whole body disappeared behind his back, the guy's shoulder blades poking out of a tight wasp-yellow T-shirt.

Daniel drummed his fingers on the wall. Should he go in? He checked his pockets. Only enough money for bus fare. He probably wouldn't get in anyway. Damn. He was about to turn away when he saw Fleur appear from behind the mass of yellow. She stalked straight towards Daniel, hitching down her skirt. Her legs were blotchy; it was cold. His mother would say 'Put some jeans on before you catch your death.'

'OK?' Daniel said when she got outside, trying hard to pronounce the words precisely.

She didn't hear him, but veered left, towards the taxi rank in front of the train station.

The guy in yellow appeared at the club entryway and made to head after her.

Daniel automatically grabbed the guy's wrist. Both of them stared at his hold. The man's eyes were bleary, the whites streaked with red lines. The guy in yellow dragged his elbow back like an oversized dart, and let loose: he punched Daniel in the chest. The air was knocked out of him.

Twin bouncers in shiny bomber jackets grabbed them both. The couple in the doorway clutched each other. The bouncers dumped Daniel face down on the pavement in a mush of chips and gravy. It made the damage done to his eye and his split lip look much worse. Daniel placed his palms on the pavement, trying to get up. Hands grabbed his elbows and hauled him up. He turned. It was the whole group of guys, bar one. The guy with the gold earring. Just let the beating be quick. Daniel pressed the back of his hand to his thickening lip and checked it for blood. Bright drops the size of pennies.

They made a circle around Daniel.

A cop van ploughed up the street and the guys sieved outwards. The van necked the corner and pulled up. Daniel made a run for it.

He swiped his face clean and collided with Fleur. He put his hands out to stop himself, palms crushing her breasts. He saw her mouth open, screaming.

'Sorry. Sorry.' He signed it too.

She rubbed her chest, folded her arms. 'God, your face.'

He grinned, split lip cracking further. She remembered him.

'I was coming back, I thought I heard fighting. Are you OK? They shouldn't be allowed to hit people. It's disgusting.'

His shoulders dropped. She didn't recognise him. She was only talking about the cuts on his face.

'Do you need anything? I can call someone for you? Maybe you should go the hospital?'

'I'm fine, my mother was a nurse.'

'I'm sorry. I can't quite . . . understand you.'

His chest felt tight. Frustration, embarrassment. 'Never mind.' He started to walk away.

'Wait!'

He sensed her walk after him a few steps, and then stop. When he was sure she wasn't looking, he stopped, hovering out of sight. Just wanting to make sure she got into a taxi safely.

She sat down on the bus station bench, purse on her knees, legs together. A guy strolled up, the one with the gold stud in his left ear. It seemed to wink at Daniel. Daniel thumped the brick. Why'd he have to be so proud? He left because his pride was hurt; Fleur didn't remember him. She couldn't understand his speech. So what? He could have stayed, talked to her, seen what happened. But he'd just left. And now that guy, that ape, was in his place.

The gold earring guy raised his hand to brush the hair from Fleur's face. Fuck. He couldn't watch this. He ran home.

Daniel pressed the intercom to the flats. He waved at the camera and the door buzzed. He tried the door; it gave. He walked up the bland staircase which reeked of plastic and food, like a hospital canteen. The smell always made Daniel feel sick. He had spent a lot of time in hospital canteens when his grandfather was ill, until his mother brought him home to nurse. He stopped before number 56. The numbers on the flimsy white door were plastic, coloured gold. It was already ajar. Dozens of his black socks were lined up on the radiator in the hallway. The cream wallpaper behind the radiator had curled up from the heat.

Daniel's mother was wearing a washed-out blue dressing gown and round, fat bee slippers. The dressing gown was spotted white where she'd splashed it with bleach. Her face didn't look right without make-up. It seemed puffy in all the wrong places, too shiny. Her hair was in rollers, though the bottom few were slack.

She covered her mouth with one hand. Her fuchsia talons were more like beetle wings than nails. She'd gone outside the lines in some places, polish flecking her fingers. She shook her head.

'Danny.' She signed as she spoke. 'Why?'

Daniel squeezed past his mother into the bathroom. He pulled off his shirt and ran the tap. Mint-sized hotel soaps dotted the cream sink.

Daniel pointed at the soaps and signs: *You steal?*

'Shut up. Come here and let me look at you.'

His mother grabbed a first aid box off the trolley by the sink, things his grandfather's nurses left behind. She picked out some saline packets and ripped the tops off with her teeth. Daniel looked away to rinse his face gingerly. His mother drummed her fingers on the sink and raised her hand. Waves. He ignored her. She waved again, more insistent.

'What?' Daniel spoke aloud. The word was just about recognisable, though the T is dropped.

'It's not stealing.'

Daniel rolled his eyes and shook his head.

'Stay still.'

His mother squeezed the saline onto the cuts around his mouth and eyebrows.

'Mah.'

'What?'

He signed: *Pain.*

'Well I'm not bloody surprised. Was this guy wearing a ring or something? Do you know who it was? Could you pick him out?'

Daniel shook his head and signed, fast and energetic: *No police. No.*

'Er, yes police.'

He shook his head, breathing out in a whoosh. He escaped the bathroom and disappeared into his bedroom. He pushed the door to and dropped onto the bed. He picked up the paper aeroplane he'd tried to give to Fleur. All those years ago. He had a sudden urge to ball it up and throw it out the window as far as he could.

His mother came in. 'You're at least going to tell me what it was about.'

He stared at the far wall.

'Well?'

Daniel put the plane down: *Boys making annoyance with girl.*

'A girl?' She signed this as well now. Then: *Who?*

He signed: *Not anybody.*

'Hm. Was it that bloody Rose you're always going on about? I bet it was.'

He fingerspelled: *F-L-E-U-R.*

'Well excuse me,' his mother said and fingerspelled the same word, '*Fleur*. La-dee-dah.'

He signed: *She's nice.*

'Honestly, Danny. How long ago was it since you even knew her? Why hang on to the impossible? I mean, is she even hearing-impaired?'

He raised his hands: *And?*

'Nothing. Never mind. But seriously, how long have you had her picture? That place you think I never look?'

He grinned, so unexpected and wide his mother cracked a smile. He winced. The cut in his lip hurt.

'We'll talk about this tomorrow, Danny boy. There's aspirin in the bathroom. Want some?'

He signed: *No thank you. Night.*

His mother nodded and drew in a long breath. 'Well I hope she thanked you at least.' She frowned. 'Hey?'

Daniel shrugged.

His back to her, he used his voice. It scratched through the column of his throat with effort. His remembered patterns of speech felt rusty. 'She doesn't know who I am any more.'

After the accident, he'd clung to the aural world. He'd hoped for a breakthrough in science, something, a way of reversing the irreversible.

52

But the hearing loss had degraded dramatically, going from mild to profound in a shockingly short time. Speech, understanding, comprehension, all drowning because of his body's failure. All because of a bird he'd tried to rescue on a garage roof, and the subsequent fall. But that wasn't true. The loss had been present, but not identified. The doctors, clicking pens, had said it would have progressed throughout his life anyway, just not as quickly. Would he have tried to rescue that bird again, if he'd known what was going to happen after the fall? Definitely. He clenched his fists again. Why had he let his pride get in the way and make him walk away from Fleur?

At least there were pluses to being Deaf: he didn't have to hear the sadness in his mother's voice.

In his peripheral vision, Daniel knew that his mother watched him for a long time before she tightened the rope around her dressing gown, and closed his door. Did she feel like a planet? The two of them making their quiet orbits around each other, the quietness coloured by sign language, those small conversations like coffee breaks in boring meetings. She'd never be quick at it, not like his Deaf friends, and so she'd always orbit around him, but never on the same trajectory.

# 10

Yugi Hamugoshi strides through Uji Corp's grey offices in a Brioni suit. Paper flutters on timid secretaries' stations. As Yugi heads to another important meeting, where he will sit at the head of a walnut desk, making black heads nod, making him feel invincible. Slightly padded at the shoulders, tapering to a slender waist, it is a fine blend of wool, cashmere and silk. It drapes off his lean limbs just so and would make him seem in excellent shape, even if he wasn't.

Yugi stops. Through the glass corridors housing plush conference rooms, where ten men await, he spies a child in the main office. Who had authorised that? He presses his fingertips to the glass. The magnet disconnects, glass becoming a door.

'Could someone tell me why that child is not in school?'

People turn around, phones to ears, coffee cartons frozen at several lips. Someone hides a steaming bowl of *soma* noodles.

'Mr Hamugoshi, sir,' the woman closest to the child squeaks. Her name is Izumi or Izanami.

He winces when she speaks.

'My babysitter . . .'

The air conditioning is regulated to turn off when the temperature reaches a certain point. At this moment its engine subsides, and the room's silence is even more profound, broken only by ringing phones. When Yugi glares at one unanswered phone, people get back to work, voices hushed.

He approaches the child who, unaware, is reading a *Manga*. The images are graphic, a nude woman being chased by a group of men. Yugi bends his head lower. This is for kids?

The child looks up. 'Don't worry, Chihiro will save her. See?' He turns the page and stabs the next square.

Yugi looks at the sticky finger. The kid's nails are jagged. In the comic book, a young man leaps in from out of nowhere, wielding a samurai sword. The following squares show him cleaving all but one of the attackers in half, and holding the girl's face he has just rescued.

But the final image is the hero, his back to an unseen attacker, made weak by his adoration for the girl, about to be decapitated. The caption: *To be continued . . .*

'Is this really suitable material?'

Izumi or Izanami smiles. 'It's all the rage. Sir, forgive me, but may I get you some water? You seem ...'

Yugi is shocked. He tries to understand why. It feels somehow difficult to breathe. 'Find another babysitter for tomorrow, we are not a crèche. Any damage your child does will be automatically deducted from your salary.'

Yugi exits through the glass door and turns right, returning to his office, not the conference room.

The woman was the man's weakness in the *Manga*. For as long as they have been married, Yugi could say this was not true of Chinatsu. She did not blink as he attempted to have sex with her. Those black, unblinking eyes. Reminding him he does not have the power to make her brow wrinkle, or make her sweat. Her mouth stays perfectly straight, she stays perfectly straight. He started having sex with prostitutes as a way of trying to rediscover his desire. But when Chinatsu became his wife she also became undesirable. She must never know what he had done; the shame would not be tolerable. He could stop, if he wanted. But if Chinatsu ever knew, he would no longer be a man in her eyes. As it is, his hold over her is slippery. This is not a welcome feeling.

He wants, just once, to show her his true self. To see her reaction to what makes him tick. What would Chinatsu do if he pinned his hands around her throat and squeezed? What colour could he turn her face?

At his desk, he stretches his legs out to their full length and opens his wallet. The scent of oiled leather triggers nerves in his stomach. Take another one of those stress pills? No, too soon. He could try again with Chinatsu tonight. Should he take one of those performance enhancers? His knee is jogging.

He smoothes his desk clean of imaginary dust. True, some things cannot be fixed; they are gone, broken, done. But some things can be. He looks at the single photograph on his desk: Chinatsu on the swing, a miniature version of the one in their hallway.

He makes a phone call.

'Any news yet?'

'Your wife has not done anything outside of her usual routine yet, Mr

Hamugoshi. Except that –'

'What?'

'She had a brief lunch with the Chinese woman, Li.'

'And you did not think to inform me of this? I want to know what she does, when she does it. Daily reports. Or do you wish to terminate the contract?'

A pause. Yugi hears clicks and clunks on the other end as his contact moves around. A metallic clinking, water rushing. He's making tea? 'I am aware of the terms of our contract, Mr Hamugoshi.'

Yugi wrings the phone; plastic creaking. 'Just keep watching.'

'Keep paying, and I will.'

The contact hangs up. Yugi hammers the receiver down, jaw clenched. The action flurries the few papers on his desk, revealing a yellow *Post-It*. It sits, this simple lemon square, eyeballing him back. He can feel the chill in the air conditioning. In what looks to be his own handwriting are the words: *Find the newspaper clipping. Important!* The last word is underlined three times. He peers closer. How had he forgotten writing that? Was he so distracted by Chinatsu that he was losing his grip? The idea made him all the more determined to resume control.

# 11

Later, Fleur would piece together the time she had missed.

Nan would have been at the hospital. She would have said things to her. Been her usual blunt self. Fleur's eyes would have been closed. Hands down by her sides, atop neat green bed-sheets. Some sort of tube had given her liquid, food and medication. It had gone through her mouth, down what the doctors described afterwards as her oesophagus, and into her stomach. Nan had said Fleur's lips were talc-white. Her hair had been so greasy it seemed gelled.

A diagonal cut had sliced Fleur's face. It had cut down from the outside edge of Fleur's left eyebrow to the corner of her mouth. As if someone had been measuring the distance from each point. It would scar. She would fondle the scar, faintly, in idle moments. When she was nervous, or at the bus stop, when she thought nobody was looking. When it throbbed. Reminding her of what Marcus had done. The scar would always be slightly visible.

Nan would have created a massive screech by dragging a chair towards the bed. If you could have brushed the wrinkles from Nan's face, like the seeds from dandelions, it would be obvious that she and Fleur were related. She'd have tried to smoke. Taken a pack of rollups from her trolley-bag and scrunched the crimped tobacco.

She'd have said something biting. 'Ere. I'll make one for you an all.

Except, oh aye yeah, you've landed yourself in hozzy. This is the thanks I get for raising you, I suppose? Haven't seen you for good on five years and this is our reunion. But here's what, you wake up and walk out of here with that pillock, I'll throw you down the stairs meself.'

Or is that what Fleur had actually heard?

And then, finally, the threat. 'You've a shit-load of explaining to do when you wake up.'

Nan would prattle on. 'So the doc, Pakistani chap, says you've got something called 'closed head injury'. Reckons you've got about forty-eight hours to wake up. Much longer and there could be complications. I'll be here. Got that? I'm not about to lose you as well as your mother.'

Or is that what Fleur hoped she'd heard?

Fleur did remember this. She was sure of it.

'Look like you're dreaming. What you dreaming about, flower?'

# 12

Chinatsu is standing before the hotel. A piece of crumpled paper pricks her hands. Yugi's name is visible, repeating over the paper. Can she really do this? Sleep with another man? Of course she wants a child. But really, she wants to feel like a woman again. The idea thrills through her. A man inside her, gripping her body. The vitality of it.

Yugi enters her head again, blocking that desire.

When Yugi had gone to work she'd fired up his computer and retrieved the article from her dresser. She'd used an online dictionary, making sure to cover her tracks and delete the history afterwards. It took hours to translate the article, and even then she only had a fuzzy understanding of it. The grammar had gaps and she was forced to imagine the meaning. From what she could understand, police were looking for an Asian man to help with their enquiries. It couldn't possibly be Yugi. Could it? But if he wasn't connected to it, why would he have the article? And if he was connected, how many more were there? Murder. A woman had been murdered. She closed her eyes and breathed out. No. Yugi wasn't a murderer. She would know, surely? Chinatsu massaged the pressure points at her eyebrows. She was tense; her fingers provoked acute pain. Smoothing out her tension, she felt suddenly seized by the need to search his office. To know. She sat, chest heaving, trying to talk herself out of it. Eventually, she planted her hands on the desk, leaving ghosts of palm prints, and started to look. She did it carefully, precisely, putting things back in place once she'd looked in, around and under them. Nothing. She sat back down, looked at the desk drawer. It would be locked, wouldn't it? Yugi was scrupulously private. She hooked her finger under the handle and pulled; it gave.

A wash of documents revealed themselves. Accounts, financials, data. Not much of interest. She tried to pat them down in the same place after rifling through and sat back heavily in the chair, swivelling a fraction from left to right. Pointless. She pushed the drawer back, and it grated. She pushed harder, panicked. What if she couldn't get it back in? He'd know.

She bent down, holding her hair from her face, to see what was getting in the way. And she knew she'd found it. Whatever it was she was looking for, this was it.

Taped to the underside of the desk drawer was jewellery. She got off the chair and angled herself under the drawer to see better; an earring, ring, necklace, the chain taped in a neat zigzag. One of the earrings stood out because it was so simple in comparison to the rest. One small stud winking like a dull, pink eye. Were these trinkets his stolen tokens of affection, to remember past conquests? Loves? Slowly, she pushed the drawer back and manoeuvred the chair into its correct location. She stood back. Did everything look right? She adjusted a leaf on the plant and went to check the clock in the kitchen.

Coming out of the office, she nearly ran into a maid who was holding a bundle of precisely folded towels. A lavender scent drifted off them. The maid gazed at the closed office door.

Chinatsu smiled. 'You can take a half day, if you like.'

The maid bowed. 'Yes, Mrs Hamugoshi.'

Chinatsu watched the maid leave, the front door click to. She thought of the jewellery. Why was she sharing her house with so many women? And most importantly, why wasn't she broken-hearted about the fact that Yugi was sleeping with other women? Perhaps because she'd known, she'd felt him separate from her. The date of the article was ten years ago. It coincided with when Yugi had started having problems. Had he just got bored of her? She tried to see herself from his perspective; some dutiful, sexless wife. A model stereotype. It was no wonder, really. She shook her head. This wasn't her fault. But did that really fit? Trinkets of affection?

Murder.

Were all the women who'd worn this jewellery dead somewhere?

Shock rockets through her body. Her stomach feels hollow and she wants to throw up. How did he do it? She pictures their faces, their half naked bodies, abandoned in some hotel room somewhere, or a darkened alley.

Chinatsu calms herself. No. It's too ludicrous to even consider. There had to be another explanation. Didn't there?

She reaches the kitchen, slippers padding over the matting. She would be late for her appointment. A strange thought corrals through her: What if she carried on with this? What if she encountered Yugi at some point, finding each other in some hotel room? Was that even possible, and what would his reaction be? The idea of revealing herself to him as a woman, not a wife, made her wet.

So here she was, standing before a hotel in an ice-blue thong and thrust-forward heels, ready to fuck a stranger for what? Chasing love? Some skewed notion of family? Duty? If she does this, lets another man inside her, reaching, finding his ephemeral happiness in the walls of her body, what becomes of that hope?

Shinjuku continues as normal around her, unaware of what she is about to do. She watches people crossing at zebras in the weakening afternoon sun. It's just about cold enough for jackets, but not for heavy coats. Couples twirl noodles at restaurants; shoppers come out of the various camera and department stores with paper bags. How many other women are about to do what she is going to do right now, this very second? Can she go through with it? The fantasy was possible, but now, stood here. . . she isn't sure.

She takes a deep breath.

She's doing this for Yugi. Them. A family. Revenge?

The Park Hyatt is an impressive building. Chinatsu checks her watch. It is silver, delicate, with a pearl face the colour of a moon. She's five minutes early. She enters the building and crosses the lobby. The hotel is like a mirror; everything gleaming. She wears a chocolate trouser suit and walks calmly towards the lifts, blending in with other business people; well dressed, but not glamorous. Madame Li would find this ensemble acceptable. In fact, this is how she advised her to dress.

She tugs at the chain Yugi gave her.

There is a bin shaped like a small rocket by the set of lifts on the left. If she hadn't foregone breakfast, she could easily have thrown up into it. What if one of the staff questions her? What if she sees someone she recognises? What would she say? She's here to meet a friend? Dressed like this? Relax. Chinatsu deposits the crumpled paper into the bin. It thuds.

The lift doors open. She steps inside and pivots on the ball of her left foot, heels together, bringing herself to face forwards. She presses a button on the keypad. As a child, Chinatsu got up to grade eight in ballet. She misses the feeling of control over her body. As the doors start to close, she spots a man at the end of the lobby. His clothes are shadow-black, but his white trainers attract her attention. Trainers in this kind of hotel? He's about to leave. Does he have a crumpled piece of paper in his hand? Her piece of paper? Surely not? The hand disappears into the pocket of his leather jacket.

Chinatsu takes a half step forward. The doors shut her in. She smiles. She's just being paranoid. The lift whooshes up and deposits her on floor 15.

Stepping onto the thick carpets she heads left, directed by the brass plates on the wall. She stops before a uniform door and is about to press the bell when she pauses, smoothes her hair and bows her head. She speed-walks back to the lift.

On the way down, Chinatsu fumbles in her purse and takes out her notebook. It is a larger version of the one she was writing in the night Yugi found her in the kitchen. She'd had to leave it on the counter where it sat. The next day, the notebook had disappeared. Not daring to ask Yugi, she'd questioned the maids. They all swore they had found no sign of it.

Chinatsu folds back the notebook's hard cover. Glancing at the camera in the lift, she writes, fingers shaking, on a clean page and in English: *Fleur.*

That beautiful name, the long loops of English writing. Where *is* she?

The lift opens before Chinatsu expects, and she hurriedly tucks the notebook back into her bag.

Heading for Shinjuku station, her mobile buzzes. 'Tea Restaurant' flashes up on her phone.

She takes a deep breath. It'll be OK. 'Madam Li,' she says.

'I hear now from my employee. Perhaps this approach not for you.'

She meets Madam Li at the tea restaurant.

Chinatsu is speaking before she sits down, 'I apologise, I just -'

'Yes, so. There is another way.'

Chinatsu's mouth goes dry. Her tongue feels heavy in her mouth. She was going to forget all about it; she obviously wasn't capable. But now she was intrigued. 'Yes?'

'You type of woman seem more accepting when you are employee not boss. Understand?'

'I think.'

'No power, not power-*full*. Yes?'

'Yes, Madam.'

'Fucked, no fucking.'

Chinatsu grips the tabletop. 'I understand!'

Eyes slide over to their table. Whispers.

Chinatsu looks down, cheeks buzzing red.

Madam Li's chuckle is the hiss of an old record player, a needle breathing over a song's end. 'This easily resolved.'

Quiet, Chinatsu is carried along by the crowds at Shinjuku station. She rides the train in silence, hands on her handbag which is a cushion on her lap. She does not notice the man in black, hanging casually onto the overhead strap. He's watching her through the door in the other carriage. Even if she did see him, with his dishevelled jaw-length black hair and adolescent features, he would just seem like any regular young boy on his way to meet a girl. Aside, that is, from the scar, sashimi-pink, curling down from his left nostril, drawing a backwards letter C across a sensuous mouth. The train rocks; a fellow passenger stands on the young man's foot. Eyes on Chinatsu, he reaches down to wipe the scuff from his bright white trainers.

# 13

Yugi Hamugoshi *is* going to play squash tomorrow, and he *is* going to meet the prostitute today.

He practises his conversation: 'Hello. Take off your clothes and lie on the bed.'

Sweat prickles under his Egyptian cotton shirt. The office is suddenly hot, isn't it? He calls his secretary and tells her to adjust the heating.

Yugi steeples his fingers on the desk. He stares ahead at the monochrome clock on the butter-cream wall. There are no figures on the clock, but the fingers indicate ten to twelve. It ticks in time with the row of stress balls on his sweeping rosewood desk which has no papers.

A voice invades the walls.

'Mr Hamugoshi, sir? I have requested the temperature be altered for you. Do you wish to have lunch catered today, or shall I make reservations?'

Yugi clicks a button and disconnects the voice. He is alone in the largest office he has ever occupied. It is the largest in the company, which is natural, given he is now MD of Uji Corp. All he'd had to do was submit to Chinatsu's father's request, and marry his daughter. After that, everything else had fallen into place.

The office has a toilet, a shower, an exercise bike, and a charcoal leather sofa which doubles up as a bed. He could live here, really. The blinds are breathing. Long, thin white fingers, or shreds of a torn dress, half hiding the streets of Tokyo, 135 floors down.

His mobile shrills and he takes it out of his trouser pockets.

'Yes.'

'Yesterday your wife went to the Park Hyatt in Shinjuku. It was a brief visit, not long enough in my opinion. However, I did collect something of interest.'

'Fax it over.'

Yugi pockets the phone and watches the flat black machine. His fingers drum the desktop until it whirrs into life. He snatches the paper. On it is a scanned image of a piece of paper that has once been crumpled but straightened out. He recognises his wife's handwriting, controlled and small. It's his name, again and again. That he is in her thoughts, even in such a strange way, is arresting to Yugi. His gut burns for a moment. He thinks about cancelling his appointment.

Yugi stores the paper in his office drawer. It is time to leave.

Yugi says, 'Take off your clothes and lie on the bed.'

The girl, she told him her name is Maria, has heavy eyelids. She looks up at Yugi from her perch on the hotel bed. She taps her hands on the mattress and stands, thigh boots creaking. She brings her hands to the neck of her blouse.

Opposite, Yugi flattens his back against the hotel wall. The dado rail juts into his spine. He can't help but watch Maria's fingernails, PVC-black, the same as her boots, as she undoes the high-collared blouse from neck to navel. The black nails travel deftly down the fabric, as though playing an instrument.

He sniffs, pinches his nostrils together. They stick momentarily, then unglue.

Maria glances up. The skin on her eyelids is so taut, Yugi wonders if blinking is painful. Canary yellow daubs the lids, her high cheekbones are 80s pink and her full mouth is pert like a cartoon fish. Her teeth are too big for her mouth. A diamond of white glints between ruby red lips.

66

Blowjob lips.

Yugi presses harder against the dado rail and clenches his teeth.

Maria half folds her blouse and drapes it over the chair adjacent to the bed. A white bra, off-colour, is placed over the blouse. Yugi frowns. A high-waisted skirt and a black thong follow. The boots stay. They finish just above the knee, and constrict the skin there, plumping it up. Maria puts her hands on boyish hips. There is a thin window behind her and to the right. The half-covered stretch marks on her hips wink silver in diluted sunshine.

Yugi narrows his eyes.

Maria's nipples are brown, her pubic hair straight but short. It's a diamond of black against the white of her cunt. Yugi imagines her after a bath, craning into awkward positions to shave her lips. Parts look scratchy, like a man's beard. Will it be prickly? He swallows.

'So, where do you want me?'

Yugi looks up. He reaches up to his throat and works the grey tie out of its silk noose. He winds the fabric around his knuckles. 'I said . . .' he has to swallow again, ' . . . lie down on the bed.'

Maria holds Yugi's gaze as she sits, skin pearly against fuchsia sheets. Using her right foot as leverage, the heel spiking silk, she shifts into the centre of the bed. She uncurls, body shuddering with the attempt to make the motion fluid. Upping the number of crunches she does would solve that. Her hair touches the pillow, coiling, before she rests her head back.

Yugi sweats. There is something exquisitely distasteful about this one.

*Thud.*

The squash ball ricochets towards Masa's head. 'Hey!'

He manages to dodge the ball - just - and gets a racket onto it. It's a fumbled strike; the ball twangs oddly off the frame. Loses pace. Yugi chases it down, takes it early.

*Thud.*

The strength in his muscles feels good.

The ball pinballs from wall to wall.

Masa misses. 'Agh!'

*B̰̰̰̰̰rrrrr.*

'Time up, old man.'

Masa keels over, hands on knees. 'I think I'm gonna puke.'

Yugi collects the ball, shorts and shirt heavy with sweat. He needs a good stretch. He strides over to Masa, pats his shoulder with the racket head. 'At least you're getting better.'

Masa straightens, rolls his head from side to side. 'You're getting worse.'

'I can understand why you'd be jealous. Good looks, money, unparalleled sporting prowess.'

'Humility . . .'

They laugh.

'You clearly cheated.'

'Oh yeah.'

They walk towards the door. Yugi goes through, holding it open for his old university pal.

'So Yugi, did I forget your birthday then or what?'

They head down the warren of corridors towards the changing rooms. He and Masa had lived in halls together, sampled Tokyo, graduated together, even started jobs together. On paper, they were alike in many ways. Except Yugi's company now owned the company where they had both originally started work.

'Yugi?'

'Huh?'

'Seemed a bit personal, that's all.'

'Just blowing off steam, you know how it gets.'

'Yeah, yeah.'

They reach the changing rooms, walking into a wall of stale sweat. Yugi pulls his shirt off and grabs a towel from his locker. He never uses the ones laid out by the club. He pulls a shower door back.

'You're just getting old, Masa. Happens to some of us a little earlier.'

Masa takes the stall next to Yugi's. 'You're a cocksucker, man. Hey, you use that number I gave you yet?'

Yugi lets his head fall back, shoulders dropping as water needles his face. He spits. 'What number?'

'*What* number?'

'Oh, that number.'

'Yeah, *that* number.'

Yugi bows his head to wet his hair, breathing through his mouth.

'They have some great girls, you know. Do anything you want. Fuck any yet?'

Yugi frowns. Whenever he blinks, all he can see is Chinatsu on her knees, the tea tray neat and ordered, her upturned eyes.

'Do you ever think about anything else?'

'Huh. You fucked one. Who'd you get?'

'I have a wife, Masa, as do you.'

'Yeah, like my wife doesn't screw around either. Everybody does it, Yugi, come on, don't be a fool. She's got a thing for this guy who works at our favourite restaurant? A waiter? I mean, come *on*. I see it. It's the way she looks at him, sticking her fucking tits out when he pours the water. She thinks I don't, but . . .' Masa's voice sounds muffled, water crashes to the tiles, ' . . . I do.'

Yugi pours shampoo onto his scalp and scrubs. He holds his left hand before him, flexes the fingers back and forth. The veins bulge on the back of his hand, invigorated by the game. They seem like worms beneath his skin. He turns his arm over. Faint marks score the underside of his wrist, like a set of drawn-on veins. Red, not blue. He remembers the prostitute, the baby-faced concern she'd shown, stroking the back of his hair when he cried into the shadows of her neck after the orgasm wracked his body.

He'd left, feeling hot and panicked, shirt untucked, unkempt, all of a sudden confused as to where he'd put that article. The article. The one he'd searched and searched for but could not find. Was it possible Chinatsu had found it? The idea his wife knew something about him, and where the knowledge might take her, zigzagging uncontrollably in her mind, gave him stabbing pains in his chest. Under the water, the scratches burn.

'Human nature, Yugi. Everyone does it.'

Yugi washes the soap from his hair. He thinks about Chinatsu, her back to him in the kitchen that night, the notebook on the counter. The faxed copy of her handwriting had been sent by the detective, his name printed all over it. Like a teenager with a crush.

# 14

Her nerves tickle her gut as she sits in bed, flicking the pages of the newspaper without reading, anxious for Yugi to leave so she can prepare herself. The thought of what she is about to do makes her heart race. She feels hot down *there*. Another man, inside her. Another man's dick. The word echoes inside her brain.

Dick.

*Dick.*

It's . . . sexy. She rolls her lips together, imagining the pressure of a mouth kissing hers.

But there's also the guilt. Husband. That word, that honour. Another one: Wife. She tries it out, aloud, in English.

'Wife.'

Can she really desecrate everything this word should mean?

She thumbs her wedding ring around and around.

Her eyes are drawn to one particular article. Her mouth moves mutely: *There are approximately 63 million women living in Japan. 42% of these believe extramarital affairs are acceptable, in certain circumstances.* She throws the paper in the bin and uncaps a tube of body moisturiser from her bedside drawer. Yugi would not like to read such things. Is she one of those women? Her and Amber?

'Chinatsu.'

Her husband's voice coming from the bathroom makes her sit up straight. Each time he speaks or she is near him, breathes in a smell of him on sheets or clothes, or sees the imprint of his lips on coffee cups, she wonders. Her mind arrows back to the article.

'Chinatsu.'

She can't help it, but each time Yugi says her name, she hopes something might be different. He'll look at her when he's talking, properly. She'll understand, with a warm rush of clarity, why her husband has this article. It won't be something horrifying. It will be something that unites them. He'll say how much he misses her, that she is beautiful, that he wants to love her to their limits, that they should try for a baby. She sets the moisturiser onto the table and hurries to him. He is standing by the sink, washing himself.

'Yes, Yugi?'

Yugi turns. 'What?'

'You called for me?'

He shakes his head. She sees the skin on the back of his neck crumple as it snakes from left to right. 'No.'

Disappointment weighs in her stomach.

Yugi is naked to the waist. He thoughtfully cleanses the muscles of his left forearm, the cloth flicking droplets onto a mirror she has recently polished.

Once, Chinatsu loved the *idea* of Yugi, in a giggling schoolgirl way. She was a teenager when he wooed her, the only daughter of one of Tokyo's most powerful men. She sees gaggles of the girl she once was as she makes her secret weekly journey to the herbalist on the Bullet. They titter behind fingers pressed to their snub noses, a mirror of herself at that age. But their fingernails are chipped cherry-black, while hers are oyster.

Yugi's experience had impressed her, those proud good looks and his impenetrable distance.

At sixteen, Yugi had made Chinatsu blush. His precise kisses brought heat to her cheeks, though he could never tell. Her mother had taught her how to make blushes invisible, through the art of make-up. She

71

remembered her excitement at making not only a good marriage but finding someone she could really love and respect. She had interpreted Yugi as a mystery, a gift she would eventually get to unwrap.

Two months after her wedding, Chinatsu realised two things: Yugi was not a gift and she would never peel back his exterior to see what was inside.

She laughs out loud. The sound bounces off the bathroom's marble walls.

Yugi flinches, cloth thudding to the floor. His black eyes examine her through the mirror over the grey sink. She hurries to the fallen cloth, bends and retrieves it. She moves to the sink to rinse it clean. Yugi does not move out of the way. Her cheeks burn below her powder as she leans around him to turn on the hot tap. The heat of the water bites her skin and puffs out into the cold bathroom air. She twists water out the cloth; Yugi twists off the tap.

She looks up, allowing a small frown.

Yugi's face is like carved wood, buffed free of any error; he has no pores, and not a hair out of place. She looks down, focusing now on the water spotting the pewter sink. If Yugi looks into her eyes long enough, will he see all her secrets? Will he know what she and Madam Li discuss? What she almost did at the Park Hyatt? What she is planning to do soon?

She notices that the soap on Yugi's arm is drying. He has fine, sparse hairs, but they are stuck down by the soap. Chinatsu takes his hand like a nurse. He faces her and she keeps his arm out straight with one hand, running the cloth down the length of that limb. She starts back at the shoulder, and repeats. Once, twice, again.

A phone rings in the office.

Yugi takes the cloth from her; she is dismissed.

She lingers treacherously, but nods and leaves. There is no point staying. She navigates the network of sliding doors until she reaches the kitchen. In this room of machines, she feels more at home. She stares through bamboo blinds and at the orchids. Behind them is where she buries the rewards from her enterprise with Madam Li. It is the place she has buried every spare note and coin since she married Yugi. Even before it was clear her marriage would not be what she had hoped. Why? Was it simply so she could have something of her own? It is where her money tree will flourish, her moonflower. If she thinks hard enough, she can see the moonflower glowing, flickering in the background like a faulty lamp. She suddenly wishes that Yugi would let her grow her hair long.

She presses the back of one hand to her throat. The skin is hot.

If only she hated Yugi.

Her husband appears, fully dressed, briefcase in hand.

'The car will be here in moments,' he says.

'You will have a safe flight?'

'I shall.'

'I will get your case.'

'Don't trouble yourself. The driver can do it.'

They nod at each other. Chinatsu touches her forearm, strokes the length of it up and down, from wrist to the inside fold. Her hand stills when she notices Yugi's attention, his eyes travelling with her movement, as though she is conducting him. He looks up, their eyes clash. She can't hold his gaze. Yugi lingers longer than usual. What does he want? She keeps her eyes fixed on the carpet; the clipped, stippled weave of oatmeal, like waves of tiny pins jutting into the floor. Why is he still here? Does he know?

She does not watch him go, but hears the squeak of the car pulling up. From another room, pretending to be busy, she hears his footsteps. Yugi gives orders in a low voice, there is the rumble of cases, the snap of the boot and the front door slamming. When the sound of the car is indistinct, blurring with the noise of the rest of the world, Chinatsu turns around.

She has her own appointment to keep today.

Chinatsu heads to the kitchen to make tea and nearly collides with Satoshi. She clasps her dressing gown closer to her body.

He looks down. He's wearing the same loafer-style shoes, large, brown, that woven ankle bracelet. His T-shirt is tucked haphazardly into the front of his jeans. Her eyes linger on that glimpse of firm torso flesh, the line of chequered underwear. He's so narrow at the waist. What would he look like without that T-shirt? Is he wondering the same about her?

'You're here early today.'

'Sorry, Mr Hamugoshi let me in this morning. He asked me to fix the tiles on the shed yesterday. It won't take long. It's my grandfather's birthday this afternoon, so I couldn't come any later.'

'That's nice. How old is he?'

'Sixty.'

That's his grandfather? Her own father was not far beyond sixty. She should not be looking at this boy like this. Nevertheless, she finds the grip on her dressing gown relaxing.

Satoshi's eyes glance downwards, stopping at the V of her breasts. 'So . . .' Satoshi says.

'I'm keeping you from work.'

Satoshi bows his head. His eyes snatch a last look at her cleavage as he leaves. Making tea, she watches him through the window. He wants her, surely. The thought makes her stand up a little straighter. She lets go of the dressing gown altogether, showing the lace of her slip.

Chinatsu is locked into the bathroom, wearing only her bra and black knickers. She can do this. She can do this. It might actually help their marriage. But the mantra is not slowing her heart rate any.

For just a moment, she can imagine she is a single woman, desirable, wanted, free to do anything she pleases. But why did Yugi look at her like that this morning? Was she imagining the accent on the look, the slight . . .? She frowned, unable to put a description to it. Perhaps it had been nothing. She puts her toes onto the folded toilet seat and paints each nail with a slick of clear gloss. Her feet leave prints that seep outwards like steam.

She lowers her knee, watching her leg flex in the mirror. Her legs are short, but slender.

Chinatsu is experimenting with looks. She tries vampish. This involves crushed cherry lipstick, narrowing her eyes and looking at herself sideways on. She tries naive. This involves pink lip-gloss and wide, fluttering eyes. Chinatsu decides her face is too aware, too much life playing across it, for this look to work.

She will just dress as a smarter version of herself. A career woman, though she would settle for a secretary, who makes tea for bosses and does not kneel before she enters the office in her husband's house.

Stepping into the grey tulip skirt she has hung up on the bathroom door, she runs her hands over the fabric. Her palms make a whooshing noise, like the sound of sand being blown across a beach. Her mouth twists; not that she has ever been to a beach. She wraps the ballet-style shirt around her middle, and ties its cream ribbons at her left hip. She tugs the knot tight and slips one foot then the other into mulberry peep-toe shoes. The sound of her feet going into heels reminds her of the sound she got when she put her mother's lacquered tortoiseshell ornament to her ear.

Chinatsu has been practising how to walk using her bathroom as a small runway. She walks from sink to shower, turns, and back again. The trick is to take your time, and expect your hips to sway. She feels sexy, almost powerful. Whenever she does something without Yugi's knowledge, like meeting Madam Li rather than going to the salon, she has more energy. But this, this is no small thing, and adrenalin has buzzed through her all morning. She doesn't feel the need to eat.

She rubs salve into her lips, which are red from trying on and rubbing off too many different colours, and completes her face. What will he be like? The thought causes a swelling of desire between her legs. The bathroom is quiet and so is the house. It is just her, Chinatsu, clicking tubs and tins.

But still, she senses something. Someone.

'Who's there?'

She waits.

'Hello?'

Nothing.

Water plinks from the tap to the sink.

She shakes her head. The overheads are bright and harsh, because Yugi has a perfect face, but Chinatsu does not like looking in the mirror. She can't put it off any longer though. It is almost time to leave. The mirror betrays the age of her skin, the brackets either side of her mouth where foundation gathers, sliding as if magnetised to her decay, and all the other imperfections she usually skips over, as though her face is a CD and she can just miss out tracks she does not care for. After frowning, her skin used to spring back, smooth and perfect. Now there are permanent dents. She once watched a vet programme that said you

75

could tell if a dog was dehydrated by pinching its fur. If it was healthy, the fur would spring back. If not, the fur melts slowly back into place. Chinatsu had spent the rest of the afternoon in the bathroom, pinching her skin, sure it was like that of a dehydrated dog.

She dims the switch, smiles in the half darkness, and regards the new face looking back at her.

'I can do this,' she whispers. It is for Yugi, really. For us. A child will knit them together, a genetic sharedness he wouldn't be able to deny. Even as she thinks it, one last glance flicked into the mirror, her face tells her the thought is a lie. It was that and more. It was a need to be alive, to be a woman, to understand what that is and means. But was this the right way?

She wished for the intimacy of friendship, for someone to share this with, and thought again of her English friend. Was that all this was really, a quest for friendship? To connect. Admitting dissatisfaction in her circles, it just wasn't acceptable. She had the idea she would be arrested by some secret police force, denounced and punished for wanting more.

Chinatsu retrieves her handbag, coat and keys.

On the Bullet into the business district, Chinatsu doesn't think of Yugi. On the short walk from the stop to the hotel, she enjoys the purposeful sound of her heels striking concrete, and doesn't think of Yugi.

She pauses before The Cerulean Tokyu Tower Hotel. It is not as impressive as the Park Hyatt, so buttered with money it looks smug, but it has been chosen not to attract attention. To all intents and purposes, she is a businesswoman and this is a business lunch. She steels herself and strides into the building.

Inside reminds her of a spaceship. It is a circular lobby, lit dramatically from above. The colours are variations of dark granite and alabaster. The hotel itself is all glass and steel. So much glass. How does it stay upright? According to Madam Li, it is the tallest building in Shibuya. Chinatsu hears her heels change sound: they go from clicks in the marble lobby, to soft thuds in the carpeted bar. She arranges herself on a stool and appears completely at ease. The right leg is draped over her left; her arms are at comfortable right angles to the bar top, fingertips just touching. But her breathing is shallow. She feels like she's run here

76

all the way from home.

Chinatsu resists smoothing her hair. She wants to check her lipstick but knows it will betray her nerves. She wipes her tongue against her front teeth, sucking. Her mother taught her poise. Desperate though she is to scan the crowd of lunchtime suits, she has been told to let him come to her. He is the one with the picture.

The bartender has a bow tie and a waistcoat. The waistcoat is the colour of Christmas trees.

'An apple Martini.'

He nods and returns with a drink, placing it on a black napkin. Chinatsu raises the glass to her lips. It is shaped like an upside-down umbrella. The alcohol smell stings her eyes. She pretends to take a sip and lowers it again.

A man sits on the stool beside her. He smells of sandalwood. She does not look over.

The bartender revisits them.

'Apple Martini, please.'

This time, she looks.

He is not Japanese, that is instantly obvious. He is a businessman, Chinese, with the kind of wealth that enables him to approach everything with calm. She can tell this is old wealth, born-into-money rather than money accrued, as is the case with Yugi. His calmness ripples out to her, and her breathing regulates, becoming less shallow.

He holds a hand out. 'Tao.'

She takes it; his palm is warm and broad. Hard. 'Tao.'

'And what shall I call you?'

She angles her head. 'Amber.'

His face is incredibly symmetrical.

They abandon their drinks and ride the elevator in silence. Her hands are crossed over her front, his behind his back. She breathes in. She has to be someone else now. Amber. Is this so she won't feel guilty for betraying her husband?

The elevator stills, the display reads sixty.

She steps out first, turns, and gives him a look she has never dared use on Yugi.

He smiles, balanced and open. He walks towards her. Straight away she knows there is something about this man that is reachable, tangible, real. She could know him. Madam Li's would-be caution rings in her ears: Men are cunning. But looking at him, she just knows.

They walk together until he stops and opens one of the doors. His shoulders are a few inches from hers. Electricity in the gap between their bodies, more erotic than any touch. She wants to close that gap. Does he use his tongue when he kisses? Her body bristles, everywhere alive, longing to be touched.

She pushes the man who is not her husband with her fingertips. His back clicks the door closed. He takes the condom from his pocket. She, Amber, takes the condom and flips it to one side.

The Chinaman's eyes question her. She doesn't blink. She won't negotiate on this. Finally, he nods and pushes his fingers into her hair. Her scalp prickles. The feeling is delicious. Now more than ever, maybe because of Satoshi, she's going through with this. She's got something to prove.

Amber leads Tao, walking him backwards towards the window. Their eyes are locked. Tao turns her, twisting her hips. Her shoulders contact with the cold glass.

Tao's kiss is rhythmic, a slow swell and lull in intensity. He parts her lips with his tongue. She traps his bottom lip between her teeth and his eyes open with a smile. Raises his eyebrows. She doesn't blink. Suddenly urgent, he brings her leg up over his hip. She can feel his cock. Reaching down, she frees his cock and angles him into her. Her stomach cinches when he enters her. His breath is quick, shoulders rising and falling, disturbing the strands of black hair that have fallen over her face, shielding half of it. Half clothed, they fuck against the window.

Tokyo runs on, the coming dusk tingeing the city the most delicate pink.

Chinatsu walks like a woman who has just had sex; controlled, shoulders back, a smile playing on her lips. Every time her eyes close, she flashes back to what just happened. She clips and unclips her purse, finger stroking the metallic clasp. She glances at a man as she crosses the zebra crossing, testing a look of pure lust on him. His mouth parts and she smiles to herself as she keeps walking towards the station, heels striking concrete. There is nothing apologetic in her walk, and it feels. . . amazing.

She rubs her lips together, in an attempt to put back some of the moisture that was kissed out of them.

Waiting for her train, she chooses to stand, not sit. On boarding, she feels bold enough to allow a gentleman on the carriage before her, despite the fact he has just insisted she go first. He watches her and his attention feels good. She chooses not to acknowledge it. One arm is raised, her hand clutching the strap, hips knocking gently against the metal of the carriage, eyes sometimes on the scenery whizzing by, sometimes on her reflection in the dusty glass. The rocking action makes her smile.

The gentleman gets off three stops later. He pauses, and turns back to see Chinatsu draw away. She keeps her eyes front, but cannot keep the smile from her lips. Her palm feels hot, remembering the heat of Tao's penis. The train clatters on. Tao. The sheen of sweat over his body like butter, preserving him like a Chinese Emperor. His smell: ginger and musk. It's the smell of aftershave and semen. The tips of her ears burn as she remembers it trickling, warm, down her thighs when they had finished. She swallows, tongue still furred with the taste of him.

Chinatsu writes his name in her notebook.

As she walks, she thinks of Yugi. He will be trapped within the bubble of a first class flight. He will be scanning the stock markets, his broadsheet open like a limp origami swan on his lap. From what she understands, he is going to kill a dying company and welcome it into Uji Corp. And all will smile and bow as he does it.

She stows the notebook in her handbag, leaving the clasp unlatched. He won't be back for a few days.

# 15

Daniel itched with nerves. He had the aeroplane in his pocket and all the words he wanted – no, needed - to say to Fleur, butterflying about in his head. Soon they'd be eighteen, the both of them heading off to university. And then it'd be too late. He couldn't lose track of her. He had a sensation that it was now or never.

Her hair was silky, with almost a pink tinge to it. Like strawberries. Her cap was thrust on her head at an awkward angle, making her ears stick out. Cute.

He waited in the queue. He had his best aftershave on and he'd shaved. It had taken all of two seconds, but it felt good. Clean and manly. And he'd put on that new T-shirt his mum had got from *Asda*. He got to Fleur's till; she didn't recognise him at first. Why would she? She hadn't recognised him that time outside the nightclub either, had she? Though perhaps she'd been drunk. This was such a stupid idea. Should he just order something quickly and dash off? What was he doing with a frigging paper aeroplane in his pocket? What a total prick.

And then her eyes changed. Recognition shaped her face.

'Daniel? H-hi.'

He couldn't hear her voice any more, not the way he used to, just shapes of sound from the hearing aid. But the shapes of sound and the shapes of her mouth matched up. She'd said his name. He felt like one of those animals in those David Attenborough documentaries, chest all puffed up and bursting with pride.

She looked nervous, gaze going to a manager-type.

'What . . . what can I get you?'

He ordered a *Happy Meal*. Not exactly butch, but it seemed appropriate. The ring on her wedding finger caught his eye as she handed over the little cardboard house with its golden Ms. He gripped the handles, but didn't take the box.

'Meet me?' he said. If she thought he sounded stupid, she didn't show it. Her neck flushed bright red, the colour licking up to her cheeks. It made the green in her eyes seem even brighter.

Fleur looked at the ring on her finger.

'Just talking,' he said.

She let go and he took the box. The manager, stacking paper cups, eyed them. Fleur nodded quickly.

'Lunch? An hour.'

She emerged with a white cardigan over her arms. It seemed exceptionally feminine in contrast to the clumpy work shoes and dark uniform.

'You're pretty,' he said.

She grinned, hugged her cardigan to her.

There was a mini retail park adjacent to the *McDonalds*, just before the bridge that led towards the motorway and out of town. They wandered to the patch of grass behind the *Kwik Save*. Daniel set a jacket down for her to sit on.

'That's so sweet.' She bit her lip. 'Who even does that?'

He wanted to say something really corny here, but sat next to her instead. It was mild and the sun warmed his arms. She smelled of flowers. Had he ever been happier than this? Who knew? Now he was sat with her, thought didn't make sense.

'What happened to you?' she said.

He touched his hearing aid.

'No. Not that. I – I meant, you changed. And then you left. I couldn't understand it.'

'I was embarrassed.'

She shook her head, and plucked a daisy.

He pointed to her ring. 'Marriage?'

'Engagement.' She gave a little half smile, then curled her fingers into her palm.

'Where are you going to university?'

She grabbed a handful of grass, ripped, the earth coming with it. Her fingernails were stained with green. 'I didn't get in. My grades weren't good enough.'

'I don't understand.'

She shrugged. 'My mother died. I hated school. Hated everything.'

What could he say to that? There was nothing that would make that better. They looked at each other and she shrugged. He was sure she understood the depth of his sorrow. He wanted to ask her about her scars. But not yet. One day. If nothing else, they could at least be friends.

Because he couldn't think of anything to say, he gave her the aeroplane. 'I made this for you. When I was a kid.' He laughed. 'Stupid.'

She shook her head. 'No! It's pretty.'

'Pretty? Hmm.'

'When you were a kid? I can't believe you still have it!"

He shrugged.

'I don't get presents. Why an aeroplane?'

'I loved them at that age. Wanted to be a pilot. Actually, I think it was something stupid like, I wanted you to know you could fly. You can still go to university, you know. There's Clearing?'

She bit her lip, smiled. 'Yeah.' She looked at her ring, and her smile wavered. Her eyes met his. 'I love it. Thank you.'

There was an awkward moment. He could feel the rumble of traffic nearby, a breeze ruffling the hairs at the nape of his neck. The smell of her sun-warmed skin.

'Teach me some sign language.'

'Really?'

She nodded.

He taught her 'Hello,' 'Goodbye,' 'Please,' and 'Thank you.' He corrected her, and she copied, getting it almost perfect.

'How do you say I love you?'

He pointed to his eye, to his chest, and then her.

'That's it?'

He nodded. 'Try.'

She repeated his movements.

'Thank you, that's good to know.'

'Hey!' She slapped him, like she used to do when she was a kid. 'I didn't mean –' She looked down at her ring again. He was dying to ask whether she loved him. That rugby-type guy he'd seen her with. The one with the gold stud, from the night at *Reflex*. But he didn't want to know.

'We're just talking. It's OK.'

'I know.' She split the stalk of a daisy, and curled its stem through the gap. She fitted the ring on her wedding finger, and showed him.

'Much nicer,' he said, signing at the same time.

'What's my name in sign language?'

He reached for her hand and turned hers palm up. He fingerspelled the letters of her name on her skin, slowly, gently.

Half a dozen lunchtimes more, they were sitting on the grass verge again. Daniel was feeling a little niggled. He'd seen the same guy around a few times now. Another rugby player type. Always in shorts. Some random tattoo stamping his calf. Could it be Fleur's fiancée? He didn't seem like the guy Daniel had encountered at the *Reflex*. Or was it a mate the fiancé had sent to keep an eye on Fleur? Or was it nobody? Most of the guys looked the same round here.

Fleur was sitting cross-legged, unwrapping the lunch she'd brought. 'Strawberry jam. Here.'

He took one, and bit into the brown bread, the jam sweet on his tongue. 'Best jam sandwich. Ever.'

She laughed, and then grew serious. 'I'm learning sign language.'

He lowered the sandwich.

She pulled at the crust of one of hers, rolled the bread between finger and thumb. 'Then you won't need to wear your hearing aid.'

'I don't mind it so much now.'

'But why should you try to be like us? You're fine as you are.'

Daniel smiled. 'Maybe I like hearing your voice.'

She coloured again and looked troubled. She was going to tell him something, and he was sure it would be important. He waited.

She licked her lips, opened her mouth to speak. Eventually, 'I'm leaving him.' She knotted the grass over her fingers and pulled, one strand after the other. 'What do you think?'

He brushed the hair from her face, traced the blush that was joining up the freckles, his fingers warmed by the heat of her skin. Her lips were soft. She tasted of strawberries.

# 16

Nan wouldn't have been the easiest person to have around the hospital wards. The nurses would definitely have had words with her about lighting up. Fleur was sure she'd heard Nan arguing quite ferociously with a nurse.

Nan's words had been like moments of clarity in the fog. Her smell, her presence, all little anchors that kept Fleur from getting too far away. Thinking back, Fleur would wonder if coma was like weightlessness. Like being in space with no ground, no markers. Nothing definite. But she'd never been in space, obviously. Yet, while filling a kettle with water at Nan's, watching the rain drip onto browning roses through the kitchen window, Fleur would wonder if she'd ever been in a coma either. Not like she'd actually experienced it, not really.

At some point, Fleur's grandmother would have got out a packet of *Rizlas*. Fleur was sure she remembered the smell of tobacco itching her nose.

'I'm sorry, Mrs Johnson. You cannot smoke in here.'

'D'you see a fag in my mouth, eh? It's to calm my nerves. Just a Placido Domingo. Not gonna smoke it.'

'Placebo?'

Nan would frown. 'English, nurse. Come on, love. Do as the Romans do, an' all that.'

She'd have popped the cigarette into her pocket to smoke in the loo later, or to poke out the window, only bringing it in to suck on.

The clouds would roll in again, the fog thicken. Fleur's feet would leave the ground, arms flailing as if in zero gravity. For a while, some moment of time that was completely immeasurable – seconds, hours, a day maybe – there would be nothing. Absolute, unnerving, *nothing*. There was not even panic at there being nothing.

Until the next thing she could remember.

Sounds. Squeaking. Trollies? Remembering *Return to Oz*. The girl strapped in, about to get electrocuted to realign her brainwaves. Electric shock therapy.

And still no panic.

Nan's voice, when she heard it cutting into the nothing again, would be hoarse from smoke. 'What's it mean if she was gripping my hand? It's that she knows I'm here, right?'

'The likeliest explanation is that it was an automatic reflex response. But that in itself is a really positive thing. We should really make a start now, Mrs Johnson. When you're ready.'

'I just need to explain, I don't want her to be scared.'

Fleur would be sure, this time when her knee was jogging, waiting for the bus to take her to the Job Centre, that she remembered Nan's exact words. Breath tickling her ear.

'Can you hear me, pet? The doctors are going to have to . . . induce labour because the baby didn't, it didn't survive, darling. I'm so sorry. They say it's too dangerous to give you a caesarean because of the anaesthetic. But don't you be afraid, I'll be right here.'

# 17

Chinatsu sits up very straight, sipping her noodle and red pepper soup from a heavy spoon.

The dinner party is at Madam Li's house. There are three couples: Chinatsu and Yugi, Madame Li and her Japanese husband, and Masa, who is accompanied by a Korean woman who is obviously not his wife. The men are dour in suits and cufflinks, rings flashing on pinky fingers. Yugi, Masa and Madam Li's husband have done business together for many years. It was at such a dinner party, many years ago, that Madam Li first slipped Chinatsu the piece of paper with her other number.

It had happened when Chinatsu had excused herself from the table, Yugi's eyes upon her back. Her chest had been tight, hot with anger as Masa had continually petted his newest 'aide', explaining what a wonderful worker she was. How quick she was to pick things up. The girl had been tall with a thick fountain of black hair and inkwell eyes. They had looked at each other across the dinner table, she and this girl, a certain sadness tarnishing the girl's smile. Chinatsu was sure she saw her shrug. How straight she had sat as Masa praised her, how self-assured.

Chinatsu had been almost unable to breathe. She'd stood in the hallway between the kitchen and the dining room, her palm an anchor on the cool wall. Attempting to regulate her breathing. And it was then that Madam Li had come.

Now, Chinatsu's eyes meet the Madam's over each of their spoons. The men talk across them. 'Oh I don't know, Yugi, women are actually capable of understanding politics. You don't give them enough credit. Isn't that right, Rie? Rie went to university in Tokyo. You know who the Prime minister of Japan is, right?'

The woman who is not Masa's wife titters. She was introduced as his aide, but Masa was not so important as to require an aide at a dinner party. She has long false eyelashes and an eye-catching butterfly watch. Can she even tell the time? Chinatsu bites her lip: cruel.

Masa pats Rie's hair.

Chinatsu grinds her teeth. She doesn't know why Masa's action irritates her so much. Because he is confident enough to do it? Because Rie looks contented as a lap dog? Or because Yugi, quite simply, wouldn't dream of it. She sucks on her soup. Yugi barely touches her in private, let alone public. At least, not for a long time he hasn't. In her peripheral vision, Chinatsu registers Yugi turn his attention on her, deliberate as a camera. She suppresses the urge to throw the spoon down. Wants to hear it clatter. Instead, she places the spoon on the bowl and dabs her lips with a napkin. Rie's spangly jewellery catches her eye. It seems lustful and inelegant. A girl dressing up like a woman.

The jewellery taped to the drawer flares into her mind. Her stomach turns over. Who *was* Yugi? What was he doing? Anger streaks through her body. She deserves to know. She wants to question him, but does she dare? What would be the consequences?

She thought again about the girl from school. Her life had seemed full of so much fear, just as Chinatsu's was; the strictness of her parents. All that regimented preparation, all in order to marry well. Her first day at that English school, there was a strange game taking place in the playground. She remembers boys and girls together, lots of eyes on her. Children pointing. She remembers the burning feeling of it. Of being embarrassed just because of herself. There's a song to the game, and one by one people are called from one team to the other. If you could break through their latched hands, you were absorbed by the team. Became one of them. Chinatsu's name is called, foreignly, but she can't break through. The knock back is violent; the playground rushes up. Her knees and palms are bloodied, the cuts full of grit. She's crying in the toilets, a place all slimy and grey, copper pipes squealing. Running her hands under icy water and aching to go home.

The English girl says her name is Fleur. She says something about boys. Her voice startles Chinatsu. It's gentle, low, reminding Chinatsu of the almost-silent scratch of the needle before a record plays.

Fleur might not be in Japan but Chinatsu has always imagined her as being there. Long-limbed and thin. Ghostlike.

'Here.'

Fleur's fingertips press and smooth the plasters. They are the colour of English skin. She strokes them over Chinatsu's arm. How yellow her arm looks against that salty off-pink. They look at each other, two smiles. And she suddenly isn't alone any more. Their single word conversations, pronounced and understood with a makeshift sign language became more fluent, spotted with dialogue, evolving to full sentences punctuated with expressive eyebrows. Their widened eyes, fingers drawing in the air, *Ah! Yes*. Chinatsu learned English quickly because of this girl, and knew at least that there was somewhere, with someone, that she could fit. When her father's secondment ended, Chinatsu never fit anywhere again.

The shrill laugh focuses Chinatsu back to the dinner party.

'Now, now, Rie, you don't get off that lightly. Just take a guess,' Masa says.

Chinatsu imagines Rie turning round to slap him, but the girl merely looks up to the chandeliers for inspiration. Eyes open so wide her false eyelashes tickle her brow bones. She is like a child trying to decide whether to have the red lantern or the green lantern at the festival. Chinatsu looks to Madam Li, but the Chinese woman stares straight at Chinatsu, not blinking. Chinatsu bows to sip her soup. Her hand shakes. Eventually, Madam Li looks away.

'Rie?'

'I know he has grey hair and is as old as my father.'

'Oh, well observed.'

Chinatsu is only aware she has spoken when the dinner party pauses. Spoons hover over china, Masa's eyebrows are stuck in surprise mode, Rie concentrates on fishing red pepper cubes out of her soup. Madam

Li's husband's face crinkles with a grandfatherly smile, performing a rocking, oracular nod. Madam Li does not look at Chinatsu. Of course, neither does Yugi, but she knows by his stillness that he is not happy. Chinatsu sits up straighter. Yugi watches her a lot lately. His new attention does not give her the flush of excitement she had thought it would.

'So, Tsung, how is business?' Yugi asks.

Madam Li's husband laughs deep from his barrel chest. 'Business is very well, Yugi, so well in fact that I hope you shall never get to know my business.'

'We have found good partnerships in the past.'

'You are no longer in the business of forging partnerships, Yugi.'

'Acquisitions are a form of relationship,' Masa says.

Chinatsu stares at him. What is this feeling she has? Masa is touching Rie under the table. Hand up her skirt, rubbing. Chinatsu can tell from the distraction in his face, the movement of his shoulder. Yes, that's it. Hatred.

'Too true, Masa, too true.' Yugi turns to Tsung. 'Then again, life surprises us, from time to time, doesn't it?'

Spoons clink against bowls. A wine glass is picked up, sipped, and replaced.

The look Tsung gives Yugi is loud and dark. Yugi smiles, and brings his napkin to his lips. Blots.

Rie tells them that her English name is Moon. Madam Li asks has she ever been to England and Rie says no. With difficulty, Chinatsu resists the temptation to ask why she needs an English name at all if this is the case. But Yugi is watching her again. It would not be wise.

In the car on the way home, Yugi pushes a button on his left and the partition rears up. Chinatsu watches it rise, like a shark cutting through the ocean. With his ring finger, Yugi irons out a non-existent crease on the crossed leg of his trousers.

'Who is the prime minister of Japan, Chinatsu?'

Her eyelids are heavy. She just wants to curl up under her moonflower and wake up in warm summer soil.

'Taro . . . Taro Aso.'

90

As her eyes droop, she is aware of Yugi nodding beside her. She's too tired to figure out what that means. And the words, she's not sure if she said them, or just thought them, 'Who are you sleeping with, Yugi? Who is she?'

She wakes up alone the next morning, unaware of how she got from car to bed.

Winter sun, cold and bright, makes rectangles on the wall next to the door. Three squares of eight. Did Madam Li try to poison her? What a ridiculous thought. She is transfixed by the squares of light. Could she step through each of those windows, and out into a more beautiful world? All she wants to do is feel the sun on her shoulders.

She rolls onto her left side. A tear makes a slow path over her nose. The last time Chinatsu cried was when she was nine and her mother shaped her eyebrows with thread, using the cotton to trap the stray hairs, then ripping them out without warning. It had made her look like a surprised Siamese. She begged her mother to cut her a long fringe, but she wouldn't.

Chinatsu sits bolt upright.

The sun is so bright that it has to be around midday. She swirls on her robe, silk cold and tacky against her skin. Ice edges the air in the house. She dresses properly first before exploring. Yugi is sitting in the kitchen reading the paper, the pages rustling.

He has made coffee, or had one of the maids do it. Steam rises from the mug. Makes patterns on the window over his shoulder. The money tree lives in the background. She took pains to make the soil level after she buried the money from Tao. Yugi will never find out, will he? Don't think about it.

She opens her mouth, has to clear her throat before her voice works, 'May I make you something to eat?'

Yugi sets a cup on the breakfast bar. His mobile is at right angles to his wrist. He is sitting as he must do in meetings, in command of the room, so poised and powerful that all are magnetised into assent.

He lowers the paper. 'We ought to talk.'

She feels chilled, cold sliding down her body. She clears her throat. 'Oh?'

91

Yugi's eyes narrow. 'Yes.'

Chinatsu nods.

'Well, I am late because I am concerned, about you.' He taps the stool next to his.

Chinatsu swallows, crosses to the stool. Her slippers do not make a noise over the tiles. She eases onto the seat and they face forward as Yugi speaks. Chinatsu's hands rest neatly in her lap. They're sweating.

'You were unwell last night.'

'I believe the soup disagreed with me.'

He nods and checks his watch. 'I carried you in.'

The words are like the steam from his mug: visible one moment, but soon evaporated. A nice gesture or a physical necessity? She can't think why she had felt so exhausted.

'I am sorry, Yugi.'

He nods and stands to find a glass. He half fills it with water and places it before her.

She looks up, turning her body towards him. 'Thank you.'

Yugi looks away. He lifts the paper. She always imagines Yugi thinks of the stocks as health checks on companies. He is interested in those that are ailing, and especially enjoys the obituaries. Beneath the paper, she sees a single, small cream tablet.

'Oh.'

'You were so ill last night you were in no state to take it. We wouldn't want you to miss them, would we? It's just a few hours late.'

'Right. Right.'

Yugi doesn't move.

Of course he hadn't stayed because he was worried about her. After all this time, how could she be so stupid? She sweeps the pill into her palm, and pushes it to her mouth. She sips the ready water. Could she hide the pill and not swallow? Could she already be pregnant? To Yugi, to the Chinaman? Would it be dangerous to swallow? But Yugi is watching, all knowing. She swallows.

'There.'

Yugi reaches down for Chinatsu's face, and pulls it to his. The touch of his tongue to hers makes her eyes open inside the kiss. If she were a stock, her diagram on those pages Yugi reads, she would have just shot up. When he pulls away, one string of saliva connects them briefly, tenuous as a spider's web. It snaps, and she closes her mouth.

'I'll be late tonight.'

'Yes. Goodbye.'

She knows the kiss has nothing to do with affection. It is merely a method of checking to see if she has taken her pill.

When Yugi is long gone Chinatsu moves from room to room. She cleans the bathroom, goes through the food in the fridge and checks the dates. She throws out all the rubbish. But her fingers curl on the bin lid and her eyes press closed so forcibly she can imagine how the lids have crinkled, how they look papery and old.

She goes into the bathroom and locks the door. She positions her palms either side of the sink as if she is about to do push-ups. She screams until all the veins stand out in her face. The maids must have heard her, have stopped mid gossip or polish to whisper about Yugi Hamugoshi's wife. Let them.

She wipes her nose and heads back to the kitchen. She takes her gardening gloves from under the sink, the mat for her knees, and the basket in which she places de-headed rotten blooms from her flowers. The brisk air stings her cheeks, her ears tingle and glow red. She dabs a dribbling nose with her gloves, plucking away soggy roses, pinching away dead leaves. She was only with Yugi once and Amber was with Tao once. The tablet could not be doing any damage. Could it?

Droplets plink onto the roses. She stares at them, little gems on velvet, tiny as tablets themselves. Is it starting to rain? The roses are fuchsia. She'd planted yellow, hadn't she?

She pulls her gardening gloves off, finger by finger and scratches her nose. Her face is wet. She touches her cheek; she's been crying. She shrugs and stands, leaving the gloves behind. Inside, she moves through the corridors, nodding at a maid or two. In the bathroom, she locks the door and her shoulders sag. She scrubs her hands thoroughly then sticks her fingers down her throat.

Once her body is through convulsing, she sits on the floor with her eyes streaming. She has a sudden, almost violent, need to be reunited with her English friend. To have that gentleness, that truth in her life again. Her cheeks heat up when she thinks of the secret they shared. She

93

remembers now. The things they had talked about, the ways they had explored each other. It was just childhood curiosity, surely. If she saw her again, would she want to do . . . *that?* With a woman? She imagines the smell of Fleur, kissing her, her mouth parting. But Fleur hadn't liked her in that way. For Fleur, it was just investigation. Was it something else for Chinatsu? Is it still? Is she . . . *that* way? The dishonour for her family would be immeasurable. But then she loved how Tao was with her body. So she was not attracted to women. It was just, as they say, a phase.

She traces her forefinger across her bottom lip.

## 18

Yugi is dithering today. Yugi does not dither. A premature baby, this set
a precedent for the rest of his life. He always had to achieve everything
sooner than expected. He always finished the reading first in little school.
As a student, he beat everyone in the hurdles, 100m and cross-country.
Each run was always that little bit quicker.

The dithering started last night at the meal, and is the fault of
Chinatsu. Sweet, innocent, naïve Chinatsu, whose name, her father once
took pains to tell him, means 'a thousand summers.' As a man who
keeps secrets, Yugi is aware when others are keeping them. Secrets are
insulators and create distance.

Yugi was always proud of the fact that Chinatsu had no distance, at
least none that he wouldn't easily be able to cross. He knows she rides
the Bullet to the Herbalist every Monday and obtains fertility medicine.
He lets her have that; it will do her no good. Yugi also knows his wife
pretends to take her contraception at night, only to flush the tablets
down the cistern at 6.13am, two minutes before his alarm sounds to
signal his new day. He also knows that Chinatsu loves him. Facts are
facts.

But there is something else Chinatsu does not know: Yugi can never give her the child she so dearly wants.

At the dinner party, Chinatsu caused him to reassess things. He can feel her growing more distant. She has more secrets. That is not really what concerns him, he has ways of discovering secrets. But *she* is different. Below her perfectly presented exterior, she is restless. More than that, at the meal, she was angry. And then, had he imagined her whisper? She asked about jewellery. And his mind darted back to the English city, the trinket he'd kept from the woman in the hotel room. From all the women. Chinatsu knew, didn't she? She must. What would this mean? What would she do about it? Why was she still here? For the first time, there is something about Chinatsu that he cannot predict or control.

After Chinatsu had taken her pill, Yugi had paused at the step. The car out front was running, his mobile already buzzing through his suit jacket, the young driver tapping his fingers out of time on the wheel to the infuriating J-Pop he always plays. Until Yugi gets into the car. Yugi had half turned back to the house, Chinatsu's kiss drying on his lips. She had tasted of ginger, and this was new. A new tablet from the herbalist? The scratches on his arm had scabbed and were now almost ready to flake away. They itched.

But instead of returning to Chinatsu, Yugi had turned back to the car.

All morning, he has not been able to concentrate. Now he's in a meeting with Jack Braff, the all-American representative of the latest company Uji Corp is in talks with.

The man says, 'Mr Hambergoshi, with all due respect, 2.2 bil is the lowest figure I'm authorised to go to. To acquire a company like ours at such a price, well, it's nothing short of ludicrous I think you'll agree. It's considerably lower than your opening offer of 2.5. Pretty sure you can appreciate how accommodating we're being here.'

Yugi's knee jogs below the desk. Jack Braff is too messy, too wide, too full of words. His brown eyes have red in them and his hair has carrot in it. A wave runs through the carrot hair and the fluffiness suggests he uses no product. His shirt is typical of Americans: open at the neck, no tie, no cufflinks, suit jacket swung around the back of the chair. His wedding ring is embedded in the skin of his third finger.

Obviously, he is loyal to his wife, not that he would have much choice. Yugi works his tongue around his teeth and swallows. His throat is dry and he coughs into his fist, crosses the opposite leg.

'Mr Hambergoshi? What do you say? Surely it's mutually beneficial for us to wrap this up today? Uji Corp are not the only company we have been considering. We have other interested parties.'

Yugi rubs the underside of his nose and places this hand flat on the desk. Uji Corp *is* the only company they have been considering. And there is only one party here for whom it would be beneficial to come to an agreement: Jack. The man is not confident of anything; he doubts he can even pick out his own underwear.

Yugi rubs his eyes. Chinatsu's unblinking gaze appears in his mind. Just a pair of eyes and nothing more, the whites like polished almonds in the darkness.

He clenches his teeth. '2.2, final offer.' He stands. 'I am sorry that we can't do business with you, Jack. My secretary will see you out.'

Jack Braff's mouth parts.

Yugi smiles, and the American stands, collects his coat and leaves.

Yugi punches the button for his secretary.

'Yes, sir.'

'Put me through to my wife please, Enza.'

'Yes, sir.'

The phone keeps ringing.

'Sir? It would appear that nobody is at home. Am I to try again?'

He cuts her off. His heart's beating so fast he should be playing squash. There's an irritating rumbling noise beneath the desk. He looks down, and realises the noise is his knee jogging up and down.

# 19

Chinatsu waits for Madam Li at the same restaurant where they first exchanged Yen.

Madam Li enters the restaurant in a flurry, scowling. Her shawl whips behind her in black tails. She almost trips up the greeter. At the table, Madam Li flaps out a napkin and rests it on her knees below the cloth. She beckons a waiter and orders *kake udon*. It appears almost instantly, as if they'd anticipated her arrival.

Chinatsu tries to slow her racing heartbeat. She doesn't know why Madam Li wants to see her. She can only presume she has done something wrong, and is in trouble.

Madam Li points her chopsticks at Chinatsu. 'This dish, stolen from China,' she says. She points at Chinatsu's untouched bowl with her chopsticks, pincering her own wheat-based noodles between wood fingers. They wriggle like flat, white worms. Her eyes do not leave Chinatsu's as the chopsticks enter her mouth, tongue curling them in. Munch munch munch. Another stab towards Chinatsu with her chopsticks. Greasy lips say, 'You no eat. Again. Hm?'

'I'm not pregnant. Is that why you wanted to see me?'

'You need variety. No fuck one man and it happen. Why I exist? If one no work, we will try you with another. You no can have sentiment.

98

Is business, yes? Emotion is dangerous, trouble, break agreement and marriage. Dishonour, you understand? Dishonour come back on me too.' She shrugs, tucks more bean sprouts through her lips. 'You think I donno? I know. You like the beautiful Chinese. It's no surprise.'

'That couldn't be further –'

Madam Li chews. 'Ya, bullshit. Next time I give you new man. Yes?'

'What do I care? As long as the outcome is the same – yes.'

Her eyes narrow. 'Hush it. I no care what you are doing after. Is better I donno. So. Listen. Each time someone new. You no afford . . . ' She fingers the grease on her lips like she's putting on lip salve and wipes her finger on the table cloth before gripping the chopsticks again. 'Nostalgia. Is business. Like I say. Yes? Otherwise, many unhappy husband. I no business. Yes?'

'Yes.'

'If no.' She shrugs and pushes her chair back. She burps, quietly, into a fist she is holding like a microphone and stands. 'You can?'

Chinatsu nods. 'Yes, of course.'

The Chinese Madam sweeps out of the restaurant. Her heels are low, but they sound like hammers as she exits. They get louder, if anything, the further away she gets.

Chinatsu pincers bean sprouts and crunches them between her teeth. Madam Li doesn't know about Tao, that they have seen each other without going through Madam Li. That really, Chinatsu calls him Tao, and he makes up for the guilt rotting her insides with his interest. She is an addict for his attention. She lives off the fumes of it, appetite erased, enjoying how he is re-drawing her into something beautiful. Her lips feel fuller, her nipples, everything does. She thinks about positions. And all the while, underneath it all, her feelings for Yugi crawl and lurk. He deserves this, doesn't he? For his lying, for his ignorance. For all his women, and what he might have done. Not just adultery. But he has hurt one of them. She is almost sure. Wasn't she?

She would actually prefer that he hit her. Does Yugi do that with his women? To be beaten in a fit of passion would be something, rather than all these years of whistling obscurity, not being considered, noticed or alive. And it would make her sing with vitality – I am meant to be, because he notices me.

Yugi deserves this, for all he hasn't done.

And if he deduces her secret, connects the flush in her face and the hum in her throat, her boundless energy, then she will confront him with his.

Who does the jewellery belong to, Yugi? Why do you have the article about that dead prostitute?

And then we will see.

On the street, walking through caricatures of people towards the station, an unshaven man reeking of rubbish and drink cuts into Chinatsu's path. She stops just short of a collision.

Chinatsu shakes her head, hurrying past him. Someone lurks in the edges of her vision. Keeping a distance. She snaps her head around. Nothing. Or did she just see the flash of someone all in black, with a pair of white trainers? Chinatsu turns a full circle in the busy street. Again, nothing. She hangs her head.

A voice explodes in her ear, eardrum buzzing.

The man who stinks of rubbish says, 'You have eyes like black widow spider. Who you trap?'

# 20

Yugi Hamugoshi is in his office, reminiscing. He was twenty-six again, five years out of university and Managing Director in-situ of Uji Corp. A bachelor, he was also scouting for the perfect wife. And, at that point, it wasn't going to be long until his new MD position was permanent. The promotion had caused ripples and cost lives, business-speaking. Some of the details surrounding the manoeuvre would always remain somewhat hazy.

This was a time when Yugi was riding high on the euphoria of success. His body always felt like it was singing with post-exercise endorphins, whether he'd worked out or not. He never found it hard to get out of bed in the morning; his eyes would ping open and a split second later, he'd sit up. The more he did the more he knew he could achieve. Chinatsu would round things off nicely. Yugi believed that every successful man required a wife that men were envious of.

He had been introduced to Chinatsu through a black and white picture. The picture was presented to him by her father, Hirari, a man who never seemed to blink. Sat before him on a bench in the park, Yugi remembers observing the man who would become his father-in-law. A squat man, he had looked like one of the pieces set before them on the chessboard. Hirari had played black. Through the game, Yugi had watched the man's fingers nip the heads of pieces to relocate them. His nails were like lobster shells; such a healthy pink. Yugi remembered Hirari using one finger to push a black Castle across the board. Yugi had nodded, pretending to admire the manoeuvre. But the Castle was like Hirari. Small but destructive, and often in the way.

As Yugi had contemplated his move, Hirari had squinted at him. It hadn't been sunny, so Hirari had done this for one of two reasons: either he had not wished his opponent to see him blink, thus revealing weakness, or the proliferation of black moles on his eyelids was so great it had made them heavy.

Yugi had directed his Bishop towards the Castle. If this threat was not dealt with, in five more moves, the Queen would be threatened. Hirari grunted. He had been smiling. It was at this point that he'd presented Yugi with a photograph of his daughter.

Hirari may have been lacking in height, but he had more natural menace than the MD Yugi had recently usurped. Apart from Yugi's own father, Hirari was the only man who had ever made him feel not quite good enough.

'Do you know the meaning of my daughter's name? Chinatsu?'

Yugi had shaken his head.

'A thousand summers,' Hirari had said. He'd gone on to tell Yugi that Chinatsu was a good and dutiful girl, always eager to please. He said she would be the sort of wife a man like Yugi required.

Smiling, Yugi had taken the photograph. Chinatsu's father had just the sort of contacts Yugi had always yearned for. With Hirari's backing, there was no way any of the partners could ease him out of Uji Corp.

Yugi had raised his eyebrows as he'd studied the picture. The girl was sitting on a swing, fingertips slender against the chains. Her head was lowered and she was smiling, a curtain of hair swept to one side to expose one shoulder. The older man's wide fingers had hooked a Bishop into place against Yugi's King. Yugi had looked up.

'Check.'

Yugi had placed the photograph down, just about controlling the tremble in his wrist. How had he not foreseen this? Yugi had neatly removed his King from danger, for now.

'An interesting strategy,' Yugi had said.

Hirari had nodded once, deeply.

Yugi had gone back to the photograph. Chinatsu's hair was black-gold, dark as the tunnels the Bullet rocketed through at night. Her eyes were free from pain. Was it time to change that? Or would she serve him better that way: innocent, unblemished and swelling with the romance that perfumes girls' thoughts?

Yugi had honourably accepted the photograph. He had always been fond of beautiful things. They had abandoned the game then, but both men know that if they had played on, Hirari would have secured a swift victory.

It should have been a simple courtship. He shouldn't have been required to make much effort. But Chinatsu, given her lack of years and experience, proved tricky. Once, he had been quite ready to renege on the deal he'd made with Hirari, despite the fact it would have spelled professional suicide. She had not been the simple creature Hirari had suggested. She was complex, maybe even a little cunning. That could, of course, be stripped out of her. Besides, not having access to Chinatsu's father's resources had been unthinkable.

Hirari had left the game, leaving Yugi at the table, hands folded over the photograph. He had been about to get up and head back to the office, when he was distracted by a scribble in the air. He'd looked up; it was a moth. He'd frowned. A Noctuidae, to be precise. Also known as an Owlet moth. They used to be found in the Imperial Palace gardens. Strange that it should have been out in the afternoon. The majority of them flew at night. He had watched its journey, thinking back. Moths are what had brought him to this bench, this business, this life. All manner of them.

Through college, Yugi had excelled in athletics and academia. His other strong subject was women. Matsuko Chen, First Year Politics, now secretary to a prominent political advisor, could attest to this. She'd once given him a blowjob in the gym's toilets purely because she was so flattered he'd remembered her name. Masa had marvelled at this, but Yugi left out the part that it was all he could do to maintain his erection throughout the process.

It hadn't always been like this. On the farm as a boy, Yugi was good at nothing. He was too slight for his father's liking, his fingers too slender and soft to dig or carry or turn over soil. The man would stand behind Yugi as he worked, shaking his head. His father would tell Yugi to leave whatever he was doing, that he would do it himself instead. So Yugi had occupied himself with other things.

The first thing he'd captured was fireflies with a fishing net one morning. He'd been seven years old and wanted them to brighten his dark room. He'd kept them safe in a jewellery box that was his mother's, the only feminine and beautiful thing in the bare farmhouse. He'd started his chores and been relieved from them. Ears stinging with the feeling of being a failure, he'd headed back to the house. But he'd remembered the fireflies. He'd raced home to play with them.

The jewellery box had been a simple affair. It was blue velvet inside and had a scratched black lacquer finish, but it had a mirror on the roof of the lid. A pearl inlay framed the mirror. He'd hoped the fireflies would've been able to watch themselves dance. But when he opened the lid, eager and still unwashed, all the fireflies had been dead.

Yugi had smashed a window, sliced open his wrist, and cried on his floor until his father found him the next morning, late for chores. He'd whipped Yugi for breaking the window and boarded it up, claiming they couldn't afford new glass.

It changed, this fascination, when he was eleven. He'd taken that first step and started to time how long each beautiful thing he stole from the world could live in the box. He'd noted the results on graph paper. Heart racing, he'd listened to their wings whispering, rasping against the velvet. And then go quiet.

Eventually, he had replaced the box with a glass jar. He told himself this was done in order to record more accurate results. Whenever he watched an insect stop its struggle, witnessed its fight diminish, his face went slack. Desire warmed his genitals. When there was no more movement, Yugi would walk to the bathroom and masturbate.

He never did it in the same room as the dead.

Years later, Yugi was given a Biology scholarship. Once at university, he had persuaded the university to convert his course to something more appropriate: Business and Economics.

Yugi often wondered about the origin of his obsession. Was it his mother's death? Nozomi, that mute image of a woman who had died during childbirth. Even his father admitted, once the second wife was safely dead, that Nozomi was very beautiful. Yugi had found a picture of Nozomi under the seat of his father's white van. It had smelled of oil and leather and metal. He'd been hunting for his latest specimen, on his back in the van's cab, his torch angled under the seat. The woman staring down at him had been so brightly beautiful he couldn't bring himself to ever look at her again.

Yugi turns in his office chair, fingers drumming the leather. When he was thirty-one, he and Chinatsu were about to be married.

Of all the beautiful things he had investigated, Chinatsu was not the most exotic or desirable, but she did possess a quiet, strange magic. She knew he had been someone else before he had achieved this position of power. And she didn't care. If not for this, Yugi might have walked away long before.

They had gone for a stroll through Jindai botanical gardens. He had planned the occasion perfectly. The forecast predicted light showers for around 3pm. The blue skies would say otherwise, so they had not brought a parasol. Yugi was dressed in a white shirt and linen trousers. Chinatsu wore a white blouse and a linen skirt that flowered out from narrow hips. They laughed at how much they matched. He could not recall the colour of her skirt, but remembered dropping back slightly as they walked to regard her shapely calves. She had narrow, delicate ankles. They would snap like a scorpion's claw, given just the right twist.

Yugi set a basket brimming with fruit on a small peak of manicured lawns.

'I have never been here before,' Chinatsu said.

'My family and I used to come here every summer.'

'Really?'

Yugi straightened. 'Why would I lie?'

She raised her eyebrows and shook her head. 'I did not mean –'

He smiled. 'Let's spread out the rug, shall we?'

Yugi watched his future wife stretch out a cream blanket. She ensured each corner was perfectly straight and that there were no wrinkles. With small, precise movements, she took bowls out from the basket and ladled in a variety of melon slices. She placed napkins next to each bowl, one apiece.

'You obviously know what you're doing,' Yugi said, kneeling.

'As do you.'

Yugi looked up, but only in time to catch Chinatsu look away. 'What do you mean, may I ask?'

She smiled, still busy choosing cutlery and snapping lids back onto the fruit boxes. 'Well, any moment now, it will rain and you shall have to protect me from the elements.' She blushes. 'Or so it is in novels.'

'Who knew beautiful women could read?'

Chinatsu looked up, a glint in her dark eyes, the only part of her flawless face that seemed real and reachable. 'You! You are. . .'

'What?'

'Trying to rile me. I will not allow it.'

Chinatsu's expression was curious. It was the first time Yugi had been unable to read a woman. Back then, she had possessed a delicate assuredness, a self-confidence in herself that said, I am worthy of you and you are worthy of me. They would both fulfil their various duties and honour the roles they would play in each other's lives. Yin and Yang.

Why was she different to other women? The insecure ones who would give blow jobs in bathrooms for a bit of validation. Was it because Chinatsu had grown up loved, as much as a daughter can be, and not counting beetles in the back yard?

A raindrop landed on the tip of Chinatsu's nose. 'Oops.'

He blinked. Oops? She said it as though she had caused the rain to fall.

Chinatsu held her palm to the sky as the rain plinked down. He could cuff those wrists with thumb and forefinger, with inches to spare. She knelt beside Yugi.

'Where did you spend your youth, Mr Hamugoshi?'

'Yugi, please. This is our. . . ' He gave it just enough time to demonstrate slight struggle. 'Fifteenth date.'

'Fifteen, really? As much as that?'

'Yes. I spent it in Tokyo, where I have always been.'

106

She looked away. Out of decency? She didn't want him to know she knew he was lying. He bristled, and felt off balance.

'We are going to get wet,' she said, taking a crescent of honeydew melon, biting. The juice pooled around her small teeth. Her lips were pink, not red.

Yugi took a deep breath. 'I ought to protect you from the elements. Purely so we can say it does happen in real life, not just the novels.'

'That would be a service.'

Yugi cupped her face with both hands. In the warm summer rain, her blouse was becoming delightfully transparent. He kissed her.

When he drew back, she was blushing.

On the surface, it was a successful courtship of which he was in complete control. According to Yugi's sense of tradition, they did not make love until the wedding night. He was surprised that he was able to adhere to his own controls. He did not sleep with anyone else until after they were married.

The phone in Yugi's home office rings. He hooks up the phone.

'Yes.'

'Mr Hamugoshi, sir. I have information for you.'

'Yes.'

'Your wife met with the Chinese woman again this week.'

'I think that may be a dead en –'

'I disagree.'

Yugi breathes in, imagining himself cleansing his body of irritation. 'OK.'

'Your wife has been rather busy of late. Sir. I believe the Chinese woman is directly connected.'

Yugi clears his throat, windscreen-wipes his top lip with the tip of his tongue and adjusts his position in the leather chair. It creaks. A train rattles the massive windows of his office. Is his wife on one of those trains? Conducting her secret life?

'I'm listening.'

# 21

Chinatsu's head is in Madam Li's lap, sobbing. She's sobbing like she is six years old and has just broken the clasp on her mother's wedding hairpiece. It's the antique amber one that she's been told, many times, she is too young to play with. Herfather, reaching for the strap he keeps hanging on the back door.

Madam Li's dress is damp beneath Chinatsu's cheek. She can smell the China-woman beneath the scratchy wool. Fabric conditioner, skin. What did Madam Li look like underneath her clothes? When she was having sex?

The Madam strokes Chinatsu's hair like she is darning socks. Chinatsu's mother never touched her with affection. Although, when father was not looking, she occasionally caught her mother's glance. She would straighten her shoulders. Her mother would nod.

Chinatsu keeps waiting for the knife to plunge between her vertebrae.

She wants to pull away. To right herself, dry her eyes and tell the Madam she is fine, not to worry, it won't happen again. They can go on like they were before. But she can't, because she's falling in love with Tao. And yet she still loves her husband. So the tears keep coming. Her neck aches from its position on the Madam's knees.

A maid enters Madam Li's drawing room. The woman's hand leaves Chinatsu's hair, wafts over her head to usher the girl away. The door clicks closed.

Chinatsu cannot sit up. But she must. With a great effort, Chinatsu straightens and wipes her tears. She raises her eyes to meet the older woman's. Madam Li's face does not display the glitter of affection or the pride of a job well done, a daughter well turned out, as her mother's sometimes did. But there is no unkindness there. In fact, there is nothing.

'You tell me now what you do.'

Chinatsu keeps her eyes on her knuckles, red as uncooked meat. Bones shining. 'I am in love with two men.'

Madam Li looks as though she wants to spit.

'This was not meant to be, Madam. This was about a child, creating a home with Yugi. What can I do?'

Madam Li scratches half of her right nostril with one short, clear nail. 'You must forget this other man. You still want this child?'

'More than anything. That is my dream.'

The Madam nods. 'Then you must not see this second love. Continue with others. It is what we plan anyway. Yes? Not difficult.'

'Yes.' Chinatsu forces herself to meet the Madam's eyes.

'Good. I book you in with new client.'


Chinatsu is watching Tao sleep, this man who is not her husband.

His watch ticks on the hotel table beside the rumpled bed, their warmth and smell trapped beneath the mushroom and craters of mulberry and cream covers. She can't help but feel a growing unease, as if she should be somewhere else. Of course she should: with Yugi.

And yet, it is Fleur's face that swims up to her. She's half the girl Chinatsu knew and half the woman she imagines her to be right now. She often thinks of Fleur as a confident figure wrapped in businesswoman's clothes, the lapels of a black suit jacket bracketing her breasts, like speech marks highlighting her wiry form. At other times, she's scuffed and bedraggled, eroded by life. In both of these images she is beautiful, elm-like. But the unsettling thing, the truth that cores Chinatsu's guts, is that the negative image is probably the true one.

Chinatsu sends out words into the night, crossing oceans, trickling her thoughts into the English girl's earlobe: 'Are you all right, Fleur?'

And no answer.

Of course not.

There is an electrical hum from somewhere, probably the drinks cabinet. It is distracting. The sound of Tao's breathing muffles the ticking of his watch. She remembers him unlatching it earlier, the heat of his wrist bringing out the smell of leather. She'd run her thumb over his skin, feeling how smooth and almost damp it was. He'd flinched like she'd burned him.

Restless, she sits up in the hotel bed, the sheets like a Grecian dress about her frame.

Tao's mouth is open a crack. His teeth are not completely perfect and betray a slight overbite. He does not look as poised or beautiful like this, but she wants details to take away and turn over in her mind.

Beneath his closed lids, Tao's eyeballs move from side to side, making the eyelashes ripple. She looks away. He reminds her of a machine. She likes the frown lines on his forehead. They are like seagulls drawn by a child. His chest is perfect, the colour of wok-heated butter. It is like planed, buffed softwood. She places a hand on his chest and he covers it with his own, a larger shadow. She moves her fingers a fraction, testing. He clutches her hand in place. She smiles.

They had held hands in the lift on the way up to the hotel room.

Tao wakes, and smiles at Chinatsu. His arms button around her. He smells of sleep and sex and the inside of bed-sheets. She feels safe, nestled in the cocoon of their brief contentment. But this is marred by the knowledge that she must soon return to being Yugi's wife. A stab of guilt. And there is that thing she is ignoring. That article, all those women. The possibility that Yugi is violent, a murderer, often seems ridiculous. But is it? Doesn't she have a responsibility to find out? She must confront him, but to do that would disrupt the spell with Tao. They are living off each other's affection at the moment. It's enough for now, this fictional space. But what about when it becomes real?

Tao delivers lines, little gifts of promises and emotion she's never experienced. Does she believe? She's not sure, but the idea is enchanting.

'Madam Li has suggested that I see other men, until I am pregnant.'

110

He frowns and the seagulls deepen. 'And?'

Chinatsu can hear the maid hoovering in the hall. 'She called it nostalgia, this feeling. An unhealthy attachment I think. That I should see a variety of men, until I am pregnant.'

'And?'

'And I agreed.'

He shakes his head. His hair's short stubble scratches the pillow. 'No.'

'Tao.'

'No. Leave him now and I will join you later. You can go to England, like we talked about.'

'It's just fantasy.'

'Until we act.'

'You're just upset at the thought of me with other men.'

He laughed. 'And you aren't?'

'What do you think, Tao?'

She is transfixed by the emotion in his eyes. She breaks away from it and shrugs, brushes the hair from her eyes. 'You're more anxious at the thought of me with a stranger than my husband.'

'You don't sleep with him.'

It is such a male thing to be affected by the physical. Despite her fears, she loves Yugi. Surely that is a greater betrayal?

'I'm not ready.'

'To leave him?'

'To leave like that. To just go.'

'What do you want to do, have a farewell party? Have him wave you off?'

She slumps back against the pillows; air whistles out of it. 'Tao, please.'

He breathes out, whether to calm himself or out of frustration she isn't sure. 'I don't understand you. How can you want to? Especially now?'

Chinatsu shakes her head. 'You can't know me if you think I want to do it. But I need to give him a reason for my leaving, other than this. You don't know him. He is competitive. If he knows there's someone else, he won't let me go. And he won't let you get away with it.'

'You think I'm not competitive?'

'You're not letting me go. That's not what it means. Being with other men, it's just to appease Madam Li, to get her focus off us. A temporary necessity. Trust me, I can do this. I can make this easier for us.'

'I want to know what you're going to do.'

She places her palm to his cheek. 'Just trust me.'

Tao puts an inch or so between their facing bodies. He rests a hand on her stomach, and she covers it with her own. 'You might be pregnant already,' he says.

Chinatsu looks down. True. What happened to her plan? Seed a child and return, triumphant, to Yugi and watch their family flower? Is this love with Tao or just total, utter relief? A little addiction, discovering that she is valuable to someone at least. 'I must get dressed. Yugi will be home soon.'

'Amber, please don't go.'

The use of her other name steels Chinatsu. She walls a small part of her heart away from him. Detaching herself from Tao, she sits on the edge of the bed, feet not touching the carpet. She knows he is taking in the curl of her hair against her jaw-line, that his eyes travel over the curves of her waist and hips. His awareness of her means that, to somebody, she is beautiful. She exists.

Chinatsu circles a fluffy gown around her and crosses to the bathroom. Tweaking the shower on, she tests the spray and steps into the heat. She tells herself she has the memories of Tao to help her through this experience. While she is on her back, she can pretend. She will imagine it is his lips sipping from her mouth. She can tell herself that Amber is the one this affects, not her. Amber is the one who holds this Chinaman in her heart like a polished urn. But she knows it's a lie.

'Are you really going to do this?' Tao asks, when she is ready to leave.

She slips stockinged feet into heels, turns. 'I have to.'

On another night, Chinatsu sits in another hotel bar, legs crossed and shoulders poised.

Her stomach feels like it's on fire. Not just about sleeping with another man, the strangeness of it, the invasion. But what if it was Yugi? Her shoulders tense. She breathes deeply. Relax; it can't be. Madam Li would never set that up. And yet, if the article was indeed about Yugi then he might frequently sleep with prostitutes. Therefore, he might frequently be in places prostitutes met their clients. Places like this hotel. Her neck prickles with sweat. She closes her eyes. What was she saying? The article could not be about Yugi. There must be some other explanation. *Relax*.

'Yes?'

Her eyes dart open. The bartender is waiting. He's wearing a green and black silk waistcoat.

She orders an apple Martini, as does the man beside her. He's overweight, face bloated. A sheen of grease sits atop his features.

Relief loosens the tension in her shoulders: at least it's not Yugi. But her tension is replaced by fear. She does not want to do this.

They ride the elevator. He stands half a step before Chinatsu. Once behind the hotel door, she takes out the condom, and he removes it from her hand. She is thinking about running for the door, tearing out of this nightmare like a dragon from coloured paper. She will board a plane and wait for Tao. Together they will knit a family.

This new man speaks: 'Take off your clothes, and lie on the bed.'

But she can't run yet. Why? What was she holding on for? Even if there was a child already, it might well be Yugi's. Unlikely, but it was possible. Was she trying to keep Tao in place so she could make a decision between the two men once she knew for sure? Raise the child with her lover, or her husband? All she knew for certain was that she couldn't leave Yugi for Tao unless she knew she was pregnant. Which meant that she still loved Yugi. Didn't she? Whatever the answer, she wasn't yet ready to leave. Tao would feel so betrayed.

When Tao makes love to Chinatsu, he bites the flesh of her upper arm, and kisses it after. He pulls her top lip with his teeth and tickles the underside with his tongue, making her cry out. She is seen and heard. Real. He reminds her of all the things she has forgotten, that she can think and feel, hope and dream.

As this other client fucks Chinatsu, he undoes all of that work with each jagged thrust. He seems to take unbearably long to climax. She is not wet and each upward movement feels like he is tearing away a layer of skin. Wrists pinned above her head, her teeth are clenched. With a grunt, he crashes onto her chest, sweat creating a temporary seal between skin. He grows smaller inside her. Pulling out, one toenail catching her shin as he clambers off her, he pads away to the bathroom. The shower hisses on and his cooling sperm leaks out of her, sticky. She is invisible.

She dresses, clicking each button closed on her blouse. The man reappears and drops notes onto the bed. He dresses and leaves. She notices he's wearing navy socks with grey trousers.

Before Chinatsu leaves, she douches and works on her skirt. She rides the train home, head against the window, scenery ticking by. The scratch on her shin feels hot under her tights. She steps off the train at her station, just registering a pair of white trainers on a young man all in black as she gets off. His jeans have been shrink-washed tight. His hair, the fringe long and spiky, covers his eyes. Chinatsu stands at the station, watching the train pull away.

The young man does not look her way once.

She begins walking home, sure she has enough time to bury her money and collapse into bed for an hour, before she must supervise supper for Yugi's return.

But the front door yawns open. Her husband guards the entryway, hands behind his back, feet apart, one looking to the east, the other, west.

Her tongue feels too big for her mouth.

'You are early.'

'I called home after lunch, and there was no answer. I was concerned for my wife, who looks very nice.'

She swallows, and heads for the kitchen.

Yugi's hand lashes out and snaps around her wrist. He pulls her to him.

What errand took you out of this house today?' His breath tickles the hairs on her ear.

'I had an appointment with our doctor. I told you, I have been feeling under the weather since the dinner party. It's nothing for you to be concerned about. Really.'

She steps forward to pass, but Yugi's grip tightens.

'Really? Shall I call Doctor Okawa?' He takes out his mobile with his other hand, flips it open.

'Have you dismissed the maids for the day?'

114

'You will answer me.'

'I was with the doctor, but not Doctor Okawa. I was with the herbalist. I – I have not been taking my medicine. Yugi, please understand, I dearly want for us to have a child and I thought he may be able to give us, me, something which might help. I know I have acted selfishly. I will not disobey your wishes again, you must believe me. And you must punish me.' She kneels and bows her head to the matting. 'You *must* punish me.'

The tears she cries are real, because she is terrified of the strength coiled behind the muscles Yugi polishes in the gym. And yet there is another, deeper feeling. Tao's love breathes life into Chinatsu, making her real. A physical response from Yugi would be something at least.

She flinches.

Yugi's fingers stroke the curve of her skull. She looks up and he crouches down to her, smelling of soap and the lavender she provides him. He slips a finger under her chin, slowly bringing it off her chest. She stands.

Yugi is frowning, as though unable to place something important.

Chinatsu can't breathe. Yugi is never confused.

He kisses her, but there is no softness to it. His teeth threaten behind the cushion of his mouth. He walks her back against the wall. The picture of Chinatsu on the swing, the one Hirari gave Yugi during the chess game, is knocked askew by her shoulder.

A draft enters through the front door, which Chinatsu did not quite manage to shut.

Children's voices float in, the squeak of a buggy's wheels.

'The door, Yugi.'

Yugi reaches down and pushes up her skirt.

'People will see.'

Yugi unbuckles and unzips. He takes both her wrists which are still sore and holds them above her head. He rips her tights with the other hand. She can feel his penis, hard against her inner thigh. Dangerous. Exciting? No. Not since Tao. There was a time when she would have craved Yugi's passion, but not now. And this was not passion.

Her husband's eyes don't leave her own. Emotionless, even when he enters her. She cries out, eyes screwed tight. Her head disturbs the

115

picture frame. She hears it clunk against the wall as Yugi continues. Her nails bite into his shoulders.

'No.'

She hears the sound of his punch before she feels it. Then the pain lights up her cheek, the whole framework of her face feels rocked, out of alignment. Her bones vibrate, and she can still feel his penis inside her, but slipping, getting soft. He draws his hand back again. She presses her lips together, stops breathing. His slap a full stop against her face. What would Fleur do? She would walk away surely, walk straight away. She had a strength, a resilience that Chinatsu envied, an ability to just get on with life, even as a ten year old.

There was one day. It was grey and chill, not unusual. The windows were blurred with rain and Fleur sat in the back with the carrier bag she used for school. There were vicious whispers going on behind people's hands. They were talking about Fleur's mother, saying vile sexual things. Chinatsu picked up her work and went to the back of the class. They said Fleur's mother had been killed because she was a prostitute, and she deserved it. Later, in exchanged notes, Chinatsu found out shards of truth.

*My mother wasn't like that.*

*It is not important.*

*It was rope. In the bathroom. Do you understand?*

*Yes.*

Chinatsu gave Fleur her school bag. She emptied out the pens that were rolling around at the bottom. She liked to watch Fleur carry it and know she'd given it to her. Chinatsu took her things home in Fleur's carrier bag and told her mother the kids at school had stolen it. She was beaten. But this did not mean that her parents did not love her.

Here is where Chinatsu knew she was different from Fleur. Chinatsu needed people, *someone.* Tao said he loved her and his love for her was strengthening. She worried about her reaction to him. The idea that she could just love anyone who loved her was distasteful.

Yugi pounds the wall above her head, jolting her back to now. He stalks away.

Chinatsu bends forward, as if she has a stitch. She breathes out, mouths an 'O' and wipes the tears from her cheek. Her bag is still over her shoulder. She straightens her knickers, hitches down her skirt and walks carefully to the kitchen. It hurts, inside. She hides the money from the last man inside a copper pan. The lid shut, sounding like cymbals crashing together. She exchanges a glance with the moonflower. It is steady, waiting, like Tao. She creeps to bed.

Yugi is pretending to be asleep. She knows.

When he really drifts off, her hand sneaks to the soft, warm space between her legs. She feels raw, the skin physically hot. She rests her hand over this place, protecting.

Before she falls asleep, there's a clatter in the front hallway. Without getting up to check, she knows it is the sound of her portrait finally falling.

As if in a dream, Chinatsu's body rises to a sitting position at 3.16 a.m. Her eyes are either so heavy they seem closed, or they are really closed and she is moving, zombie-like: hips swivelling to bring her legs out from under the snow of the duvet, toes white as cooked chicken in the darkness. Her feet meet the carpet, knees taking the weight. She pushes up, stands. Quiet as a ghost, she heads for the kitchen as if pulled by string. Yugi remains undisturbed.

The drawer opens, the lids of her eyes are still drawn, the top and bottom eyelashes meeting, crimped through sleep, reminding her of crushed spider legs. A low rumble as Chinatsu opens the drawer. Her arms are white, too, as a body in a casket, or someone freezing. A fresh pad comes out. She clicks a pen.

Chinatsu writes, without the lids of her eyes ever lifting.

The moonflower watches her write:

*I die at 3.16am, in that time between yesterday and tomorrow. Love isn't enough.*

Chinatsu's eyes open to see her hands are black from soil. She is on her knees. The scent of the earth is in her nostrils, the earth itself in her toenails. She brings her hands to her face and sees it has become engrained in her fingernails. A westerly wind has made gooseflesh on her skin; her bare shoulders tickled by her hair which is awakened by the breeze. Her knees are gritty with soil. In her hands are bags of Yen. The moonflower, her imaginary plant, the flower of all her hopes, the place that kept her secrets and would provide the means to escape if this all went wrong, has been ransacked. She puts her hands in the earth and quickly rights the orchid that marked the moonflower's place. She tucks down their roots, pats the soil like a made bed. Will the moonflower survive in there? Or is it gone for good? Does it matter anymore?

Chinatsu glances at the sky. It is still dark, a black ceiling with no upper limit. Clouds surf this picture of blackness. There are faint shapes in the sky like torn paper, edges occasionally sharking over the moon. An odd star shines through, a cyclops here and there, watching with a white-cold glimmer of ancient menace.

She brushes off the soil as best she can and hurries into the house. There's so much to do before Yugi's alarm.

## 22

Fleur would later think it was Nan's constant sighing that helped bring her back. Or kept her anchored to the real world. Either that, or it was irritation. The desire to be able to tell the woman to shut up and stop moaning about everything. Her neighbours, their cars, how clean their cars were – or were not.

Nan sighs. This time, she's stroking the back of Fleur's hand. Fleur can't feel it, she doesn't think she can anyway, but it's surely the sort of thing Nan would do in this situation.

'Time's ticking on, flower. They say it's good you're breathing on your own at least. Nothing's getting worse. But you can't stay like this, you know that don't you? Ten days. You listening to me? Come on, squeeze my hand.'

Fleur turns her head in her grandmother's direction.

Is this how it happened? How she came back? Small responses that piece together until she finally 'woke up?'

Nan slaps her knee. 'I knew it. I know you're listening. I know you're waking up. Them, they ain't so sure, but I know. You wouldn't leave me like this, would you?' She leans over and strokes Fleur's cheek with a crooked finger.

'Bloody Marcus has been. Scarpered when he got a look of me.'

Marcus? How had she reacted to that?

'Pretty sure I saw that Derek bloke shuffling about here an' all. Probably shouldn't be telling you that. Shouldn't say this, in case you can hear. Course you can hear. Still, someone needs to stop that fella. I'd a fair idea something was off with him, when he and your mum were going out. But your mother wouldn't listen, would she? Always knew best, could never get through to that one. So many fights we had about you. I know we don't talk about it, but just so you know, I'm sorry. I didn't know what was going on, you don't think about that stuff do you? Don't want to anyway. But if I made a complaint, I was scared you'd be taken away. And I was terrified of what they'd do to your mother.'

Had she been angry then, hearing Derek's name? Or afraid?

Nan stops, her nostrils flaring. She screws her mouth up so tightly it looks like she's gurning. She clears her throat. 'I've seen him about with a new missus. Got a little girl she has an' all. Someone needs to stop him. But eh, don't frown, flower. It'll be all right. And don't fret about the baby. I know, I know, but you've the rest of your life to find a good and decent man. Haven't you? You'll have happiness, be a mum one day. A bloody good one. You've just got to wake up.'

No. The overriding feeling Fleur would later have, when piecing this all together, was anger.

# 23

Yugi Hamugoshi is white.

It is obvious something is off-kilter from the moment his alarm sounds. He swats the alarm, aiming for the off button, but it won't stop screeching. Blaring like sirens. The sound hurls around his head. He hits the alarm again, and it clatters off the bedside table, dangling inches from the floor by its electric cable.

All is quiet.

There are no birds singing, no sound of Chinatsu rumpling the bed-sheets as she gets up moments before him to switch on his shower and prepare his towels.

And he knows.

Already he knows.

Chinatsu is not there at all. She's gone.

He pushes his feet into navy blue slippers, positioned carefully at his bedside. Had she done this for him? He can't remember doing it the night before.

Yugi heads to his office and slides open the door. Everything is as it should be. He taps a pile of documents into alignment with his right forefinger. A stray note creates tension on his linear desk. From Chinatsu? No. It's from a maid:

> Sir, Mrs Hamugoshi apologises but received
> a message from her mother late last night.
> Her father is unwell and she will be in touch
> shortly. She says to tell you not to worry.

Yugi crumples up the note in his fist. He will get his secretary to call and check with Chinatsu's mother but he is fairly certain of the response. The note goes into the bin. The flippancy of this action defies the adrenaline coursing through his system. Why hadn't the maid woken him to tell him? It was unacceptable.

He tweaks the sleep out of his eye with the middle knuckle of his forefinger. Yugi is walking quickly now, from the office towards the kitchen. Chinatsu's portrait is leaning against the skirting board. A metre or so above the top of the picture is the dent in the wall from Yugi's fist.

He grits his teeth.

Yugi rounds the doorway, eyebrows up, ready to smile and say good morning.

But he knows.

The kitchen is empty.

Instead, there is another note, or what Yugi initially takes to be a note. He approaches the counter warily, the garden still black and shapeless through the window.

The note says: *I die at 3.16am, in that time between yesterday and tomorrow. Love isn't enough.*

He holds it up, his fingers pegs at each corner. His shoulders drop. He knew, of course he knew, but now he is certain: Chinatsu is not at her parents. The note dives downwards. It's cushioned by a momentary updraft, reaches the ground, and is still.

Yugi Hamugoshi is also still.

What, or who, has taken his wife from him? He bends down and picks up the note. Screws it tight into his palm. Whatever, or whoever, caused this, will pay. *Somebody* will have to pay.

# 24

A snake is ripped from her throat.

Beep . . . beep . . . beep . . . beep . . . beep . . . beep . . . beep . . . beep . . .
beep . . .

   'What, honey? What are you trying to say?'
   Where is the cat?
   'I – hang on. Wait, I just can't understand, Fleur, start again – what?'
   Cat. Kitten. Kitten!
   'You should rest, Fleur. Back to sleep, come on. Shh.'

Beep . . . beep . . . beep . . . beep . . . beep . . . beep . . . beep . . . beep . . .
beep . . .

A collection of images and emotions, all like flashcards.
Marcus, face a demon of fury.
   Fear exploding, separating through her body.

Relax, relax, accept it, the impact will hurt less.

The kitten.

She's going to die.

She screams.

She can't hear anything.

Nothing.

White.

Gingerbread. A house blackened, wrinkling up with fire.

Stink of sugar and . . . meat?

A girl at the top of the stairs, her face a skeleton, eyes black and empty.

White.

Beep . . . beep . . . beep . . . beep . . . beep . . . beep . . . beep . . . beep . . . beep . . .

'Fleur? Can you squeeze my hand? And now focus in the direction of my voice. Good. Fleur, can you tell me how old you are?'

The words are in her mind, but won't move to her mouth. Her throat won't connect.

'How old are you?'

Thirty.

She opens her mouth. Pushes, pushing.

'How old are you, Fleur?'

'C-c . . .'

'Yes? Keep trying.'

'*Cat.*'

'Good. It's a good sign she's able to articulate.'

Exhausted, sleep again.

Her mind pops open. She feels like Fleur, but has only just remembered her Nan. It's like the woman just winked into existence, fully formed, a pop-up birthday card. Ta-da! I exist. Complete with a back catalogue of memories she already knew, but had neglected, and were suddenly dusted off.

'Nan!'

'Here, love. Here I am. Let's calm down, eh? Just lie back now. Shh, shh. It's OK isn't it? See? You're here. You're all right? Not going nowhere. Christ, girl, like the devil's after you.'

Her chest is hyper; rising, falling. She can't understand. Her thoughts are slinking through mud, slow and prehistoric, some sort of sandworm. They can't – won't – quicken.

'Shh. Shh.'

It slows. Razor blades in her bladder, a mad itch in her wrist, the metallic pinch. Her throat has been sandpapered; it feels covered in thousands of paper cuts.

'Here, don't pull on that, love, eh? Might be what's keeping you with me, God hope.'

Sleep drags her back under.

Beep . . . beep . . . beep . . . beep . . . beep . . . beep . . . beep . . . beep . . . beep . . .

'Nan!'

'Jesus! You're gonna put me in a coma in a minute.'

'Need to . . . I need . . . I have –'

'No, no. You just need to relax and get better.'

Don't listen. She'll forget. She needs to remember. There was something she was supposed to do.

It's exhausting, changing the gears in her head. Her memory is a boulder, her back against it, shouldering it up the hill.

Baby. A little girl. Her. What?

Her eyelids are weighted, her mind falls away. Something she is supposed to do.

# 25

Chinatsu is still looking for her husband. She can't quiet the fear simmering in her stomach. Even now as the plane begins its descent and she wriggles her jaw, feeling as though there are bubbles in her ears, she's looking. Is he on the plane, or just behind?

Did she put enough distance between them? Had she thrown him off, just slightly, with the phone call to the maid, the little lie about her father? Doubtful. Her mind jarred, like a blip in a heart-rate monitor. She'd left her writing in the kitchen, hadn't she? Nerves pulsed through her. She couldn't even remember what she'd written, but he would have found it. What was he thinking? Had he already called her parents? Could he be on his way? Oh God. She looked at her phone, but it was blank: they'd been told to switch them off. Could she chance turning it on now? Of course not, that was ridiculous.

Her plane had boarded exactly one hour after Yugi's alarm was set to sound. If he'd come to the airport, he might even have caught her, standing in the queues, flinching as she saw a million would-be Yugi's in the crowd. Will he be waiting for her as she steps off? Does she want that? She tugs the lap belt, closes her eyes.

The noises on the plane faded into the background. In that quiet moment, she recognised another feeling sitting heavily inside her. Disappointment. She *wished* Yugi had come after her, that he cared enough to come after her and get her to change her mind. The reality was he would come after her, or Tao, in one way or another. It was just a case of how, and when.

She sees a spider line, invisible but strong, connecting her to Jiguyaoka, Tokyo, the moonflower and home. It winks in the sunlight, stretching, tapering off, becoming as thin as can be, doing anything to maintain their connection. It is only a matter of time before it breaks, isn't it? If she got straight back on a plane to Japan, this invisible line would be baggy. It would never snap back into shape. Equally this person she is right now, aboard this plane, can never go back either.

Could she?

That heart-stopping, gut-wrenching, exhilarating pressure of taking off. She had experienced it just twice before. Once when she went to England with her family, where she met Fleur, and once on the way home when her father's secondment ended. The shocking force of lift-off – rocketing upwards, levelling out into smooth, clean sky.

And now they're landing. She imagines the sleek plane sinking below the clouds like a submarine, or a shark, slow and soft. They're pointing towards the ground now, hurtling for it. She grips the seat, swallows, her ears pop. The plane touches tarmac. She inhales sharply. The plane pitches forward, wheels screaming, plane bouncing, connecting properly. It's then she realises just how fast they're going. She holds her breath, until the force that's pinning her shoulders to the seat finally slackens.

It was amazing.

## 26

A plane cuts swiftly through the night sky. Yugi looks up, but can't see anything except a throng of stars, gold in black. He hears the plane's engines growing more distant. Until there is nothing left of them.

There's a strange feeling in his stomach.

He keeps swallowing.

Would Chinatsu go that far to escape him? If so, she'd have been on an earlier flight, surely?

Yugi has not been to work today. He has not taken any calls. He has dismissed the maids and, instead, has re-read the words his wife left on the kitchen counter top. Over and over. He has convinced himself that she is sick, and needs help. After that, there must be punishment. But first and foremost, he has a responsibility to go to her aid. He has had words with his own detective, the boy with the white trainers, floppy hair and black ensemble. This boy has come back to him with a name: Madam Li.

Later, Yugi watches this woman, a dragon lady coiled beneath a fuchsia lantern in the night. Madam Li. All that is missing from the image is for her legs to be crossed and Buddha like. Across the street, Yugi cannot hear. But it no longer matters. He is aware of the China-woman's game. In front of Madam Li, her poised back presented to Yugi, is a woman with waist-length black hair. Such long hair is not proper, tidy or convenient. A tourist steps back from his inspection of leather bags, right onto Yugi's foot.

English people are so fat.

'Sorry, sorry.'

Yugi's fingers curl. He takes a few steps to another tarpaulin stall, lit by lanterns and hosted by Thai children.

The tourist markets around the tacky restaurant housing Madam Li are lined with puffy white faces. They are longer, more cumbersome than the Japanese, ambling in trios, sometimes sets of four or five along the strip. Even their families are excessive. Their golf-ball eyes marvel at what they must see as delicacies: strips of octopuses, fish eyes in pots. They point with tapered fingers and huddle together. They should try these delicacies, instead of gorging on clotted old meat. The English people all looked swollen. It was a distressing sight. Perhaps an alteration in diet would mean they would then walk with something more akin to grace, and not all die of heart attacks at the age of fifty.

Yugi's father lived until he was ninety-seven. A stubbornness that was typical of the man. On his deathbed, he gripped Yugi's wrist like he was trying to leach the life force out of his son. Yugi had plucked his father's diseased fingers away, and covered his own mouth with a linen handkerchief. His older sisters were there, the ones to his father's first wife. They looked pained when Yugi covered his mouth. Then again, they too appeared malnourished, dying.

The son of the mistress, his sisters had thirty years on Yugi. They all looked about to die. He does not know their husbands' professions, but they had clearly not provided well.

When certain his father was finally and definitely dead, Yugi walked from the falling-down peasant house and the cloying sweet scent of death did not stick to his Armani suit. He had needed to see the man's last breath. Just as he had needed to see the primly outraged looks from his sisters. Their poor, unreachable brother.

All of them could die in their sleep for all he cared. Where had they been? What had they done for him with their new families and shiny children?

Part of him had wanted to scream this at them, that it was too late for sympathy and pity and care. But that was the point; it was too late. He left the house feeling lighter and, almost, cheerful. Now that he was nobody's son, nobody's kin, he could be whoever he wanted to be. Do whatever he wanted to do. Without guilt.

'This watch suit you, sir? Give you deal for 30,000.'

Yugi lifts his eyes, and pushes back his suit sleeve. He taps the face of his Omega. 'I have one.'

The child's eyes skip to someone more viable. Yugi's smugness drifts.

'Here. Boy. I'll take it. I'll give you 50,000.'

The boy, teeth too big for his lips, looks to his darker skinned and smaller sister. Her hair is gypsy-curly. She shrugs. The boy holds his hand out.

Yugi turns away. The lantern light, though soft, rockets through his vision, ricocheting each time he blinks. He needs anchoring, to feel balanced.

'Sir. Mister!'

Yugi crosses the border to the next stall. What is he trying to prove? His wife leaves him, but he can pay 20,000 Yen over the odds for a fake watch?

This wasn't how he'd carved out a global, Top 100 business.

One of the white people turns and speaks. There is an upturn to the end of the predominantly monotone words. Yugi speaks the bare bones of many languages for business. His English is strong and he can translate, but does not wish to this evening. English, and its sluggish blocked plughole of words, is not on Yugi's agenda.

He returns his attention to Madam Li and her newest recruit.

The woman reigns like an Empress at the gaudy restaurant. Their meal is over and the woman with the sheaf of hair, like water polluted with black ink, says her goodbyes. Without even seeing her face, Yugi knows who she is: Masa's wife.

Yugi smiles and dips out of sight. . This information can be used to his advantage in several ways.

130

# 27

Weird. This is a dream. And so familiar. She's been dreaming it for
weeks. Yes? Yes. She'll wake up now. Now she knows it's not real, but it
spins on. She doesn't want to stay. Wake up. This house has her. It is
alive. Hot. A baby's howl shrieks through the walls. Fire-smoke scratches
her lungs. Stink of gingerbread. Mum's jangly bracelets echo somewhere
upstairs, the smell of Shake n Vac and dust and meat. The stairs. She
doesn't want to go up. Upstairs  mum is spinning, bracelets jingling. But
she climbs, climbing. Climb quicker. The stairs will burn away. Quick!
Her hand touches the banisters for balance. Ouch. Fire. The wood is
sickening, twisting. The walls are bulging, boiling, sagging. Singe-smell of
marzipan. Black ahead, all white behind. The white. Please no. Don't see
her, don't see mum. No *please*. Mum turning, twirling from the sky. She
keeps walking. The bathroom door. Closed, now open. Mum? It's a little
girl, head bowed. Just her crown, the slip of soft child-hair. It's herself,
then someone else. Who? The head rises. She's going to see. Who? *Who?*
The girl's baby face is skeletal. Black and dark. Dead.

Blink, blink, blink. Her eyes feel gritty. It's as if her eyelids are cardboard, creaking open and closed. A wave of emotion travels over her body: shoulders, skin, bones and toes. *Something* is happening. Her eyelids are wet, now wetter, the sadness is obese. Inescapable. She moans.

'Fleur? You're awake?'

The voice – whose? Nan's, that's right – reaches Fleur over the stinging electric buzz of machines. She'd got used to all the beeping.

It feels late. That time between All Hallows and Halloween.

She forces her chin to dip: Yes.

'The doctor said to encourage you to speak.'

Fuck off. She raises her eyebrows. Say hello. Say how much you've missed her. 'Shit.'

'Excuse you. What's with the language?'

Nan reeks of cigarettes. The smell claws at her stomach, which feels hollowed out. A cold, damp cave made out of some strange carved wood. And it's not just hunger. It's something else. Her cheek sticks to the wet pillow.

'Stink.'

'What? Who?'

'*Stink.*'

'You obviously need your rest.'

'Fuck.' It's not what she wants to say. Yet there is anger. It's hot. She wants to hurt someone. But not Nan. Or does she?

Fleur sees Nan's bent hands wipe her face, which is ribbed with age. The lines are disconcertingly deep. Her fingers are crooked. Fleur knows the tips are as rough as if Nan plays guitar. That familiar clawed look, her bones knitting together with age and arthritis. Her fingers find Fleur's hand. She's icy.

'Off.' Frustration pinches her; it was the wrong word. Her eyes water. She'd meant to say sorry. She jerks her arm, at least something responds, but it whacks the cupboard. Pain flowers under her skin. But the sensation, it's a relief. Feels good. The water jug glugs over, whooshing onto the floor. A cup spins to a standstill.

Nan stares at it. 'I'm going to get the doctor.'

Fleur forces her fingers to grasp. 'You tell me. What happened?'

Nan's gaze flicks away. She licks her lips. 'You don't remember? Marcus?'

Marcus, Marcus . . . Marcus. Another person blossoms in her head, buds of knowledge: Her ring catching on her work shirt, a hand on her swollen stomach – swollen? – the fear of him. The hurt, because once it was love. Once she was grateful. Heat. She forces her hand to her stomach, trying to piece it together. It still feels swollen. It hurt a little. Why?

Nan sits back down in the chair and shucks forward, chair legs squawking. 'You argued. The doctors tell me you'd fallen down the stairs. Do you remember falling?'

Did she? She steers her mind back to this person she is now aware of called Marcus. She imagines herself falling. Yes! She remembers. And Marcus' face. It was twisted, so full of hate.

'Fight.' Fleur closes her eyes, tired, too much effort.

'What did you fight about, Fleur?'

Leave me alone.

'If you dare go back to him, if you *dare*! Vege - vegetation, that's what. That's what I had to hear! No. Don't even try Fleur. It's bad enough the baby, but if you go back, well then, it'll be . . . after a bloody coma – *coma* - I swear I'll lock you in the house. No way I'm losing two girls. You don't think I've been through enough with your mother? You really have to do this to me? Wait, no, hang on. I'm – I've just been so worried. You worried me, flower. I was so scared.'

The words are too much. Rushing in like the ocean. Coma. Baby. Vegetation?

Shock. Jagged as smashed glass. The last moment she remembered was telling herself to relax as she fell, to accept the fall. And then she came to. Here, in the hospital. Blinking and sore and sad, exactly the same as she'd left. Just *seconds* later.

But it hadn't been seconds, it'd been days. Maybe even weeks? How long? And her body had changed, time had passed, people had been living, moving, speaking, *worrying*. And she'd been left out of the loop. Something had been taken that could never be put back. Just time. She'd never fill in that blank, never knit it back together in a way she could understand.

The loss she felt yawned out before her. Like her mother, something that would always be missing.

But there was something in that lost time, wasn't there? Something had been there, in the gap. But she couldn't grab hold of that idea, and make it real. Her brain hurt. What was she even talking about?

The second thing that sank into her was a drooping sense of failure. Is this what her life has come to? An episode in a soap opera, viewers curling their lips in distaste at her weakness. Her typical white-trashness. How could she have thought she'd ever be better than this? Escape this town? Live happily ever after. Make something of herself. No. She'd just repeated her mother's life, a train clicking over the tracks.

At least her mother had killed herself, rather than having a man do it for her.

God.

The shame was hot. She kept her eyes closed, needing the dark.

With effort, she forced her tongue over cracked lips. It didn't help much.

'Sat here every goddamn day, keeping all manner of shit away from you. Can you believe Derek came here? Derek? Can you imagine? The fucking nerve of him. And that Marcus. They won't be back Fleur, I'll promise you that for nowt. I told that Derek exactly what I'd say to that new woman he's seeing if he came back. She's got a kid you know, young lass, still in knee socks.'

Derek. She homed in on the name. Derek, Derek. An explosion in her belly. A racing panic.

She'd been unable to move and *that* man had been in here. Alone? What had he done? And then not just him. Who else had touched her? Who fucking else? Who'd looked at her, dressed her, washed her? Had he done anything? She would never know. Who could she ask, who would know? Just the thought of it, the possibility made her want to fold in on herself and retreat. She wanted to tuck her arms and legs into her body and go back there, to the coma place. Where she was safe.

She shook her head, face contorted in quiet tears. She frowned.

And that was when she realised. The reason behind that pain in her stomach. Another life came into her awareness, like Nan and Marcus. The baby, her baby. But it was gone. Her mind wants to be blank, wants to be numb. The desire is working; she's not thinking any more, not feeling. What did she feel about the baby? The answer came back: nothing.

Nan sighs. 'Ay, flower. Let me get the doctor, eh?'

Her Nan disappears, muffled little stamps in the quiet – she's probably got her slippers on. She'll have made herself right at home, some God poetry out on the bedside table, that magnifying glass she uses to read. Fleur feels like her bones are made of wine gums.

Nan comes back. 'Be here as soon as. You OK, flower?'

'Mum.'

'You want to see her?'

She closed her eyes.

A stretch of silence.

Fleur's nerves itch. The quiet is dizzying. The idea of tripping into another gap, waking up with more lost time. Her life, some ridiculous DVD, skipping and arbitrary. The desire for Marcus right then, for love and care and warmth, or just some familiarity was an embarrassing, awful ache. If only. But . . . no. And that loss, too. And then their child. Too much. Too, too much.

'The police will want to talk to you soon I expect. It's your chance, flower. Do the right thing, eh?'

Her memory shocked back to the *McDonalds* staff room. Daniel. A rush of images come to her, like a film trailer. The aeroplane, the grass verge, plucking daisies, smiling up at him, his fingers, solid, tracing her name on her palm. Kissing. And then he died. Oh God, he died. Just before she could be with him, just before she was about to leave Marcus.

The guilt she'd carried with her since that day. She'd been so weak. She hadn't left, and she should have, for the memory of Daniel.

Nan touched her hand. Fleur moved hers away.

And then something came back from the gap, the white.

Daniel's face, shining in the tree, twisting, inverting to a skeleton. Her Japanese friend infused the space. She drew the affection they shared for each other around her. Make me breathe. But there was a voice in her head, and it was Chinatsu's, compelling, urging: You have to help her.

Fleur blinked, tears stopping. Help who?

# 28

Chinatsu observes her freedom through the grubby hotel window.
There's an English language school directly opposite. She can see the
students, possibly French and Italian, milling around outside the school
on their breaks. Smoking and laughing, screwing their noses up at the
English sandwiches. Their laughter occasionally reaching through the
windowpanes. They look like such good friends.

Fleur. She could go to find her today. But she has never navigated the
London Tube and neither does she have any clue where Fleur might be
living. Besides, she and Tao have already decided that she must not take
unnecessary risks. Yugi might already be here. Or, at least, he might have
someone looking for her.

Chinatsu's world is quiet and she has lots of time to think. The hotel
is purposefully discreet. She has discussed this with Tao. It would be
much easier for Yugi to find her in a big hotel where he would be likely
to have contacts. If only this wasn't the case. The room is like a musty
attic, stale and over-scented with potpourri. She can taste the perfume in
the back of her throat.

The journey from the airport to the hotel had been an assault. She'd
wanted to switch off her senses. One of Tao's associates had met her at

the airport with a cardboard sign and her name: Amber. Not exactly what she'd wanted to see when starting over in this new place, but it was a little more discreet than using her married name. Tao's associate spelled his name slowly: O-M-A-R. He looked to be from a place like India. He had purple lips and a turban piled high on his head like a woman's towel after a shower. Beneath his aftershave, he smelled strongly of dusty spices; she didn't like it.

Omar put her in a taxi and gave the cabbie directions. A brief panic flared in her stomach; he could be sending her anywhere. What if Omar was really Yugi's associate? What if –? She calmed herself by patting her nose with powder in the toilets. In the mirror's watery light, she looked sick. She clicked the compact shut and stowed it in her purse. She breathed through the fear, pulled an image around her that made her feel safe. The taxi is a tank. The driver is a security-guard keeping her safe from all these pale people, their different smell, their large litter and the full scale spread of their tumbling, epileptic language. She recognised Coke cans in gutters, but they also seemed foreign. Even the Yellow 'M's of *McDonalds* looked a different shade. Or was she just imagining it? That and the different shading to the sky and the light? Nevertheless, the off-yellow 'M' and the slightly altered Coke cans were a sign of home. She felt tied to the boutique streets back home. The taxi chugged along, bouncing her in the cab. The leather squeaked from her grip. Stay calm. She placed her hands in her lap, knees together, her palms leaving a damp print on the leather seat. The print seemed to unpeel. She stared at it, somehow disgusted, as if that print was herself, disappearing.

She heard her mother's voice: Shoulders back, child. A man must never know how you are feeling. This part of you is only for you. Understand?

Taking a deep breath she watched England pitch by, grey and harsh, striated with sections of glitter and lights, layers of grime. The dizzying blur of this capital.

The language was coming back, from talking with Fleur all those years ago, her private study of it as a child.

*Please. Sorry? Hello. What? No.*

Sentences were vague, a soup of foreignness, but words shone out every now and then like light on water.

137

Finally reaching the hotel room, Omar gone, she clicks the door and tests the lock.

And. Breathe. Out.

Kicking off her heels, her feet smell of tights and shoes that have been left on too long. She breathes in. The scent of herself is somehow comforting. Sitting on the edge of the bed, hands under her legs, she wriggles her toes. Clear nail polish winks through taupe tights. She wiggles her big toe, forcing the bone to click. She does this over and over in the quiet hotel room, to the rhythm of a ticking clock.

Looking around, there are signs of the familiar, a strange bed but a bed nonetheless, things she recognises and finds English words for: 'wardrobe', 'bedside table', 'toilet'. There are square packets on the tiny sink opposite . . . *soap*. She explores the bathroom: the bland bottles in the shower: *shampoo*. It was real life in miniature. Similar, but not the same. An echo. She longs for chopsticks, some *miso* soup, *soba* noodles, Shiseido shampoo. Starving, she'd had to buy sandwiches at the airport cafe. She'd forgotten how heavy on the stomach English food was. Japanese food was so much lighter. To be Japanese. What did it mean? It's a different face, a landscape coloured in another tone, alternate shades of culture, behaviour, the kids so exhaustingly in *fashion*. Not like here, where they blend, blend, blend. But she can be OK here, in England. It was just a jigsaw piece away, a missing shape of land between Japan and the UK.

Then why do it? Why go somewhere else to be the same?

She takes her mobile, newly bought, out of her handbag. It clicks against her compact and lipstick. There are only a couple of messages on the phone, both from Tao, replying that he had got her new number and would call her tonight. Another one tells her to be brave. The exact words are: Be brave, Amber. She reads her own messages to Tao, Amber's Tao, then sets the phone on the bed next to her. Yugi's number would never flash up on this phone. Her stomach feels tight and sore. Seconds later, the light on the LCD screen is dark. She turns towards her bag again and finds her notebook.

She writes: *In England. Have walked along grey pavements that sparkle with phlegm. Some of the spit-shapes look like Japanese characters. I think I saw the one for love.* She sighs and thinks of the name: Fleur. They were so much closer to each other now.

# 29

Yugi Hamugoshi is feeling creative. In his left hand he has a pair of hairdresser scissors, his right hand snug in silk pockets, one hip contacting the wall's edge, his right knee bent in an oh-so casual pose.

Also in Yugi's possession: an appointment for 3pm. Of course, the appointment has been made in another name, a man already vetted by Madam Li's little operation who he has paid off. This project of the China-woman's is about to be unravelled, stitch-by-stitch, unless she tells Yugi what he wants to know.

But first, he needs to send a message.

Yugi can smell the polish on the windows as he looks down two-dozen stories, watching Tokyo on mute. The floral scent is so irritating it makes his nostrils itch and shoulders tense. He breathes out. Being so close to the window he can feel the chill from the glass investigate the hairs of his cheek. His breath fogs over the pane, forward, then rewind, erasing as if he'd never breathed.

The hotel door clicks open and Masa's wife walks in.

Later, at home, Yugi runs the shower hot. Scalding. He raises his chin to the water, eyes closed, teeth bared. The water eventually runs clear. He presses a button and the shower quietens. The house seems like it is holding its breath. No noise. Not a thing.

Yugi pats himself dry, the sounds he makes interrupting the quiet. He rests the towel around his neck and dresses in grey silk pyjamas. The house seems to whistle with silence. It is cold. Chinatsu must have adjusted the heat in the evenings. He had never felt the slight ice in the air like he did now. The cold smoothes over his ears as he walks to bedroom to get his toenail clippers.

*Click. Click. Click.*

He gathers up the crescents of nail and scatters them into the toilet bowl. He checks his fingernails, raising his hand to the light. A speck of blood? He raises the clipper.

*Click. Click.*

'Ah!'

Yugi's own blood slips over his fingertip. Pats onto the floor. He plucks tissues from a box that looked to be getting low. Chinatsu would not replenish it. Yugi wipes up the blood and flushes blood and nail away. The sound of him wrapping tissue around his finger seems tremendous.

He goes to bed, tapping lights off, on, then off again. He lies on his side of the bed, nose and ears cold. Blood seeping into the tissue on his fingertip, blinking in the darkness.

# 30

'Good morning, Fleur. Can you be remembering the word I asked you to
remember? Fleur?'

'She's always arsey when she's not had any breakfast.'

Fleur glares at her. 'F'koff, Edna.'

'I don't think that was the word the doctor asked you to remember.'

An image assaults her. The little girl's eyes bore into her from the top
of the stairs as the gingerbread house goes up in flames. The girl's skin
like blackening plastic. An image of her own child, too-tiny, malformed.
Pitiful. Her chest heaves, but she controls the urge to be sick. Why is
there no sadness about her baby? No ocean-roll of grief driving over her,
stealing her breath. Was it because she missed it? The baby disappearing
while she was away.

Fleur sniffs. What was that? The scent of sweet spice tickles her
memory.

Gingerbread house? She squeezes her eyes against the image of the
burning child, her fingers trying to curl into fists. But her fingers would
only bend at the tip. Where did that image come from? Who was that
little girl? Dreams?

'Don't do that.'

Nan's bent fingers touch Fleur's hand. She intends to twitch her elbow to piss Nan off, but her knee jerks instead.

The doctor clicks a pen and writes something.

Fleur rests her head back, heart racing. Why is she acting like this with Nan? Really, there's a massive part of her which feels overwhelmed with gratitude. It's been years since she lived with Nan. The woman hated Marcus. She'd cut all ties with Fleur until she 'came to her senses'.

'That's a good reflex, Fleur,' the doctor says. 'But you don't want to hurt your grandmother. She's been very good to you. Are you angry?'

Fleur shakes her head, then nods. It's incredibly difficult just to get her body to do what she wants it to.

'Can you tell me why?'

'Needs her Weetabix, that's what. They serve some right slop in here, doctor.'

'I know. This is why my wife is always making me a packed lunch.' He smiles.

'Paki.' She wishes she could clamp her hands over her mouth. Why had that come out?

'Now Fleur, this is not very nice,' the doctor says.

'It's not his fault, flower.'

The doctor looks at Edna, then back at Fleur. 'I want you to remember these words. Apple, Banana, Peach. Can you repeat these words?'

She wants to roll her eyes, but the effort this would take would be immense. She forces everything to work: jaw, voice, tongue, mouth. 'Apple. Banana. Peach.'

'Can you say that backwards?'

'Peach . . . Banana . . . Apple.'

'And at what age was it again that you started working at *McDonalds*?'

'Sixteen.'

'And what was the word I asked you to remember for today?'

Fleur frowned. And thumped her legs. The doctor sprang up to catch her hands. Nan covered her face.

'It is very good you are strong, but you mustn't do this to yourself, Fleur. Do you understand? It is like this at the beginning, but we will be

143

making progress. I know the questions I ask you might seem frustrating, but we are trying to keep your brain active.'

He let go.

'Dirty fucking paki.'

'Now in many cases, a patient will have a change of language or behaviour. It is normal, and settles down with most people. But you must be trying to be stopping this. It is rude. The word I want you to remember today is 'Fleur'. Can you repeat it?'

Fleur turned her head.

'I think that means we are through for now. I'll be back later, Mrs Pearson. Fleur.'

The doctor left.

Nan whispered, 'He doesn't smell of curry the way the rest of them do.'

It seemed a bad thing to say, but Fleur laughed.

She heard the doctor's voice echoing in the hallway. And someone else's. Nan put a cup to her lips and Fleur took in water. Some of it dribbled down her chin. She tried to hold the cup. Tried to remember. Her hands shook. She knew the doctor's face, but wasn't sure if he'd just been here, or not. She listened.

'Officers, I have to advise you that this is not a good time to be conducting your interviews.'

'But she's awake, isn't she?'

'Her verbal skills are not as they were before the trauma. In my opinion, your questions will only frustrate her and could lead to some distress.'

'But she can speak?'

'Yes, but –'

'We won't be long, sir. It's an important matter, as I'm sure you can appreciate.'

There were thuds as heavy boots sounded over the floor. There was a woman. Her brown hair had a little orange in it, like an owl. And a man.

Her memory woke up, firing and supplying. A jolt of electricity bolts through her chest. It was the same man, the officer she'd told about Derek. Wasn't it?

She curls her fingers around the water cup and hurls it at the officer.

144

# 31

There's a thump upstairs. He freezes, looks up. Chinatsu? It's just a tick in the house.

It bothers him, but Yugi fears the house, especially at night. Even when all the lights are off, there's a glow coming from somewhere. He'll get up, padding through the corridors, feet hitting the floor like a dripping tap. He'll check each room, turning off every plug socket and appliance. But the light will remain on the fringes of his consciousness, glowing like a waxing moon. Chinatsu's absence has made the house seem enormous, reminding him of the sky threatening rain when he was a boy in the fields. When he's in bed trying to sleep the silence seems unnaturally large. He cannot discover where Chinatsu keeps the lavender oil. He calls his driver to take him to the gym and runs like a machine until his throat is raw and his stomach convulses. When he goes home after the gym he no longer needs the lavender oil to sleep.

It feels like the house is just tolerating him. The bathroom gives him water and the kitchen provides tea. The maids, gossiping in corners no doubt, leave everything prepared. He sits on the same stool as when he gave Chinatsu her pills, when he kissed her that day. His anger rises up like heartburn. He disconnects from it, sips tea, and sets down the mug and looks around. There is nothing to see. The dishes are all clean, the house is swept; everything is in its place. But the walls seem too sharp, or too close.

Yugi checks his watch. He starts. The crocodile strap seems as if it has come alive and started to mesh with his skin. He looks again; it's just a strap. He is expecting a visitor. The last time Yugi took a day off was when he got married. The honeymoon was permanently delayed. Chinatsu hadn't made a fuss. Yugi is the CEO of one of the Top 100 trading companies in the world. The company brings in 70 billion US dollars a year thanks in part to Yugi's streamlining. He had meant to buy Chinatsu some jewellery to appease her, perhaps pearls. His secretary had selected the most gauche diamond earrings and Yugi had had them sent back. A whore may need to sparkle, but a wife need not sparkle to shine.

His mobile goes off. He answers it on the first ring; it's the second person he's expecting.

'Hey, man,' Yugi says. 'How's things?'

'Shit.'

'Why. What's up?'

'It's my wife. She's been attacked.'

Yugi bends, bares his teeth to the stainless steel kettle. He runs his tongue over the centre two. Straightens and tries to sound surprised. 'What? Shit, Masa. That's terrible. Are you at the hospital?'

'All night.'

'I'll be over right after my meeting.'

'Thanks, Yugi. I could do with a friend.'

He hangs up and takes another sip of tea. Winces; it's a little bitter. The phone goes again.

'I here.'

'Then ring the door bell.'

He cancels the call and waits. Eventually, the doorbell chimes. Yugi takes his time, first putting the cup by the sink, then smoothing his olive tie. He pulls back the door, bringing forth the scent of perfumed powder, lilies and winter.

'What you want, Mr Hamugoshi?'

'Guess.'

'I should call police.'

'No. You really shouldn't. Would you like some tea?'

'I would like this over soon as possible.'

'Then you had better not refuse my hospitality, Madam Li. I am not a forgiving man.'

Her nostrils flare. 'No sugar. Now, Mr Hamugoshi, what you want?'

Yugi smiles. 'We are both businesspeople, Madam Li. I anticipate our being able to come to some sort of arrangement here.'

'Get fucking on with it.'

Yugi pulls the scissors out of his suit jacket pocket. Madam Li's gaze follows the blades. Yugi rests the tip on his bottom lip, and taps. He crosses to the vase of roses Chinatsu had cut days earlier and arranged in the kitchen. He cuts the head off one and catches the full, but thinning bloom, in his palm.

'You tell me where my wife is, Madam Li, and I don't cut down your business head by head. Now, are you comfortable with those terms, or should I keep cutting?'

'I tell you nothing.'

He spreads his arms. 'Your decision, but perhaps you want to take a while to think this over. Does your husband know about your clever little enterprise?'

'I not know where your wife go. She not tell me. She just leave.'

'Perhaps that's true, but you know who she's gone with. While you're thinking about whether or not to be agreeable, maybe you could ask Masa's wife what she would recommend you do?'

The China woman's face seems calm, her fly-black eyes are hostile and steady. There's a slight tremor in her hands.

Yugi smiles. 'You have been to visit her haven't you? At the hospital?'

# 32

Chinatsu sits outside a *Café Rouge*, eyes narrowed against the cold. She's bundled up in grey woollen trousers, a mustard polo neck, and a single-breasted black coat. She should get a beret, shouldn't she? Set it at an angle. Be artful and foreign.

Her hot chocolate steams and the pages of her open notebook ripple back and forward, as if the breeze is indecisive. This café and surrounding restaurants remind her of home. The mix of Spanish, Italian, American and French is similar to the streets of Jiyugaoka. Even as the buses wheeze past like great lumbering robots, spilling assorted colours of people, it's still hard to believe this is The West. The place that Tokyo mimicked.

But she feels more at home here. She's just another foreigner no one really notices. In Japan people can tell at a glance just what part of the country you're from, they can glean your status from overhearing a snippet of conversation and the likely trajectory of your life. In Japan, she is much more aware that she is just a little different. And more than a little unwilling to accept those rules.

She raises the mug, wincing as hot chocolate burns her top lip. She clamps the fluttering pages of her open notebook and, pulling her collar close to her neck, writes: *Amber is craning to see what I see, crawls up out of that dark place in my body. To be me? Will she chew through me from the inside out?*

Chinatsu taps the pen against her lip. Her attention is distracted by a girl with copper coloured hair who's just got off the bus over the road. She seems truly English with pale, pale skin. What is the description for them? English flowers? The girl, a head above most of the women, and far taller than Chinatsu, wears a beret. It suits her. Hair loose around her shoulders like a living, shining pashmina. She's slender and a little too thin to be healthy. Although Yugi, Chinatsu is sure, would find her appealing. Striding through the crowds, the girl's body seems to cut out a gap. Creates a walkway, as though other people feel they should make way. She is heading in the direction of Chinatsu's hotel. What's her destination? Chinatsu watches her, a forward presence, intent on her goal while the rest of the people window shop and dither and chat and gossip and attempt to cross the car-clogged road.

Recognition pulses. Fleur? She half stands. She should call her name. But how ridiculous would that be? Calling out to some Englishwoman who reminds her of an old friend. Or rather, a template for what Fleur might look like now. She misses her. The closeness they had is a gap that will never close. Does she miss her more than Yugi?

Chinatsu flushes hot. She remembers the things Fleur told her, what her mother's boyfriend used to do in the night. She remembers wiping away her tears. And the times they'd touched each other. Her stomach contracts; shame.

*Let's pretend we're married.*

*I'm the wife,* Fleur said.

In later life, Chinatsu had read that girls do this. It was innocent and explorative. But the thrilling sensation that fired through Chinatsu's body as they'd touched was something she'd never experienced with Yugi. She'd had stronger orgasms with Tao but the connection she'd felt with Fleur had never been surpassed. Tao wasn't her friend. Did that mean she was a lesbian? Was her failed marriage her own dishonour? Sweat made her underarms sticky. Half of her never wanted to see Fleur again, to come face to face with what she'd done and felt.

Chinatsu can't see the woman who looks like Fleur any more. She frowns and writes: *a white girl-woman, chopstick thin, arrowing through these streets, hair a shield of bronze. How can I get this sense of purpose?*

Feeling stupid, Chinatsu tugs out the page and balls it up.

Later, when it gets too cold to sit outside, Chinatsu counts out the right change plus the correct tip and joins the crowds on the streets. She falls into the rhythm of the general mass of clicks and thuds of shoes and boots. She has no real direction in mind.

## 33

The corridors are painfully white. Yugi realises he's frowning and tries to relax. His shoes are clapping the floor in line with his heartbeat, reminding him he's nervous. Yugi Hamugoshi, nervous? Crazy. He tries to walk to a different rhythm. A line of colour down the centre makes negotiating the labyrinth easier. It's all Perspex and beeping and squeaking-shoed nurses. The old Yugi would not find this difficult. Since Chinatsu left, so many things are unravelling.

Eventually, he locates the ward. Masa, his back to Yugi in a private room, senses him. His old friend's shoulders stiffen.

There are people in this world who have a presence about them. These people talk, and others listen. Yugi is one of these people. When he walks, it's as if shadow drapes the path behind him, as if the air rings with over-focussed silence. Something from a movie.

Masa's black head turns and his shoulders drop. He says something to the nurse before coming out.

'Yugi. Man, I'm so glad to see you. I could really do with a friend here.'

'What happened?'

'She's not making much sense. Some psycho cut loose on her, that's about all I can gather. Called the ambulance from a hotel room.'

152

'And what was she doing in a hotel?'

Masa shakes his head, unaware of the connotations. 'Not gonna know that for a while, she's pretty drugged up. To be honest, I don't care. I still have my wife.'

Yugi thinks about that, as if the words are a challenge. I still have *my* wife, but you don't have yours. Except, Masa didn't know about Chinatsu leaving. Nobody did. Yugi's anger feels out of control. *Like Chinatsu.* The thought taunts him. He clenches one fist, forcefully calming himself.

'Was she raped?' he asked. Yugi watches the frown confuse Masa's face.

'Er . . . I dunno. They didn't say. They would've told me if they'd found any . . . signs, wouldn't they?'

'So what do you think she was doing in a hotel?'

'Yugi, what are you getting at? I seriously can't think straight right now.'

Yugi shakes his head, and touches a hand to his friend's back. Masa's skin is cold through his shirt, but he smells of the gym, even though he'd have had no time to work out. He'd have come straight from work and not been home. The tie is loosened; the skin under his jaw seems saggier than last week, his stubble's a day old. Could do with brushing his teeth too.

'You know me, I just want to get to the bottom of things. But you're right, your wife is here. That's all that matters. May I look in on her?'

'It's not a pretty sight.' Masa laughs.

Yugi frowns. How could Masa find anything funny in this situation? But the laugh had been more of a yelp, like a dog shot with a pellet gun.

Masa lowers his head. 'Sorry, sorry. I was just thinking, if she heard me I'd be a dead man.'

Yugi rubs a hand under his chin, shaking his head from side to side. Stubble tickles his palm, briefly blocking the sound of the various heart rate monitors nearby. 'And do you love your wife, Masa?'

Masa looks at Yugi. 'What?'

'Do you love her as a woman, or as a wife?'

Masa tugs his earlobe. 'I don't. . . You all right man?'

153

Yugi smiles so his teeth are showing. 'Forget me. It's been a rough week, not to detract from your situation. May I say hello?'

Yugi is already aware of the distance that has opened up between him and Masa. It is a gap that can temporarily be filled with the right words and competitive squash but for Masa, their relationship will never be quite the same. He won't know why it's different, but he'll think: Yugi unnerves me; Yugi's changed. The reality is, the gap has been there all along, but it had benefited Yugi to pretend it hadn't. Did he care? He was losing so many things, what was one friend?

Yugi steps into the private room. He thinks of the fireflies in the jewellery box again, wings fluttering. Masa's wife stirs. Her eyelids struggle to open, the lashes like lightly glued cobwebs. They open enough to glimpse him.

Yugi leans in close. 'I was doing you a favour, really. Masa is a friend. He wants a wife, not a whore. I think that was the deal? What if someone else had booked that meeting and not me? Do you want to end up like my wife?'

She frowns, perhaps still unsure of who he is. Then the realisation sets in. Her mouth parts. Her eyelids peel back like blanched tomato skin. Her scream comes out as a whistle. But she's screaming from deep inside her body. The veins in her neck pulse.

Her mouth is working. He moves closer, breath touching the rim of his ear. 'Please. Please don't hurt me.'

In the middle of all the scratches and bruises and welts and jagged shorn hair, she actually looks quite beautiful. As if she was so delicate she should have been protected. Was this Masa's fault? Had she turned to other men because of something Masa had missed? Was this also Chinatsu's reason? Or were women just looking for more money to spend on the things they lusted for? The desire to know Chinatsu's reasons flamed inside him.

Masa's wife rolls her head away, seeming too exhausted to even be afraid.

'Why did you go to other men?' he asks her. 'Is it really just the money?'

Her head rolls back towards Yugi. She sighs and tears slip down her cheeks. 'Don't hurt me.'

154

'If you tell me why, I won't.'

She swallows with difficulty. 'He just . . . he just doesn't see me.'

The door unlatches: Masa. 'What is it?' he says to his wife. 'Are you in more pain?' He looks at Yugi, 'She's due more drugs.'

Yugi observes his friend, usually so willing to smooth the clay of their relationship. He claps Masa on the back. 'My friend, I shall be out of town for a while.'

As he is walking away, Masa watching, Yugi's phone rings. He checks the screen, smiles. It is the China woman.

# 34

Fleur wakes up in her own bed. It's the terrace. The hospital is gone; she's all better now. She's ludicrously happy. The spring feel to the air is exhilarating; it's nearly summer. She rolls onto her side, the pillow soft and warm and safe. There's a noise. Marcus whistling. A *Stereophonics* song. They'd both had the album when they met. The song is playing faintly on the radio, too. She hears snatches of lyrics in between Marcus bumping about in the kitchen. There's the smell of toast and hot butter.

She hums along, starts singing.

Marcus walks into the bedroom, a plate of toast smeared in Marmite. She wrinkles her nose. His face flickers like a TV losing signal. He goes from being Marcus to Daniel, then Derek.

*This isn't real.*

The thought cuts into the dream, a sad breeze sneaking through cracks in a windowpane. This is just a dream. She's embedded within this unreal nest. She's the soil woven into place by twigs and matter. There's no way to break out. But she has to.

The dream closes over her awareness. Becomes true again.

She's on her back in the bed. It's winter cold. Marcus is fucking her. And she loves him, but then he is Derek. And the love spills over into what Derek is doing, polluting. In that moment, she loves Derek. And then Marcus is Derek is Daniel. And her body and her heart stretch out, and Daniel makes love to her, smiling and golden in a way the movies made her dream about. It's too beautiful for her to bear.

And then his face goes dark and dead.

She screams.

The scream rips through the clearing. The moth scribbles, the fly dances. Her hands are freezing, a face bubbles under the water. Fighting back. She keeps her grip, keeps her nerve. But he wrenches out of the water.

Daniel.

Her fingers curl, strength doubling. She thrusts him back under.

Fleur wrenches back to reality. To the bleep bleep aeroplane food sick warm poo wee and medicine smell of the hospital. Her wail opens up and out of her throat, tearing along the corridors in the middle of the night, maybe touching each patient. Chasing them towards death. She feels as if the hospital is holding her hostage. Her body is holding her hostage. It won't do what she tells it. Fleur quietens herself through sheer resolve. She can't help but think of the fact that her body has always been for other people, and never her own.

It is time to change that.

Fleur rolls onto one side, hand over a still slightly-swollen stomach. That hard but empty space.

# 35

'Hello?'

The man's voice is soft. If his voice was made of anything but air and vibration, Chinatsu imagines it would be furred, like the grey-white underside of a leaf. So soft she could tickle it.

Chinatsu steps to the hotel door. The emergency instructions on the back are written in English, French and German only. Air tickles her face as she pulls the door open. The corridor smells of cooking, butter sizzling in a wok.

'Amber.'

Tao has a mobile to his ear, but his face is the Eastern sun, the rare silk, paprika spice. His beautiful clothes look out of place next to the dough-coloured hallway. The oily, pockmarked walls.

'Hello, Tao,' she says in Chinese.

He raises his eyebrows, closing the phone. Such an easy and open smile.

'Who was that?' she asks.

'Just business,' he answers, quickly.

Chinatsu frowns, but Tao wraps his long arms around her. She stands, arms cupped to her chest, covered by him. The warmth of desire wells up inside her. That itch to strip off all her clothes and be as close as they can be. They help each other out of trousers and underwear. Tao pulls her blouse off from over her head, arms up like a child, her hair gently resting between her shoulder blades.

Bed. Lying down, she takes in the lines of his body. His hips, muscles, the exciting sight of his penis. Hard, because of her. She smiles, keeps his gaze as he fits himself between her legs, not closing her eyes as he enters her. He brushes hair from her eyes and they begin.

There is air coming in from the window, its thin curtains drawn back. Buses whoosh by, the bleep of pedestrian crossings and police sirens. All of the outside coming in to touch them.

'Are you cold?'

She shakes her head and grips Tao's shoulder, pulling him to her. His hands cup her buttocks, keeping her close. Making love. It feels so good she wants to curse, but she bites down on his shoulder instead. When Tao comes inside her, his body stopping, forehead sticky against hers, she imagines the moonflower weeping milk into the soil. In that far off land she still calls home.

He spots kisses over her forehead and cheekbones. They turn onto their sides, Tao fastening her tight to his chest. He traces figures of eights over her hip, but his body grows heavy over hers, arm a leaden weight over her chest. She hears the altered pattern of his breathing, stronger on the breath out.

She blinks for a long time after Tao is asleep. Tao did not notice the difference. To him, she's still Amber. Suddenly cold, she pulls a free section of duvet over her naked body.

What has she done coming here, with him?

# 36

Yugi Hamugoshi isn't straight any more. He needles a pressure point on his forehead with his first finger. 'Just deal with it, Mai. I shan't be returning until I've finished what I've set out to do here, so everything will have to wait.'

'When shall I reschedule your appointments for?'

'Defer them to Lu, and if they can't be dealt with that way, just postpone them.'

'And what reason shall I give for the delay?'

Yugi reels in a breath. 'How long have you been working for me, Mai?'

'A year and two months, Mr Hamugoshi.'

Yugi holds the phone away from his ear. Another breath. 'Tell me, Mai, was that the question I was really asking?'

Yugi hears Mai inhale. 'Sir? Oh. Yes sir, I'll deal with it, no need for you to be troubled.'

He claps the phone shut like a pair of maracas. The first class lounge is as big as a lawn, but as sparsely populated as a graveyard. A portly businessman plods towards the massage section. To Yugi, all Westerners remind him of prawns on a griddle, ready to implode. Pop. Their presence discomforts him. They must be so ill at ease in bodies that do not function as they ought.

As he waits, he recalls a time when Chinatsu was open and readable. Is it the roles they felt they must play that are responsible? They had fit into being husband and wife like tea into china. Every day Chinatsu ran the house, brought the tea, removed his coat. Her silence was new to start with. The girl he had first met told him his eyebrows were thin as an old man's, and what is it with that fashion? And then she'd flushed and called it a compliment. Really, she'd meant he was strong enough not to follow such rules. She bowed her head, cheeks pink. Her hair was getting long then, far past her shoulders. A fiancée has long hair, a wife does not.

Is Chinatsu still with this man Madam Li revealed is called Tao Chang? He never expected her to do this. Had he ever really known the woman who shared his bed? Was a person defined by who they are with or who they are without?

Tao Chang. Property Mogul. Prominent Chinese hotelier with headquarters in six countries worldwide. A man who owns hotels. How can such a man know how to give Chinatsu a home? Yugi grips his mobile. It's so thin it's like a razor to the innards of his palm. And why does he still want Chinatsu after this? Whore. Wife. Who is Chinatsu? Thanks to Madam Li's digging, he knows where to go to find her. He'll ask her these questions face to face. He'll punish her for her deviation. And the man. Calm filters through Yugi. He knows how to harm a businessman. The man will be in the red within weeks.

And yet, if he's honest, Yugi has no real idea how he will punish Chinatsu. How much would ever be enough?

Yugi knows he is the one who's empty. Madam Li says she suspects that Chinatsu is pregnant, that many women run when they are with another man's child. Mistaken loyalty. Chinatsu, pregnant with that Chinaman's child. But she's still his wife. If they divorced, now they had met the ten-year threshold, the prenuptial decreed that Chinatsu would receive fifteen percent of Yugi's future earnings, annually. As far as Yugi is concerned, whatever is inside his wife, belongs to him. And he would retrieve it, by whatever means necessary.

161

A woman's voice informs him it's time to head towards the departure gate.

He straightens; hamstrings tight. He needs a run, but his routine is off. Everything is since  Chinatsu left. She was the china, the pot that kept the liquid warm, that cradled its contents. What becomes of a pot without the tea?

# PART TWO

# 1

Fleur gasps. The heat of the shower is good and right. The scalding water burns her shoulders and scalp. She doesn't soap her stomach, but watches the water run freely over the flat surface. She doesn't want to touch that part of her, which is practically back to normal. Just like she's supposed to be. Fleur ducks her head under the water and squeezes her eyes shut, holding her breath. Images of Daniel sequence through her mind under the cover of skin.

Discharged.

Nan took the word to mean she could breathe a sigh of relief. Fleur was OK. No more mollycoddling.

Fleur signs the paper at the *Job Centre*. She looks at the white square where she'd scrawled her name. Her signature looks wrong. Untidy. She doesn't write like that. She feels at odds with herself, crawling with unease. Somebody else had signed that paper. But that's just because things still aren't back to normal. Not yet. Her body feels cumbersome, slow. Like a fat old arthritic. She wants to beat it into working properly. Move. Do what you're told.

It's been two weeks since she left the hospital and moved into Nan's place. And things just aren't right. Is it because she doesn't really have any of her own stuff? She hadn't wanted to go back to Marcus' house, be confronted by what he'd done, and what she'd put up with for so long.

To look at those stairs. And now what was she supposed to do? Thirty years old and living with her Nan. No career, no boyfriend, no prospects, three pairs of tatty knickers to her name, one with the elastic gone.

Marcus keeps calling her. She is oh-so tempted to answer the phone, just to be warmed by something familiar.

But, no.

Everything felt out of sync and out of place.

It wasn't supposed to be like this.

The woman at the *Job Centre* speaks slowly, meaning she has said this before and Fleur has missed it. 'What was your most recent post?'

Fleur narrows her eyes, focussing. 'Post'. She knows that word. She dredges up its meaning. Mail, letters, box. No. Job, career, post.

The *Job Centre* woman taps her pen. Pat-a-pat-a-pat-a-pat-a-pat. Fleur claws her attention away from it.

Her phone buzzes; Marcus again. Her stomach rolls over. 'Decline'. She'd have to get a new number, when she could afford it.

Interview!

'Ah, right. No. No post. I mean, I don't remember. Oh wait, yeah. I think. . . well I did have one. I think? Will it say on file?'

The woman is looking at Fleur differently. She should explain about the coma, but it feels like giving away too much. She wasn't full enough, steady enough, to just be giving stuff away. The woman purses her lips, fingers click over the keyboard. The monitor splashes alien light across her face.

*Primark* is stuffy. Full of cripples and the work-ravaged. She's one of them now, had been all along. No sense fighting it. She's at a circular table full of knickers. Full pants or thongs? Her stomach should be larger now, she should be buying a bigger size. Instead, she picks up a pair of plain white full knickers. Size 8. She shuffles to the counter, aware of how loose her jeans are. That little gap between her stomach and the brass button. You could fit your thumb down it.

'One fifty, love.'

'Ninety nine pee?'

'Eh?'

166

She struggles to pull out the label. Apart from 'Made in India', it says £1.50. She's only got a pound. The rest is for bus fare.

'Oh. Changed my mind.'

The cashier sighs, stashes the knickers on the back wall of things to be returned to the floor. 'Next.'

In the pub toilet, which is unsettlingly close to the door covering the kitchen, a pink poster screams 'Absolutely no drugs!' The cubicle smells of marijuana. There's a yellow poster on a brown-streaked wall. Shit? It's advertising Prawns and Maria Rosa sauce. Screams, in bold black letters: Knowhere does it better.

Fleur wipes, flushes and washes her hands. None of the soap dispensers work. The water is icy and jangles her nerves. She feels like cutlery in the wrong slot, the fork in the knife section, knives with spoons.

She sits at a small circular table. It's quiet and the chef leans over the bar, chatting up a forty-something barmaid. Fleur puts her mobile on the table in front of her, a blank face. She wipes the condensation from the panels of the *Coke* glass. Squeak. Other people eat quietly around her. Cutlery scratches, elbows like crickets, people mumbling in tucked-away corners, most of them old and alone. They reek of pointlessness. Her phone lights up: unidentified number. Her stomach tightens. Was it Marcus again? She wouldn't answer it. But what if it was about a job? She could afford the drink now that she hadn't bought the knickers. It would be nice to be able to have both. And her own place.

'Yes?'

'Fleur, it's John from *McDonalds* Two.'

'Hello.'

'Hello to you. You're supposed to be at work right now?'

'Am I?'

'Yes. Ten-Six.'

'Must've slipped my mind.'

There's grumbling; she's not worried. John is going on using words she can't quite follow but there's friction in his voice. He rolls to a stop.

'So we'll see you tomorrow at eleven, yes? Think you can manage that? We're all sympathetic to your condition but –'

'Yep.'

She presses the red button, puts the phone down. Her fingers squeak the glass. Condition. They say that when you're pregnant. Except she wasn't. There had been a baby, but now there wasn't. Just like there'd been a coma, and now there isn't. She sips the Coke, the alcohol in it tickles her throat. Wait? If she had a job, why'd she just been to the *Job Centre*? Had she forgotten about that? When would her brain be back to normal? She shook her head. Fuck it, who cared? The old Fleur did.

A bell jingles as someone walks in. He's thickset, ex-rugby probably. They mostly all were round here. He's the same shape as Derek. Did she put that thought there? To hurt herself? Unusually, the thought does not bother her. There are some pluses to feeling out of sync. Fleur gets up and goes to the table the man has just sat down at.

'Hey,' she says.

He looks her up and down. Finally, a nod, 'Alreet.'

The man's flat is just out of town, towards the hospital. Not the hospital she'd woke up in, but even so, it's not a comfortable location. It flickers in the corner of her mind, moon-bright. Hospital, hospital, hospital. She waits for him to kiss her. He doesn't ask if she wants coffee or tea, but just takes off his jacket. He looks her up and down as she's sitting on his cheap Ikea couch. There's stains on the cream fabric. She rests her hands in her lap. He comes to sit next to her. The couch creaks when he leans over for a kiss. Cold tongue. Tobacco taste. His hands grip hers in something approaching romance, except his thumb is a strong band over her knuckles.

He pulls back. Helps her take off her jeans and her last clean pair of knickers. Is this quick? This *is* quick. She shrugs.

The man doesn't bother with her socks. She watches him unbuckle. Blank in the eyes. It's four o'clock and the daylight is wintry, dishwater-weak. His legs are smooth, fine haired and muscled. She sees a glimpse of his stomach, pale as bacon fat. Solid, but with a rump of fat at the hips. His dick is semi-hard and curves to the left. He opens her legs with a firm push to her knee.

168

All she can hear is the couch creaking as he pulls up her hips to meet his thrusts. His concentration is fascinating. As if he's building something in a workshop. Frowning at the vice not being quite straight. It hurt when he entered her. For some reason that seems right, as if she should. Flashes of Derek appear in place of this man's body, like subliminal advertising. He cuffs her neck. She covers his hand: squeeze harder. Hurt me. The blood rushes to her head. The tip of her nose tingles. She slaps his face, hard. His eyes shoot open, pupils expanding. She slaps him again. His strike back is a reaction. Fire flames her face. He's losing rhythm. She grips the wrist at her throat tighter and he gets a determined look. Pushes her head to one side. An orgasm crests and spills as her face is inflamed by fire. He lies inside her until shrunk, sperm cooling against her thigh and spiking the late afternoon air. She feels him looking at her, turned away and crying, catching her breath. He gets up and goes to the bathroom.

Later, she looks in the mirror at Nan's. There's a line of burst blood vessels on her cheek. Peering closer, she sees the forks of broken veins under her skin. Daniel is behind her. She spins. Nothing. Fleur bows her head and covers her face.

'Leave me alone.' Her breath tickles her fingers. 'Leave me alone!'

Unable to breathe she darts out, takes a bus and is knocking on the man's door at a few minutes to midnight. He frowns, face limp with sleep, then opens the door. She dumps her jeans, crawls onto all fours.

'Fuck me.'

He does, her forehead tapping the headboard.

'*Fuck* me.'

He uses her hair as reins.

'Fuck me fuck me fuck me.'

This time, she's crying before he's finished.

# 2

'Ready?' Tao asks. His limousine looks as out of place in this back street as his suit did against the hotel walls. He stands beside the open door, waiting.

She takes a last look up at the hotel building.

The person she was sometimes, Amber, is broken-hearted. She doesn't need to be her any more, but there is a sense of sadness, of leaving someone behind. There are shadows on Chinatsu's heart, like clouds on the moon. Or liver spots staining ageing skin.

It won't be long until Yugi finds her here. He's coming for her, she can feel it. His precise footsteps vibrate through the earth with all the power of those lizards thudding through old movies. Why doesn't that terrify her? Does it make her feel important? Is that what she wished he would have done all along? Chase her and prove how important she was? Except Yugi's motivations for following across the oceans could well be to punish, not reclaim.

She pulls the strap of her purse over her head. Her suitcase has already been forwarded to the new apartments Tao has picked. A couple of pigeons pick about at crumbs near his feet, grey heads reflected in the leather of his shoes. His fingers slip over the back of her hand, his thumb tickling the underside of her wrist. *Is* she ready?

Chinatsu gets into the car like a lady, sitting first and drawing her feet in afterwards. The movement is not quite fluid, but graceful nonetheless. This will get harder to do, as the months progress.

# 3

Smoke scribbles up to the Artex ceiling, veiling the room. Nan never crosses her legs. She has both set firmly on the ground, feet apart. Fleur watches her. Nan hasn't noticed her come in. The older woman rests the wrist of her smoking hand on her knee, flicking the butt with her thumb every second or two. Smoke makes the photograph in her hand look hazy, wreathing over the gold frame as if trying to charm it. As Fleur gets closer, she sees the woman in the frame is smiling. She's wearing a cerise silk maxi dress and has over-plucked eyebrows.

'Who's that?'

Nan jumps and her cigarette falls onto her lap. She swears and scrabbles for it, resting it in the nook of her glass ashtray.

'It's rude to creep up on people. You don't recognise your own mother?'

'No need to bite my head off.'

'Well, maybe she did look different. Before that Derek one. What kind of person hates cats? He's got a daughter now, you know? Not his own, mind.'

Derek. The name is like a gunshot. Fleur forces her heart to slow. One. Two. Three. She catches her breath. Yes, she knew that. Nan had told her in the hospital.

Nan taps the ash off her cigarette. 'Never trust a man who wears denim bottom and top.'

Fleur nods. Four. Five. Six. Seven. Eight. She's OK. One night she counted to one thousand. She counted in the boiler cupboard at mum's, or in the bed with the blankets up to her nose at Nan's, as she tried to memorise the cracks in the ceiling. Anything so she didn't have to think about Derek.

'Cup of tea, love?'

'If you're having one.'

Nan heaves herself off the chair. She carries her weight around her middle, like a rubber ring full of sand.

Fleur follows her into the kitchen, Nan's slippers stick-sticking as she walks. The kitchen hasn't changed at all. Still the same brown melamine cabinets, the patched lino Nan once drew hopscotch on in yellow chalk when it was raining and mum wasn't well. The white plastic clock above the grill on the gas cooker, gone brown with the heat.

Nan runs water into the tinny-sounding kettle. Fleur clicks on the back ring using the lighter; the handle is greasy. Nan hands her the kettle before opening the fridge. Fleur puts the kettle on to boil.

The fridge light is the colour of Vitalite. Bathing under the light is a tub of Stork, two green boxes of eggs, piles of unspecified meat wrapped in Co-op carrier bags and an authentic glass bottle of milk with a blue and silver top.

Ask her, ask her. Fleur opens her mouth. She wants to know more about Derek. What happened to him, where he is now. She's a grown-up. Nan can talk about it now, surely? There are a dozen tins of Smart Price cat food in the fridge.

'Who's the cat food for?'

'Cat.'

'You've got one?'

'Nap.' Nan plucks the milk out and puts it down on the counter-top. 'Have a whiff of that, will you? It's just to be on the safe side, in case any turn up. Innit?' Nan grabs out an open tin of cat food. 'Look how juicy that is. You could eat that yourself, I'll bet.'

Fleur pulls back. 'Pass. Ta.'

173

'Give it here.' Nan snatches the milk bottle and Fleur notices scratches on her hands. Nan's fingers curl too far inwards, as if calcifying.

Fleur nods at the scratches. 'What d'you do?'

'Been pulling nettles.'

'With gloves, I hope?'

Nan shrugs.

Mum had had scratches. Red, not white. Little knife marks decorated the most sensitive parts of her: the inner arms, thighs, between her toes. Fleur had painted her mother's nails once. Decorated them in *Barbie*-pink. That's when she'd seen them. Mum had smacked the back of her hand and shouted at her for staring. She'd darted out the room and back to bed, hauling the sunflower-yellow duvet over her head. Her mother did not follow; she'd had a date. When they met in the bathroom the next morning to brush their teeth, they didn't talk at all.

'Here, your tea.'

'Ah, yeah. Ta. Not with it today.'

Fleur gulps tea. It burns down her throat. A dream she doesn't remember having swims into mind. Drowning. Always drowning. A little girl's eyes in the water. Fleur's own chest burning from the pressure of holding her breath.

Where were these images coming from?

Nan stirs her own tea, spoon ringing in the mug, before dropping it in the sink. They go back to the sitting room.

'Want the telly on? *Columbo's* about to start.'

'I'm off out in a sec, when I've finished this.'

'Work?'

Fleur bites her lip, twirls an earring around in its hole. 'Yeah.' She nods. 'Yeah, I'll be back late. See you tonight.'

Nan switches on the set, twists the volume low and sits down. The cigarette has burned out in the glass ashtray. She lights up another. Nan turns to watch the opening credits of *Columbo*. She's positioned a black and white TV set at the head of the smoked glass table; the top of it is grey with dust. The table has a poinsettia tablecloth draped over it. Fleur winces. Guilt. Who has Nan been spending her Christmases with while she was with Marcus? She gets up.

'Better be off now, Nan. See you later.' A shiny ornament on the window ledge behind Nan catches her eye. It's squat and bulbous. 'You serious about this Buddha stuff then?'

Nan looks to where she's pointing. 'Should look into it.'

'You're a Christian.'

'But it's all the rage. Madonna's into it, in't she?'

'I think that's Kabbala.'

'She doesn't half look good though.'

'Mm. See you later.'

'Take a brolly from the laundry room. It's going to rain.'

Fleur's phone vibrates; a message. She opens it: *I miss you so much. I wish we could go back. M.x*

# 4

Yugi snaps his phone shut, clipping off his secretary's irritating voice. Apparently, the favours he's calling in to ruin the Chinaman's business are not all working. The man is well liked. There are other people he can try, those not guided by such resolute morality.

He focuses on the café over the road and assures himself that what he is doing is completely normal and acceptable. He's just a concerned husband keeping an eye on his possibly pregnant wife. His fingers curl into his fist so tightly the knuckles shake. Even he knows that's not true. He knows he should be able to say, Darling, let's talk about this, it's not too late. He'd bet this Chinaman, the bastard usurper who's fucking his wife, would be able to say that. Because what, he has Western sensitivities? Rage swells inside him. He adjusts his shoulders and tries to lean back in his chair. Relax. But he doesn't even want to talk to Chinatsu, he wants to. . . what does he want? He doesn't know. This feeling is alien. His knee jogs below the table.

He wants to make her pay for doing this to him.

She needs to feel the pain he has known.

But he can't take his eyes off Chinatsu. This woman, his wife. Whore of the modern world. She wears tall heels like the Westerners; they are not demure like those of modest Japanese working women. They are too long for her body and spoil the grace of it. Women like Chinatsu should not wear shoes like that.

'Sir –'

'No.'

'Yes, sir.'

The waitress scurries away. Yugi rotates the knife on his table, flipping it onto its side. And again, like some dead, metal fish. He thinks about his arrival in London. He'd received a clipped phone call from Madam Li providing him with Tao's location. He headed straight for the hotel where they were living. Living, not staying. He had been faintly aware of this man in business before now. A caricature of a man, paying for sex. And yet, Yugi has done the same. The difference between himself and this Chinaman is that he knows how to find a good wife. And yet, perhaps they are equals in this too? The Chinaman had obviously seen something in Chinatsu, just as he had. But what? Was it the same thing Yugi had wanted from her? Disappointingly, it probably was not. Yugi nudges a person obstructing his view. Out of the way. The person's response is very high-pitched; Yugi tunes it out.

The Chinaman must think affection is love. He will have convinced Chinatsu of this too. But it is not. Love is honour, and duty. Love is burying the person you have this emotion for, no matter how much you hate them. This is why he returned home to the farm when his father died.

Memories of the bare funeral and his half sisters' bleak, hollowed-out faces with their witchy eyes watching his every move fill his mind. He shoves it away.

Yugi has not done what he intended to do in London. He planned to come here and retrieve what belonged to him, put this man in his place, and return home. He would then attend the primary Okshawa takeover talks in person. Now he would have to do them via video conferencing. This would probably mean losing the account. Would Chinatsu enjoy knowing that she is, potentially, worth billions?

But here is his wife in high heels, walking the streets without any shame, in broad daylight, despite the fact she's just come from another man's bed. *Adulteress.*

And yet, there is a sadness about her as she sits in the café opposite. The words RAINBOW CAFÉ partly obscure her face.

Yugi is not at all certain what Chinatsu is thinking. He bites down on surging anger, controls himself until the feeling plateaus and stretches out. He takes a sip of water as Chinatsu pushes her food about with a fork. Even the bottled water tastes wrong here. As though laced with chlorine. He signals the girl and asks her to boil this water and add some hot lemon. She looks confused, but nods and takes the water back.

A van rumbles past, spewing up papers from the gutter. When he looks again, Chinatsu is gone. He fights a moment of panic. But this is not an issue; he knows where she's living.

The girl returns with a squat bowl of water. Slices of lemon float in it. He waves a hand. 'Take it away.'

'Sir? Well, might I get you something else?'

Yugi settles back in his chair, wood creaking. He crosses his hands on his lap, regards this girl with renewed interest.

A red bus swishes past the window, sheaves of water surfing up. Has it been raining already? He glances skywards. If it has, it's definitely about to again. The air feels oppressive and expectant.

The waitress raises her eyebrows, polite smile stuck in place as she waits for Yugi's reply. She glances around, changing her weight. Her smile widens. For a Westerner, she's more petite than most, which is more likely to do with a stringent diet than her natural form. His thumb rubs the inside of his palms, would she look like a Matisse, or a Giacometti underneath those hideously baggy clothes?

# 5

Chinatsu draws her fingers through her hair; it's definitely growing longer. It's now past her jaw line and tickles her neck like a new lover who's still enchanted with the scent of her skin, the things their bodies can do together.

She looks in the mirror much more now. Her skin seems warmer and brighter. She's decreased the amount of powder she wears. Many English women seem to forego make-up altogether. She's not sure she wants to go that far.

Tao is rarely in the hotel. He tells her, with a smile, that this is their home for now. Maybe you'd like to live in the country? She tries to call it a home in front of Tao; he owns the building after all. In her head, it's a hotel. Not permanent. Like him?

She doesn't know him yet. The thought makes her panicky. She believed she did, or that Amber had known all she needed to know. How stupid her invented character seems in this country, as if the light is too harsh to take the fantasy. Tao does not seem to mind. In all honesty, he seems to have no awareness of the distance between them. Distance had been between her and Yugi too. Yugi definitely did not mind. Perhaps all men are like this, solid and removed with the women chasing, always wanting to close the gap. The men, getting further and further away.

Mistake.

The word jolts her.

Has she just swapped one man for another? Her gut feels heavy. The word resounds in her mind as she goes about her business, putting on smiles for a new man. She can make this work. She will regain the intimacy she had with Tao in their stolen moments in Tokyo. She must. If this doesn't work, what was it all for? Although, perhaps all Tao really wanted was a companion. Or a woman who would perform both wifely and domestic duties? He obviously did not believe in maids.

Chinatsu has risen early this morning to attend to things for Tao. She dresses while he is still asleep, choosing black silk palazzo trousers and a plain white top. She pushes her feet into turquoise slippers, washes her face and does not reach for the make-up. Tao prefers a more natural look, particularly during the day. She does not need make-up, he says. All men have quirks; she must get used to his.

She bought the slippers from Harrods, but with Tao's money. With Yugi, she had an allowance and a card. Tao leaves money. She knows what that means. But it's not the same now, as when he used to give it her. Is it?

She investigates the kitchen, having become better acquainted with the placement of cutlery and glasses and pans in their various drawers and cupboards. More often, she finds the items she expects when pulling open a door. She prepares eggs, carefully whisked, with the perfect amount of milk and pepper. The mixture sizzles when she tips it into hot fat. She stirs it with a wooden spoon, and brews the coffee Tao prefers. This is something she still needs to experiment with as it doesn't seem to be his perfect blend. It can't be quite right, because his body doesn't relax after the first sip, the way Yugi's did after tea.

Outside the sky is thick with total cloud. If she looks down she can see the private garden. It belongs solely to the penthouse. It has a bench and strips of grass in a square. She could plant things. A different sort of plant than the sad beauty of her moonflower. Maybe she could make rainbows of colour. Was it allowed?

She takes Tao the eggs. At first, he looks surprised and pleased. And then a frown creeps onto his balanced face.

He touches her shoulder.

'Chinatsu, you do know this is not your job?'

She lowers her head as he eats.

'Are you sad here?' He gulps back coffee.

She has questions, but is unused to expressing herself.

'I love you. You know that?'

Tao says this, each morning before work. A car does not come for him when he is going to work, only when travelling. Most days he uses public transport. Seeing him check to make sure he has a thing called an Oyster card makes her feel proud.

She nods.

He lingers, sets the coffee down on the bedside table and smoothes his lilac silk tie. The colour makes his already bright complexion fresher. His skin is so elastic, so supple it is hard to imagine he'll ever look older than mid thirties.

'Chinatsu, you can say what you feel. I'm not some overbearing husband, am I?'

Is this part of the problem? The husband part, at least.

'Are you bored? Is that it?'

She shakes her head.

'Then are you afraid? He won't find you here, I promise.'

Oh, he will, but this does not make her afraid. Because this is inevitable. 'No.'

'But you're so different, so distant. It's worrying me. Would you like me to do anything?'

Has he finally noticed the gaps? That she is distant because he doesn't have sex with Amber any more, but makes love to Chinatsu. This woman he thinks he knows. Which of the two women is she really? Does she even know herself? 'No. Nothing.'

He checks his watch and sighs. 'I must go.'

'Yes. Have a good day.'

'And you. There is money in the kitchen, should you need it.'

As he runs down the stairs, grabbing his own briefcase, getting his own coat, she sinks onto the bed. What is she supposed to have a good day with? His money? It's not her job to take care of him, he's pointed this out, but she has no other purpose but to spend his money and grow their child. She has done the test now and what she had believed was right. She is pregnant. Most of her is certain the child is Tao's. A small

181

part of her will not stop asking the obvious question. But what about that time with Yugi?

Chinatsu looks around the beautiful penthouse and sighs. The more alone she is the more she wonders what else she could do with her time. The less laws there are, the more she thinks about Tokyo, her routine, and Yugi.

In Tao's world, there are limitless opportunities, and nothing to do.

The smart hotel they are installed in overlooks the largest expanse of green she has ever seen. She has the urge to spray and wipe every leaf and blade of grass in the park. That would keep her busy for a while. But then what? Perhaps she could get a job, or would that be too hard?

In Tao's keeping, she is free to leave their floor as she pleases, as well as the hotel. He never questions her about what she has done, except out of polite curiosity. When he has to leave town on business, he does not even hire a maid. He trusts her. Even though she may well be pregnant with Yugi's child. She must tell Tao. Soon.

The days blend into one.

One evening, just before he is about to fall asleep, she tells Tao the news of the child. He wraps her up in so much love and kisses she has the urge to free herself. Wash him off and sit alone with her child and her thoughts. But she cannot. It is a beautiful thing. His happiness for them is lovely. If he has any questions about the paternity, he does not voice them. Perhaps he does not care. They stay up late, talking about the future, knitting plans. Tao is always in some sort of contact with her. An arm around the waist, a kiss to her nose, the stroke of her belly.

Another morning. Tao has made sure she will not cook. He sits at the table room service has prepared. She had blushed as the staff positioned the breakfast things. They'd had maids at home but it now seemed strange to be waited on. She surveys the strawberries and fruit, pancakes and croissants. Tao takes coffee and sweetens it for himself. She plucks grapes, bursting the skin with her bottom teeth. Their sweet cool taste fills her mouth.

'How are you and the baby?' Tao asks, looking up from his newspaper.

It is in Chinese so she can't read it. The pages are thin as rice paper. She looks at the pictures; they seem to be of wars and money. 'We are well, thank you.'

'Well?'

'Yes.'

He raises his eyebrows. 'Nothing else to say?'

'I answered the question.'

Tao puts his paper down and reaches for her hand across the linen. 'Amber – Chinatsu.'

She stiffens. 'Yes?'

He sighs. 'You have no morning sickness?'

'I have morning sickness at 1pm. Twenty minutes. Then I am fine. There is really nothing to worry about.'

'You are so precise.'

She looks up. 'You would like more coffee?'

He shakes his head.

'Can I prepare anything for your trip this afternoon?'

Another shake.

She sighs loudly.

'Amber, just relax.'

She places her palms flat on the table. The cutlery clinks. 'That is not my name. My name is Chinatsu.' Her breath is shaky. 'Amber was the name I used for my men.'

Tao raises his eyebrows. His lips press together. 'I apologise, it slipped my mind. I have had a busy week. And it's a beautiful name. Does it have any meaning?'

It means a thousand summers. Yugi would know this. 'No.'

Tao stands and presses his fingers to her cheek. 'You look so beautiful this morning.'

There is such warmth in his expression, an openness Yugi never possessed. Yet she feels completely disconnected from him. Who is he? Why does he want her? It makes no sense. How many times had she yearned for such affection from her husband? Yet here it is, freely given, and she shrugs it away. Was Yugi's attention so much more precious because of its rarity, or because she truly loved him?

*Mistake.*

Chinatsu swallows. Her life made her think of learning to bake with her mother. Like when you fold too much egg into the cake mixture and you are either too gentle or not gentle enough; it curdles. Just falls in on itself.

Did she really want Tao, or did she just want a child? Should she leave him, too? And what? Find Fleur and be with a woman? Ridiculous. Her stomach flips over. It wasn't just the embarrassment of the things they had done together, how they had explored each other. It was something else, something she had tried so hard not to think about. One day Fleur had been absent from school, when she came back there were bandages on her wrists. Had that been Chinatsu's fault? She grips her stomach, wincing at the memory.

On the day Tao flies to Hiroshima on another business trip, Chinatsu locks herself in the bathroom and takes extra care with her appearance. She thinks of the first time she prepared her face in Yugi's bathroom for her first encounter with Tao. Her fingers shake as she tries to line her eyes.

Will getting a job be as simple as taking a blouse to the till and saying, 'This please?'

Apparently not.

A few hours later, a woman behind the black desk in the echoing lobby takes her time looking over Chinatsu's outfit.

'I would like job. . . *a* job, please.'

Ice-blue eyes travel up and down Chinatsu's body, stopping at her mid-section. The pregnancy could not be so noticeable just yet? Perhaps, somehow, they just know. Some of the women who don't give her jobs are nice, some not.

At the end of the day, her feet are sore and swollen, but it's faintly pleasurable. Working women must feel like this at the end of the day. She's sat in a Café Nero, one that's tucked away from the main bustle of shops, occupied only by a handful of businessmen and women. Perhaps her job is simply to have this baby. Is she wrong to want anything more? To have a reason to paint her lips and wear stockings each day?

A woman with a face full of freckles flashes by, a blur of copper hair seeming so bright it could almost splash Chinatsu's eyes like sun spots. Fleur?

A high-chaired child claps its hands, a giggle like strings of popped bubbles. Its mashed-up food clatters to the floor, distracting Chinatsu.

She looks back at the window; the woman is gone. Was she seeing things?

The day is perceptibly darker.

Chinatsu takes out her purse. In the back, buried deep and folded into four is the newspaper cutting, the one about the prostitute. As though undoing tricky origami, she unfolds it and smoothes out its creases. They spring back. Why had Yugi had this? Was this small square of words the reason for everything? Was this clipping why Chinatsu had finally left her husband? The feeling of not knowing him, of never being able to know him.

The air hissed with rain.

As the streets grew slick Chinatsu realised: She needed to know. Was her husband capable of such a thing? Of *murder*?

# 6

On the third time with him, he gets a name. Andrew.

They are panting. They have orgasmed. Affection is creeping into his eyes when he looks at her. She's not just a thing to fuck any more. He likes her because she's kinky. She'll do all the things they do in porn films. Like and lust turn to love. It's that easy for men.

She lies there, thinking of the ghost life she should have had. The one where her baby is growing, where she would be lying in bed with Marcus. And yet another life, Daniel holding her as she is pregnant with their first child.

Fleur sits up. Naked, she walks to the bathroom. She's patting mouldy-smelling water onto her cheeks while thinking she should probably move on. She does not want to fall into a relationship. What would be the point of that? The thought of Daniel is thick and physical, like a presence. She pushes him away.

*You have to help her.*

The voice is without echo, without a breath on her earlobe. But she spins around, hot. There is no one there.

'Hey, babe. You coming out any time this year? I'm good to go again.'

Fleur looks at her arms, turning over her wrists. The stark white scars on her wrists. Had she meant to kill herself then? She isn't sure. She'd

186

just wanted the pain to stop, or for a different kind of pain to distract her. She is definitely too thin now. She looks down at her breasts; they seem sucked and saggy. Her arms are covered in sunset-vibrant blotches. Scratches on her hips, bloodied crescents where his nails had dug in. She closes her eyes.

*Help her.*

'Shut up.'

'Well fuck you, too.'

She pulls her clothes on and watches Andrew as he speaks. It doesn't seem to be anything important. She stares at the glass of water beside the bed. Water, over her face, up her nose. Not breathing. Not being *able* to breathe. She wants to feel the release of the glass shattering, of freeing it. Her muscles itch for it. She picks up the glass, hurls it at the wall. Water slops. Glass bursts over the wall like an egg.

Andrew pins himself to the headboard. 'What the fuck?'

She shrugs. 'Sorry. I dunno. It's been a difficult month.'

'Are you fucking crazy? Get out you fucking crazy bitch.'

'Crazy?' She laughs. 'You mean, because I fucked you.'

He bolts towards her, bottom jaw mean-set. She knows that look, and what comes after. She doesn't flinch or cringe. But it's like a bulldog catching up with a squirrel. It doesn't know what to do when it's got it cornered.

'Huh.' She clicks the door behind her.

On her way out, she checks her phone. Eleven missed calls, five messages. She reads the last one: *Fucking bitch. U need to know wot u put me thru.*


'You look nice.'

'Don't bother.'

It's a Goth pub, far away from the throb of student night at Baa Bar. There's someone with a Mohawk that tickles the doorway arch, wearing boots that reach his or her knees. Fleur notices the swelling of breasts below the cut-off lumberjack shirt. She raises her eyebrows. Most of the women, or those who closely resemble women, have pale faces and Edwardian red lips. The kind found in paintings.

Madonna's *Like a Virgin* squeaks out of the juke box.

187

All the rest of them look like motorcyclists and they all seem to know each other.

'What's the matter, bad day?'

Fleur takes her hand from her cheek. 'Men like you?' She tilts the whisky back into her throat. Swallows.

'Do you mind if I sit here?'

She looks at him properly. He's like an extra from an 80s bike movie. He's wearing a shiny waistcoat over a white long-sleeved t-shirt. His hair, what he has of it, is plaited into an ash-coloured plait down his back. A thick gold earring drags his left lobe down a quarter of an inch further than the other one.

'So, what's your ship called?'

'Ship?'

'You must be a pirate dressed like that.'

'You don't like me.'

'A psychic pirate. Shiver me timbers.'

'I wouldn't mind.' He raises one eyebrow. 'No? Too soon?'

'Too disgusting.'

'I can buy you a drink though.' He picks up her empty glass. She can see the imprints of her lips ghosting the rim. He inserts his nose. The pores are huge. 'Jack Daniels and lemonade, right?'

She shrugs. 'If you want.'

He comes back, boots heavy over the wooden floor, which is laid out in planks. Gary Numan's *Cars* replaces Madonna.

He puts the drinks down in the ring-marks already on the bar. She pulls her glass towards her.

'Ta.'

They sip at the same time, and replace. Now he's sat, legs apart, jeans smelling of diesel and stale sweat. His gut pokes out his waistcoat.

'I bet your boyfriend doesn't know you're out here. I bet he wouldn't like you talking to me.'

'Look. Sorry, but this is really not going to happen. Let's just say I probably need a bit of a break.'

'You saying I'm ugly?'

'As a moose.'

'I watched this movie on bestiality last night. Got a stack of em.'

188

Fleur pulls a face, drained her glass. 'Thanks for the drink.'
'Something I said?'

She hurries out of the pub into the quiet side street. The door clatters behind her. Her breasts are sore and heavy. She folds her arms under them. Could she be due on? When would her periods get back to normal after the pregnancy? Her breath jets upwards like smoke. The cold pinches her nose.

Is someone watching her? She looks up. Around. A shadow flits, darker than black. Still and soft.

A car whooshes past the head of the street, tyres dipping into the dregs left from an earlier shower. The headlights briefly light up the road, before it continues down the main road. The shadow's eyes flash green.

Fuck's sake. 'Here, puss puss. Pss pss pss.'

The cat does not blink.

She's jolted by a memory. That day in the sunshine, the kitten on the bin, the stairs. And then waking up. Without a baby.

The pub door opens, digging her spine. 'Oi!'

'I knew you'd be waiting.'

'Oh bloody hell. Get lost, yeah?'

He's wearing a jacket now, the shiny type bouncers use. It smells of metal and cigarettes. His furry hands dip into an inside pocket. Metal glints.

'I like you. You're interesting.'

'You're after a shag, that's what.'

A bus hums past the main road. Fleur looks for the cat but it's gone.

'I do think you're beautiful. I'll treat you really nice.'

'Huh. Not my thing.' Who was saying this? The words were coming out of her mouth, but this wasn't her. It wasn't how she wanted to come off. Really, she wanted to tell this guy to buzz off in a polite but definite manner.

He smiles. Teeth bright in the dark.

'I'll hold you all night.'

She pulls a face, starting to get unnerved.

'Come on, why don't we get out of the cold?'

'I like the cold.'

'Have you ever fucked in a meat freezer? My kid brother's a butcher. I've the keys to his shop.'

'That's fucking crazy.' But a flare of erotic pleasure warms her groin. And it's good, to *feel* something again. She's not like that though, wouldn't do that.

'Joke.'

'Right.' When is he going to go? She looks around. Is there someone here to help her if he won't get lost?

He covers her body with his, pinning her against the doorway.

'And you're the most beautiful thing I've ever seen.'

Thing.

She grabs his arms, ready to push him. His breath is bitter and warm. He presses a thumb through her lips, pressing on her bottom teeth and forcing down her jaw. It tastes of salt and soap.

She wrenches away. 'Get off.'

'I know you want me. I know it.' He grabs her wrist.

She shoves him and runs up the street, hails and piles into a taxi.

The latest message from Marcus: *Why aren't u answerin my calls?*

Getting to Nan's is a relief. She showers. Turns the dial right up and lets the water scald her. Breath puffs in the cold air as she gets out of the shower. Coming out of the bathroom, tiptoeing over the creak in the third floorboard, a figure emerges to her left.

'Shit! I did try to be quiet.'

'Been awake all night. Do with talking to you tomorrow.'

'I've got things to do.'

'If you want to stay here, you'll make time. Is that clear?'

Fleur clutched her towel; it was starting to gape.

'Right?'

She gritted her teeth. 'Right.'

Going into her bedroom, Fleur flops angrily onto the bed. She grabs up her phone. Drafts a reply to Marcus. *Because you're a twat.* She saves it without sending.

# 7

Yugi hasn't shaven today. It's rare to see a beard or even stubble in Japan. Here, men care less about their appearance, or at least seem to cultivate an appearance that suggests such an attitude. They sprout hair all over the place. Furry arms, long hair, beards. It is unclean. Even their coats look like dead animals. The meat excised, skin thrown haplessly about their shoulders. And the women. They are equally unkempt. The waitress at the restaurant had clearly never met a wax strip in her life. It was positively barbaric.

Yugi peers at the mirror and wipes a smudge from it. The maid has not cleaned it as thoroughly as wife could. His finger squeaks.

The waitress is on the bed behind him, naked and prone. He jumps, turns around. Nothing. She is not really there.

It was the first time he hadn't been able to perform, with someone other than Chinatsu that is. Was it because she wasn't strictly a whore, someone in his employ? Because of her thick thighs? What? She'd undressed, rolled back onto cheap sheets. He'd unzipped himself, hard until he met her vagina. Her fingers gripped his cock, shockingly cold, her thumbnail a snagging pain on his skin. She directed him to the right place. He'd pushed again, but softened. She'd held him at the base, just tight enough, working her hand up and down. But it was useless. She'd unstuck her palm from his penis.

'That's all right,' she'd said. 'We can just cuddle?'

He'd zipped up, face pinched, and gone to find his wallet. Thrown down a sheaf of English bills. Just barely seen her brows knit and her mouth open.

Now, Yugi places the old-fashioned blade to his cheek, one side of his face soaped up. Stops. He lowers his arm, blinks, and unbuckles again. He pushes his trousers and underpants to the floor and lowers the shaving blade. As if bidden, he pulls a sprig of pubic hair between his forefinger and thumb. Each taut hair seems to pull a bubble out of his skin, so the hairs look like balloon tails, all gathered together. The bubbles could be poison, an infection. A rash from one of the women. He feels his skin for bumps; it's smooth.

So Yugi pulls his hair tight and cuts.

The first cut makes him wince. The hair is rough and resistant. He continues to pull and slice, getting closer to the skin beneath it all. There is soon a nest of soft hair covering his feet, tickling his toes.

His groin feels itchy. The cut hair prickles against him. The skin beneath the jagged hair looks newly slapped. He's getting an erection, foreskin tightening, penis lifting. The slit down the centre looks like it's been sliced with blunt scissors. His mind conjures up an image of his wife and her new lover, her being fucked from behind.

And then the memory of that prostitute, the one he'd scoured the English papers for any titbit of news. He had wrapped his fingers round her throat, pressing hard, harder as they'd had sex. Though never particularly open with Chinatsu, keeping this from her had put such a distance between them. It had been like the world changing shape, the oceans parting on separate tectonic plates.

Yugi doesn't feel in control. He must gain this back in any way he can. It's time to let Chinatsu know that he's here.

# 8

Chinatsu's hands shake. The piece of paper that came in a plain hand-delivered envelope this morning, slipped between Tao's Chinese newspaper and a variety of bills that she puts in his study, was written in her own hand. It contained one word: Tao. She would have only written that back home, in Japan.

Yugi. She puts the paper into the bin, then pulls it back. The lid thuds closed. Her heart is racing. She's too hot. Should she call Tao, tell him to come home? No, that's ridiculous, but. . . He's here. Yugi is here.

She puts a hand over her stomach and one to her back. It's the sort of ache that makes her want to curl up in bed. Guilt washes over her. She imagines it trickling down over her organs like slow-running fountains. Is this her penance? That she'll never be allowed to live in peace? Chinatsu breathes out and out and in. She scratches her stomach. The skin is different in one place, where her nail dips in a little deeper. Her child has already etched a single stretch-mark into her body. Or is it Amber, dying, nearly dead, putting up one last fight to crawl out? Crazy.

Chinatsu goes to the bathroom and rubs cocoa butter into her stomach. She doesn't want any more stretch marks.

Hand massaging her belly, she thinks of her child as frozen in time. Like her stomach is a freezer compartment. Time will surely catch up one day, and she'll suddenly be old. A mother. That state of being she'd wanted for so long. Why isn't she full with pride? Things weren't supposed to feel this way. She'd thought the moonflower would glow in the dark, attached to her through an invisible umbilical cord. But the moonflower is sick. She can see it, wilting and weak. There's a click in the bathroom.

Is someone here?

'Hello?'

Her body alert, she looks around for the source of the noise. She sees her make-up brushes in the holder on the shelf. She'd used them earlier, to lighten the dark circles under her eyes. It was probably just the brushes falling into place.

Chinatsu is asleep on the couch when Tao lets himself in. He tickles the underside of one foot. She pushes herself up.

'Tao?' She moans and rubs her eyes. 'I'm messy. You should've told me you were on your way.'

Tao looks amused. He strokes back the mess of her hair. The action, so intimate, makes her want to back away, like a stray cat that won't let you stroke its head. But she holds herself in place.

'I called, but you didn't answer. You must be exhausted. Come on, no cooking tonight. Let's go out for dinner.'

The restaurant is Japanese themed, decorated with tourist-Japanese colours. They've aimed for a foreigner's notion of authenticity. The waitress' kimonos are not tied. She watches them clump about in platforms. All wrong. Generally speaking, the kimono does not suit the frame of the Western woman. It would be as if she wore sports clothes.

Chinatsu sets down her chopsticks. The cook is clearly not Japanese either.

Tao swallows, and puts his hand atop hers. It makes her jump. What's wrong with her?

'Yugi never did that.'

Tao stops chewing. He looks at his hand and removes it. This is the first coldness through anger, rather than general unfamiliarity, that she's felt from him.

194

'I must go to Manchester tomorrow.'

Chinatsu raises her eyebrows. She often knew Yugi's itinerary six months in advance. Not out of consideration, but simply due to his devotion to preparation.

'I should like to come with you.'

She expects disapproval, or outright hostility, the checking of her presumptuousness. Tao dabs his mouth with a napkin and settles it back on his lap.

'You are different here.'

Chinatsu looks down. She grips the table to steady the nausea. Amber is inside her, eyes glinting in the dark. A low growl revs in her throat. Was she going insane?

'This is not Tokyo,' she says.

Tao laces his fingers together, resting his chin upon the crutch he has made. 'Meaning?'

'We are all different with different people.'

'And in different places?'

She shrugs, in that small way mother showed her was acceptably demure. She lowers her chin.

'Chinatsu.'

She looks up.

He smiles. 'Nothing. Well, I am not in Manchester for pleasure of course, but there are much galleries.'

She smiles at the slight flaws in Tao's Japanese, far more superior than her own attempts at Chinese.

'Perhaps we could go to the theatre in the evening?' he says. 'Something called *Dirty Dancing* is on.'

She smiles. She has seen the advertisements too. 'Yes.'

'Would you like that?'

She nods. 'It would be nice, I think.'

'Really?'

She considers. 'Have you ever skated, on the ice?'

Frowning, Tao says, 'Once, as a boy. I seem to remember falling quite a lot. You want to do this?'

'It might be fun.'

'Maybe after the baby.'

Her smile fades. Surely skating would not harm the baby? 'Yes, of course.'

More food comes. Chinatsu tries not to be disconcerted by the untidiness of the waitress' uniforms. She concentrates on looking content, even though she feels hideous. She's starting to feel clumsy. Are her cheeks getting puffy? How much more bulbous would her stomach get? It was a gentle swell at the moment, but it could become enormous. As they wait for the waitress to position bowls of rice and sour dishes, Chinatsu pushes a finger against her cheekbone, testing. Tao laughs. She places her hand in her lap instead.

She can't hide the feeling that Tao is really Amber's lover. He is Tao, and Chinatsu has stolen him. Once, Chinatsu knew what honour was. Honour and duty. She prided herself on it; the routine of being the good wife. Now she's pregnant and flirting with a man to whom she's not lawfully bound but now completely connected to. It is a disgrace. Isn't it?

'Why do you want me, Tao?'

He looks at her, dabs his mouth and nods. Reaching over, he brushes away her hair and traces the outer edge of her ear. Yugi had done a similar thing once, except he had straightened one of her diamond earrings. The most curious feeling; a small metal bar rotating inside her earlobe.

'I have thought on this,' Tao says.

'And?'

'Well, do you like stories?'

She looks up. 'Is it a good one?'

A smile. 'You should like it.'

She nods.

'Well, I've had a life of complete and total privilege. Materialistically, I have never had to struggle. You feel terribly sorry for me now, yes? I can tell.'

'It sounds like an extremely tragic story.'

He taps the table with one finger. 'Privilege can feel. . . confining. Do you understand? They do say what, beauty is a curse?'

She wants to guffaw loudly in the manner of Madam Li, but presses her lips together. 'My mother might disagree with that, Tao. To mother,

196

beauty is a daughter's only saving grace. Without it, I would be married to a pig farmer.'

'Not if you were rich enough.'

'But I wasn't. So instead I became a prostitute.'

Tao laughs. The first wide-open, unguarded laugh she has seen. He opens his mouth so wide she can see the troughs of his molars.

She feels proud of her joke, but tries not to show it.

'But you're not. . . *that*, any more. You never were, really.'

'Oh no?'

He looks pained.

'Never mind. Please continue with your story.'

He rests his chopsticks. 'Very well. From as early as I can remember, my life has been mapped out. At this age I will go to this school, at that age I will follow my father into business; at this age I will marry Jiao. She was like the China vase, beautiful, refined; empty.'

Chinatsu frowns. Why doesn't she like this reference? She raises her eyebrows: jealousy. 'How terrible.'

'But Chinatsu, this certainty was so unnerving. To be my own man and make my own way, have a wife of my choosing, I had to break with all tradition. This is not the way of every Chinese family any more, obviously. But mine aspires to the restoration of such traditions. I knew that if ever I expressed my disapproval, I'd never see my family again. But I wanted to see the world, give it beautiful buildings – don't laugh –'

'I wouldn't.'

'Well I wanted to do something so completely out of the ordinary, except I wasn't cut out for engineering.'

She twists the diamond in her ear. Yugi would never admit to weakness.

'And you know, I really thought it would be my father who wouldn't forgive me. But he was a self-made man, he built his company from the ground upwards and I think he understood my need.'

A woman, laughing like a hyena, attracts Chinatsu's attention. She's large as a bear and her clothes are all too tight. The man she's with is exceptionally groomed and exceptionally attentive. Such an odd match. She smiles; it's nice to think the woman is loved for herself.

She looks at Tao. 'So your mother disapproved?'

'She saw it as total betrayal and, for her sake I think, my father would not see me either. She left the room when I was saying goodbye. That was the last time I ever saw her. My father has started to write emails in recent years, but they're all about work.' Tao smiles. 'Like bulletins.'

'It is good of him though.'

He nods. 'Each new country I visit, I send my mother some trinket. A hair piece, an ornament, a necklace.'

'She does not acknowledge them?'

He shrugs. 'I would prefer an alternative to this, but I needed to pursue my own path. And still do. Maybe one day.' He picks up his chopsticks and taps them on the rice bowl. Tap-tap, tap-tap.

It sounds like a heartbeat.

'There is always hope, Tao.'

'And yet, the choices I made had further consequences. I have not had time to search for a wife, and though I have a family, I don't. Really. I started to wonder if I would ever have this.'

'So you bought one instead.' Her mouth falls open, shocked at herself. She watches his reaction. What would Yugi have done with such an insolent remark?

Tao bursts out laughing. The sound is overly loud, gauche. She cringes. Even the hyena-woman looks over.

Moments later, Tao looks sad. 'As a boy, certainty is too much of a prison. I had everything and nothing. As a man, I had everything and nothing, still. And neither did you.'

'We are just conveniences to each other?'

'No. We were both lost, and grateful to find warmth. Is that too much poetry?'

She lowers her head. 'I suppose not.'

'What is the point of life if there is no one to witness it? Look up, hey? I think I might spend my whole life trying to decipher these thoughtful looks you have.'

'So you want to conquer me. Stake a flag through my navel and call it Tao-land.'

Again that laugh. It is not as uncomfortable this time. His shoulders bounce and the sound is warm as it comes from deep inside his body. She's smiling.

'I want you because I'll never know you, not totally. I'll never be sure you'll stay, or if you will love me the way I do you. Why that expression?'

'Nothing.'

'Something. Definitely.'

'Then that is my mystery. You'll have to find it out, won't you?'

His eyes crinkle as he smiles. 'You are not my wife, so you have made a choice to be with me, and you do it each day. I like this uncertainty.'

She adjusts her dress, making sure the bra straps are in line. She crosses her legs and smoothes her hair.

'So thank you.'

She frowns. 'I don't understand.'

He shakes his head. 'That is *my* mystery.'

He places his hand over hers again, removing it quickly. Has he remembered her reaction the first time? She's a bad wife and an ungrateful lover. Tao is open and gives glimpses of himself that Yugi would never allow. And through this whole confession, Tao's easy outpouring, all she can do is wish Yugi had done this. For her, Yugi was the mystery.

Feeling sick, she brings the chopsticks to her mouth, reminding herself to chew slowly. She has heartburn. Either that or the acid in her chest is Amber, returned. But for what? To chop down anything she cultivates here, a poacher raging through thick jungle, hacking a clear path. How can you stop something you created?

Later, before bed, Chinatsu is brushing her hair in the shared master bathroom. It has two sinks; his and hers. Tao comes up behind her. He wraps his arms around her waist and kisses her hair, chin performing a mini massage on her scalp. 'Do you love me?'

He says it so quietly she can pretend she missed it. She takes his hand. 'I feel tired tonight.'

He masks his disappointment well, and they head into the bedroom and get under the sheets. She resists as he pulls her into his arms, wanting to pull him towards her instead. He looks up, but she pulls again so his head rests against her shoulder. She strokes the soft crown of his head, the tips of his ears and the growing stubble of his cheek. His skin is smooth as hazelnuts.

'I will be a dutiful mother.'

199

'Yes,' Tao says, breath hot against her breast and smelling of mint. 'I am certain of that.'

The baby kicks.

# 9

The sun is on Fleur's eyelids, exploring her. Daniel used to explore her
like that, just in the way he looked at her. They'd never had the chance to
touch, not in that way. His expression had always been so gentle and
warm. Daniel. He's here. He fills that gap between sleep and waking.
Was he real, or just smoke and imagination?

Either way, she doesn't want to wake up, but can feel her body
surfing towards it, the layers of sleep peeling away.

They are stood outside a house made of gingerbread. It's been
burned, but is still recognisable as a house. She spots a pond in the
distance. Before the pond she can see what looks like cows. They seem
to be sleeping, or dead. The grass is like Astroturf.

She focuses on the pond and is suddenly there. Ripples skate over the
pond's surface.

Panic tightens her chest. She's going to have to watch him die. Again.
Each time is different. Why? Why does she have to keep seeing this?

The water sploshes, the lazy yawn of a slow front crawl. Daniel is . . .
swimming. He rises from the pond, butterflies dancing in the clearing.
She has an impression of his body, a thatch of hair at his abdomen. A
line down his chest. Those shoulders, straight clavicles. A fairly solid

chest punctuated by brown nipples and framed by lean arms. Somehow, he's older than he was when he died. More of a man. The idea that Daniel is still living and existing somewhere, filters in and sets. His closeness, his wetness, next to her. Dripping on her sun-warmed skin. The affection in his eyes is challenging. Does she deserve someone who loves her? Who really loves her?

*You're swimming in there?* she says. *I thought you'd be afraid of water.*

He frowns and shakes his head. *What is the point of being afraid?* He rests his thumb against her mouth. He removes it and draws close, fits a kiss inside the envelope of her mouth.

A ribbon of laughter. Fleur breaks away from the kiss. A little girl is playing hopscotch to their right, hopping on one leg then two.

*Help her.*

She wakes up, pillow damp. She wonders if it was the water dripping from his body that's made it wet. Then she wakes up properly and the illusion is no longer there. The pillow is just wet because she's been crying.

The smell of burned toast rises up from downstairs. She hears the trundle and beep of the bin lorry working its way down the street outside.

Sighing, she heaves the cover aside. Her feet thump along the landing and down the stairs. She ties the knot in her thick dressing gown. There's a bowl of steaming porridge competing with Nan's cigarette smoke on the dining table.

'I feel like Goldilocks.'

'I've put sugar in it.'

Fleur sits at the table, rests one foot on the leather chair. 'Ta.'

'Not sleeping well?' Nan taps some ash on a saucer.

'Why say that?'

Nan sucks on the roll-up. Smoke plumes out of her nose like a dragon. A pensioner dragon that makes porridge and sucks on roll-ups and watches *Columbo* and *Kojak*. And meddles. The porridge bulges as she prods at it.

'Work?'

'I quit. Or was sacked. Not sure. I might've had to be in today. I'll find something else.'

202

Nan is nodding, tapping the cigarette. 'And so what's with all that?'
Fleur frowns.

Nan points the cigarette at Fleur. She realises the top of her dressing
gown has slipped. She blushes, knowing what must be on show. The
marks from sleeping with Andrew. Sex marks.

She clutches the gown to her throat. There's no sense denying it.
Nan's seen it all before, with her mother.

'It's how it starts, you know.'

'I dunno what you mean.'

'Right.'

'Whatever.'

'Fleur. Your mother. . . well, anyone would think she just didn't like
herself. The bruises I saw. The things she let them do. Sleeping with any
random men who so much as winked her way. I'll get you sectioned
before I let you go the way of your mother. Tell you that now.'

'I'm not crazy. I'm just confused.'

'S'what your mum said an' all.'

'Fuck's sake.' Fleur stands up sharply, slams the spoon down in the
bowl. A blob of porridge slaps onto her cheek.

Nan looks at it; they look at each other. They both suppress smiles.
'Just don't do it to yourself, flower.'

'I won't. I'll stop.'

'How?'

Through gritted teeth, 'It's not an addiction. I'll just stop seeing this
guy.'

'If you're getting hurt on purpose, you're afraid of something. You
were always safe with me. I don't get it. What's there to be afraid of now
Marcus is out the way? He's not bothering you is he?'

The words are jagged in her insides, the harmonics of a guitar,
resonating with her earlier dream. What's to be afraid of?

'I'm gonna get washed, got things to do.' She starts to leave, pauses.
'Don't worry.'

Nan nods, head turned now to the television. She twiddles with the
knob on the antique set, shifting between stations.

# 10

Tao is worrying about leaving. Chinatsu can sense this.

Chinatsu can don Amber's skin, zip it to her neck, act as ventriloquist for the enchantress. She raises an eyebrow. Tao knows this dance well.

'But nothing,' she says. 'I will be fine. What, are you worried I will not return?'

It's six thirty in the morning. Tao is softly leaving a different hotel room, smooth and striking in his suit. He is so flawless an image. All grace.

The hotel walls are geisha red.

'I am merely concerned you will get lost in a city you've never visited. Why must you find a problem in that?'

If she wasn't so frustrated, Chinatsu would laugh. This argument? It was almost amusing. 'I did manage by myself in London, when you were not there.'

He's not looking at her properly. 'You know, there has been a lot to restructure, Am – Chinatsu.'

There. This is what the conversation is really about. She softens her voice. 'And I appreciate how much you have done for me, naturally.'

'And what I will continue to do?'

'OK.'

'This child. I thought marriage was many years away for me, if at all –'

'I am already married.'

Tao pauses, his back to her. He has a pair of pyjamas, folded by his own hands, close to his chest. 'Well, I am running late for this meeting.' He puts the charcoal pyjamas in a Samsonite case and clicks it up. 'Do contact me if you require anything.'

Chinatsu has never enjoyed watching people walk away. She has a memory of getting lost in a department store, her mother oblivious, threading further and further away while she struggles through the adults, her mother drifting like a helium balloon. In sight, in sight, then gone. The utter panic of being completely disconnected from everyone.

'Tao?' She sits up in the queen-size bed, silk and wool around her naked skin. Her strength is in the delicacy of her shoulders. She lets the silk slip, knowing Tao will see and be moved. Somehow, it will reignite that inclination to protect that most men have. For a globally successful businessman, he is wonderfully naïve. She could never coerce Yugi out of an argument by using her body. Not that arguments were ever a factor in their household. Is this, with Tao, something positive?

He comes back to kiss her forehead. The sound of the kiss is ugly, because Tao loves only what he sees of her. Yugi would see through this posturing. And yet, this odd arrangement, with a man who arranged to screw an upmarket whore, has such a strange sense of honour. He is the utmost gentleman. A man of his word. He has given up so much and she cannot really fathom why. She thought it was the sex, that Amber made him feel alive. Did she remind him of the body he walks around in? What it could do and feel? This is what he did for her, made her real instead of the ghost in the house. But now she's not so sure. She does not know Tao but perhaps she can pretend to until it fits, for the family she has craved so long.

'There is much to resolve and really, I have no time for this conversation. I have made incredible sacrifices for an unstable premise. If this was a business deal, I would have weighed up the situation and decided it was not a good prospect. There is no balance.'

She raises her eyebrows, but otherwise keeps the surprise from her face. 'There is not.'

'Which, ironically, is why I am here. Business is legalised gambling, do you agree?'

She shrugs.

'Now is not the time to hold back your opinions. I know they are there.'

This irks her. Does Tao know her well, after all? She was not sure she liked this.

'But I'll tell you something. I won't be a father to a bastard child. If it is to be in name only then I will not proceed with this, though you will be provided for, naturally.'

She blinks. 'In name only? Are you proposing to me, Tao?'

'Why would I, when you've just reminded me you still belong to another man?'

Amber would have said, Well that didn't bother you before. Chinatsu says, under her breath, 'I belong to nobody.'

The conversation is over. Tao is not sure what he's heard and will go away to process it, but she can tell he knows it's not good. 'You have my number.'

She folds her arms over the covers and relaxes her posture. 'Should I dress for dinner later?'

'You may eat out or order room service. I have much to do today.'

'Tao.'

'Yes, Chinatsu.'

She kneels on the bed and with a deep breath that seems to saw out through his shoulders, he comes to sit beside her.

He nudges her with his elbow. 'Go on.'

She shakes her head. 'Have a good day.' She doesn't look up when he leaves. She hears the firm, muted footfalls of leather on wool. The door clicks closed like her mother's tongue when she made mistakes. Mother's tongue would be cramping if she could see her now. Did her mother know by now? Sense her daughter's departure from their homeland?

A clock ticks somewhere in the suite. Tick, tick, *tick*. She covers her head with a pillow, too tired to go in search of it.

She wakes once or twice and when the day is brighter, she's not certain whether they had the conversation she remembers now.

Standing in the bathroom, the light is on, white and bright. Natural light floods in, overwhelming the artificial lights. She makes up her face. Earlier, she'd pulled back the blinds and looked down onto the street. Tokyo streets look the same from this height, though British ones are less dense. The cars are different. *Gaijin* – foreigners – fur the concrete. Except here *she* is the *gaijin*, safely entombed in this plush square of sky.

Manchester is a city of angles and anonymity. More personal than London, it's like a cubist painting. As though Braques has emerged from his twentieth century resting place, spat on his charcoal and sketched the cityscape on a Starbucks serviette. And then he has torn up the serviette, thumbed the fragments about like a paper Rubik's cube, and created Manchester. Its buildings are all mixed up, the old with new, modern with traditional, run down slums with elite office complexes. It was not like this at home, with Tokyo's uniform geometry.

Should she find Fleur today? Chinatsu smiles. She knows no more about where her old friend might live than she did yesterday. It would be a pointless pursuit. And yet, the desire to revisit the old school, their old places, itches.

In the bathroom, Chinatsu pencils in the gaps of her sparse eyebrows. A faint memory of the door unclicking while she was in bed. Had Tao come back? Was she imagining this? She can't remember now if it was a dream, or the truth.

She doesn't know who she is, or why she's so afraid. How can she love Tao when she doesn't know who he is either? He is different here too. So which is the true Tao, the one in the hotel rooms in Tokyo? That man seems like a fantasy now; so far away as though it had never happened at all. This life, the one that was supposed to be the fulfilment of their dream, is somehow lacking. And yet also more than what she could have dreamed for. How can she be Tao's wife when she's still so connected to her husband? She swaps the eye pencil for a lip one and draws a nude line around her mouth. She slots it back in the holder, clicking against other tools and picks out a brush. She fills in the lines with lipstick, watching her mouth work itself into strange angles to reach all the places.

Faintly, she remembers asking Tao how this could work when she has no answers. Did he reply? She's sure his warmed-honey voice clouded around her. A voice which, if she were to close her eyes and paint, she would colour fossilised amber with the sun shining through. His answer?

That's the thing about mysteries, he'd said. They are there to be discovered.

She cannot remember who says the last part, if anyone, but she chooses to keep the memory as real and not a dream. It gives her confidence for the day.

She doesn't do a thing all day in the city centre, except use her disjointed English to navigate her way to and from art galleries. Not knowing the language makes it, strangely, easier to speak to people. She gets versed in picking out the types of people who will help her. She wanders around art galleries, feet tapping in the echoing spaces, smiling at the older English people who are mostly alone. They seem rich, hands behind their backs at times, both men and women, smelling of spice and lavender, wearing Chanel box jackets and looking like things from films.

She likes the mile high windmills, the fountains, the huge TV screen. In Tokyo, people take no notice of the technology. It's just part of the landscape. Here, people interact. Children run screaming through the fountains, workers stop to watch screens at lunchtime. What are they eating from those yellow plastic troughs? She sits on the cold bank of steps before the screen for the afternoon. She cuddles a cardboard cup of decaffeinated coffee and tries to make sense of the sport. She grasps the name of the sport after a while. Cricket. Translates it into Japanese, hoping the word will stick.

Over the hubbub of sirens and language and laughter and piped TV, Chinatsu hears bells. They must be for churches. At four, the smell of pizza makes her want to be sick so she gets up, aching slightly, wriggling her toes against the soles of her shoes. They've gone a little numb and tingle back to life. She looks around for a toilet. She follows the metal tram lines on the road into the train station. There must be one in there.

It's been hours since she's spoken to anybody, and feels in a bubble. If she bumped into someone and had to speak English now, it would be all wrong. And yet, there are Japanese faces everywhere. Boy students with bleached blonde punk dos that look ginger and their jeans loose and

208

revealing striped underwear. Their parents would not be proud of where their tuition funds had gone.

She walks through one of the station's open mouths and collides with a girl who is too skinny for her English frame.

'Sorry.'

'Not a problem.'

Chinatsu pauses. This has happened before, very occasionally, in Tokyo. An anonymous face in the crowd becomes one she half-recognises. It had happened more often lately, since she'd started with the men. Would she bump into one of them on the streets as they're cosseted with wives, their bubble pricked? What's equally strange, is that the other girl has stopped too and turned back. She wears a beret at an unflattering angle and has a mass of freckles, like rain on glass, unhidden behind make-up. Chinatsu can feel the powder on her face; it seems to stiffen her responses. The woman's eyelids seem swollen, as though she's been crying. Or maybe she just has a cold.

The woman smiles at Chinatsu. The smile is a question, but is meant for her. It is not the smile of a coffee shop person giving you change. It feels to Chinatsu like she is stopped; people are wheeling by the two of them, this way and that. She smiles back. The air all around smells of lavender.

Chinatsu thinks of Fleur. Could *this* be her? Somehow she doubts it, but she makes it true in her mind.

Yugi is behind her. Her eyes widen. The ground tilts. The world booms in her head. There's an announcement: bing-bong. The words thunder into her brain and try to break out of her skull.

'...passenger announcement...'

Chinatsu covers her face with her hands. Sinks to the floor. The announcer is for a cancelled train, voice free of any regret. It's too hard to blink, to stand. No space for thoughts, just feeling. And this unsteadiness is transmitted by a megaphone, blaring in her head.

The woman with the red beret is gone. Here again. Gone. An image paused and undecided, flickering between present and future. Or is that herself? Yugi? Or Tao? She wants to vomit.

People's heels, boots and shoes thump past her. Dinosaur feet. Her eyes screw up against the pain of sound.

She gets to her feet a hunchback. Straightens. She can see her misshapen silhouette imprinted on the door of the station bar. She places a hand over her stomach, as if it will fall off. Or her baby will get out.

'Here. I went to get you a drink. They wanted to charge me for water. Can you believe that? Come on, let's get you sat down.'

It's her. This girl that smells of lavender. She touches Chinatsu's shoulder and her hand sparks through the silk. She directs her head towards a bench, which the girl, two heads taller and far narrower, flicks clean of newspapers. She sits a hyphen's distance from Chinatsu.

She wants to ask, Are you Fleur?

'What happened there?'

Chinatsu stares at her mulberry and chocolate boots.

Her head falls to one side and her expression softens. She looks away, as if catching herself.

Chinatsu tries to straighten, so her body isn't such an apology, but it feels too hard.

She nods. 'Do you think you should go to the hospital? Make sure everything's okay?'

Chinatsu shakes her head.

'How're you getting home? Not on the train? I don't feel right leaving you.'

She swallows, as if this could rebalance her unsteadiness. Cold sweat spreads between her shoulder blades. 'Phone.' The lie doesn't taste good. 'Husband.'

'I'll wait with you?'

'No, no.' Chinatsu raises the phone Tao gave her and dials a random number. She speaks in Japanese to static then holds up her right hand. 'Five.'

'Well okay, if you're sure.'

Before, the woman's first smile could have been friendship. Now they are strangers again.

'Thank you very much.'

The woman gets up like she is pregnant. That reserved way of standing, pushing from the calves up. But it is not so pronounced. She could have imagined it.

The woman pats her pockets then scrabbles in her rucksack, retrieving a plastic pen and a piece of printed paper. She flips the paper over and writes on the back, using her knee as a rest.

'Just in case.'

She hands the paper over. They shake hands lightly, the paper crumpling and in the way. The woman fishes in her pockets again, and puts a type of sweet on the bench.

'Sugar might help. It's opened, but I haven't touched it. Honest.'

Chinatsu looks down at the paper, feeling emotional. This is just hormones. With the numbers, there is a word.

'Karen.'

Oh. She wasn't Fleur at all. The knowledge is startlingly upsetting. Chinatsu points to herself. 'Chinatsu.'

The woman nods. 'Well, careful.'

Karen walks away, arms close to her body. She looks stiff; as if aware she's being watched. Does Karen have a money tree, an escape plan, a moonflower? Or has she just escaped and is beginning to blossom? Does Fleur have one? It hits her again that this is Fleur's country, the north especially. She is getting closer and closer.

This is also where the prostitute died.

Could it have been . . . could Yugi have . . . ?

This time, she can't finish the idea. Can't stomach it.

Chinatsu has the strangest feeling of a tightening noose. Yugi is here, right now. Isn't he?

Karen falls out of sight. The station hall is awash with jaundiced light and seems abruptly desolate. Chinatsu closes her eyes and hopes for a baby girl.

She has another resolution: she will discover the mystery behind the newspaper article. Because if Yugi did have anything to do with it, then people should know. And Yugi should be punished. She is not doing it because she wants to exonerate her husband. She is not a flower, and Yugi is not the sun.

211

# 11

Yugi is remembering. 'But this is what I want to do, father. I have a scholarship to the university, so it won't cost you a thing. I will be able to make my own way in life, and look after you and your wife when you are older.'

In his memory, Yugi could see the red veins cutting through the whites of his father's eyes, the shape of stretched springs, as he looked towards him in the kitchen's cave-dark. It was before dawn and there were chores to be done. There were always chores to be done. No matter how much he scrubbed, Yugi's nails were rimmed all around with black before the day even began.

Yugi looks at his nails under the brash train station overheads. His nails are scrupulously clean, except for a line of red under the middle finger of his left hand. How had he overlooked that? How had it happened? As if in response he becomes aware of a raw circle of pain on the underside of his wrist. He examines it. There's a mass of scratches like the veins in his father's eyes. He'd scratched in half-sleep, a small, purposeful destruction. He struggles to regulate his breathing. Glances around. Nobody has noticed.

The things Yugi could have done with that waitress, if he hadn't been spoiled with nausea. She has thick limbs, like a Matisse sculpture. She would enjoy his attempt to remodel them. Her skin smelling of milk and moisturiser, nipples too-large for quite dainty breasts, like splodges of ham. Her vagina would be obstructed by a mess of pubic hair. He'd make her wash before he'd go there, enjoying the thought of shaving it bare while she sleeps. She'd liked how his fingers would cuff her wrists, how he'd knead her broad waist. He would take her from behind, something grotesquely sexy about seeing her cellulite as he plunges into her, the spill of her stomach over his arm. He'd make a fist around her small throat. Her choking sounds would make him fuck her all the harder.

But she'd enjoy the pain he inflicts. Somehow, this would make it cruel; unsatisfying. She is so young.

He'd thought about being like this with Chinatsu. That desire to curl his clean fingers around her throat and squeeze until her toes tingle and her head swells up. Pop. Brain raining down like confetti.

But he never touched Chinatsu in this way. Dozens of faces, all prostitutes, reel through his mind like clothes whipping by on a walk-in closet, activated by remote. He can't seem to switch them off.

Yugi uses a toothpick to clean his nail, his shoulders loosening only when the red is gone and disposed of. He sanitises his hands with a travel-sized bottle of hand wash, the kind they have in hospitals.

The frustration he felt that last morning with his father, the knots of anger at his inability to communicate his thoughts in a way that would get him what he wanted, is exactly how he feels when looking at Chinatsu on the train station bench. His wife's body has been distorted by another man. He desires to rid her of that mutation, to force her body back to its usual state.

He leaves the seats by the tram link, mostly hidden by a billboard advertising *Coca Cola*, when Chinatsu heads out of the station. He follows, passing under the train station clock, shadowing other commuters who believe they have something to walk fast for. The pace of this city is so slow. Nothing like the flashing, spasmodic revolutions of Tokyo. At the station's exit, Yugi ignores a man in blue proffering a paper.

Yugi has always been able to see further ahead of him than most. It's how he charted his life and how he became so successful. It had not occurred to him that his wife could also plan so well. He watches as Chinatsu window shops, walking leisurely. She checks the road before crossing. She sees the man who is about to collide with her when he is inches from her face. Yugi had been aware of this potential collision from ten metres away. The man seems to be someone who enjoys collisions with women.

Yugi's fingers curl. Restraint, restraint. It wasn't the right time. He wasn't ready to confront her yet. He wants to have something over Tao. He wants that man's business to crumble, a spray of dust from an unsettled brick, before the inevitable avalanche. But it's not happening.

And then he sees them, his wife and that Chinaman, meeting accidentally on the way to the hotel. Yugi steps into the shadow of a *Starbucks* alley to watch. He sees how their faces wake up with recognition. How they check for cars, bodies almost revving with anticipation. They cross the road. He knows it's going to happen, cannot prevent it. Seeing that man kiss his wife, he chokes with rage. Chinatsu turns her mouth to the left for the kiss, and suddenly there is a gap in Yugi's anger. His wife's small aversion is a tiny square of hope.

And yet, Yugi's wife and the Chinaman walk away with their shoulders touching. The Chinaman moves her to the inside of the path. He does it by taking her fingers as if he is about to lead her onto the dance floor. Why? Yugi's shoulders sag as he realises. It is a protective movement. So that Chinatsu is away from the road and out of danger. The Chinaman truly cares for her. Why bother? Why pursue this? Why not just leave and take another wife? They are easy enough to come by.

Yugi is about to turn away, when he sees Chinatsu stop. Her palm touches the Chinaman's face. She draws him close to her. They kiss again. Tao grins. Yugi's breathing is getting faster. Half of him is still considering letting this go. He is beaten, isn't he? But the competitor in Yugi, that drive which had always pushed him into first place, kicks in.

He presses himself against the brick of the alleyway, watching. His breathing ragged.

# 12

When she closes her eyes, Daniel is pointing like a mime artist at the menu board. He has hair the colour of halos and eyes so blue you could fly kites in them. Her memory of him is too bright and too cruel. She can almost reach out and touch him, smell his skin and hair. Almost.

Fleur took the bus into the city centre. She wants to be away from herself and who she's supposed to be. Possibilities of the person she could be flit through her brain as her head presses against the window, bus jouncing, hips swivelling to its rhythm.

She window-shops in the day. By four, evening is settling in at the base of the city's buildings. Lights are coming on in preparation. The bleep of pedestrian crossings, lights winking, car headlamps a dull amber. Commuters' cheeks are red; winter can't be far off. There are workers in expensive coats and thin scarves. Grubby bearded people selling *The Big Issue* in every spare corner. There's a frost in the air. There's something nostalgic about it, or something exciting. Change?

The green badge of a Starbucks attracts her attention. Its inside is damp and warm with other peoples' breath and body heat. She orders a hot chocolate and finds a table to herself. It's expensive. She counts out the coins and reluctantly hands them over.

OK. So think.

*What is there to be afraid of?*

This is the only line looping round her head. The ring of a planet, an advertising banner circling her eyes. She takes out a pad and starts to make notes.

Writing: the dream, the gingerbread house, Daniel. The little girl. Who was she? Herself? What is there to be afraid of? She underscores this. Because there is something to be afraid of. She's been afraid her whole life. Of Derek, of people knowing about Derek. Not telling the truth.

The realisation is like a slug to the gut. She's afraid still. She thinks of herself falling, the thud thud thud of her ribs down the stairs. The brutality of the sex she'd had lately. Trying to forget the past in the craziest of ways. And Nan sitting with the picture frame, the one with her mother inside the gold frame, alive and beautiful. Before she hanged herself. Before Fleur found her in the night, stumbling about trying to find the cause of that creaking noise. Her toes had been such a curious blue against the pink polish. What had Nan been saying about Derek again? *What kind of person doesn't like cats? He's got a daughter now, you know?*

Had she been dreaming about Derek's daughter? Is that what she was supposed to do?

A man appears in the coffee shop doorway. He's got a backpack and looks like a retired catalogue model. For like, Argos or something, but still.

Once he's ordered, he comes to her table. She stiffens. That's a bit forward.

'There are no other seats, do you mind? I won't be long.'

She forces down her suspicion and looks around. He's right; there are no free tables.

What is there to be afraid of?

Fleur smiles. 'Sure.'

He sits and pushes his bag under the table. They smile at each other again, knowing that the table is too small for them to just ignore each other. She looks at the dots of red under his stubble. He has a strong jaw and there are polka-dots of black stubble at his nostrils.

'Cold,' he says. Mimes a shudder.

Lame. Fleur smiles. 'Yeah.' Not exactly much better.

'Thought we were going to get away with it this year.'

She frowns.

'Been so mild.'

'Ah, right. Yeah.' Come on. 'Good job though, am not a fan of all that slipping and sliding. Leave that to Bambi, thanks.'

He laughs, a real laugh. Her cheeks go red.

The window behind them steams up as they talk. What is your job? Where do you live?

'I'm trying to find something new,' she says. 'I feel like I got stuck, you know? Thinking that's all I can do.'

'That's admirable. I hope you do.'

His compliment is nice. She hasn't felt that little warm flush of someone being kind for no reason since Daniel.

She shakes her fringe out of her eyes, a little self conscious. 'What about you?'

'I'm a policeman.'

She sits back. Would he know? Would he be able to check up on her? Find out what she'd said about Derek if he ran some sort of search. What would he do when he knew? Leave?

'People often have that reaction. Don't worry, I'm one of the good guys. So clean I squeak. Kind of a joke between me and the guys. Got into it after being a salesman, the dodgy dealings going on there are far worse than anything I've ever encountered in the force. '

She nods. 'Really? God, I'd never have thought that.'

'Yeah, well. Just decided to get out of it one day. Got a degree a bit later than usual, and then a totally new career.'

'That's admirable. So where do you live?'

'Salford Quays.'

They talk about the area for a while. How a lot of people don't like it but that he loves being close to the theatre and just far enough away from Manchester. And the view. At night, he says, the lights wink on the water and it's quiet and still and serene. Very calming.

She says she's never been.

They ride the bus back to his house in Salford Quays together in silence. They look and smile at each other every now and then. Her palms feel sticky. Should she really be doing this? She actually likes this guy. Or is she really just going to look at the view? Fleur's head is against the window again. Cars drone past. It sounds like it's raining.

The policeman lives in a proper house in a proper estate. It's new and small and sort of American looking. Really, it seems a place for families. Those with more money than she or Marcus would ever have had. For the first time, the loss of her child aches through her bones and body. A yawning grief. So powerful, it could close right over her, sewing her up inside. She breathes in, tries to shed the feeling. It's almost too hard.

He has a shiny car in the driveway. Its registration is up to date. He has a flat screen TV, computer games piled up over DVDs, mainly comedy, opened bills on the kitchen surfaces. She tiptoes around, nosing, as the kettle rattles towards boiling. His house is clean but not too tidy, and not too messy either. She doesn't feel neat enough for this place. Her upbringing, her small- townness, is stinking out the house. She smoothes her hair back, tries to hide the hole in her sock between her big toe. There are pictures of his family on the wall. Family Christmases, barbecues and birthdays. She's never been to a barbecue.

He's clinking spoons and stirring more coffee. Do they both know they won't drink it, or is it just her? She expects the video games to be football and boxing; but they are fantasy things. They often have Vikings on the front, or some sort of warrior, heroic quests. It is geeky, and somehow cute.

There is a cat; she can smell it. She hadn't expected that either.

There are suddenly too many nerves, a surge of them about to short circuit her out.

A smile, and he hands her the mug. It burns her palms. With Andrew, it had been easy. Her in control. But this was different.

They sit on the leather sofa. It's chocolate and the material is cracked but still expensive looking. Their knees point at each other. He puts down his cup. She keeps tight hold of hers as he kisses her. Finally, she can relax. She knows how to do this stuff; it's the small talk she's not good at. He takes her mug, puts it on the coffee table with the TV guide – no *Sun*, no *Daily Mail*, no 'Babe' magazines – and kisses her again. He pushes her flat with his body. The arm of the chair digs into her back.

*The McDonalds staff room. Those other policemen.*

His tongue tickles her upper lip.

*The woman police officer, exchanging glances with him.*

He nips her bottom lip, painfully.

*If there is anything else you can help us with.*

His hand covers her throat, but is just stroking. She pins it in place and puts pressure on his hand. Hard. Harder. He pulls back, eyes questioning. She kisses him. Her hands find his jeans button.

He sits back, couch creaking. 'OK.'

'What?'

'How about we go out for dinner?'

'Eh?'

'Food? You like tapas?'

'What's that?'

His presses his lips together, but the smile is good-natured. 'It's Spanish.'

'I know.'

They separate and he puts the television on. Some American show that is meant to be funny. He doesn't laugh much either. He sits there, just dumb-fucking sits there with his arm around her shoulder, while she's all tense and straight. What did he want her to do? Finally, the show finishes and she can make her excuses. He takes her number, gives him hers.

The taxi purrs up outside to take her to the station.

'It was nice seeing, well, meeting you,' he says. 'Call you later?'

'Uh. Yeah, whatever.'

A kiss on the cheek. She sits in the cab, slams the door and doesn't look at him.

What is she afraid of? As the taxi pulls away with a 'station, love?' she hits on it. She is, was, and always will be afraid. Not of Derek, but herself. The fact she hasn't resolved this. She didn't tell the truth. Didn't properly report him. Derek has always been this strange skeleton, a framework for how she's acted and maybe, for who she's ended up with. Until now. She's still thinking as she automatically gets on the bus, moving further away from the city. It's not guilt for Daniel that she needs to sort out, not really, it's guilt for Derek.

What other little girl's bedroom is he creeping into right now? Who is he forcing to be still? Who is hiding in the boiler cupboard, burning the backs of their legs?

She takes her pad out the bag and writes: I am a horrible person.

Her phone is buzzing in her bag. It couldn't be the policeman already. It would have to be Marcus.

# 13

Fleur. The girl from the train station moves through Chinatsu's mind like an aftershock or, strangely, the lulling laps of an orgasm calming her body to sleep. She half-forgets what the woman looked like, though she is thinner than most. She stands very straight. It wasn't her childhood friend obviously, but that doesn't matter.

Chinatsu rides the empty lift, whirring up towards an empty hotel room. But Fleur is with her. Was Fleur as lost as she was? Or did she follow the signposts in her life, never unsure, taking large strides in comparison with Chinatsu's own small and shuffling footsteps. Her small feet. For some reason, Chinatsu thinks that she does not. And it is sad.

She will find her. A strange thought ticks about her brain: If I find Fleur I will find myself.

Pain jolts her stomach. Shocked, her cheeks tingle. Heat prickles between her shoulder blades. Perhaps this child already hates her for bringing it into the world under such dishonourable conditions. Or maybe there's something really wrong?

The key card doesn't work. She tries it again. Nothing. Has Tao come to his senses and evacuated her from his life? One more time, and the door gives. Relieved, she gets inside. She can smell lavender. She hates that smell. Except, she doesn't. Lavender reminds her of Yugi. Could he actually be in here? Don't be stupid. But the worrying thing is that she still does not hate Yugi.

Chinatsu crosses to the window and bows her forehead to the cool glass. She knots her hands behind her back, like the old people she'd seen in the galleries. She closes her eyes, dizzy, giddy.

Manchester plays on below her, this small city, whirring away. It's dark outside and strobe lights slice the sky. They reveal the buildings opposite like erasers clearing spaces in the dark. There are lots of women, girls really, shining in flimsy fabrics and oiled skin. The men are untidy, shirt tails on display. Englishmen have no finesse, they are not gentlemen and this is strange. Their belts never go with their shirts, their shirts are boxy and starchy, with creases folded into them. The girls wink and glitter and attract. Such extravagant displays for such untidy men.

She stands back, forehead cool, and places a hand over her stomach. She wets her lips and squeezes her eyes shut. Mother would not be able to breathe around such women. Did her mother now know that her only child was no longer in the land of her birth? That she had abandoned her duty and her husband, and is pregnant by a Chinaman? And more, does she know that she enjoys it?

But is she enjoying it?

Chinatsu never spoke to her mother on the phone, but communicated through letters, and even those were rare of late. A part of Chinatsu knew that her mother could tell what she was hiding, even if all she spoke about was the garden and the house and Yugi's business. She could no more hide from her mother than she could hide from herself. Did she feel me leave, like an eclipse, a strangeness to the day, a subtle change in the light? Her mother. It is only now, pregnant, that Chinatsu understands the air of constant disapproval between the two of them. Because her mother had been a teenage girl, before she became a wife.

Mother once accompanied her on a visit to the doctor for a sore throat. Chinatsu wore no bra and made sure her blouse was white. Perhaps Amber was inside her even then. She kept her school blazer on and her arms crossed until called into the office. She went alone.

Should she? Shouldn't she? She took off her jacket, burning from the possibility of his gaze.

After this appointment, she changed doctors, requesting a female one. This pleased mother.

The doctor had been too polite to gawk. The men here are the opposite. They gawk and gawp and their mouths open and close, eyes bulging like fish in the tanks of the restaurant where she first did business with Madam Li. And women are meant to be dutiful for this? They are no peacocks these men, there is nothing resplendent in their cheap shoes and, she presumes, artless conversations.

Does Fleur dress up at night like the girls twinkling below her, all strewn together like clusters of pretty lanterns in the trees for local festivals? She doubts it. Fleur may be as much a foreigner in this country as she is.

The rowdiness from below rises up to meet her. The clock ticks, Chinatsu watches. Does she miss not having had this sort of free life, to dress up and attract men? Honestly, no. The ticking echoes her pulse. It seems to go faster. She does miss the friendship that seems to exist between these links of women. It's something she hasn't understood since Fleur. Tao returns upon the tick of eleven with the click of a door.

He does not speak as he moves about his business.

He does not notice her by the window.

He takes off his tie, and his shoes.

He goes to the bed.

'I'm over here. Did you have a good day?'

'Oh! You startled me. I thought you'd be in bed. Yes, productive, but not good. I won't bore you with it. What are you doing all alone in the dark?'

'Please. I want to know. Bring a chair, sit here.'

She hears Tao sigh as he hauls a chair to the window. He sits.

'And?'

'A little more forward.'

'Ch –'

'Just, please.'

He moves to the lip of the chair, and she gets up off her own chair to stand behind him. His shirt whispers as she moves her hands over his

223

shoulders. She feels them relax and imagines she is the iron, smoothing out creases on bed sheets. She can smell the starch.

'Now tell me,' she says.

Tao talks about his day as she pushes her hands over his shoulders and down his arms, again and again.

'And yours?' he asks later, 'What did you do?'

She stops. Her body hangs with this question, but that he even asked is amazing, and makes her momentarily sad for the life she had before. And glad for this one. Yet her life is so much less vital than Tao's. It's embarrassing. She's tempted to make up the importance of her day. She saved a puppy from being run over. There was a bomb scare in a gallery. In reality, the most significant detail of her day was the girl who got her water at the station. What use is that to a man? And she should certainly not trouble him with a silly stumble.

'I should like a job.'

Tao turns in the chair. She wants to stroke the question out of his face with her hands, to tell him it's not his fault, this is something she lacks, but cannot muster the action or the words. Tao is not Japanese. Would he feel as threatened as Yugi if she wanted to work? How far do his boundaries extend?

'You are not happy?'

'Not so far, I see.'

'Hm?'

'It is late. You should rest. Will you be taking a bath?'

'Stay here. Why do you want a job?'

How can she say that her time just slips away? She feels like she's standing in front of a mirror, an unkind sketcher drawing age deeper into her face. And yet she never has and never will contribute to the world around her. She will pass through this life, leaving not a mark in its fabric, not a footstep to be washed away or mourned over, affecting no-one. She is still the ghost in the house. 'You have done so much for me. I ought to contribute. I wish to.'

'You are pregnant.'

'And what after?'

She can read the thought in his face: I don't understand. This thought is in the blink of his coffee-brown eyes, the crumple of his brow. His

Chinese skin is oiled and too youthful for a man of his years. Will he always look under thirty, with her ageing faster and faster alongside him? He doesn't have to say it.

'Then you shall raise the child.'

'And after?'

'Perhaps we shall be blessed with another. It's been such a long day.'

'No.'

He rubs his thigh and lowers his head.

This is the time to stop, when the patience runs dry and you have been told what a long day they have had, and that you can discuss it in the morning. And this never happens, because they are out of the house before you've had a second to speak.

'No.'

She holds her breath.

Tao breathes out.

'What kind of job would you like?'

His voice is cracked from fatigue, but her heart races. His response is exciting. It is new, and unexpected.

'I haven't decided yet.'

'I could ask around. There might be something in the London office.'

'No! I'm sorry.' She shakes her head so her hair swishes against her shoulder blades. 'I should like to figure this out for myself.'

Tao nods, his lips pressed together, chin dimpled. She has a longing to put her finger over these temporary creases in his skin. This means he doesn't approve, but is at least attempting to keep that to himself. She really could love him, in a different way, a different kind of affection than the one Amber nurtured for him. It will just take time.

The moonflower may be dying, on the wane and about to return to the earth, but perhaps this is not a sad thing. Perhaps it is just because she no longer has need for it. Tao can be her sun, but she is her own planet, making her own gyrations.

Tomorrow, when Tao is working, she will go back to the small town and explore.

Her Chinaman kisses her, strange to feel his lips reach hers from below. She feels suddenly sick.

225

# 14

Yugi is enclosed within his hotel, the one close to the Hilton, where
Chinatsu and her lover are staying. They have clearly tried to cover their
tracks. The Hilton is not Tao's chain of hotels. Yugi has not been
sleeping well at all. Tonight won't be any different. He cannot find
lavender in the shops anywhere. Does she get it in oil or spray form?

He dreams about dying, just being unable to breathe. His brain
doesn't wake him up. He becomes a ghost in his dream. He wakes
sharply in the blanket folds of night. Panting, he thinks that the dream is
a lesson to teach him to live. That he has been a ghost in life. To show
him where he has gone wrong. Westerners, they are obsessed with God.

In the middle of the night, fingers wrap around his throat. He is
suffocating. Eventually, he struggles to a sitting position, clumsy with
sleep. Eyes sore and narrow, he fumbles about for his watch on the
bedside table. His fingers bump into a glass, upending it.

'Shit.'

His pulse is hammering. Yugi wipes his lips. They're crusty. He
swallows, trying to get the bad taste out of his mouth. It felt sore, as if
the dream was real. Someone really had been trying to strangle him.

226

Yugi touches his neck, still breathing hard. Cars surf past the hotel window. The wind rattles a squeaking sign somewhere. It is the memory of Chinatsu and the Chinaman that is making Yugi's sleep so restless. That image of them kissing. Of his own wife stopping her lover for a kiss. *Needing* that kiss. When had Chinatsu ever expressed that kind of affection for Yugi?

Chinatsu loved the Chinaman. This is clear now. It is this thought that makes Yugi feel like he is suffocating. It is Chinatsu who is strangling him in the night. But Yugi would show Chinatsu and her Chinaman who really had the power. If he could not hurt this Tao Chang in business, he will cripple him emotionally. He will take Chinatsu away from him, whatever the cost to Yugi himself.

# 15

'You're going where?'

'Out.'

'With?'

Fleur scans the clothes she has. She has absolutely nothing decent to wear. She edges past Nan to the wardrobe. 'For.'

Nan sips her brew, sucking on her fag before she's even swallowed. 'Eh?'

She feels sick. 'I have a job interview.'

'You have a job.'

'No. Interview. I didn't go in for the job, remember? Think I'm fired.'

'Fleur –'

'I want something different, OK? I can do something different.'

'Not with that attitude.'

'Well thanks, great thing to say.'

Nan's nostrils flare, smoke sighs out. 'You're just –'

'Like my mother. Yeah. Except I never killed myself, did I?' Even though she'd tried, she mentally added. Shame flamed up as she remembered the bite of the razor on her wrists. 'Maybe it'd help if you

228

didn't keep reminding me about that. Or is that what you're trying to do?'

The expression on Nan's face was like dirt, staining and something she didn't want to see. 'Don't you come back to this house if you've got that kind of attitude, missus.'

'Believe me, I wish I didn't have to.' She slammed the door.

She's in the Goth pub again. It's in the lull just after lunchtime. There are a few bikers in with laptops. She's ordered a cranberry juice. No alcohol. She looks at her mobile. Who does she want to call her phone more? The woman from the student assistance interview she's just been on? Or the policeman guy? A thought crept into her head: Marcus.

A guy positions himself in the gap next to Fleur's stool. Fleur stares at her drink. Déjà vu or what? The guy glances at her and looks away briefly to order a drink from the barmaid. He gets very close to the barmaid, then rests his wrists on the bar and looks back over. His voice is surprisingly soft.

When the man's drink comes he takes a sip from the small glass. She can smell the cranberry from here. Buying the same drink. How original.

A text flashes on her phone. She's saved him under 'Copper'. It said: a bit hectic to call. How are you? I've booked a table for tomorrow night. Send you the details later. Hope that's okay. If not we can reschedule. Have a great day! X.

The warm feeling in her stomach is odd. She suddenly wants something alcoholic.

Fleur glances over, may as well tell him to bugger off and stop looking.

He's a little small and has a lean face with a compact mouth. There's something refreshing about how clear his skin is, despite the lines around his eyes. His dark hair is spiked in a mini, more sedated version, of the Mohawk. There's a hole in his left nostril for a nose-ring which has been taken out. She can smell coconut, most likely the styling wax used on his hair.

'I'm not interested,' Fleur says. 'Just so you know.'

'I'm Joe.'

Fleur nods. She faces forward again and presses her thumb to her glass; it's still warm from the dishwasher.

'Bad day I take it?' Joe says.

Fleur smiles tightly.

'Not up for talking about it then eh?' Joe smiles. It's the opposite of someone who has a lot to hide; he shows all his teeth. There's a gap between the front two. It's kind of cute.

'Don't think she's your type, Joe,' the barmaid says, giving Fleur a wink.

Fleur looks at Joe; he's gone a bit pink. She notices that his face, plain and clear, is made up of quite delicate angles. His eyebrows are fairly thick, but his eyelashes are long. Fleur looks at his plaid shirt, rolled up above small, but well-defined biceps. His arms are smooth and completely hairless. She resists a desire to test how soft they are.

And then she notices the swellings of breasts beneath the distinctly lumberjack-looking shirt. 'Oh. Right.'

'Yeah, I'm a dyke.'

'I'm so sorry.'

'That's cool.' Joe takes another sip of whisky. He – she – has twin silver rings on her thumb. 'But *I'm* fairly happy with it. Just so you know.'

Fleur presses her hands to her face. 'So. . . so it's J O, not J O E?'

Jo nods.

'Short for?'

'Johanna, so you should really call me Yo. Don't ask. Mother, total hippy.'

'Mine too.'

'Oh yeah? What d'you get?'

'Fleur.' She rolls her eyes.

'Excellent. Flower power. D'you give her hell for it?'

'She died. Hung herself actually. Dunno why I told you that. Sorry. I'm not even drinking.' She laughs. She's aware how tight and scary her voice sounds.

'Probably the last thing you need to be apologising for. You know?'

Fleur presses her lips together. She's about to cry. She can't cry, not now. What she definitely shouldn't do is think about the colour of mum's toenails again, that painful purple-blue, swelling through the sugar-pink of her nail polish. And the sound, not the tinkle and tap of her bracelets, but the creaking sound of her swinging gently. The same one the bed made when Marcus was having sex with her, or when he adjusts position in his sleep. Whenever she heard that she'd be awake instantly, expecting to look up and see her mum's purple-blue toes.

The tears pass, and she can speak again.

'Air?'

'Huh?'

'Air?'

Fleur nods. There's something about following Jo out the pub that makes her feel looked after, even though Fleur is a good few inches taller. The glass collector makes way for them, with Fleur behind. Jo holds the door and waits for Fleur to go out first. She smiles, feeling kind of girlie. Weird, but nice. Is this something she's looking for? Maybe it would be close, intimate. That friendship she'd always looked for, had missed so much since her Japanese friend went away.

'Not too cold,' Jo says.

'No.'

Their feet whisper over the grass to one of the beer garden's benches. It's wet, and the moisture dots the golden suede of Jo's boots. There's no one out, except a couple of smokers at the front door. Their voices are cloudy, cut through by a scream or shout from the clubs down the road. That and the thump of the bass. Every now and then, a car swishes past the main road.

'Pretty.' Fleur nods at the cheap blue fairy lights that are knotted into the eaves of the tables' umbrellas.

Jo laughs. 'Yeah.'

They sit on the benches next to each other, and face the solicitors' buildings opposite the quiet side street. She folds her arms; her breasts are sore and heavy. Still hasn't had a period. Her breath streams upwards like smoke and the cold pinches her nose. Should she text that policeman back?

Jo leans in, nudges her with one arm. Her soft arms are backed up by solid muscle. There's the briefest itch of electricity between their bodies.

'How bad could it have been, really?' Jo asks.

'Sorry?'

231

'Your day. It's only midday, there hasn't been time.'

'You wouldn't believe me.'

'I'm an accountant. D'you believe that?'

Fleur frowns. 'Erm. No?'

'Key-rect. I'm a psychologist, specialising in CBT. Do some lecturing at the uni in Manchester as well.' Jo laughs. 'And no, I don't dress like this for work. And I'm not 'reading' you right now either.'

'Which one?'

'Met.'

'Ah right. That's great. Well I'm just a waitress. Well, I was. But I just had an interview, but I dunno.'

'Well, the waitress over there is studying for a Masters in Forensic Pathology. Two kids, spaz of an ex. I used to work in construction. Only did my degree when I was twenty seven.'

'That's kind of amazing, actually.'

'No. But everyone's got other stuff to them, or they don't. Whichever. It's about what's right for you.'

'I don't think I understand that.'

'You will.'

Fleur looks at Jo. Jo stares ahead.

'What's CBT?'

'Cognitive Behavioural Therapy.'

'Oh.'

'Hear all kinds of stories. Won't even charge you.'

Fleur shakes her head. 'It's OK, I don't want to talk.'

They sit. Fleur scratches one knee through her jeans.

Jo turns to Fleur, and strokes her cheek with one thumb. Her ring is cool over Fleur's skin. The touch is gentle and unobtrusive. Her body wakes up in a way she hasn't experienced before. That little sting of excitement, swelling her clitoris. She keeps looking at Jo's lips even though she knows she shouldn't. They're thin and ridiculously pink, even without any make-up.

'Is this too much?' Jo asks.

Fleur shakes her head.

Jo's mouth meets hers softly. She catches the tang of cranberry and bite of toothpaste. A stitch of hard, dry skin catches. Fleur isn't sure whose it is. Jo's tongue is a shock, warm and wet, the inside of her mouth tastes of tobacco. She kisses firmly, rhythmically. Eyes closed, a flash of Hollywood-white teeth appears in Fleur's mind. The smell of cut grass. Eyes to fly kites in.

She jerks back and presses her lips together.

'OK?' says Jo.

'I'm not. . . '

'Me either. I'm bi.'

'I meant, I shouldn't be doing this. I'm not with it at all.'

'It's okay.'

Fleur sticks her fingers under her legs, raising her feet off the ground. Does Jo shave her underarms, or is she hairy like a man? She remembers Marcus' fingers twisting clumps of her hair. And fucking her, as she stays as still as possible. That could be the rest of her life. She thinks of Daniel's smile, warm and open and welcoming. Or this could be her life. Couldn't it? But not yet. The only person in her mind at the moment was that little girl from her dream. Derek's girlfriend's daughter. If Derek was hurting this girl, the way he'd hurt Fleur, it would be Fleur's fault.

She deadlocks Nan's front door, checks the back and then pushes at all the windows. Nan always leaves them open after smoking. She has no idea what's out there. Creeping upstairs she runs a bath, gets in and washes herself without cleaning herself down there. She's never liked touching herself in that place. Exhausted, the lure of falling asleep in the bath is overwhelming. But the idea of waking up freezing cold with her hair sopping wet makes her heave herself up.

Coming out the bathroom, tiptoeing over the creak in the landing, she senses a figure to her left.

'Hey.'

'Hey yourself, madam.'

'Look Nan, we need to talk. Just let me get changed. OK?'

Nan turns away to water her Yucca plants with a washed out milk carton. Its long, long leaves are brown like pond reeds and make whispering sounds. She grunts. It sounds like an agreement.

# 16

Today was the day Chinatsu was supposed to go to Fleur's town, to navigate the train systems and wind up where she had begun. But she doesn't feel up to it. She feels heavy. Normally, Chinatsu likes the weight of the child in her stomach as she walks around; it grounds her. But today, she feels like she's dragging chains. By now, the moonflower is just a faint flicker across oceans, yet she has something else growing in its place. She has started to like the heaviness in her breasts, the tenderness of her nipples. Every painful shift of fabric against them reminds her of her body, the pregnancy. She's taken to wearing silk.

But the other her, the one she ghosted away into an ill-fitting compartment, like a magician's assistant, is gnawing out of her. Chinatsu is certain. Amber's bones are breaking and brittle, she is dying, but she will use every last particle of energy to emerge. A dying demon butterfly and Chinatsu, the husk she will leave behind.

Just her imagination working overtime. Chinatsu knows that's not true and yet the thought is powerful and intensely scary.

'What is the matter? Is it the baby? This city?' Tao had asked before leaving for work. 'We will be back in London soon. This deal's just taking a little longer than I thought.'

Chinatsu is tempted to tell him that the woman he fell in love with is eating their baby. She assures him it's purely nausea, and is normal. It is not. Something is very wrong.

Amber is killing them. That's crazy. She's going crazy.

Chinatsu had wanted Tao to come back before he even closed the door. To notice that something was wrong.

There is a pain inside her and her vagina, the whole area, is numb. Doesn't exist. Amber is walking through her body. Waiting and ready. Chinatsu pulls her mobile off the table. She calls Tao, but it goes to answerphone. Who else can she call? She wants her mother. The longing is sudden and overwhelming, as painful as it was impossible.

The numbness is spreading, seeping, cold. She takes a herbal pill for the pain.

# 17

Yugi is fully clothed as he walks his fingertips over the naked girl's throat. She chokes and shirks away. A flicker of a smile and fear.

He thinks of doing this to Chinatsu, and keeps his erection.

'You're very mysterious,' she says. She's a whore picked up from the streets at the back of the train station. She has dark hair and a lithe body, so thin her clavicles are like razors. She looks like she might stop breathing any moment. He looks at the bruises on her legs, great fists of things. Things he hasn't done to her. Her hair is black as Chinatsu's but stripped of sheen, where his wife's was almost slick and glassy.

Yugi lies on his back. The girl's nipples are inverted. How can she not be ashamed of this mutation? He throws the sheet corner over her body.

She kicks it away. 'We should get started. You know?'

Yugi gets up from the bed to look out the hotel window. He sees a car park in brick and black and yellow, a chain of red lights winking on and off up the spiral. He hears the girl scrape over the sheets as she flips over and flattens out on her stomach, looking at him.

He turns. 'You should stop this.'

She pouts, legs bent and feet waggling. He has a desire to bite her instep like it's a dog bone. She throws the pillow she's had stuffed under her chin. He catches the ear of it with one hand and throws it back. It hits her square on the nose.

'Ow!'

'Why do you want this life?'

She frowns, stops all pretence and even lets out her stomach. 'Right. Well this is clearly a no-goer. You owe me a tenner, mate.'

'Men who will just use you and beat you. Do those men pay you? Why can't you get a normal job? Is this really so much easier for you?'

She sits up and crosses her legs. Her skinny frame reminds him of a grasshopper. Her stomach does not even sag when scrunched up like this. She bites her thumbnail, gnawing like a tin-opener. 'You're freaking me out.' She stamps her hands on the bed, gets up, starts to dress.

'You will damage yourself if you continue in this way.'

'Seriously?'

'Or somebody else will damage you.'

She pulls on her tights and tears two ladders in her hurry. She works her dress over her head. Half of it is not pulled down. She grabs her boots and purse, tries to dodge round him.

'Let me past.'

'You could be a waitress.'

'What the fuck? Get *out* of my way.'

He slaps her, and stares at his hand.

'Yeah. Typical. It's always the fucking foreigners isn't it? So fucking repressed.'

'I just wanted to be with someone. My wife is here with another man.'

'Mate. Like I fucking care.'

Yugi grabs the girl's wrists. It's easy to walk her backwards, to throw her on the bed. Easy to rip a gash in her tights and drag aside her underwear. So easy to unbuckle and fuck her. Feel her tight, body resisting. His control. His temporary power.

But he lets go of her wrists. There are bands of red around the skin there. Her veins are in relief from the pressure. She is still standing up, panting. Her fear changes to anger and contempt, a seen-it-all-before shake of the head. Her lemony perfume invades his nostrils and catches in his throat. Her scent invades him, making him feel unclean.

237

He thinks about Chinatsu. He had done enough waiting, enough watching. It was time to act. She was *his* wife and he would have her back. She would always belong to him.

The prostitute attempts to leave but Yugi snags her wrist. Her throat, where her pulse flickers. Someone will feel his strength. Someone will not disobey him. 'Not yet,' he says to the prostitute. 'We've not even started yet.'

# 18

Fleur had tried to talk to Nan about Derek. The discussion had flared and caught, exploded into fireworks. It was always the way. Why didn't she have patience any more? She used to be able to put up with anything. Now, she snapped when things didn't go her way. What right did she have?

The more she walks, the slacker the tension. The anger weakens and her shoulders relax; she feels like a boxer, dancing out the anxiety. Forcing back the pinch of tears. She'd been in the wrong, snapping like that then slamming out. It was the sort of thing Marcus would do.

She wipes her nose. There's a schoolboy tying his laces on a bench before the Catholic school at the top of Nan's road. What was his life like? Was he wasting time tying his laces because he didn't want to go home? She remembered that feeling.

But there was one thing Nan had let slip: where Derek worked. Whether he still worked there was another matter. She turned, spied a bus approaching traffic lights. She ran for the stop and caught it just in time.

'Beech Hill, please.'

The supermarket rolls by as the bus heads towards the back of the town centre. They by-pass the new gym, wheezing up the slope towards the collection of factories. She dings the bell and gets off before a large sprawl of concrete. The blocks remind her of massive slabs of cake. She smells for the briefest of moments the spice and cinnamon of gingerbread. A steady stream of black splurges from chimneys. Her stomach flips.

It's cold; she pops shut the buttons on her coat. Now what?

Three times she's been in and out of the Texaco at the corner of the industrial estate where the factories are. The Pakistani has his lips pressed together as he sells her a third packet of chewing gum.

'Thank you.' He looks over her head.

She wanders out, bell ringing, fingers numb and arthritic.

She's been watching the traffic coast up and down the road for a good couple of hours, looking for signs of life, freezing her arse on the bus stop bench, pacing around. Waiting. She doesn't feel in any emotional turmoil, as she'd expected to. She's completely calm, as if this is what was supposed to happen. She's supposed to be here, waiting for Derek. But what the hell was she going to say to him?

Fleur rises up onto her tiptoes and controls her muscles, inching slowly back down to the ground.

Her phone buzzes. Oh God, Marcus again. But it's not, it's a number she doesn't recognise. 'Hello?'

'Hello, Fleur?'

Her stomach jolted. 'Speaking?'

'Hi Fleur, it's Jenny from the interview yesterday. When would you be available to start work?'

'I'm sorry?'

'We have a few students needing support from next week. Would that be too early?'

'Er, no.'

'Great, I'll post you some forms and email you the details. OK?'

'Yeah. OK. Thanks.'

Fleur has a smile on her face as she tucks the phone back into her pocket. The smile wipes when she focuses on the grey blocks of oversized cake; the factory is letting out. The roads around the estate are clogged now with people picking up loved ones. The troop of people reminds her of dwarves coming home from work except they're all different shapes and sizes. Old women and youngsters in jeans and white trainers. Men, old and young, trudging up the hill, smiling for people in waiting cars. With people collected, there are U-turns and horns and the estate starts to filter down to stillness again. Fleur keeps watch from the bus stop, chin on her palm. There's no fear or pain, or panic, her body is curiously relaxed.

Perhaps she doesn't expect to see him.

Perhaps she expects this to be a wash-out; she'll have to try again. Keep coming back and back.

And then her body tenses like it's been zipped straight. It's him. The man who came into her room. He is cased in fat and age, but she can pick out the person she once knew. Her mother's boyfriend. The person who'd had the most impact on her life.

Fleur gets off the bus stop bench. There's a gnawing in her stomach, as if part of it is missing. She looks at this new Derek, padded with fat as children pat snow onto snowmen. It is hard to feel anything. Are her emotions on catch up? Will they hit her full force any moment now?

He smiles, completely unaware of her. A blue car circles around the neck of the road and pulls up next to him. The driver is a woman with frizzy brown hair and a chewing gum pink jumper. Derek gets in the passenger side. The woman places her hand flat on his cheek and kisses him. The glint of her wedding ring catches the light and sends strobes of nausea through Fleur's stomach.

The girlfriend?

Despite Nan mentioning this, she hasn't expected Derek to be knitted together into something happy. With someone who was completely innocent of his past. She shouldn't pursue this, whatever *this* was. The past is the past and now she has a new job. She can move on, away from Derek and Marcus. There is no point to this. Maybe she could even get to university? People do that nowadays, like that copper, study later on in life.

Daniel's face beneath the water. Eyes open, blinking. His expression is compassionate but challenging. Conscience?

As the car drives away, she spots a sticker on the back: *Child on board!*

The muscles in her legs wilt. She crashes onto the seat, so hard her teeth hurt.

241

# 19

She wakes in a shell of pain. Bleeping. Hospital? What about the baby? The sounds reach her, an incessant tick, as if through a brick wall. It feels like there's a tremendous weight resting on her legs. She can't move. Why can't she move? She has to sit up, got to ask about the baby.

And Amber.

She's like a relentless chick, pecking through the shell, peeking out, desperate to emerge from the mucus to air her matted wings. Who is in control of this body now? What will she do with me? A tigress prowls the gates of Chinatsu's barriers, testing each for a loose hinge, clawing. Chinatsu knows that's not true, but her brain seems to have no strength, it wants to be absorbed in this fantasy. Where she doesn't have to think about the baby not being here any more.

She opens her eyes to find Tao's smile. He no longer has that youthful, Zen look, as of a Buddhist who finds balance in the world, regardless of its poisons, the skin so elastic she thought he would never age. It looks loose, and pale. She has done this.

His fingers slip into hers, they tickle her palm, but it's like she's wearing an oven glove.

'Why?'

She shakes her head. Everything hurts.

242

'Why did you do this to yourself, Chinatsu? You could have told me you were so sad.'

What is he saying?

'They found pills, Chinatsu. Painkillers. You took too much, far too much.'

No!

'Don't get upset. I'm not angry. We will deal with this, OK? What? I can't hear you.' He comes close. She smells the oil of his hair.

'Yugi. Here.'

'Here?' He frowns. 'I once had a phone call from Madam Li, warning me that he knew. She asked me where we were staying. But, it was just. . . well I thought it was just conversation. She was warning us, I thought? I. . .'

Chinatsu turns away, blinks. Who cared? What did any of that matter now? She turns back.

'Baby?'

Chinatsu knows there are tears spilling from her eyes as she waits for his reply. They're sliding down her cheeks, being absorbed by her hair. But she can't feel their track on her skin. She's numb. Her heart speeds up. She closes her eyes, and calls for the moonflower. The joy it brought me, the possibilities and hope. She can't feel it, can no longer see the glow. Barren.

'The baby's fine. He is strong, like you.'

'He?'

'Don't sit up. Lie back down.'

The contents of her head sieves.

'They did a scan.'

'He?'

'He's well. But you have to promise you will relax. I don't think your body can take much more stress. I didn't even notice, I'm sorry. How thin you look.'

He's blaming himself. This makes her want to cry even more. She barely has the energy to do it.

Tao squeezes her hand. She sees the action but the faint, tickling feeling she gets from it does not correspond.

'She's got me.'

243

'Who?'

She shakes her head and coughs, rests her hand on the slope of her belly.

'Who?'

'Yugi found us.' Could he be here now? Could he take the baby? What would he do?

'Please calm down, please don't do this. I hate seeing you like this, in here. Think of our child.'

She shakes her head. Her throat swallows without her doing it. She splutters, the action taking her by surprise. 'Not crazy.'

He strokes her hair back and sighs.

She tries to shirk away, but her neck won't listen.

'You're just tired and stressed. I understand why you're scared; Yugi is a powerful man. But he's not here, Chinatsu. We would know, surely. But I see how scared you must have been now, to do that. I'm the one who's supposed to keep you safe.'

'I know, I know . . . '

'Shh.'

Her eyelids weigh heavy.

'Yugi.'

Eyes closed, she hears his inhaled breath, imagines it cycloning over his molars, curling down his throat. He's working hard not to hate her and walk away from this. If she'd lost his child, he wouldn't be here at all. Maybe he's wondering if she's talking about Yugi through fear, or because she desires him and needs him there. How can he know the truth, when she does not?

Tao loves her.

He thinks she's crazy.

No, Tao understands her, he sees her.

He'll put her in a mental hospital.

No.

She doesn't know if it's a dream, or a sleeping thought that tell her; the baby dies with the moonflower.

She wakes up still in the hospital bed, strapped in by holey blankets. Her mind is full of sunshine and Hawaii and friendship. Dust and dry grass, a dog slumbering in the heat. She blinks. The room itself is still, white blinds closed. There is what she presumes to be a bathroom behind a brown door. Something drip-drip-drips away. Chinatsu swallows, her throat swollen from the unrelenting dry-cold of this place. It hurts to swallow. Tao is still here, asleep in the single armchair by the windowsill. His face looks slack.

Something has changed.

The stubble around Tao's chin has increased. His coffee-coloured shirt is lined and now looks the colour of decomposing food. The room is musty and needs airing. She smells herself in the room, the way her body gets when she hasn't washed. There are now three empty cardboard coffee cups on the windowsill next to him.

Chinatsu's brain skips to Yugi. Does she miss him? No, of course not. It's just, she always imagined that in serious circumstances Yugi would be the one asleep in the chair. No. She's weak, not thinking straight. She's come to love Tao. Looking at him, she's touched by how much he must love her. Shocked at how easy this seemed to come for him. She ought to love him for that, at least.

But he is still a stranger, a stranger in the room with her still baby. Still.

She knows it's true. Her body agrees.

Her eyes close and open. 'Tao?'

He stirs, eyelids unstitching. He rubs the sleep from his eyes with his fingertips. 'You're awake,' he croaks into fingers, rubbing his face.

'It's dead.'

'What?' He half raises, sits back down. 'The baby? What? But they checked. There was . . . they did the scan. Everything's fine.'

She makes her fingers go straight and holds them by her hips. She can't place them over her belly. She resolves not to touch her own body again until it's out.

'They must check again. And then induce.'

'You are. . . '

'Asking you to do one last thing. Get the doctor, Tao.'

'What? You –?' He swears in Chinese. 'What do you mean? You're twenty weeks, it's not time.'

'It doesn't matter!' She hears the craziness at the edges of her voice and draws in a rattling breath.

'But –!'

'Just go!' The scream rips at her throat.

His face, creased and colourless as over-washed rags, drains of all its blood. She imagines it trickling into the terminal inches of his fingertips, like the water plinking down the long radiators of their penthouse apartment, weighing down his arms. But his fingertips are white.

Tao pauses briefly, then nods and strides out the door. It's the first time she's seen him look ungainly. His spine isn't straight, his neck's jutting out. His boots clump against the floor, tapping a ragged heartbeat away.

He leaves the door ajar.

Nurses laugh softly in the corridor just to the right. There is a howl somewhere in the distance, an alarm going off and a herd of feet. She hears the squeak and rattle of trolley wheels and their contents, glass and boxes.

A bomb is about to go off in her body. At any moment, her mind is going to explode and the grief will shower her like fireworks, burning for years to come. The structure of her thoughts will change; everything will be double-checked and cautious. She can't imagine having spontaneity again, not that she had much of it. But now the world will always be cold with sharp edges, never sturdy, that period of waning autumn and winter beginning where the trees aren't anything in particular. Jagged, like broken black glass.

And she'll never ever want to wake up again. Every day will be a struggle.

But for now, she's got to hold everything in place. She knows she won't get through this if she comes undone.

She still has to give birth, doesn't she? To her dead baby.

And then?

She can't think of that.

And then?

A boy. She hates Tao for telling her. Hates him.

246

She moves her head. A soft laugh at the back of her skull. It's beginning.

I did this, I ate your placenta.

You killed our child, Amber.

You are me, Chinatsu.

Amber has her baby, her body. She'll finally get to claim her lover. Will realise her dreams to stretch her wings in this city far away from Tokyo and home and Yugi. Amber has won. That's not true. None of this is true. She shouldn't let herself think these things.

Chinatsu wills her dormant moonflower to glow like cold embers, to blow over its ashes like a Native Indian harnessing fire, and reignite.

Nothing.

Tao re-enters with the doctor.

He says things and his hands touch the dead part of her that must be excised. He nods and she doesn't listen to his words, just watches Tao out the corner of her eye, watching her. Tao covers his face with his hands. He's crying.

Weak.

She turns her head away.

Many people fill the room, and take her to another.

Drugs.

It takes hours, or days, but maybe just minutes. There is nothing but the pain.

'Push! Push! Nearly there! And breathe! One last push!'

Her body is exhausted. Her skin is ripping and the mass is jammed and. . . Her screams ring in her ears forever afterwards. She'll always feel the sound of them, raw in her throat.

After the birth, all is still. The doctors and nurses are also, briefly still, before they leave. And Tao looks away from the thing she has carried.

Her child does not cry and she does not get to hold him or stare at him and suck up all the detail to imagine what might have been, how he would have grown. Perhaps they offered, she can't remember. But she sees them examine the small redness. She catches a brief glimpse of it; it looks like a mutilated hamster. They whisper to Tao, conspiring. He is sweating and thin, they say that they will have to do a post-mortem to determine the cause of death. But she knows, Amber killed the baby. She deserves to die.

They work down there, cleaning, stitching.

She's in the hospital bed, still strapped in by holey blankets. She blinks and she is in this still room with its closed blinds and tap drip-drip-dripping in the bathroom beyond the brown door. She swallows, her throat swollen from the unrelenting dry-cold of this place. And Tao is here, asleep in the single armchair next to the windowsill, his face still slack.

'Tao?'

He stirs, his eyelids unstick and he rubs the sleep from his eyes. 'You're awake,' he croaks.

'Our baby is dead.'

The air whistles over his molars, air over distant mountains, to escape from his mouth. 'Yes.'

And everything falls down.

# 20

Yugi can't breathe. As he tries to harness the strange breathing pattern, he's aware that what he's feeling is panic.

He's seen his wife being taken away in an ambulance. He's seen the lights flashing without sirens, not because the sirens were quiet, but because his brain has turned them off. Because it cannot process more. He has seen himself, outside his body somehow, a black-suited figure, crumpled shirt like some downtrodden detective, trying to hail a taxi. Trying to follow. But the ambulance swims away, rippling cars and buses and bikes. And she is gone.

He loves her. Yes. Despite everything, Yugi loves Chinatsu.

And now this woman, who he loves, might be dying.

There is more than one hospital in this city. Where would she go? What should he do?

Indecision roots him to the spot.

'Spare change?'

Yugi looks at the tramp. He's bearded and grubby and in a yellow visibility vest. He's holding a magnifying glass in one hand, a *Costa* coffee cup in another. Fingerless gloves. Yugi looks him over. Why has nobody taken care of this man? Why has he gotten into this state?

'Are you married?' Yugi asks.

The tramp shakes his cup. 'Spare change, fella?'

Yugi fumbles for some change. Drops copper into the cup.

The tramp peers at them, presses his lips together. 'Have a nice day.'

Yugi looks down at his own clothes; there are grease stains on his shirt. He buttons his jacket and combs a shaking hand through his hair.

The woman Yugi loves might be dying. Right now. Someone knocks into him. A faint 'sorry, mate' drifts backwards. He staggers. What is this feeling? It was like when his father was dying, but more insistent. He remembers the moths in the jewellery box, how he transferred them to the box to die. The powdery flutter of their wings. Like the snap of washing in a breeze. Death.

But this is different to all of that.

The woman he loves – *loves* – might be dying. And he doesn't even know where she is, where to go.

Yugi droops. His back hits the wall, the front of a building. He isn't sure which. Just something solid to keep him steady. He sinks to the ground, wrists dangling from his knees, blinking.

A siren slices through the city, roaring close, then sewing its way around buildings and traffic out of the centre. Yugi heaves himself up, brushes his trousers. He hails a taxi and says 'hospital', hoping it will be the right one.

Perhaps he has something in common with that tramp, or will in the future. What is the real reason he's wanted to kill Chinatsu? Isn't it because he loves her and she has hurt him? Or that he's tried to love her in the only way he knows how? Delivered some approximation of a feeling that other people understand implicitly. But did Chinatsu really need to be punished so severely? Perhaps they had both just been lost. Perhaps he simply needs his wife back. Yugi grinds his molars together. No, that is not it. He has tried, for her. He has loved, for her. And this is what she does to him?

He would not allow sentimentality to get in his way. He would find her, and watch and wait to see if she is dead. And if she is not, he will do what must be done.

# 21

Someone is watching Fleur. She can sense it, the eyes on her. But where? Who? Is she just being paranoid? She's sitting at the bar of the restaurant the policeman has booked. There is nobody else there except herself and four members of staff. Of course she's imagining it. But her back has been itching, a creeping sense of needing to turn around. On the bus, at the cash point, the walk here. Are the staff wondering if she's been stood up? Her hair is too fussy and pretty. Why did she put it in plaits? She isn't twelve. She loosens the little plaits and just lets it hang.

'Your hair looks nice.' He touches her shoulder as he sits next to her. 'The waves.' He nods. 'Pretty.'

She bites her lip and clears her throat. 'Thanks.'

The bartender shows them to a table. It's all flickering candles and dark corners. Thankfully, another couple walk in and Fleur relaxes a little. She's had to go into her overdraft to take money out to pay her half. Stupid. She feels so obvious; too try-hard. He's dressed much more casually in a jumper and faded jeans. She wipes her lipstick off discreetly as he looks at the menu.

'OK?' he asks.

She feels dizzy. What is she doing in this situation? What is she even doing on a date? He is being nice and didn't want sex, when it was blatantly obvious she would have gone along with that. So what was this about? Nothing was definite, and she didn't like it.

They order and eat. She has a couple of drinks and he has one beer and then water. Everything joins up when he says, after not letting her pay half for the bill, 'Would you like to come back to mine?'

There is another quiet car journey. She does not feel like being amenable, or playing the chatty girl card. And it is strangely OK. His voice eases into her thoughts as the car coasts over black roads.

'So what's your story?' he says eventually.

She smiles and tugs the seatbelt away from her neck. 'What's yours?'

'School, College, Uni, The Police, Engaged, she ran off with all my money – and my best mate.'

'No.'

'You think that's funny?'

'No!'

'Look at you, laughing.'

'It's the way you tell it.'

He smiles, indicates off onto the slip road. She likes the sound of the steering wheel whooshing against his palms.

He nudges her knee aside and fits himself, clothed, between her legs. The bed-linen smells of lime. She reaches up to kiss his throat. He presses his forehead against hers, anchoring her to the pillow, catches her top lip with his teeth. He's hard against her leg, and she actually wants to make love to him. She wants him to undress her, touch his skin, feel that hardness inside her. And fall asleep in his arms. Because it fits, it makes sense.

And that's confusing. Some stupid dream. The dream she could have had with Daniel.

Her emotions are firing, erratic. Dizziness.

Soon, it's going to be hard to breathe.

He finds her hand and fits his fingers between hers, pressing her arm over her head. His thumb circles her palm. 'Do you want to?'

The words are strange, and she realises it's because she's never heard them before. Marcus never asked. She nods; she does. Yes.

252

There is just the sound of clothes whispering against skin. They help each other and he lowers her back. She puts a hand to his cheek, and he doesn't look away. He meets her eyes, like he has nothing to hide. Fleur is the first to look away. He kisses her, soft then crushingly hard. She hides her eyes, as if not to see her own pleasure. His touch is painful, his fingers between her legs, circling and dipping; she's never felt that. Her nose stings; a new and strange emotion is whirling under her skin and in her brain. What is it, what is it?

He moves away and it feels like loss. Her body gets cold. She touches his arm as he is turned away, to keep a link, so she won't be spinning out there on her own. He fits the condom with one hand. The rubber smell tickles her nose, but it's a good smell. Good because it means he has been respectful and she is worth that respect.

It's almost too much. She tries to pull away. His fingers tighten over her knuckles.

'What is it? What's wrong?'

She shakes her head. A succession of people flash into her mind: Derek, Marcus, Andrew. Can this be a good thing?

He strokes her hair out of her face. His touch so unbelievably gentle. She winces.

'Fleur? Hey, we can stop. It's too soon. There's no rush, I know I pushed it. I like you, you know?'

She nods.

'Do you like me?'

She nods. Her eyes are stinging, slightly wet. She forces back the emotion and curls her hands around his neck, drawing her back to him. As the pressure of their kisses strengthens, he gets harder, and more urgent. She puts a hand between her legs, finds him. Watches, her eyes on him as he enters her. When the sensation becomes too intense, she squeezes her eyes shut and moans.

Warmth spreads through her whole body. His hand is tacky in hers, the fingers loosening as he drifts further away into sleep, the catch of a slight snore every now and then. She blinks in the darkness, replaying it. Sex. It doesn't have to be painful. She doesn't have to be fucked. It doesn't have to be love, but her body can feel other things. It is capable, she is capable. It is allowed. The tears roll off her cheeks and soak her hair. This new feeling is scary. She loosens their fingers completely. She dresses and leaves.

The next day Fleur is outside the Texaco again, on the corner near the bus stop that overlooks the factory. She glances around, still unable to shake the feeling that someone is watching her. Is that just because she feels so suspicious, watching someone else? The policeman calls her phone for the third time. A text message pops up after he rings off. She is about to read it but a second one pops up in its place: Marcus. More threats. She shakes her head, fires back a message: *contact me again and I will call the police.* She waits, stomach tight, for some vicious reply. Nothing. She sees Derek crest the corner on the opposite side of the road.

There is no car today. The woman is walking. Her young daughter gripping the woman's right hand. The girl has small, precise footsteps. She reminds Fleur of a helium balloon.

Derek kisses the woman, holds his hands out for the girl and a hug. Fleur's stomach tightens. As it begins to drizzle, they start walking down the hill together. She catches a familiar scent. Is it the factory smoke meeting the rain? Whatever, there is a definite smell of burning in the air. Is this her imagination or is it really gingerbread? Like the house from her dream?

The girl turns around and stares directly at Fleur.

It might be crazy, but Fleur is sure this is the girl she dreamed about. The one Daniel told her to help.

Fleur swallows. The light on her phone switches off, catching her attention. She glances down and thumbs into her messages. Another Marcus message probably. She deletes the last text without reading it and pockets the phone. She stares ahead at the girl, watching Derek and his wife get smaller and smaller down the hill.

The girl has the same walk she did. Same stare, same face. Blank.

And it's her fault.

# 22

The world is grey.

No, it is grey with sticky red, the colour of her hamster baby, the colour of sweet, tacky barbecue sauce on grilled chicken.

Tao will not go to work, so she has even destroyed this for him. He says it's still the same day and that he might go tomorrow. She doesn't understand. It's been ages. Hasn't it?

She killed his child.

Stillbirth is more common in women over thirty-five. The information is fed to Tao who spoons it to Chinatsu. They examined her placenta, he said. The shape of it was like the misshapen baby she had produced. Getting out that mass of blood was like giving birth, again. To something else still and useless. They said, Tao said, that the placenta had peeled away from the uterus, meaning that the baby was deprived of essential oxygen and nutrients.

Her body broke the baby.

It was hungry. Starving. It couldn't breathe. It suffocated in her body.

She ate the placenta. Amber's words, but Amber is her creation, the person who gave her the courage to leave and seek happiness with a new family. Had she ever really wanted that? Her stomach squelches when

255

she thinks of it all, literally spasms in. The very thing, her, that was supposed to nourish and protect her child was lacking. She is faulty, toxic. She abandoned her moonflower which glowed through the dark nights in her Tokyo garden. It cradled her dreams and kept her alight. And she left it behind. And now she is being punished for this desertion.

There's some commotion, an Englishwoman's voice. Tao pushes it away, disappears for a while and it is gone.

'Who was that?'

'You're awake. Do you want a drink?'

At some point it's not the hospital any more, it's the hotel again. The radiators trickle. Tao, or the machinery, has turned on the heating and those long metal bars will heat up and glow.

She's rotting amid the mountains of dark blankets in the bedroom. Their silks are clammy against her skin. Even they do not wish to touch her.

In films, the woman would admit at this point that she has never cried. And when she cries, she will be saved.

Chinatsu has cried out all the fluid in her body. Tao brings green tea. She hates him for making her want to cry even more, but the heat of the tea is good in her mouth.

The sheets are soggy, the pillows damp and disgusting. They will grow mouldy, if Tao did not steal in from time to time to open the window, allowing air to slice through the drapes. She smells cheese and herbs from the restaurants below; she wants to be sick, but has no energy. Sometimes, rain smatters the glass, blown in waves, and aeroplanes roar through the sky. They're so close to the airport here.

And then Tao comes to close the window.

He is the ghost in the house that she once was. Preparing, planning – plotting? Is she Yugi?

He's coming now. His feet position themselves outside the door, toes like fingers. Go away. She stares at the door, the buttery wedge of light around the wood. Can she keep it closed with the power of her mind? She created a woman, a thing that ate her placenta, so why can't she keep the door closed?

The door opens, pushing over thick woollen carpet.

She sinks into the covers, like going to the bottom of a pool, and squeezes her eyes tight shut.

'Chinatsu? Would you like some tea?'

He waits.

Go away.

He creeps to the bed and sits.

Away.

'Can I come in?' He taps gently on the cover over her face, her breath making it heavy and hot. He peels it back.

The placenta had peeled away from the uterus.

She opens one eye; the hallway light is unnecessarily bright.

'Hi,' he says.

She looks away, tears needling her swollen eyelids. She can barely close them, and has to breathe out of her mouth because her nose is stuffed up.

'Look at me.'

She doesn't move.

'Damn it, Chinatsu! Look at me right now or you can get your belongings and leave today.'

She waits a beat, then glares.

'I didn't mean that. I'm going back to work. While we're still up here there are some other clients that I can – anyway, I won't bore you with the details.'

She flinches. But she wants to tell him not to go anywhere, that just having him in the house, patrolling the hallways, makes her feel safe. She eases herself into a sitting position. The nightgown slips off her shoulders revealing her left breast. She looks down at it, lifeless and flat.

'It's what I do. I need it, to be busy.'

'I'll get out of your way then.'

He hooks the nightgown sleeve back up onto her shoulder, fingernail scoring a short white line on her skin. Her leg itches, the memory of the toenail scoring her ankle. The man she slept with to ensure Madam Li's suspicions were not aroused.

Tao withdraws his hand. 'I don't want you out of the way.'

'It is fine, really. I expected this. You were with me because of the baby. There is now no baby. I appreciate everything you've done, really, you have been more than wonderful. . . but –'

'Your nose is running.'

She raises the blankets to hide her face. Tao wipes the bottom of her nose with his thumb. His eyes almost disappear when he smiles.

She can't smile yet. It wouldn't be correct. She bites the duvet instead and more tears sting her swollen eyelids.

'You can't think that's the truth? Hey? I've completely changed my life and obtained the bad will of a man as powerful as your husband. For what? People don't do that just 'to provide'. Do they?'

She grinds her teeth into the cover. The fabric squeaks.

'I chose this, and you. I see things through. Don't leave me, Chinatsu.'

She glances up.

'I'm not trying to take anything away from you, but I lost here too. You must give us this chance. Yes?'

She takes a deep breath and sighs into the fabric. Guilt clouds thickly over her. He lost too. It might not even be his child. Have been. It might not even have been his child.

Tao takes the cover from her mouth and pulls her to his shoulder. She breathes in the scent of lived-in cotton, the warmth of his body beneath the polo shirt, the planes of his chest hard and reassuring against her cheek.

'Yes?'

His breath whispers over her hair. By the smell of his breath she knows he hasn't eaten any breakfast. He smells hungry. She must get up and wash. She must feed him, he still needs her.

She nods. 'OK.'

She could tell him about Amber. About her fears that Amber will take her over and destroy their life, no matter how hard they try. That there is a dark part of her that will never let them be happy. Tao is understanding. He could help, couldn't he? Or maybe she is crazy. Maybe she does just need a doctor to crack her head open and put everything back in its right place.

'Tao?'

258

'Yes?' He strokes her hair, his touch making her scalp prickle. She can smell the grease of her own hair; he should not have to touch a woman in such poor condition.

'Have there been any phone calls for me?'

'No. None. Were you expecting any?'

She shakes her head. 'I'd like a bath, I think.'

'I'll run it for you.'

'It is a woman's job.'

He nudges her and leaves. Moments later, the taps squeak and she hears the water flooding in.

She heaves off the covers and pushes her feet into slippers. She smells of oil and blood. Perhaps she's imagining that. She closes the bathroom door, smiling, but pushes Tao out. She does not want him to see her still-swollen stomach.

Sighing, she gets into the bath. He has also provided bubbles and the hot water holds her, steaming out the poisons of her body. She tries not to look at her stomach and keeps her eyes on the tiles when she leans back. Hot water seeps into her hair. It will be OK in time. But half of her doesn't want it to be OK. It should hurt forever. She closes her eyes and thinks of her moonflower, and its nostalgic glow. Could she plant a new moonflower here? A sunflower perhaps, one of promise and hope and everything that is positive.

The dirt leaves her body and sticks to the sides of the bath. But the real badness is inside, isn't it? Amber. She cannot tell Tao, won't tell him. But she must get rid of Amber. Find a way to excise her, cut her out. How? She must be stronger, cleverer, and quicker. She submerges herself under the water, swollen stomach providing buoyancy. Water plugs her ears. Bubbles pop out of her nostrils, her heels clunk against the basin.

But where is Yugi?

## 23

Yugi is getting ready for the most important meeting of his life. Honour will be restored to his family name, and balance to his life.

It would appear that he is physically incapable of hurrying. There is a sense of weight over Yugi that was never there before.

All of his buttons are wrong. The dry cleaning rattles like gifts to unwrap. He picks up a new shirt; the one he tried on first is discarded in a heap at his ankles. He glances at it. He frowns. The Armani shirt is shaped like a person, only the person has been melted out, like the snow on the farm.

He removes his gaze and, working upwards, fastens the new shirt as though he is sewing himself in. He stops. The buttons are refusing to listen. Just as his contacts have been refusing to listen. Yugi was under the impression that he was a powerful man, that he made things and broke things and people bowed under the weight of that fear. It seems that people are reluctant to puncture the Chinaman's good will. Yugi was never really the man he thought he was.

His forehead is like a page of Braille; the sweat stands out. He wipes it, gathering the moisture onto one finger and flicking it away.

As he observes the buttons his chin digs into his chest. He feels the soft pouch beneath his chin. Yugi has not been going to the gym and the ratio of his food intake is all out of proportion.

The fight with the buttons continues until Yugi nears the crest, entombing his chest in white linen. It's possibly not the best colour shirt for this meeting.

He pauses again, pulls at a stray piece of cotton which is poking out from the top.

It stays firm.

Yugi lifts the razor from the bathroom shelf. The glass is green and clean, ringed only with the imprint of his electric toothbrush. If Chinatsu were here, it would be spotless before he noticed.

Heart picking up pace, he brings the metal in line with his nose and draws down. The metal nicks. Bright bloodspots flower on his upper lip. He'd forgotten to cream up. He splashes his face and starts again.

Done, he inserts his feet into clammy leather. His toenails jut against the tip, forcing the nail bed back into itself. Can a nail grow backwards and return to the body?

Yugi circles a jacket over his shoulders and, soles sucking against warming leather, bends down for his briefcase. Only he knows there is nothing inside it; it is empty.

Empty. Just like his wife is now. He has been to the hospital. Watched her through the window. Saw the Chinaman sit and sleep by her side. Has been edged out by nurses, concerned at his unkempt state. He had seen the emotions on his wife's face; the Chinaman's defeated slump. He should have felt elated by the knowledge that she had miscarried, but he wasn't. Nevertheless, the Chinaman must still be punished for meddling in Yugi's affairs. He has no doubt that Chinatsu will return to him now, because now he has noticed her. He sees her, just as the Chinaman did.

Yugi tugs his suit jacket so it sits perfectly on his shoulders, exits his hotel room, thumbs the circle for the lift. Ready. Riding it down, he thinks of all the prostitutes he has slept with over the years. The women who have created this gap in their lives. There has to be some way of finally closing it.

261

# 24

It's raining in the park. She remembers a dream about Daniel, of being underwater, dancing, her clitoris warm and swollen. Sun splashes the surface like a greeting. She just has to kick up, *up*. And her face will kiss the sun and Daniel and . . . good. There is just one more thing to do, one more thing to find. Where is it? She rolls in the water, hands guiding her body. But it is murky and she cannot see.

Is it the rain that reminded her of last night's dream? The rain spatters Fleur's umbrella as she watches Derek from a distance. He is sharing a black umbrella with his little girl. Is it actually his little girl? Or is he snuggling in on a one-parent family, the same way he did with her mother? Her chest feels tight with pain. Does she even know what she's going to do?

The rain eases off. Fleur pulls the umbrella down.

She watches.

Derek is standing behind the girl. He steadies the metal arms of the swing for her to fit into the seat. Fleur's eyes concentrate on his hand at the small of her back. Push. She struggles forward. Push. She flies. Push. It goes on. The girl never smiles. It's going too high; she can see the swing frame creaking, jumping off its legs. Fleur's stomach wriggles. The

262

chains buckle in mid air. The girl drags her feet on the ground – once, again. The third time, she catches her foot and spills onto the sand.

Fleur starts forward, but holds herself back. She sees Derek's hands over the girl, righting her, brushing the sand from her face. The limpness of the girl's body until he stops touching her. Is she making that up?

Her phone buzzes. She turns away, walking fast, needing to be away. Could this be Marcus? She checks the number; it was the policeman. Marcus hadn't been in touch again. Part of her puts a tick against her actions; well done, she'd got him off her back. She'd done that. Another part is sad because it's yet another dead end. Something done, finished. She holds the phone to her ear.

'Hey.'

'Oh. I was rehearsing what to say to your voice mail.'

'What would you have said?'

'Something about hoping you were all right after the other night. I haven't scarred you in the heat of passion. A mis-timed joke about pressing charges.'

'Ugh.'

'Yeah. I know, sorry. So . . . *are* you okay?'

'I need your help. I think. Or something. Can we meet up?'

# 25

Chinatsu sits upright, eyes blinking in the darkness. She swallows, it's such an effort to slow her racing heart. What was she dreaming about? The images collect together. There was a baby made from metal that beeped when it had a dirty nappy. Its faeces were metal too, slick with brown juices. She had cleaned it up. But the baby did not want her breast. It had no need of her whatsoever. It would not feed from her body, so rusted and died.

She keeps blinking, trying to push away the dream. She wishes Tao would open his eyes. If he does, maybe it would mean they are meant to be and will survive. She won't have to go through with the plan she has half formulated.

Tao's stomach gurgles like the radiators in the penthouse, liquids creeping and trickling from one organ pipe to the next.

Something hisses.

The smell of egg noodles clouds the room. It doesn't make her feel sick; that surprises her.

They leave Manchester for London at the end of the week. Tao's business and her baby are both concluded.

She has no idea how many days have passed. She lives in the night and has no day. When it is day she slants the blinds and turns on the lamps. When Tao gets up to go to work, she opens the blinds and makes filtered coffee; he will not regularly eat a proper breakfast no matter what she says. He kisses her with dry lips.

One night, he reached for her, half awake. His body was hard and strong against her stomach. She feels a butterfly of desire, but when he puts himself between her legs, his jutting penis is obtrusive. Her desire falters. She imagines a minute version of Tao's penis stabbing a butterfly into submission, a pin slicing through the fur of its abdomen. The thought seems to wake Amber. She eels through the water of Chinatsu's body, full of fast passion, a viper willing her to slip so she can open her mouth wide. She thinks of Fleur, not wanting sex, but companionship. Friendship.

Chinatsu blinks through until the morning, and pretends to be asleep when Tao wakes and sits to briefly look at her, before easing the covers back.

Someone is trying to start their car below. It finally sparks and drives away.

Tao has become her Yugi. She gets up when she hears the shower running. She prepares a flawless face for when he leaves. She kisses him goodbye with warmth. As he walks out the door, one smiling look over his shoulder, she hates him for not knowing.

'See you later. Relax.'

'Oh yes.'

She hears the muted ding of the lift as the door clicks to a close. She pauses, waits, then heads to the bathroom to transform.

She knows where she needs to go, and what she needs to do.

# 26

'Nick. Thanks for meeting me.'

'Yeah. Course. You sounded . . .'

'Weird?'

'I was trying to avoid language like that, but . . .' He shrugs.

Fleur smiles. She's half stood to greet him and now sits down as he slides into the red booth of the café. 'It's good of you to come all this way.' It sounds cruelly formal, especially when she knows the face he makes when he orgasms. Relax.

'I'm working here – tonight at least. Plus I wanted to see you. It did worry me, you leaving like that.'

'Sorry.'

'Yeah. So, how –'

Fleur pushes away a mug of half-drunk tea. She folds her arms. 'Why'd you stop?'

'You don't exactly look like you're ready to chat.'

She hunches forward. 'Sorry.'

'Better.'

She smiles. Purses her lips. 'So, firstly. Formal apologies for vanishing on you.'

He nods, lips pressed together. 'Second?'

Nerves make her breathing ragged. 'I have a problem.' She rubs moist palms with her thumbs. 'I think I know someone who's . . . abusing someone. And I don't know what to do about it.'

He raises his eyebrows and sits a little straighter; police mode. 'You tell the police.'

She bites her lip, nods. Without looking at him, she says, 'But I'm scared.'

'That's understandable, but the process is anonymous.'

'Mm-mm. No. That's not it.'

'Then?'

'I know this guy.'

'If the police ask him to come in, he won't know you're the one –'

'No. I'm scared because I can't explain what I know – what I think I know – without. . .' Her face heats up, her bones feel searing hot. Spit it out. 'Without talking about myself.'

Nick looks up from fingering loose sugar granules on the table. He looks at her, nonplussed.

'This is hard,' Fleur says.

He dusts his hands off and nods. 'OK.'

She forces herself to hold his gaze.

He tongues his cheek, folds his arms on the table. 'I think it's important you tell me this.'

'It's just. . . I haven't.'

He puts a hand over hers. 'If you tell me, I'm obliged to report it if it's related to current abuse. I think that's what you want?'

'Yes.'

'Do you want to go somewhere else to do this?'

'It's OK.'

The waitress brings Nick's coffee and they spring back, thank her, and move together again. He doesn't put his hand back.

'Maybe I should explain why I left like that?'

'It'd be nice.' He sips his coffee. 'I'm listening.'

She looks around and leans in, lowering her voice. 'It hasn't been . . . er, gentle? Before?'

He frowns, mouths. 'Sex?'

267

She nods.

He breathes out. 'Right.'

'Well it was unexpected, confusing.'

'I think I understand,' he says, frowning.

'OK well, I was also quite caught up with following this guy which, shit, that sounds criminal. Maybe. . . I just, oh I don't know.'

'Fleur. Start over, what's been happening?'

Her stomach flips; her name sounds delicate in his hard tones.

'The man I've been, well, following, he was my mother's boyfriend. A long time ago. I know it sounds crazy but really, I need you to believe me. Because I've just got no clue what to do about it.'

'This man, what did he do?'

It was like going into another mode. The story wanted to be told and told to a person who could do something about it. It seemed desperate to get out. Perhaps because of this, she didn't feel the sense of shame she thought she would. She cleared her throat. 'He watched me. I don't remember much else, other than this total dread. Like, this constant fear. I used to hide in the boiler cupboard, hoping he wouldn't find me. Stupid.'

'What else?'

He was being completely professional now. 'I think other things happened, I remember bleeding.' She didn't dare chance a look up to see his reaction to that one. 'I think something's happening with the girl he's living with. I saw them in the park and she just, it's sounds ridiculous, but she looks just like me. Not in the face or anything. I mean. . . how she is. I'm sure there's something going on and if I don't talk about what happened to me then they won't investigate that, will they?'

Nick opens his mouth.

She puts out a hand. 'But that's not it. There's this guy, his name is Daniel. He died around here. I mean, it was years ago but I remember seeing someone who reminded me of Derek following him that day. I'm worried that Daniel's. . . death is something to do with me.'

'That is complex.'

'What do you think? Should I report it? Will something happen?'

'Professionally, I can't talk you through this. I don't want to influence your choice or indeed your statement, should it come to that. But personally, I would report it. Any allegation of abuse, specifically, would have to be followed up. It's duty of care. But. . . '

Fleur rocks against her seat back. 'But what?'

'The problem always lies in having enough evidence to make a conviction. In these sorts of cases you're really reliant on the accused making a confession. Unfortunately, that's quite unlikely.'

She lowered her head.

'Statistically,' he said gently. 'Most will just admit to something they anticipate as minor. So they might not get a conviction, but they will get a caution. And they'll have to sign the Sex Offender's register.'

Fleur winces. She takes a deep breath. 'I think he's the one who killed Daniel. I really do.' It was strange to talk about Daniel as gone like this, when in her mind he was ever present. She was scared that the more she talked about him in this way, the more distant he would get.

'Nobody's going to judge you, you know, if you report it? Don't be afraid.'

She sits shaking her head, tapping her first two fingers on the tabletop.

Nick wraps his fingers around her hand, stilling her tapping. 'Anything helps, Fleur. Think about it, if you'd given a statement years ago, perhaps he'd never have been around that kid.'

She plucks her hand away from his. Gets up to go.

'Fleur.'

The chair legs scrape the floor.

'You've got to stop leaving like that. Come on.'

She opens the door. The cold air zings against her face and sucks her breath away. Nick comes outside, putting away his wallet.

'Money. Right. Sorry. Totally forgot to pay.'

'What're you so afraid of? Are you going to let all that stuff stop you from having a life? We have only just met, but whether it's with me or not, everyone's entitled to be happy. Are you just not going to bother letting yourself?'

She turns sharply. 'You're right, we don't know each other. You've an awful lot to say about something you don't understand. We fucked. And that was it.' The word seems to solidify in the air before her.

'No,' she hears him say as she walks away, 'that's shit.'

269

She'll deal with Derek in her own way, confront him.

# 27

The lipstick comes last. Chinatsu uses a brush, the fibres bending as she pastes the red lipstick over the natural pink of her lips. She's almost ready. Isn't she? Can she go through with this game? She rubs her lips together, evening out the wax. Walking from the bathroom to the hall, her tights whisper when her calves accidentally brush against each other. The fabric lines her legs, keeps her toes together. She hasn't pulled the tights up quite right and can feel a pocket of air between the tights and her knickers. The moonflower is just a flicker, a vague awareness now. An ember of snow-light, phosphorescent in a satin-black darkness. Please? Anything.

The moonflower no longer speaks to her.

She has drawn her face into the shape of Amber's.

Tao would prefer this woman. No, Tao would not agree with this. Tao will not know.

Tao is not her keeper.

She runs her palms down the grey tulip skirt, wraps the ballet-style shirt around her middle and ties its cream ribbons at the left hip. She tugs the knot tight twice and slips one foot, then the other, into mulberry peep-toe shoes. She looks at the world from a more confident height. She doesn't smile at the sound of her feet going into heels, although it still reminds her of that shell-to-the-ear sound.

In order to rid herself of this evil, Yugi must see it. She must repent to her husband. He must disinfect it from her body.

Her heels echo over parquet flooring.

With each step, she hears the thought 'Crazy, crazy, crazy'.

What is she doing?

The irony of the situation is almost amusing, but the chemicals of her failed body make things greasy and hard to define. She heads for the door with purpose, playing dress up for her husband the way she once did for Tao. Her hips will not sashay the way they did that day.

One way or the other, she will be herself again. Honourable. Forgiven. And the pain will stop.

She halts before the lift and presses the button. A halo of red appears around the metal circle. The lift's doors draw back and Chinatsu steps inside. Her fingers are loose, as if they're not her own. She can't seem to curl them together. They hang from her sides, limp. The lift whirs and falls and she and Amber fall with it.

Chinatsu half wishes it would never stop, because when it does, she has to begin the end of her journey. She has to push her resisting limbs and ignore the pain still operating in her body. Was that pain physical or just emotional? She has to bring her body along the streets and before people and through her memories. Yugi is here. She is revealing herself for him, and knows he will find her. The clipping she had taken from Yugi, which seems so long ago now, is sat in her purse. Is that prostitute's face blinking up at the chinks of light from the darkness, like her moonflower, waiting to be discovered, opened out and read?

The lift stops and her body seems to move of its own accord. This was good and right. It would finally, finally be over.

# 28

There's a crunch in her stomach as if something had fractured. Fleur has just realised where Derek might be going.

This morning he's been to *Greggs*. He's met the woman from the car for a drink in *The Moon Under Water*. He's picked something up at the Post Office and been to the bank. No sign of the girl. It's sunny, just like it was that day.

Fleur has kept over the road from him at all times, behind passers-by, four or five heads away. She stops to pause at windows when he slows down. She feigns interest in the shops, then gets back on his trail when he gets going again. He doesn't know she's there. Would he even recognise her now?

Anger drenches her body. It's hot, acidic, her breathing shallow. On the verge of not being able to find oxygen. Panicking. Is this what it's like to drown?

So many things she has to say to Derek.

My mother wouldn't have killed herself if it wasn't for you.

I know you murdered Daniel.

What are you doing to that little girl?

And the unspoken question, the one she's never uttered: Do you know, do you have *any* clue, the smallest, remotest idea, just what you did to me?

Derek passes the *McDonalds* just as she reaches it. Cars sound like surf on the road. They keep walking. There are less and less people to hide behind. Here is where she'd thought she'd seen Derek following Daniel. Here is where she'd pushed that thought to the back of her mind. It wasn't really Derek. She was just imagining things. After all, she hadn't seen him for about ten years. But she could have made sure, couldn't she? Why hadn't she followed, investigated, made certain that the uncomfortable feeling in her gut was just that? That there was no valid reason for her to be afraid. But the truth was, she had been afraid. And had been her whole life. The worst thing was her intuition had been right. Hadn't it? The reason Derek was walking towards the pond must have something to do with Daniel. But what? This wasn't the day Daniel died, but it seemed important. Why? The answer tickled around at the edges of her brain.

Maybe Derek was just on his way to somewhere else? This time, she wouldn't let Daniel down. This time, she'd find out.

Fleur's throat is dry. Her lips are sticking to her teeth. She forces her breathing to regulate. Her head feels light, as if she hadn't eaten all day. She's focussing. She doesn't need to be afraid of this man any more. This man should be afraid of her.

Past the *McDonalds* they go. She glances at the restaurant, her reflection splashing on the glass doors. Past the embankment, towards the bakery. There's a delivery lorry turning. A breeze rattles crisp leaves in the park opposite. Her head pulls to the right; she can see the terrace where she used to live with Marcus. Was he in there? She can just make out an England flag in the back bedroom and imagines him watching the football with a can of Stella, caught up in the game, silently furious. He always seemed to be furious about something. What if he saw her now and followed? What is she doing in this place?

Fear is like something sliding around her throat and squeezing tight. Her shoulders hitch. Turn around. Go back. She pauses, then pushes on. No. She's going to confront Derek. The breeze reaches Fleur's face, fingering her eyelashes. She has to wait for the lorry to turn and indicate out, toe tapping. Had Daniel done this?

A rush of fear: If Derek really did murder Daniel, could he do the same to me?

The lorry is clear now but she can't see Derek. She clenches her fingers. Whatever the danger, she has to do this. He can't be allowed to get away with it. She quickens her pace, passes under the bridge. A wave of cold shunts down her arms. Her whole body is drenched in icy sweat. She's at the clearing. Heart hammering, breath quick and light, her shoes tap against a nest of leaves as she steps inside.

# 29

Yugi regards his wife, conflicted. He is known within business circles for quick-fire decisions, the rat-a-tat-tat of orders. Yugi Hamugoshi is not the type to shrink away from firing people, to delegate the trimming of the fat.

However.

*This* is no longer the ghost of his wife. This is something, someone, entirely different. Yes, he had felt her changing as she walked the walls of their house, something bridling within her, a fistful of fingers wriggling in her womb and venturing out. But who is this person?

Something flutters beneath the surface of his wife's face. Chinatsu. Her name means a thousand summers. Her lips are red, not pink as they used to be in his home. Mutation. The colour on her lips, that edge to her hip, the disconcerting energy to her eyes. Here is the truth.

Is the woman he married still caged within this body? Did he ever really want to be with that woman? Did he want to be with the one he sees before him now?

The desire to punish Chinatsu for her betrayal rears up, stinging. She brought such dishonour to his family, disrupting all he has built.

It's all falling down.

But where is she going? He is intrigued by her legs striding with purpose, how she scythes through a crowd. People move for her. She is . . . attractive to them. Perhaps she is exotic when contrasted with these white faces, people plugged with fat. Did he really need to travel to another country to be aware of his wife's appeal?

He forgets about Tao. Tao is unimportant. Tao could have been any man. The realisation fits, making total sense. This situation is between Yugi and his wife, always has been. And that is how it will end.

Chinatsu moves direction, seeming to change her mind abruptly. She heads towards the station now, silk among nettles. Yugi is drawn as if hypnotised by her scent, wanting, needing to possess her. Have all of her, for himself. And to make sure nobody else could have her.

# 30

The air in the clearing is thick and quiet, almost syrupy. It's warmer in here. She thinks of coming out of the shower, being naked. Incredibly vulnerable. She's so close to him right now. Derek, the man she had been so afraid of all this time.

A part of her can't quite believe she is here. Is she really about to do this? The gulf of years between what happened and who she is today swirls away, turning down a plughole. Suddenly she's that girl again, burning the back of her legs in the boiler cupboard, praying he won't cross the room. Hoping he won't pause before the gap of light where she can see him, smell him, that he won't pull the door back in a whiff of dust, meat and leather.

Fleur rakes in a breath, eyes fixed on Derek who is rooted by the pond. He looks bloated as he struggles to bend over and kneel. What on earth is he doing? Does he still smell of meat?

The water whooshes; Derek's fingers spoiling the pond's surface. She can smell warm earth. Dankness; the smell of underwater.

Say something. *Speak.*

She opens her mouth. 'Hey you' is on the tip of her tongue but she frowns when she sees Derek take something from his pocket. It's white. She creeps closer. What is it? Derek places the object on the surface of

278

the pond. It looks bizarrely fragile in his swollen hands. The object doesn't sink. A rush of understanding fires through her chest, like being electrocuted. Her fingers tingle.

It's a flower.

She closes her mouth, realising at that moment how dark the day is. The flower seems to be emitting the faintest, subtle glow as it rests on the water. Some small diamond in the coming dark.

Why is he here? The answer she's been scratching round for crystallises; it is Daniel's birthday. She frowns, checking her dates. Is that right? Why would Derek know, or care, about that?

Fleur's anger unravels; all her intentions dissolving. She's not sure why she's there any more. She is invisible and without purpose.

Is Derek not a man to hate?

She turns, backing away, heart starting to gallop. He could turn around any second. Any moment now. Eyes wide, she steps to her left, turning her body. Some stray piece of wood *clicks*.

'Fleur?'

It's instinct, pure and simple. Hating herself for it, she runs.

# 31

Chinatsu returns to the town where she first met Fleur. The train journey is a total haze. The landscape changes from grey to brown, concrete to fields then orange brick. This was the place where she half fell in love with Fleur. A different love to the romantic, if she was totally honest. Fleur was the friend Chinatsu never forgot. She was the one she longed for. The girl who seemed so perfect and yet was so damaged. She remembers how they plotted to do away with the man who was hurting Fleur. They'd hatched schemes to get him arrested. We could steal the most expensive ring from H. Samuel and put it in his coat? We could paint his car red and say he'd run someone down? Then he'd go away forever. They'd been joking, obviously, but as the train slows Chinatsu rubs the finger where her wedding ring used to be, thoughtful. She thinks she would have done it, done something anyway, so Fleur could be safe.

What if she met Fleur again while she was here? Unlikely, it was a fairly large town. But what if? Could she really look at her old friend, knowing she'd left her there to suffer? Would the guilt be in Chinatsu's eyes; the reproach in Fleur's? Would it somehow ruin the memory of their friendship?

Nevertheless, Chinatsu had felt compelled to come here; it was a desire that had to be met. Besides, when would she get the chance to see this place again? A thought struck her. Was this town the real reason she had planted the moonflower? Was the whole plan actually to do with Fleur? That was ridiculous, surely, and yet there was some truth to it; she was searching for something in her life. A connection she'd felt here that she wanted again. Could she really find that in Tao, or was she fooling herself?

The decades had not changed the town all that much.

Chinatsu hails a taxi from the station. Something itches on the edge of her consciousness. Is Yugi following, or does it just feel like he's always with her?

The supermarket is much bigger than she remembers; it has a field for a car park now. The people seem to be fatter than they are in Manchester. The houses look tight and stingy. There are England flags hanging outside various windows. Why? The amount of houses seems to have quadrupled, a plague of orange-brown brick. Bit by bit Chinatsu matches how the area looks now with how she remembers it.

The taxi whizzes under a bridge. She looks left. What was in that little thicket there? She's distracted by the indicator blinking and is thrown to the other side of the car as it banks round the corner.

The car halts. 'Mesnes School is just on the other side of them railings. Entrance round the corner. Not much of a tourist trap.'

The engine shifts in pitch. It reminds her of the aeroplane.

Chinatsu hands over gold and silver coins. 'I am not a tourist.'

She slams the door shut behind her and frowns. Is that true?

A breeze loops through her legs, sieving into 10-denier tights. The taxi performs a U-turn and heads back towards the town and the train station from where she's just come. She doesn't head towards the school. She's waiting. For what?

The answer meets her before she has time to think about it.

'Yugi,' she says.

From behind her, her husband speaks. 'I see you.'

She turns around on a peak of hope. Hope? But Yugi isn't here. There's just an old car slumbering down the road, straddling bumps she assumes are to stop people driving too fast.

281

She clenches her fist to ease the cold from her fingers and pulls the newspaper clipping out from her purse. She spreads the page; it's buffeted by the breeze and feels alive, as if about to spring.

The prostitute's face is grainy, made up of fading ink dots.

Wait. She's putting the clipping away when she sees a flicker on the edge of her peripheral vision. Yugi? She's sure that's him; she recognises his gait, his smooth and precise way of walking, the blur of his dark hair. Instead of going towards the school she heads for the clearing. Had Yugi been following her? Was he trying to hide in there? The clipping flaps in her hand as she heads up the street and ducks into the nest of trees. It is shower-warm and fragrant with damp soil, plants and flowers. Midges drift. There is something exciting about the darkness. A bubble of excitement expands in her stomach, this small flicker is the most she's felt in ages.

She will soon be rid of Amber. The pain will stop.

Or, she will thrust the newspaper clipping in her husband's face and then see who must be forgiven.

# 32

Yugi had watched his wife from the clearing. Why had she come here? She'd noticed him and turned, and he'd slipped further into the clearing. What had been flapping in her hand?

Now, the breeze mounts and slithers through his hair, the air close against his scalp.

Chinatsu, I am not the man of honour you think I am, the husband you married; I have strayed from my duty, I have slept with many women, I have killed. *Killed.* I am responsible for the fact that Masa's wife is in the hospital. And I cannot stop, even now. I am weak. How can you love me?

There is a thrill in this revelation. A sickening, shocking thrill. It is like stripping all the clothes from his body. Tearing the pristine, white shirts from his arms. Feeling the fabric tense and break in his palms.

'You will see me,' he murmurs, fingers finding the buttons on his shirt. Thumbing them open. His jaw clenches. 'You will see me.'

He removes the shirt. The fabric is feather-soft as it falls from his shoulders and down his arms. The air licks his skin, his shoulder blades, stirring the hair at the back of his neck. He pulls the tongue of his *Ulysse Nardin* watch strap. It thuds to the floor. His thumb rubs his wedding ring, curling it around his finger. He pulls that off too. *Thud*. It lands on the leaves at his feet.

But clothes are not enough. Yugi raises his arms. He stares at his fingers in the darkness. They seem to have become twigs. Bent, misshapen. Things that perpetrate crimes. His arms are twisted and angular. Black, as if they had been set alight, ravaging the skin from bone and charring the bone black. Mirroring the blackness within him. The darkness of his birth that was responsible for killing his beautiful mother. That killed the moths in the jewellery box. That killed the first prostitute in England. That murdered again, and again. And again.

A darkness that would kill Chinatsu.

Because this was his nature. It could no longer be denied.

A woman in his wife's skin enters the clearing. He presses himself back against a tree, folded into its shade. His wife looks almost mythical, disappearing into darkness. She's searching for something, someone. Him?

'I see you, Chinatsu,' he whispers, following.

# 33

Chinatsu angles her head. What is that? She walks to the water, focussed on the glow of white light in the centre of the pond. She is drawn. Upon reaching the pond she kneels and touches the water. It swishes between her fingers, cold.

It is the moonflower, come alive to guide her through this encounter with Yugi.

Pain clutches her abruptly, suffocating. She feels the pain of her loss. The child, leaving Yugi, the upheaval of her life. Being with another man. And then an idea formulates. She could bathe in the water of her moonflower, immerse herself and be cleansed. Plant a wish as they do in the river at New Year. Or, she could sink to the bottom, feel the water all around her, and never come up. She blinks in the darkness. This last idea is the one that makes sense. If she can rub herself out, none of this will have ever happened. There will be no more pain, no more dead child, no more emotional exhaustion. It won't have to hurt any more. She frowns. But does she really want to die? Kill herself? She isn't sure, but she does know she wants it all to stop. The water will make it all stop.

Chinatsu stands to her full height and starts to remove her clothes. Soon, she is standing naked in the clearing before the pale moonflower, an elm of white. Not shivering. She steps forward. The water kisses her toes, pools between them, slips over her skin and up to the ankle. Ice. She steps, one foot after the other. Sludge is gritty, cool. Up to her shins, her knees. She can't breathe. Amber scrabbles. She wants to explode out of her body. Chinatsu forces herself forward. She can't wait for it all to stop, at least for just a while, for everything to be still and quiet. The water licks the tops of her thighs, her vagina. Slides in the groove between her hips and stomach. Turns her body to frost from the outside in.

One arm outstretched she heads for the moonflower, but it is drifting further and further away.

Her stomach cinches when the water meets her bellybutton. Higher, higher. Her stomach is much less swollen now. The water reaches her ribs, like crenelations in rocks. It cups her breasts, working her nipples to peaks. Higher. Up to her shoulders, neck, chin, fingering her mouth. She kneels slowly, the moonflower almost in reach, fingers outstretched for it.

And dips below.

The water encloses her, fills her nostrils and ears, the closed lids of her eyes. Warm, still, peaceful. Just as it should be. The world sounds different beneath. She opens her eyes, stinging, in the murk. Her eye finds the moonflower, and it keeps her safe.

Her child's face rears up to hers. Though she would not hold it, would not look, she knows it is hers. But the baby is a rotted skeleton, still tethered with rags of skin.

She screams without opening her mouth. Panic attacks the walls of Chinatsu's body, desperate to be uncaged.

Strong arms fasten around her waist. Her body is hooked, propelled backwards. The moonflower reels away from her. She reaches out for it. She cannot go back to the painful reality of life.

Yugi's voice sounds in her ears. 'What are you doing? What are you *doing?*'

Her husband's words travel from his mouth, and drift over hers. Is he real? Is he here?

'Chinatsu?'

His breath walks over her lips, even at this distance, that familiar scent of his breath.

She is not afraid. Yugi is here, and has saved her from herself. It is what she always wanted; to know how much he cared.

He is unravelling, just like she is. Who will they be under all of that? Better? She could tug a stray hair from his scalp and he would twizzle around on both feet; clothes, skin, him, coming away in strips, revealing – what? A boy with wise eyes and ambition who wanted to be a bigger man?

'I . . . see you,' she says.

Her mouth feels full with Japanese, like cotton balls swathing her gums, her eardrums bursting with the sound of it. Yugi's face bends over her. Her body racks, sputters. She snorts out water, coughing and retching, wanting to curl up and protect herself.

'What are you doing, Chinatsu? What were you trying to do?'

She rests her head on one side, against the earth. 'Want it all to go away.'

'All what?'

Why does he care so suddenly? The Yugi she knows has no concern for her emotions. But his breath warms the cold on her face, tickling the drying hairs on her cheek. Water drips from his chin to her shoulder.

'This. The baby.'

She focuses on Yugi, feels his body against hers, solid and strong. 'How can you even look at me?'

'You are my wife.'

Tears burn the edges of her eyes. Isn't this what she'd wanted to hear for so long? And yet, it is tinged by a cruel undercurrent. Is Yugi a murderer? She could not love that.

'Did you kill that woman?'

He draws back. Chinatsu sits and clutches at Yugi's shoulders. 'Did you kill that woman? Did you kill her?' Yugi doesn't move. She thumps his arm. '*Did* you?'

'Did you love that Chinaman? Did he fuck you better than me?' Yugi seizes Chinatsu's hair and curls it into a knot. 'Did you like being a whore?'

She smacks him. Her muscles sting with the violence of it. His bones clang and ring beneath her fingers. She claws his neck.

He's panting, staring her down; wild. This is new. Yugi, real and damageable. A rumpled shirt. Neck scored by her nails. Bleeding. She'd thought one day she would see his layers disintegrate. He would blur, crumble and be left shining; the man her youth had promised.

Yugi's skin is glowing, the blood making his complexion extraordinarily healthy. She flinches when his hand reaches out for her. But he doesn't hurt. He strokes her neck and sighs. He leans back against the floor, elbow touching her bicep. They look at each other.

His hand goes to her mouth and thumbs a caress over it. The nail holds her bottom lip, plucking.

Yugi's face goes from still to shockingly alive, leaping with anger. He forces her into the mud, fits himself between her legs. He's hard beneath his trousers, which are wet and reeking of pond water. In her mind, this is happening before Tao, before England. It's what she'd always wanted. For the moment, she won't let reality intervene. This is true. She reaches down and unzips Yugi. She needs to feel him. There's suddenly the electric shock of his skin against her. He urges, and will be inside her any moment, any second. The tightness, the gorgeous amazing pain and thrill and beauty of him inside her. She moans.

At that moment, all she can think about is the man who is waiting for her in the home he is trying to create. As her husband's penis is urging inside her, the true reality invades; she is in love.

'Tao,' she whispers.

They look at each other in the mud and the darkness, Yugi knotting her hair. His eyes narrow. She sees the anger swell and flame.

'I killed that woman.'

She's panting. 'What?'

Yugi presses her shoulders into the dirt.

She pushes against him. '*Answer* me.' Crying, fingernails dig into his skin. Why had she craved a man like this, when Tao was there for her, so open and willing? She needed Yugi out of her. Now.

Yugi is nodding. 'It's true.'

Her throat tightens. She wants to be sick. She strains against him. Hits, writhes, kicks, claws, bites. Anything to sever their connection. Finally.

Her panic seems to anger Yugi. He doesn't like her resisting. Doesn't like the fact she has her own will. He wants to overwhelm her wants. He's never loved her for who she is. Not like Tao, despite the secrecy with which they began. Yugi moves inside her. His face is twisted. He's more excited, more driven, more terrifying than she's ever seen him. It's sheer and total fear that means she gets her foot up onto his knee. She drives down, wincing, free of him. She rolls away, searches in the leaves for a weapon. Her fingers stub something hard. She picks it up. It's a good weight. Eyes open, she cracks the stone over her husband's head.

'No!'

Leaves shake like a tambourine as Yugi drops back, limbs settling. Still. But he's not dead.

'Ai,' Yugi croaks, on a whisper. It doesn't mean I love you, but Love. He repeats it, over and over.

Love. Tao. She has a sudden and total wish for his safety and strength. She sobs, 'Tao.'

The leaves rustle again. Yugi is conscious. Her husband's hands spring around her throat, fastening tight. Her scream rips through the trees and the darkness, the close intimacy of the woods.

# 34

Flying through the trees, Fleur stumbles. Pain jags up her ankle. Her throat is raw, pulse sprinting. Everything's out of sync. She's going to hyperventilate.

'Fleur! Wait. Fleur!'

*What are you afraid of?*

She comes to a dead stop.

'Fuck!'

Derek stops just inches from her face.

She can feel him breathing, hot, onto her skin. It's the inside-of-tissues hot, of Fleur's bedroom when she's sick and her mum has made chicken soup and drawn the blush-pink curtains. Her mum's bracelets jingle as she brings glasses of orange squash and rests a clammy palm on Fleur's head.

Inside the boiler cupboard hot.

But it's no use. Her mother still leaves and *he* comes back.

She pushes the memory away. 'Why're you here?' she asks the old Derek, the one in the woods. 'Why did you leave that flower?'

'It's good to see you. Been so long.'

She clenches her teeth. 'Why did you leave that flower?'

He shrugs, sweat glistening on his forehead, picked out by whatever light was still left in the sky. 'Knew of the lad.'

Fleur sneers. 'Liar.'

Derek's feet rustle in the leaves underfoot. He half turns, sighs, turns back.

'Why can't you just tell the truth?' She sees his fingers clench and relax.

'I don't know what you're talking about.'

'I know you followed Daniel.'

He laughs. 'Jesus. Don't be fucking ridiculous. Besides, I didn't do nothing.'

His mouth seems twisted, as if he's had a stroke and it doesn't work properly. Her lips part, her heart speeds up. *Say it.* 'Does your girlfriend know? Wife, whatever? Does she know all about you?' She wets her lips. 'Does she know what you like to do?'

Derek's gaze zooms in.

'What's that little girl's name?'

Fleur chokes. Derek's hands are round her throat. He hooks her leg from underneath her. He's on top of her. What's happening?

In the distance, she hears sounds of lovemaking, gasps of desire. Her stomach wriggles with disgust.

'I was looking out for you, you selfish bitch. Didn't have to, did I? What was it to me? The lad was following you, obsessed. I owed it to your mother to look out for you. Didn't I?'

His fingers smell of iron, not meat. He relaxes his grip, fingers unsticking from the skin of her neck. He heaves off her; relief. She can breathe again. She sucks air in, throat feeling tight and raw. Could that be true? She feels completely and utterly deflated. And yet, something's not right with that explanation. What is it? Why can't she *think*?

'Was giving the lad a warning, to stay away from you.'

Chest heaving she sits up, totally confused. A warning? Twigs and burrs spike her legs through her clothes. Something's wet, soaking through her jeans. She dreads to think what. It smells dead. She brings her knees to her body. 'What's her name?'

She feels Derek's attention on her, heavy.

'Eh? You what?'

291

'That little girl.'

He swears and she thinks of Marcus, how his anger could build and coil – lash. She shouldn't say anything else. She should get up, brush herself off and leave. Get away from this man. But the memory of Daniel is close right now, insistent.

She blinks. Derek is a dark figure across from her. Although he's sitting down she can feel the tension glowing off him. 'So do you go into her room too?'

She imagines that Derek will strike her for this. Really lay into her. It will be a pain so sharp and clear, a fire exploding in her head. Making her bones vibrate. But he does not touch her; she is unharmed. She stares at Derek, just about making out that his right hand is curled into a fist. He wants to hit her. Is he about to? Would she have to run?

Her mind shows her the possibility. Fleeing through the trees. A fast-forward snapshot. She would be aching with the effort, scratched to bits, fear streaking through her. His hand would seize her head. Her head would jar back and she'd lose her footing. Then what would he do? He'd start kicking her. Boots would smash into her face, stomach and skull. And she would know it was over, the world was going dark. She might die in the same place as Daniel.

But Derek is still. Knuckles still clenched. She *should* run. Yet one thing rushes through her mind: she's weak. She didn't fight him then and she doesn't want to fight him now. She's still afraid.

Her whole body is on pause, numb with indecision. She can't move. Her thoughts are crawling. Slow, slower. She wants to close her eyes, rest her face against the earth. Just feel warm and safe. She wants to give up.

A scream slices through the trees.

It gives Derek pause. He seems to dance, unsure. Stay or go?

Moments later, she hears him scurrying away. He sprints away, feet sounding light over the leaves.

Fleur watches the man who has abused her, not just as a child, but throughout her whole life. Running away.

She looks back in the direction of the scream. Go and see? No. She should get out of here as fast as possible and call the police. But there. Again. God, it's a woman. Would it be too late by the time she goes to call for help?

What should she do? Disgust settles over her. She never fights. She remembers.

Right before it happened, Nan and mum are arguing. Fleur is in bed, reading her mum's Mills and Boon. Nan's been downstairs while mum was out with Derek. She's been chain-smoking and watching old films on that portable black and white she carries everywhere, the sound blaring. But it's not annoying, it's safety. And then Mum and Derek come back, voices drifting up from under the carpet. The clink of glasses. Mum's voice is high and happy for once. Nan shushes her, the disapproval low and mumbling. It's not long before something smashes.

The front door slams. The letter box rattles. Fleur ducks under the curtains. She sees Nan marching away, breath puffing in the night because of the cold or her cigarette. She's got her cream bobble hat on and the socks she uses as gloves are white picks in the darkness.

The desire, the need for Nan to come back, is a pain in Fleur's stomach. If Nan stayed over Fleur could stay up and watch those old films too, Nan sucking away on her roll-ups. But she was gone.

Fleur's eyes go to the door. Cold, she creeps out of bed and edges into the boiler cupboard which is hidden behind a glossed white door in her room.

Not long later, when mum has cried herself exhausted, the bedroom door glides open.

'Just saying goodnight, flower. Hey, where'd you get to then?'

She leans back, trying to keep as far away from the door as possible. The massive water tank is covered, but a bare spot on the pipes pricks her back through her nightie. She squeaks.

A floorboard creaks. She scrunches her eyes. Please. Don't let him find her.

Air swirls as the door rushes back. Strands of her hair reach out towards him.

'That racket upset you did it? They're still friends, it's just a little fall-out.'

He smells like meat. Bacon and blood and clotted things. It's a sweet, cloying smell that gets into his fingers. He chops up animals for a living and gives them to mum for presents. She thinks he's great.

'Come on, let's tuck you into bed.'

Fleur crosses the floor to the bed, the carpet crispy beneath her bare feet. Her pulse ticks in her throat.

'You can't get into bed with that nightie on, love. You'll end up all hot and sweaty. Take it off and lie down so I can tuck you in properly.'

She looks behind her, hands curling the nightie's fabric.

'Come on, love. It's all right. What d'you think I'm gonna do?'

She pulls her nightdress off and stuffs it under the pillow. Reaches for her duvet.

'Now, hang on. That's for me to do.'

But Derek does not reach for the duvet. He stands behind her, smelling of sweet, dead things and smoke and winter cold that's stuck to his denim jacket.

'You don't tell anyone we like each other, do you?'

She keeps her hands by her sides, shakes her head.

'People'll be jealous of what we have. But it's not bad, I'm only helping you for when you're older. I'll never let anyone hurt you, Fleur.'

But Derek did hurt her. And the pain of Daniel's loss waves over her, so fierce it's hard to comprehend. Right now, she wants to cry, drown in forgetfulness. But that scream. Cautious, she steps forward.

'Hello?'

She's heading closer and closer to the pond. Fleur clears her throat. 'Hello!'

A blow to her stomach, a kick to her head. Just two little touches, yet wildly painful. Beyond anything she could have imagined. Keeling over, she drops to her knees, rolls onto her side. Is there blood in her mouth? It's as if her body has been lit up and she's on fire. Is it? She quells the thought. Her bones feel mushy and useless. Her skin itches with pain, throbbing in time to her pulse. She should get up. And who is screaming? She has to help. Get up and give that statement, for Daniel, for that little girl. For herself. She can't walk away from this. And yet part of her is content to let go and lie there in pain. Come on. She grips her stomach, staggers up.

'Get away.' The voice, gruff and masculine, stops her dead. 'It is none of your business.'

He's a dark shape ahead of her. She's breathing too fast.

She could see the woman on the ground now. Oh God, what had he done?

'What have you done?'

He rushes forward, she shields her face. Another dizzying blow. She drops to the ground, as if he's wounded her so badly she can't stand. But she's trying to get his attention off her. She tells herself the pain doesn't hurt, waits it out. The man turns his back, returns to the woman. Fleur's anger sparks at the other woman's weeping. She isn't afraid, but furious at this man. How dare he think he could do this to a woman, and that she would just walk away?

She heaves herself up again.

'Get off her!' She scans the ground for something solid and heavy-looking; a weapon. She kicks her feet around, stubbing her toes on a rock. She grabs it, runs for the man.

'I said get off!'

The man is flying towards Fleur too. She's lifting her arms, hauling the stone high over her head. A flash of shock as he notices the rock hurtling towards his face. He can't break the trajectory, the collision inevitable. There's a sickening thud. Squeamish, she drops the rock. Jumps her feet out the way. The man drops to the ground, mute.

There's a rustling sound, a woman moaning. Fleur darts forward. Guided by the wink of light coming off the glassy pond. Before the pond is the woman. Splayed out and naked. But she's moving. Fleur can hear the leaves rustle as she does.

She strips her cardigan off and covers it lengthwise over her.

'It's going to be OK. Can you get up? Come on, we need to get out of here.'

'I can't.' The words are foreign-sounding. They only come out as a whisper but it's a sound she knows implicitly, a timbre to the voice she just seems to feel and understand. But it can't be her, that would be too weird.

'We have to go. What if he's just knocked out? What if he wakes up?' Even as she's speaking Fleur starts to feel dizzy. Her head throbs. She pitches forward and forces herself upright. Focus.

The woman finds her hand. Her fingers are ice cold. 'I can't.'

'Then I'll go and get help. I'll be back straight away, I promise.'

'No. Please.'

Fleur sighs. If she lies down and waits with this woman she'll pass out. Willpower is the only thing keeping her upright. They have to survive. They would survive. Fleur can only think of one thing to do; she'll have to carry her. She reaches underneath the woman, wriggling her arms under her knees and around her back. She steadies herself. Lifts her as though she's a weightlifter; straightening up from the knees. Doesn't get an inch. They topple over together, a tangle of limbs.

'I'm going to try and drag you.'

Fleur tries. She pulls from the woman's shoulders and the woman tries to help, pedalling her feet on the ground. They're getting closer. She can hear traffic. The whoosh of tyres on the road.

'Come on. Come on.' She's saying it to herself more than anyone.

But it's no use. After what seems like a marathon they collapse onto the ground for a second time. The pain in her head is beating, pulsing. The blow finally catching up with her. Dizziness convulses through her body. But they're almost out of the clearing, almost safe. The failure is too cruel. Fleur throws up. Freezing, she starts to shake. The woman's arms find her. They hold onto each other for warmth.

# 35

The light is so bright. Not golden, but silver. Moonlight.

'Daniel?'

The words come out wispy. It's too painful to speak. Too tight. But it is warm. Why? She is still in the woods, isn't she? How can it be warm? She feels completely and totally safe; nothing can harm her here. This warmth means she is cared for; she is loved.

The emotion is so beautiful and so unexpected, she collapses into tears. There is no more pain because he has taken it away.

'Daniel,' she whispers, smiling.

She knows it's him, taking care of her. He is not in the *McDonalds*, under the bridge, swinging a *Happy Meal* box, playing pool with his friends, or painting aeroplanes. They're not living a life together in a street with shiny red cars, hose-pipes and children's bikes. He doesn't come home with a briefcase, a hard hat and a smile.

But somehow, he's still there, still alive. Because that is Daniel's warmth encircling her body, creating a bubble of safety and reassurance, soaking up her pain. He lives in those places she doesn't know or understand. One day, she will.

She breathes in.

The pain in her body suddenly ignites. Dynamites up and explodes in a shock that creases her face. She bares her teeth, a moan leaks out.

'It's OK.' A woman's hands reach for Fleur, drawing her up and onto her feet like a rope, gentle and firm.

The moonlight glows gold, a cloud scuds across the sky, too fast.

There is a sound like crickets, bleating in the grasses.

The woman's hands are slender and pale. Her graceful fingers interlock with Fleur's. She is naked and beautiful, covered only by Fleur's cardigan. Her fingers a knot, the woman tugs Fleur through the leaves. Her feet make no sound over the leaves while Fleur's rattle in the undergrowth, body feeling as though her blood is stiff. So hard. So *hard* to move, to keep going forward.

Her eyes are heavy-lidded. Her joints feel rusty and hot and she watches the woman's dark hair breathing over her pale shoulders. The woman's eyes are oriental; liquid black. Her cheekbones and the whole shape of her face is sculpted with exquisite delicateness, as if from real china.

One day, we'll live in Hawaii.

'Is it really –?'

Liquid eyes turn on her. The woman's head angles, her perfect brows arching.

The buzz of traffic zips extremely close. Fleur hears chatter, a whoosh of static. Something electrical. A high whine, then more static. Some sort of response. Blue lights whip her vision. She shields her face. Something cold and wet nudges her hand. Dog? There's a roar of noise and goings on, she can barely pick it apart. What's happening? What is all this? Automatically, she shields the woman's nakedness with her own body.

Before everything goes crazy, before the police move in and take over, Fleur looks back at the Japanese woman. Holding hands, their hair tangled up in each other's, they smile.

Fleur winces.

White. The light attacks her eyeballs.

Medicine smell, warm food and baby smell. Wee.

Beep. Beep.

The squeak of rubber shoes.

Visitors chatting gently.

Tickle of cigarettes.

The twinge of pain – needing to wee. She works spit into her mouth.

'Na – Nan?'

'You obviously have a fondness for this place, eh, flower?'

'Chinatsu?'

'Who, honey?' Nan stands so the chair scrapes back. She looks white, scarily so. There's a startling amount of green in her brown eyes. The colour glitters in her white face.

Fleur shakes her head. 'Nothing. It doesn't matter.'

'You shouldn't speak. Save your energy. They'll be wanting to question you.' Nan smoothes her hair back.

She wakes again, not knowing how much time has passed. There are the same beeps and smells, but a wall of black awaits her.

'Nick.'

'Your Nan called us, worried about you. Said you'd been talking about Daniel a lot, thought you might have gone to the pond to reminisce.'

'How is Chinatsu? The woman I was with?'

'Being treated. Alive. About to give a statement against her own husband.'

'Husband?'

'From what she says, you both saved each other there. I have to hand over to my colleagues. OK?'

Nick goes to leave. She catches his hand briefly, snagging a little finger that she hooks in some kind of hold. He glances back at her. With this strange grip, they shake hands. He nods.

A female policewoman enters the hospital room, bulky with all her black gear. She's blonde and friendly. 'Hello, Miss Pearson. Are you feeling a little better?'

'I'll live, thanks. I want to make a statement about Derek Matthews.'

'Let's start at the beginning.'

# 36

He bursts out of brown water. Sucks air. A degree of tension in the boy's face relaxes, like the slackening of a tensed elastic band; oxygen, life, momentary relief. He is *not* going to die.

Water splashes, drips – *flies* from his face and off the umbrellas of his shoulders, windows of reflected light curving in each droplet, mirroring the sun. The blue-blue sky. His sandy hair is dark, suckered close to his skull. He bends to fit a hearing aid that's lying on the bank. It is not a pond, but a beach. His feet hit sand, become powdered and milk-gold. He walks along the beach, past children and balls and sun cream and melons baking in the heat, vendors, sunbeds, jet-skis. His hands are in his shorts. He's smiling. He has all the time in the world.

The coast of the ocean becomes a Tokyo skyline, blushing deep damson and salmon as the sun sets. The moon is up now and he's a silhouette. Walking the beach, walking the world, always walking.

Fleur rouses towards wakefulness; the slight pressure on her hand causes a slim ring to kiss the insides of adjacent fingers. She opens her eyes and looks to her left. Smiling, she's kept safe in the smile of the man next to her.

'I hear Japanese weddings involve a lot of karaoke?'

She squeezes his hand, smiling.

'How did they meet again?'

'Mm, let's just say it was something of an unconventional meeting. Chinatsu and Tao wouldn't ordinarily have met, so it's lucky really.'

'Cryptic, aren't you?' He tickled her.

She laughs, slapping his hand. She looks over at him, wondering, a hand on her stomach.

His eyes are questioning, his smile inquiring.

She shakes her head.

Their future is something distant and unset.

'Will I have to sing?'

'Relax, Nick. There's nothing to be afraid of.'

The plane begins its descent. The Tokyo skyline comes into focus. Beyond the concrete and lights of the airport, Fleur sees a runway and a sky so blue you could fly kites in it.

Sarah Dobbs is a lecturer in Creative Writing. Previous work has been broadcast, performed and published by the BBC, Bolton Octagon and Flax. She is currently at work on her third novel and is co-writing an English and Creative Writing textbook for Anthem Press. You can follow her on Twitter @sarahjanedobbs

Acknowledgements: Thanks go to: Professor Graham Mort. I honestly can't believe there is another teacher who has had so much impact on so many people. I'm grateful to be just one. To Dr Lee Horsley for helping it all to come together. Funds for Women Graduates (FfWG), whose generous grant enabled me to finish my PhD when it was starting to seem impossible. Dr Martin Coleman and Dr Jonny Powls for guidance on the 'science bit'. Yes, I have taken creative license and, yes, errors are mine. To all those who kindly acted as case studies, allowing me insight into the realities behind this fiction. This novel is partly about the importance of female friendship, so thanks to all my friends, for cake, handholding, laughter, sparkle and bravery. To Unthank, who took a chance on a novel that I have been trying to write for most of my life. And finally, to you, M.

Lightning Source UK Ltd.
Milton Keynes UK
UKOW050126240712

196463UK00001B/32/P